Richard Savage

An Exile from London

A Novel

Richard Savage

An Exile from London
A Novel

ISBN/EAN: 9783743340930

Manufactured in Europe, USA, Canada, Australia, Japa

Cover: Foto ©Andreas Hilbeck / pixelio.de

Manufactured and distributed by brebook publishing software (www.brebook.com)

Richard Savage

An Exile from London

AN EXILE FROM LONDON

A NOVEL

BY

COL. RICHARD HENRY SAVAGE

AUTHOR OF

"MY OFFICIAL WIFE," "HER FOREIGN CONQUEST,"
ETC., ETC.

COPYRIGHT

LONDON
GEORGE ROUTLEDGE AND SONS, LIMITED
BROADWAY, LUDGATE HILL
1897

By RICHARD HENRY SAVAGE.

Uniform with this Volume.

MY OFFICIAL WIFE.

THE LITTLE LADY OF LAGUNITAS. A Franco-Californian Romance.

PRINCE SCHAMYL'S WOOING. A Story of the Caucasus—Russo-Turkish War.

THE MASKED VENUS. A Story of Many Lands.

DELILAH OF HARLEM. A Story of the New York City of To-Day.

FOR LIFE AND LOVE. A Story of the Rio Grande.

THE ANARCHIST. A Story of To-Day.

THE PRINCESS OF ALASKA. A Tale of Two Countries.

THE FLYING HALCYON.

THE PASSING SHOW.

A DAUGHTER OF JUDAS.

IN THE OLD CHATEAU. A Story of Russian Poland.

MISS DEVEREUX OF THE MARIQUITA.

HIS CUBAN SWEETHEART. By Col. R. H. Savage and Mrs. A. C. Gunter.

CHECKED THROUGH.

LOST COUNTESS FALKA.

CONTENTS.

BOOK I.

THE PAPERS IN THE CASE.

BOOK II.

PERSONALLY CONDUCTED.

CONTENTS.

BOOK III.

"WHERE IS THE PROMISE OF MY YOUTH, ONCE WRITTEN ON MY BROW?"

AN EXILE FROM LONDON.

BOOK I.

THE PAPERS IN THE CASE.

CHAPTER I.

LUNCHEON AT THE LAWYERS' CLUB.

THREE men were gazing contentedly at each other over the debris of an "up-to-date" luncheon, in a cosy room of the Lawyers' Club, when the senior, hastily consulting his watch, settled himself down in his leathern armchair, and then, lighting a cigar, said: "We have just half an hour. I've a directors' meeting at 40 Wall, at 2 o'clock. Go ahead, now, Isidor."

The person addressed, promptly produced a pocketbook, and then drew forth a letter. "Reed id yourselb, quied, first," he said, "und we hab Moses's obinion, lader." Isidor Blum strolled to the window of the room and silently contemplated the superb water vistas surrounding the irregular pinnacles of lower New York City. That great fortress of Mammon, known as the Equitable Building, never sheltered three more devoted worshippers of the Golden Calf than the trinity called together now by Isidor Blum to "dalk over a little drubble!" And No. 120 Broadway never knew a sharper trio.

There was no doubt of the financial solidity and

physical well being of Isidor Blum, Esq., senior partner of Blum Brothers, of New York, New Orleans, Fort Worth, El Paso, and Tucson.   A shining exemplar of the American evolution of the Hebrew trader; at fifty-five, Isidor Blum's robust form, superb dark eyes, and luxuriant blue-black hair and beard still attested the oriental splendor of his picturesque youthful comeliness. The easy bearing of the man, his natty attire of richest commercial smartness, the selected diamonds, his jingling chatelaine of Masonic emblems, Pythian badges, Odd Fellow's charms, and Mystic Shrine tokens, all attested the fact that Isidor Blum had "arrived."

More than all these external hints, the firmness of Isidor's financial *pied à terre*, was shown in his doting familiarity with the gray old "coyote of finance" now closely studying the letter, and his lofty domination of Moses Dalman, the listening lawyer, who was leaning his head on his hands, and while concealing his face behind the blue smoke of a Perfecto, was mentally making a new entry in his fee book.

"I must go do Garlsbad soon!" thickly muttered Blum, turning from the window whence he had caught a suggestive glimpse of the *Fuerst Bismarck*.   "June dwendieth!   Nod so much dime to lose."

"This matter looks serious," slowly said William Bent, gazing at the letter of "Brother Morris," from Tucson, Arizona.   "We've held on to that property for a long ten years.   Here it is, ninety-two, and we bought in eighty-two.   Now the railroad comes right up to us, and—when, by Jove, *the mine turns out to be a mine*, we can't afford to lose it.   I've got to take a look over the Northern Pacific, and you're going to Europe, you say.   Better let Dalman take it in hand."

"I must be in London on July fifteenth," resolutely said the lawyer.   "So, don't count on me being here after July eighth."

"Dat's jusd in our hand!" chuckled Isidor Blum, "and you, too, gan see de Senador in San Francisco, Bend, on your vay home.   Now, vad do you say, shall we bud the whole in Dalman's hands on choint agound?   You see, you and the Senador are von hallf und Blum Broders, de oder!"

Old William Bent tossed the letter over to the law-yer, "See what you make out of that, Dalman," he said in a rasping voice. "It looks to me like a mighty bad business, and, I think that we should act at once."

Tall, lean, and erect at sixty-two, with a cold gray eye and a smooth shaven parchment face, William Bent was a priceless recent gift from California to the Imperial City of America. For forty years, William Bent had been judiciously engaged in "discovering good things for other people," and suavely distributing these same "good things" among the trustful investors of two hemispheres. He had early learned the golden rule that the whole secret of success in life lies in refraining. He always "refrained" from losing his own money in the vast operations which had gained for him a majestic toga of directorships, trusteeships, and fiduciary offices of great profit to himself. A fro-zen calm, a ministerial manner, a hard-headed "horse sense," and a callous heartlessness, habitually pre-served his equanimity. Lost to all human emotion, save a few carefully nursed private vices, and an un-dying rancor toward his enemies, he allowed the hope-ful to quietly drift within the reach of his tentacles, then, with tightening grip, extracting the last drop of their golden circulation. Even his hat, broad brimmed and sober, had a sacerdotal air, his sober attire befit-ting either a modest poverty or untaxed millions. His favorite boast that a gripsack, an overcoat, a check book, and an umbrella were a financier's complete out-fit, proved that if he cast an eye on the good things of this world it was only a cursory, oblique glance, and, probably, veiled from the observation of the madding crowd. Dim tradition assigned him the rudiments of a family in prehistoric days, but they had drifted slowly out of public sight. His later incursions into family life were only silently veiled approaches upon the do-mains of others! This particular capitalist belonged to the mysterious guild who "arrive at the Fifth Ave-nue," and, after registering, are never heard of above Canal Street, save when some unhappy accident brings their names into the headlines of the "modern jour-nals," and their "counterfeit presentments" before the gaping multitude.   The veil when drawn aside, usually by the deft hand of the lawyer, frequently presents the old, old tableau—"Trustful womanhood, and the hard hearted veteran admirer!"   Nice, quiet, old gentlemen these !

"Who did you say your partner was, Mr. Bent?" briskly snapped out the lawyer, as he smoothed out the letter with his lean, nervous fingers.   "Mr. Blum called him 'the Senator,' I think," concluded the advocate.

The old man gazed for a moment at the audacious lawyer.   "You may as well call him, *Mr. Cash!* That will do just as well.   I have his power of attorney, and, I will act for him in this little deal," replied Bent, frowning slightly at the indiscreet Isidor Blum, who was complacently finishing his *café noir*, and smacking his lips over a *pousse café.*

Isidor Blum delightedly contemplated his own successive rise from a vicarious cotton-grabber in the Semitic camp following of Banks's army, to a New Orleans trader, then, a New York wholesaler, and now, he was the proud head of a chain of aggregated Blums, with their tentacles firmly fixed on the effluent and refluent trade of New York, New Orleans, Fort Worth, Texas; El Paso, and that pearl of country cities, Tucson, Arizona.

Isidor Blum, ignorant of the imprudence of dragging in a Senatorial name, was proud of the hungry tribe of cousins and brothers who had gathered since the piping times of the war, from Frankfort, Breslau, Vienna, and Budapest, yea, even from Warsaw and Cracow, to aid in distributing all profitably sold articles of use or ornament over that broad zone of the United States, now tributary to the Blums and their international tribesmen.

Nothing too great for the ready enterprise of the prosperous Blums !   Cotton presses, country stores, cattle ranches, army contracts, mail-routes, mines and freight and post-routes, were under their direction, and, at Tucson, Arizona, Morris Blum, the crystallization of their family keenness, towered over the whole lower strata of Blums.   He was the very Benjamin of these sagacious invaders, and he gleamed "Like a diamond in the sky."

For Brother Morris was the head and front of the "dollar-snatching movement" in southern Arizona, and the spacious halls over Blum Brothers' "Palatial Golden Rule Bazaar" were the headquarters of all the various local societies of Tucson. While Isidor Blum had cheerfully in the war days exchanged ammunition and quinine for the priceless cotton with confederate generals, and tobacco and cotton with his champagne subsidized Union friends engaged in "*putting down the rebellion*" in return for "right of way" between the lines—so, the Benjamin of the tribe in Arizona judiciously dealt with all the Mexican rebel generals and Apache chiefs—"on the sly"—as well as the "constituted authorities" of Uncle Sam.

A dashing American-bred Blum, young Morris was "in it, with both feet," to use the words of a Tucson frontier admirer. His lucky speculation in laying out and improving a cemetery, afterward sold *en bloc* to the lethargic Christians at a great profit, was only equaled by his aplomb in joining the Episcopal Church "in order to grow up with the country," and advance the moral interests of Blum Brothers. Holding up the family flag at Tucson, he was always ready to contract for any salable goods, from a fifty-stamp mill down to a baby's sock, and equally prepared to sell a hundred horse-power compound engine, or a personally selected "corset cover." The adroit Morris Blum was justly uneasy now about the future of the Condor Mining Company, and had sent on a warning note of alarm to the great Isidor. The lion of the tribe of Blums had received a few private words in a mixture of Yiddish and patois German, which, so far, he had not divulged to the old money-seeker who was his "pardner," with the judiciously veiled "Senador."

"It's chust as well do see how de old man agds, first," mused Isidor. "I mighd buy him oud ! Und we haf de whole mine."

"I think this whole thing should be put in one man's hands—*at once !*" said Moses Dalman.

"Of course, professionally, I'm willing to give you an

opinion," crisply said the lawyer. "I am ready to act for you—but you are soon to go one way, and Mr. Bent another, therefore, I think that Morris Blum, at Tucson, is the man to handle the whole affair!"

The Christian and the Hebrew money sharks were now gazing silently at the oracularly immobile face of Moses Dalman, counselor, of the New York Bar.

"Vell! Do mage a beginning, I redain you for Blum Broders," heavily said Isidor, closing his eyes, dreamily, and stealing a furtive glance at William Bent's ashen face.

" *That's all right!* " curtly broke in Bent. "One lawyer will do—*of course.* Charge the whole thing to the Condor Mine! Now, Isidor, I will telegraph out to San Francisco, after we have had a private talk, but, if we can agree better, let Morris run the whole thing, under Dalman's direction. There's got to be some pretty fine work done! What do you do to-night?"

"Ball—at the Progress Club—do-morrow, annual dinner at the Bnai Brith, but, Vednesday night I gom up to you at the Fifth avenue, Bent."

"All right," said the American. "And, Dalman, you had better come up there, too. We will settle on a plan. Morris Blum would suit our side."

"Den dat's all righd," sighed Isidor, warily. "Chust dell us now, Boses, your firsd idea."

Dalman had finished reading the letter for the third time, and, conscious of his "fat take" to come, alertly faced the problem. His eye-glasses gleamed over a hawk-like nose and a pair of steady, merciless eyes.

Slim, compact, yet vigorous in figure, with a lean, hardened face, a cold, ringing voice, and a watchful manner; the student's brow was wrinkled far too deeply for a man of thirty-eight. An ingraft of Jewish blood upon the Americanized German, Moses Dalman was a type of "Younger New York up to date!" An *elève* of the public schools, gliding, eel-like, through Columbia College, and then fastening, leech-like, upon a "confidential practice," Moses Dalman was already a rich man, while yet on the sunny side of forty. Bold and aspiring, confident of his pull with the courts, and his power over a jury, secure in his thorough knowledge of both law and practice, he was down town, an absolute economist of time and speech; Spartan in his business habits, never making a needless enemy, wary and close-mouthed, his vigor and unscrupulous professional skill had made him invaluable to his clients.

Moving in the open—between the lines of religious antipathy—he mingled in the best non-sectarian society, his club memberships being judiciously regulated as to both party and creed; with a businesslike system, he "showed up" after dark, as an all-round "good fellow," sitting behind a bottle or a poker hand, with "as firm a nerve" as any man in Gotham. Two things, as luxuries, he as yet abjured—they were the Scylla and Charybdis, which he had so far warily avoided. "Love and politics only pay on the higher levels—as a supreme dissipation for those who can afford them"—he sententiously observed, "what is easily obtainable is always valueless!" Which mixture of cynicism and practical sense veiled the sybaritic luxury of his sensuous nature.

"Time enough for all that, by and by," mused Moses Dalman, with a complacent glance over his fee books. He was grinding out the golden grist.

"This matter may grow into a very ugly one," said Dalman, slowly commenting upon Morris Blum's letter. "But, there's only one thing to do, and that is, to find this missing fellow, Walter Ryley, at once! If he is in New York, then I can get at him, that is, if you authorize me to go ahead. It will cost a little money."

"Neber mind about de money," broke in Isidor Blum, "I bay all de disbursemends out of mine own pogid."

"Here is the whole thing in a nutshell," calmly continued the impressive lawyer. "You are in control of the 'Condor Mining Company' now covering the old Live Oak and Magnolia claims, in the Tombstone District. You are all right for the ownership of an undivided half in each of these claims. You've also had the two claims properly recorded in the name of Walter Ryley and Hugh Dalton in eighty-two.

"Ryley sells to you his undivided half, and the bill of sale is properly recorded, and you have had the two claims properly surveyed and patented, and kept up the assessment work.

"The mine is surely going to be very valuable! But, there is this to observe: Hugh Dalton's title to an *undivided* half of the two claims, and the conditions of your bill of sale, force you to keep up all assessment work, free of charge, on Hugh Dalton's half interest. That's a clear contract, and you dare not legally incorporate this mine, as you are only trustees for Hugh Dalton's interest.

"Moreover, Morris Blum writes now that Hugh Dalton killed a Deputy Sheriff in the row with the Earp gang—then, skipped out to Texas—and was, himself, killed later, at El Paso, in a gambling saloon! We could easily fix up a title to that interest, that is, Morris Blum and I, could, in time," mused the lawyer with his eyes fixed full upon Isidor Blum. "They do these things pretty easily down there in Tucson. I had some business there last year. But," and Dalman's voice hardened, "*now*, comes in this Walter Ryley's devilment. He drifted over to London, in the mine-selling fever after the great Tombstone discoveries, and there sold, or pretended to sell, a lot of Arizona 'wild cat' mines. He is supposed to be knocking around New York, now, a mere human wreck. Was a high roller in San Francisco, New York and London, once upon a time, the old story. An English firm of solicitors, 'Carstairs, Lyon & Carstairs,' of Sheffield, England, write to the Postmaster of Tucson for information of Walter Ryley, who sold an interest in the Live Oak and Magnolia mines to one Chandos Brandon, mining broker of London, in eighty-three. Ryley never returned to Tucson, after going over to El Paso to find Hugh Dalton."

"Now," said Dalman, "Morris Blum writes to your London agent and finds that this man, Chandos Brandon, is dead, an insolvent debtor. There is but one thing to do, gentlemen. *These English fellows must never find out Mr. Walter Ryley!*"

All three around the table nodded their heads. "It

was a judicious move on Morris Blum's part to have his chum, the Postmaster, write these people that Walter Ryley was dead!"

"Killed by the Apaches during Geronimo's raid! That will throw them off the track."

"What do you advise us to do?" asked the wary partners.

"Let me first try to trace out this fellow Ryley, if still alive. Turn the whole thing over to Morris Blum and myself, for the present. The English lawyers may drop the whole affair. They will probably call it 'quits' on a bad job."

"*Here, you are wrong!*" vigorously protested wary old Bent with a reminiscent flush of anger. "An American will go into a thing on a margin, make a deal, and then soon forget the mine and even its name, sometimes in a week. But I've found that the Englishman buys out and out, and always some blamed fool or another will turn up at the last and *sift the whole thing*. If there's a mine there *he'll have that;* if it is *only a ledge of trap rock*, he'll build a mill and then pound away at it for awhile. Yes! *I've had trouble with them.* You'll surely hear of these chaps again. Now, *I've got to go!* Go ahead, Isidor! Give Dalman your orders, I'll write to-night to the other chap, my friend! *Don't spare money.* If it's a good mine, as Morris says, we can stand a few thousand. *Shut them out*, beat them at all costs, only keep our name out of it. Morris can meet them down there if they turn up, and either bluff them, or fix the thing. *Put up a 'cold deck' on them!* Dalman, you had better trace the whole thing while you are over in London. I'll stand in. Now, remember, to-day is Monday, we meet Wednesday night at the Fifth Avenue."

Grasping his hat, the old shylock hurried away to the elevator, anxious to escape a ten-dollar fine at his meeting.

Then Isidor Blum sprang up and locked the door. "*Read dad! Boses!*" he tremblingly said, giving his fellow Israelite the few reserved lines of "Broder Morris." The lawyer whistled sharply in his surprise when he deciphered the confidential scrawl. "*By*

Jove! a million in sight! We must find this Ryley, Isidor."

"Yes, und blay a fine game vid dis old Bent und de Senador, Boses. I'll dell you all. Ve must have de Condor Mine, de gontrolling inderesd for Blum Broders, und, if you gan work old Bend und de Senador oud, I give you a good share, und dey vood the bill when we buy dem oud."

"Isidor, I'll get away and find this poor, ruined loafer, if he's alive. Don't you ever let old Bent see that letter!" excitedly cried the hawk-nosed lawyer. "I'll stand by you, *thick and thin.* I'll post you on the sly." He whispered a few words, and Isidor Blum roared:

"Oh! dad vas a good choke. Arresd dis fellow, Ryley, und lock him up. *Keep him quied!* Led me give you a check now. You spege to me *alone* ven you find him. *I don't give noding avay to Bend.* He's got blendy of money *now*, und de Senador has stole himself rich. It is ——" He leaned over and whispered a few words, whereat Moses Dalman laughed, as he pocketed Morris Blum's letter. "Go on, righd away out. Moses, find dad fellow. I bay for the lunch."

Isidor chuckled over his "good choke," gayly.

And, with the sly gliding of a wolf, Moses Dalman darted away to the elevator, and betook himself to the haunt of a friendly legal luminary on Centre Street. "If I can only get this fellow Ryley, then there's a fortune in this for me!" mused Dalman. He had coolly taken away the semi-Yiddish scrawl that told Isidor Blum of what Morris Blum had discovered in the mine. "We have covered up the drifts, plugged up the diamond-drill holes, and cut down the whole working force. We only keep Bill Murfee and the four men who cross-cut the ledge and worked the drills. They are all now at the mine, and *Bill lets none of them leave*, even for a moment! Their letters are slyly stolen, and no outsiders can see them. *They are safe!*"

As Moses Dalman sped away to begin his search for a needle in a haystack, he furtively dallied with the tempter, now whispering, "If I find the title in this fellow Ryley, I might get hold of this half the mine *for myself.* It's a good thing, *anyhow!* If he had a power of attorney from Hugh Dalton, though this thing may be already gone forever, we must bluff them—fool them—or fight them!" And, in half an hour, twenty men were searching through the slums of New York for the *ci-devant* broker, Walter Ryley, while Moses Dalman sought out his mining and stock friends to gain any hint of the whereabouts of the once prosperous Californian speculator. This done, Dalman turned homeward.

Moses Dalman was distraught as he slowly sought his office eyrie in a tall Cedar Street building. The elevator boy noted his gleaning, gray eyes and the set lines of his vulpine face. "Putting up a job on some poor devil! That's what yere up to, Mr. Moses Dalman!" mused Fergus O'Connor, a great expert in dime novels, cigarettes, and cheap Bowery theaters. There was a nervous lifting of heads in Dalman's office as he entered. Two saucy-looking, drab-colored typewriter girls redoubled the speed of their clicking instruments, and the office boys sprang to an attention. It was *le "reveil du lion"!*

"Tell Mr. Levy I want to see him at once," sternly said Dalman, as he clashed his office door. His face was clouded with anxiety.

"Beg pardon, sir! Here's a telephone message from Mr. Isidor Blum. Wants you to dine with him to-night at his house—to talk over some business. I was to call him up and answer."

"Say that I'll come!" shortly answered Dalman, dropping his head on his hands, at his table. The Condor mine had, for the present, driven all other matters out of his head. He looked up sharply, as Abram Levy, heavy, rotund, and of an overhanging head, sullenly entered. Levy, legal assistant, and responsible office drudge, had early resigned himself to beer and cheap dissipation. An encyclopedia of practice, a "hustler" in the lower courts, a walking directory of New York, he kept barely even with life on Dalman's fifty dollars a week, knowing full well that his name never would ornament the ground-glass doors

where "Moses Dalman," in ominous black letters, indicated the shark's lurking place. Blunt, burly, and
devoid of scruple, he butted away daily as the office
battering-ram at the brunt of Dalman's detail of drud-
gery.   Full well he knew that he never would escape
the tenacious clutches of his stern-eyed employer, his
junior by five years.   His life had burned out early!

"Where do the Pacific Coast mining fellows hold
out here, Abram ? " bluntly queried the successful
lawyer.

"Wall, Broad, Exchange Place, Pine, Cedar, and
all the little holes around there," grunted Levy.

"I'll not be back this afternoon. *Look out for everything !* " said Dalman.   "Telephone to me up at
Blum's house, 968 Lexington avenue, if anything oc-
curs. *I dine there !*" answered Dalman, filling his
cigar case, turning the knob of his private safe, and
leaving without a word.

As the "boss" disappeared, Levy grunted: "You
brute ! You would not even give me one of those
cigars if I slaved fifty years for you ! " and he lurched
lazily back into his den, where a broad paper-littered
table offered him a tempting field for "original re-
search."

Mr. Moses Dalman could time his drudges to the
half-hour, and his bitter, aggressive domination was
an ever present silent goad to the resentful toilers in his
"mill of the gods," and so, the "office business" ran
on.

For three long hours, Moses Dalman "dropped in"
here and there, wherever he could trace the broadshouldered, soft-hatted wanderers of the West, with
their clothes of frontier cut and hugely overgrown
golden watch chains. A word with a policeman—a
cigar to a janitor—and a few tips at some third-rate
drinking saloons, sufficed to give him a faint "view
halloo" on the trail of Walter Ryley, the much
desired.

The janitor of the Consolidated Petroleum and Stock
Exchange at last furnished the bustling lawyer with a
sure pointer. The hospitable advocate had taken his
man across Broadway, and loosened the guardian's

tongue with the best of Bacchus's outpourings, the truth-compelling whisky!

"Ah, yes! I remember Walter Ryley very well. When we opened up in 'eighty-eight,' in the new building, he was then in high feather! Back a few months from London, he still had a good deal of money. Had an office with old Colonel Harper, of Arizona. They did a good deal of stock business; firm name 'Harper & Ryley.' *All busted up now!* They used to take their luncheon at Billy Mulholland's, over in South William Street. Like as not, old Harper is hanging around there now. He's gone off to rags, and Ryley became a regular 'bum,' poor fellow! *Drink and women soon did the business for him!* All that gang of California and Western operators are 'on their uppers' now. You can buy a clothesbasketful of mining stock with a ten-dollar bill to-day. The jig is up, as far as they go." The janitor paused for breath and another drink.

"What sort of a looking man is Ryley?" carelessly asked the secretly delighted investigator.

"Well, he is a tall, heavy-set fellow, with side-whiskers, dark eyes and hair, smart and cunning enough, and used to be a heavy swell after he brought back some money from London. But, Good Lord! He may be in the Potter's Field now. I haven't seen him for some years. Find out old Harper. He will surely know about him, if any one does. Harper keeps a grade higher up. He strikes an old friend for a five-dollar bill now and then, and, if Ryley is alive, he would surely nose it out, and get a half of it, for Harper's a good old soul."

While the janitor recrossed Broadway, with a handful of good cigars, Moses Dalman soon sought out the headquarters of Billy Mulholland.

Picking his way down South William Street, he pushed the swinging half doors, and ignoring the attractions of the windows, with their museum of pictured dead prize fighters, passée actresses, and extinct Fenian heroes, he faced a burly, purple-mustasched boniface, whose yellow diamond shone truculently across the bar. It was "*the Mulholland*," himself.

Billy Mulholland, recognizing the legal aspect of his visitor, cast a reassuring glance at his ice pick, and the revolver lying ready by the cash drawer, but he broke into a broad grin, as the acute Dalman judiciously ordered the best in the house, and bade his host join him. It was the first legal customer who had ever "blown off" the house!

"Colonel Harper? Oh, yes! *It's about his regular time.* Take a seat. He always comes in for an evening toddy, and a game, in the back room." Mulholland winked aimiably in the direction of the private room, whither a bare-armed young ganymede of ferocious aspect was bearing a tray of drinks.

Pondering over the favorable situation, Moses Dalman now became anxious to strike while the iron was hot. A possible double cross lay threateningly before him.

"Here's old Bent, a sly, old manipulator. He surely knows every Pacific Coaster in town. He might easily run down this Ryley, and either spirit him away or else, buy his silence. And the Senator, the hidden partner! I suppose he rushed these mining patents through for the Condor. He has been for a long while mixed up with Morris Blum in the fat Arizona mail contracts. I must keep Ryley away from the whole lot, certainly, *until I have done my work.* Blum Brothers evidently want 'to throw' old Bent and the Senator in this deal, for Morris and Isidor are hiding this rich strike of rich, rotten gold ore! If I get to Ryley first I warrant that *they won't throw me!*"

He was interrupted by a joyous shout from the Mulholland, and in five minutes "Colonel Harper" and the lawyer were gossiping like old friends. There was some pretense to a faded sobriety of dress in "the Colonel's" garb. He clung to his title, his heavy crooked cane, and his present appetite for drink, with a vast store of stirring reminiscences by flood and field. Reversing the valves of his cross-examining skill, the fact trickled out of the gray-bearded old wanderer that Walter Ryley was a vicarious visitor at Einstein's Empire Lodging-house on the Bowery.

"I've not seen him for some months, but he always

makes his headquarters there, sir," pompously said the well-warmed-up old tippler.

With a deft skill, Moses Dalman poured out the "oil of gladness," and changed the subject, until Colonel Harper was an overcharged "Ancient Pistol!" Borne off at last in triumph by a trio of card players to the back room, the Colonel swept away the change of a five dollar bill, which mine host, Mulholland, at a wink, laid down before the jovial old rounder. It was an innocent tribute.

"Don't let the old boy want for a drink *now and then*," said Dalman, as he rang up a coupé and slipped a second five-dollar bill into Mulholland's hand. "I will come and see you again."

The Irishman nodded and winked amiably as he "set them up" in good-bye.

"Now, what's that devil's little game I don't know," murmured the host, as he saw the keen-eyed stranger whirled away uptown. But, he loyally fed up his "ward in chancery" with the "blue ruin" of South William Street; in fact "Ancient Pistol" was soon so surcharged, that he was a volunteer lodger that night in the "poker room," for Mulholland gave good measure, and he scented the return of the gray-eyed man, who was so free with his money

Colonel Harper was maudlin, and only played a mechanical game of poker, long before Dalman leaped out of his coupé at the door of D. D. Bryce's "all-night open" legal den, deftly planted in a near juxtaposition to the frowing Tombs, on Centre Street. He dashed into the "reserved sanctum," with a business-like air, but with a secret triumph in his crafty heart. "That old 'snoozer' is so drunk now that he will never recall the man who looked up Ryley," mused the eager wolf, now hot on the trail of his destined prey.

"See here, Bryce! I want your very best man for a few days. One of your rounders, a man who knows the Bowery!" cried Dalman, as he burst in upon the principal's reverie of an approaching golden tide of fees!

"What for, Mose?" was his chum's curious query "What's up?"

"Never mind! I want him, *at once!*" snapped Dalman.

"Ah, I see! Professional honor! *Secrets of client, and so on*," sneered the legal spider, touching a bell. "*Send in Yakey!*" shortly said Bryce. "There's your man, Moses!" laughed Bryce. "Now, you owe me a favor. Remember: *Don't spoil Yakey's beauty!*" But the two men had disappeared into a cubby hole room of the den, whence wires and telephones connected with all the punitive and eleemosynary institutions of Gotham, and also with sundry side wires to the outworks of D. D. Bryce's system of snares for the unfortunate client. Bail, divorces, alibis, and other "easements" were kept "on tap" here, day and night, to allay all the pangs that flesh may fall heir to! *All this for those who could pay well!*

"Do you know the Empire Lodging House on the Bowery?" demanded Dalman, eyeing the promoted waif of the streets, who was at once the bully and "sleuth," par excellence, of Bryce's Great Moral show. "Yakey," a carrotty-haired giant, laughed a gurgling laugh, "I should smile. I put two hundred voters in there for 'Wet Dollar Jones' last election, and I staid there two weeks, *superintending my colony.*"

"Good!" snapped Dalman. "Are you solid with the night clerk?"

"*We were schoolmates,*" grinned the aspiring member of a profession dignified by Coke, Mansfield, Marshall, Story, and the extended family of Choates.

"Get your things, then, and come with me. I want you to stay there a week, on half work and double pay."

"*I'm all ready, Governor!*" grinned Yakey, throwing on a coat. "I'll need a little ——"

"Precisely," interrupted Dalman. "Here's a hundred dollar bill," and then he led the way to the coupé."

"Tell the fellow to stop and wait at the nearest corner," remarked Counselor Dalman. "I want you to keep your eyes open now. Who's this night clerk?"

"*Pal o' mine when I was 'crooked'!*" simply said Yakey. "No name, *to speak of!* He's 'done time,' *the same as me!* You see, my boss selected me from a 'State Institution,' on account of my 'intimate knowledge of metropolitan life,'" he roared, in high glee.

"*A judicious selection!*" blandly remarked Dalman, studying the pitiless, glassy blue eye, debauched face, and knotted fists of the young man who had been a "terror" while serving as "puller in" for a Baxter Street "Gentleman's Repository."

"How am I paid—*by the day or job?*" drawled Yakey.

"I want you to put up at the Empire! Don't leave the house for a minute till you get hold of a fellow named William Ryley, who hangs around there!" sternly said Dalman.

"*Oh! Ryley, the Lush!* I know the cove," sniggered Yakey. "It's no easy matter. *He's an occasional!*"

"What's that?" sharply said Dalman.

"He hangs out there, but only when he can't keep full in some saloon. Tall fellow, black hair, broken-down mining man, always 'on the bum.' I know the bird, and he's ugly and foxy when drunk, too! Old Einstein has cracked him once or twice with a black jack. They'll 'do him up,' *for fair*, some day. Now, give me yer orders," said the unabashed Yakey.

"I want to get to him, day or night, as soon as I can! There's my house address, my club, my office! *Don't leave him a minute!* Send a messenger boy for me at once, *when you find him!* I'll come to the office. You tell the boss and the clerk it's your lay. Keep my name dark. I will come instantly. Keep Ryley in hand, give him all he wants, but keep him sober enough to talk—*that's all!* Do you follow me?" demanded Dalman.

"I'm dead on the game, Guv'nor! Hello! Here we are. Wait a minute. I'll be back," said Yakey, for the coupé had turned out of Grand Street and was dodging the cars upon the flaring Bowery.

The gaudy shops were in full blast, yokel and human waif idly wandering along there with thug and harridan. Keen Semitic faces peered out from fortifications of old clothes, brass watches, Peter Funk auction displays, and singularly abandoned looking female loveliness glared down from window and "poster," calculated to bring a shudder to Anthony Comstock and a cavernous sigh from the lugubrious Dr. Parkhurst, who grimly vetoes all "cakes and ale." The Bowery was in full bloom!

"*Hell's whirlpool!*" mused Dalman, as Yakey glided away to where an overhanging cheap transparency bore the huge lettered inscription: "*Empire Lodging House. Beds 15 cents. Single Rooms 25 cents.*" It was a retired abode for gentlemen of reduced means.

In five minutes, Yakey returned. "Our man is out on a bender; struck a few dollars and is doing the grand, but he'll turn up busted *in a day or so!*" the spy reported.

"*Damnation!*" growled Dalman.

"Ye won't have to wait long. He left a valise of old traps with Ben Solomon last night. He bought a new coat. He's a high roller, *now, you bet.* I took a private look at the gentleman's baggage. Old papers and such. The things only strapped. I've put Ben dead to rights. You'll do the handsome thing by us, *I know!*" fawned Yakey.

"See here," said Dalman, "Fetch me that fellow's valise and I'll give you fifty dollars now, and a tenner to stop your friend's mouth. I'll send it back to you *within two hours!*"

"Hully Gee! Wait, I hope I won't have heart disease. *Back in a jiffy!*" exclaimed Yakey, who sped away, returning in ten minutes with an old-fashioned two-handled leather valise. The firm grip of the youth upon the battered portmanteau only relaxed when Dalman pushed a roll of bills into his hands. "*There you are!* Remember! Hold on to Ryley, and treat him as if he were a 'certified check,' till I see you. I'll be back at my rooms at eleven."

"Drive on!" signed Dalman, as he whispered to Yakey: "Don't spare my money. Never lose him a moment from sight. Here, give me the number of the Empire. I'll send my own man with this thing before nine o'clock."

On his way to his splendid apartments in the gay "Thirties," Dalman stopped the vehicle, sprang out, and sent a telephone message to the sybaritic Isidor Blum.

"Detained.   Don't wait dinner.   On hand at eight sharp," he piped off, and then with his own hand, he bore the coolly abstracted valise into his front hall.

"Be here at eight sharp!" he cried, tossing the happy driver a five dollar bill.   "*I'll have a job for you.*"

"Now for a voyage into this fellow's past!" mused Dalman, as he bade his valet bring him a stiff brandy and soda, and drew his curtains.   "Come in at eight sharp when the carriage is here!" cried Dalman, as he dismissed his servant, then, locking his door, he emptied the contents of the absent Ryley's valise bodily upon a table, whence he had swept all the costly litter, with one quick jerk of the covering.   His heart was beating in high hopes now!

"*The papers in the case!*" laughed Dalman, as he sipped his brandy and soda, and lighting a cigar, proceeded to a careful scrutiny of the poor belongings of the man who had sunk from San Francisco's Big Board to the level of a Bowery guttersnipe.

An hour later, Moses Dalman laid down the last of the documents with a smile of triumph.   His microscopic eye had easily fathomed all the secrets of the heterogenous mass of papers, and a few letters and a ponderous diary with a faithless Chubb's Patent Lock were already locked up in Dalman's private jewelry safe in his lounging room.

Sharply ringing the bell, he dispatched his valet to the Bowery with the antique valise which had yielded up its treasures.

"Just leave it at the office, take the first coupé and get back here *at once!*" directed the exultant lawyer.

In the halt hour of the man's absence, Dalman closely studied a faded document indorsed: "General Power of Attorney," Hugh Dalton to Walter Ryley, dated Tucson, Arizona, in the far away eighty-two. "Notary Public's seal," mused Dalman.   "If that fellow, Ryley, did not record this, I am good for a half a million, unless Morris Blum has lied to his brother. A week in London will give me the whole game! Mum's the word!"

When Moses Dalman drove up to Isidor Blum's

Lexington avenue mansion at half past eight, he tendered his apologies for delay.

"Dond menshun id!" chuckled Isidor. "I haf wridden brivately do Borris. We will ged away vid ole Bend und de Senador."

Three hours later Moses Dalman drove slowly homeward in a secret glee. "I have befogged Isidor Blum," he grinned, as he mounted his stairway. His valet in waiting handed him a little note which roused him like the golden voice of fortune.

"Give me my revolver! I'll not be home for some hours! Go to sleep!" said the exultant Dalman. He caught up a light top-coat, and descended the stair in joy, for Yakey had scrawled the words: *"Got him here —drunk—in my room."*

CHAPTER II.

A DEAD-BROKE BROKER.

IT was midnight when Ben Solomon, the night clerk, haled the drowsy Yakey out into the stifling atmosphere of a third story hallway in the rickety frame building dignified by the name of the Empire Lodging House. Counselor Dalman placed a warning finger on his lip, as Yakey uttered a grunt of surprise. "I wish to see what he looks like! *Only a glance,*" whispered the lawyer. Holding a battered tin candlestick, Yakey led the way to an eight by ten compartment, where two cots, a cheap bureau, with its ten-cent looking glass and broken pitcher, furnished the "separate sleeping room." It was a squalid abode— the haunt of thief and convict.

Prone upon the straw mattress, still half dressed, lay the wasted form of a man, yet on the sunny side of fifty. "*It's him, sure enough,*" hoarsely murmured Yakey. "An', *there's his whole outfit.*" He kicked the battered valise under the bed. "He's safe for the night." Holding the candle cautiously so as not to awaken the sleeper, Moses Dalman studied his wasted face at length, and turning around motioned to the door. He had mentally photographed his victim.

Once in the hallway, he bade Yakey follow him to some safe place, after giving positive directions to Ben Solomon, to guard the recovered jewel so opportunely raked out of the Bowery mire.

Mr. Ben Solomon, in a red shirt, with its sleeves rolled up, was eyeing the open ground floor doorway, a *Police Gazette* in his hand, a presentation cigar between his lips, and a heavy blackjack lying on his desk at hand. A half opened drawer showed a knife and revolver ready for instant use.

"I'll bounce the life out of him, if he tries to sneak away!" hoarsely muttered Ben, with a wink to Yakey. *"I'm game for his nibs!"*

"Where is there a decent saloon with a private room?" curtly demanded Dalman. "I want a bite and a sup, and now, I'll give you your cue."

"Billy Schwartz's, corner Hester Street," growled Yakey. "Right good joint! I'm solid there! Come along!"

In ten minutes, the stolid Yakey was master of his employer's simple instructions. "This man must not leave your sight till I have done with him," sternly said Dalman. "When can you get him around here to-morrow morning, so that I can stroll in, on my way down town, and fall across you both?"

"*Nine o'clock*," nodded Yakey. "They'll turn us out then and I'll bring him in here, to this very room. You see there's really good eating and drinking here." Yakey swept his hand proudly in compliment over the quickly spread table, "An' I can 'corral' him here for a week on the quiet, if you will only foot the bill. I'll be hanging around here at nine sharp, all ready for you."

His employer nodded, well pleased.

"That's the plan, and I'll open out on him, and come in again between five and seven!" said Dalman. "You're to tone him up, and keep him sober until I tell you to let him go—then, perhaps, you can rush him all you want to! I want him to forget me—after I've done with him!" gloomily concluded Dalman.

"That's easy—*dead easy!*" significantly said Yakey. "A good dose of 'dope'—*a rap on the head*—and then

—*over to Bellevue he goes !* Turn him loose here on the Bowery, with a few dollars, drunk—*at night*—and the very next thing you'll hear of him is *hanging on a wire in the pickle tub over there*"—he turned his thumb eastwardly—"waiting for some one to give sixteen dollars for his cadaver—for the saw-bones. That's the end of the Bowery bum!"

Moses Dalman quickly swallowed the remaining half of his "special" brandy. The ashen hue of his face was a tribute to the Israelite's inborn aversion to lethal violence. "Mind you, I want him *to take his own chances !*" he whispered. "*You understand me !*"

"Dead sure! You are to know nothin'," practically finished off Yakey. "*But, he gets done up for fair, all the same*, see! Why, all I've got to do is to tow him down to the Barrel House, here, and leave a two-dollar bill or so loose around his clothes! *He won't bother us no more*, see! Those night harpies will take him over *on the East Side*. An'—they don't come back from there—*floaters—see !*"

"All right, I've heard enough of that. Now, you are not to lose sight of him a moment. Let no one tackle him 'on the confidential.' How will you keep him busy ?"

"There's life enough on the Bowery for us! Ten dollars a day'll do the trick," cheerfully said Yakey.

"Then get back to him *now*. Remember that you get fifty dollars a day if you fill the bill, and *nothing, if you don't*," replied Dalman. "I'll walk up the Bowery alone now, and jump on a Fourth Avenue car when you're well away. You know your orders ?"

"*I'm dead on !*" gruffly said Yakey as he vanished through a side door, first imparting a valuable secret. "You're king high here! I've posted Billy Schwartz. Friend of mine, see ? But keep your trap shut. Don't let any one pull you into a game after you leave, and always keep a shut mouth. Den dey'll let you alone."

"*I know New York*," grimly smiled Dalman, as he lingered a half hour in converse with certain gay damsels who had flitted into the back rooms; and then, leaving a gracious memory and a broken ten-dollar bill behind, he sauntered out and, lynx-eyed in his self-control, paced measuredly up town, past the haunts where men and women were vigorously undoing the good handicraft of Mother Nature. He shunned the voluptuous attractions of the " Victoria Loftus's Troupe of High Kicking British Blondes "; he demurely passed " Shooting Gallery," " Elysian Theater," " Harmonia Concert Hall," and several other resorts where the " gifted artistes " unceremoniously mingled with the audience, when their "turn " was achieved, in search of stray admirers, and the drinks, which were the local substitute for the laurels of applause. " *It's about as near a hell on earth as possible !* " mused Dalman at last, leaping aboard a car and speeding away to the equally vicious but slightly more decorous Tenderloin.

" Man is the legitimate prey of man," mused Counselor Moses Dalman, as he regained his " sumptuous abode" with the consciousness of duty well done. " *Yes*, and *woman also !*" he added, with a mental corollary that his projected scheme to trick both Bent and the Senator, as well as " Blum Brothers," was the crowning triumph of a life spent in much useful invention and judicious solitary cogitation.

" I do not see how they can get away now," mused Counselor Dalman, as he laid his tired head upon his pillow, with which comforting mental assurance he slept the sleep of the just, being " wearied out in well doing." And, a mile away, the bloated bully Solomon and the stolid Yakey laughed over the little impending drama on the Bowery, while above them the wreck of what had been a man of fairest prospects wheezed and tossed in the vision-haunted restlessness of the drunkard nearing his doom. This was but a "modern instance " of that easy descent to hell, which seems to be the *auto da fê* of the unrecorded lost souls; the devil's "unearned increment " of those who take up the battle of life, at first, fired with youth's high hopes and arbiters of their own destinies. For many roads lead downward, and few onward and upward, in the crowded purlieus of Vanity Fair. The pace that kills is the popular gait nowadays!

Counselor Moses Dalman was early astir on the

morning after his surreptitious exploration of the broken down speculator's last bit of personal luggage. During his bath, and while disposing of his morning coffee, he ruminated calmly over the Condor Mining Company's affairs, for he felt that he already possessed "a controlling interest," thanks to the documents so deftly abstracted. He already nourished a dull resentment against "Blum Brothers," and that old human octopus, Bent, as well as the vested partner, the "Senador." He had gazed enviously upon the splendid possessions of Isidor Blum in the magnificent Lexington Avenue house, excepting in his sweeping greed, only that portly dame, Rebecca, be-diamonded like Queen Esther, of happy renown, in all her glory. He was willing, however, to allow Isidor "a controlling interest" in the Oriental pearl of all his tribe, and the young horde of Blums, just reaching the age when they could "fix values" beyond a doubt, in all cases of property liable to pawn or chattel mortgage. The leadership of all the aggregated Blums of America was Isidor's proud personal right, but *as to the Condor Mine*—"*c'était bien autre chose.*" The fact that Blum, Bent & Co. proposed to coldly rob the "confiding British investor," gave to Moses Dalman's projected campaign a spicy flavor of poetic justice. He represented the "bears in the woods," who poured out to wreak a tragic vengeance upon the wicked boys who once thoughtlessly jibed their elder with the remark: "Go up, thou bald head!"

Any remaining shred of conscience not plucked away in the wild offensive and defensive melée of the New York courts, was "temporarily shelved" by Dalman, when, with a tranquil heart, he sat down at half past seven, to an hour's study of several papers, selected by him to build up the card "Castle in Spain," which his fancy had founded in his dreams of the night.

"It is my duty, *to myself*," he mused, "to see that old Harper, Bent, or 'mine frent Isidor' do not fall foul of Ryley and pluck him away from me! Perhaps, Yakey may find the right way to effectually bar that dangerous possible intimacy. If old Bent should dig up 'Colonel' Harper, and set him on the trail, I might be 'defrauded of *my just rights*,'" grinned Moses. "And, I will see to that! I must! And yet, I must not let Yakey gain a hold upon me! Such things as 'blackmail' and 'extortion' are heard of, even in our own Imperial City!"

Moses Dalman was ever alertly alive to his safety and public reputation.

Leaving his morning mail untouched, Dalman ran over all the London diary of the speculator, with occasional cries of joy. "He must have been a man of some good parts before he 'closed with the bottle' for the last death grapple! What set him off on the downward road? Success or failure? Wine, women, cards, and high life? or, the gradual 'letting go' of a disappointed man? Some turn of black luck—the unfavorable dwindling away of the market? Woman's cajolery? Man's betrayal, or the bursting of the whole western mining bubble? Poor, old, broken-down bummer!" mused Dalman. There were the usual newspaper slips, pasted in here and there, recording the many sunny days in the life of Walter Ryley, Esq., of London, New York, and—the golden West! Memorandums of checks showed that Ryley had once moved goodly sums. With a critical sigh, Dalman turned to several groups of letters, after once more examining the full general power of attorney of Hugh Dalton to Walter Ryley. "It is strange there are no letters from Hugh Dalton," said the puzzled schemer, as he ran over the documents, wherein his practiced eye could easily trace the fate of the Hugh Dalton interest in the Live Oak and Magnolia claims. There was nothing to show the formation of the Condor Mining Company. "That's Blum Brothers' work, and shows the trail of that slimy old crab Bent, and—de Senador," grinned Dalman. "They wiped the other things out of existence, and now, 'hold the fort' under a changed name! But here is the usual 'kick' of that golden ass, the British share-buyer."

A dozen or more letters, dated in eighty-three and eighty-four, addressed to "Walter Ryley, Esq., of

Ryley & Harper, New York City, U. S. A.," gave the alternating phases of hope and despondency in the mind of Chandos Brandon, stock broker, who had evidently purchased the Dalton interest upon Ryley's glowing representations. The period of disgruntled complaint seemed to culminate, and the evidences of a "shunting off" of the whole investment upon another, closed the correspondence.

"This fellow's address is valuable—*9 Bishopsgate, E. C.* That's good," growled Dalman. "Now, for the fat sheep who was sheared later by Brandon him-self. This story tells itself!" laughed Dalman.

There was no mistaking the fiery energy of Mr. St. John Gladwyn, whose dozen or more letters, evidently unanswered, concluded with a comprehensive anathema written in "eighty-five."

"A pretty hot communication, and, *devilishly well written!*" laughed the counselor. "The old gentleman evidently relieved his feelings, no doubt!" Mr. St. John Gladwyn's vigorous threat to proceed against both Ryley and Chandos Brandon "jointly and sev-erally," for the considerable sums invested, was the peroration: "I do not wish to believe that my friend Brandon has duped me, and swindled me out of the very considerable sums which I have been led to invest, but *your* silence, and *his* unwillingness to bring *you* to book, leaves me no alternative. I have instructed my solicitors to take the necessary steps to effect a recovery, etc., etc."

"That's the song of the plucked bird, always," laughed Dalman. "I have one anchor only to hold to, that is, Brandon, for the peppery old fellow writes, 'you can always address, "care of Chandos Brandon, Esq., stock and share broker, 9 Bishopsgate, E. C. London."' The old duffer was probably a gudgeon from the coun-try, and came up regularly to town, to harry Brandon. In fact, here is a pleading letter, the last, from Brandon to gain a plausible explanation of the stoppage of the mills of fortune." Dalman put the valuable papers away in his safe. "*Now, for Walter Ryley.* I will get him *disposed of,*" prudently murmured Dalman, "and then, off to London, to untangle the British title. A few hundred pounds may place me *in loco* both Brandon and Gladwyn! It all depends on the power of attorney being recorded. *I must look that matter carefully up!* I have two strings to my bow, when I bend it, and if I *don't* gain by the flute, I *will* by the fiddle, for that half of the Condor Mine *shall be my own*, I swear it!" With which cheerful adjuration, Dalman slipped out of his "sumptuous apartment" in a very modest guise for a man whose fees were thirty thousand dollars a year. "I must not startle him with my external splendor," mused the artful Moses.

On his way down town, in a Fourth Avenue car, Moses Dalman pondered over Isidor Blum's evident anxiety about the future of the Condor Mine. The Hebrew millionaire had urgently prayed him to search untiring for the much desired Walter Ryley. "You see, Boses, I don'd vant old Bend to ged ahead of Blum Broders. Ged ready for your drip to London. Loog oud for dis vellow Ryley. I god a glerk in old Bend's office vod vatches him for me. His ledders und his visidors. You see, old Bend was de New York end of de Senador's dam'd rasgalidies. He don'd risgk his buplic name, de Senador. Oh, by Cheminy! No, nod a leedle bid. If you ged dad vellow Ryley, you mage reddy for London—ad vonce! I'll vatch old Bend here. I chust bed you he wrides now brivately do Tucson und London, und we must drow him off der track, you see?"

"Yes, I see the point!" had cheerfully answered Moses, with a mental rider, "*and I'll sidetrack Blum Brothers, too*, until I see just where I come in, too, for *this pudding is a fat one*, and I believe poor Ryley was probably swindled out of his half—*at bottom rates*, perhaps paid in whisky and 'hand-me-down' clothes from 'Blum Brothers' Magnificent Emporium' in thirsty Tucson!"

Moses Dalman, of the New York Bar, the Mount Moriah Poker Club, the Perennial Riding Club, and the "Jung-Arion," drifted quietly into the Hester Street side-door of "Billy Schwartz's" at nine o'clock. A crowd of small tradesmen, "overnight" clerks, and "theatrical gents," with the first crop of early morning "Bowery suckers," were "lined up," facing the four busy barkeepers who "builded better than they knew," sin, disease, murder, and shame, in the gleaming poisons swirled around deftly in the cocktail glasses by their nimble fingers. It was the devil's headquarters, with Delilahs galore at hand.

A touch, a meaning touch, on his arm told him that Yakey was true to his tryst.

"*Have something!*" perfunctorily said Dalman, with a generous sweep, indicating the "easy boss," who lounged up at the nod from Yakey.

"*Mr. Schwartz*, my friend *Mr. Levy!*" growled Yakey with the grin of a Ward McAllister. "Hold on, Levy! I have another friend here."

"Bring him up, then, by all means," hospitably remarked Dalman as Walter Ryley, unsteady in gait, and red of eye, slouched out of the private room.

In the easy companionship of the "saloon," the four men soon drifted into a desultory chat.

"Order some breakfast," remarked Dalman, "I want to have a talk with you," meaningly signaled Dalman to Yakey, and then, the three strolled into the private room, taking their seats at the round table sacred to "poker," when not in use for "private refections," or used when the transit of the Bowery Venus "of the period," erratically occurred.

While the viands were preparing, Moses Dalman drifted into a mock proffer of steady employment to his stool pigeon Yakey. "My brother writes me from Fort Yuma that he wants a man to go down to Tombstone and watch a mining property which he has, out there," began Dalman.

"I've got a good billet in the coming election," growled Yakey. "Plenty of money! I don't care to go so far away. I want to get a regular place as keeper in the Tombs," continued the unabashed liar. "Perhaps, Mr. Ryley here, might go?"

Moses Dalman keenly watched the glimmering fire of interest in the drunkard's neurotic eye. "I used to know Tombstone—some years ago," aimlessly rejoined Ryley, his trembling hand unconsciously feeling for the absent glass. Yakey caught the motion and ordered up another round, as Dalman contemplated Ryley's shiny Prince Albert coat, dented derby hat, and the pitiful social pretense of a soiled paper collar peering out over the high-buttoned lapels. The ex-broker's hands were thin and emaciated, his draggled side whiskers drooped feebly, and, innocent of wrist-bands, his arms leaned heavily on the table. "I might, however, find you a good man, Mr. Levy," said Ryley, "and, I could tell you all about the 'lay of the land' out there and post him up a bit." Moses Dalman's cold, cruel eye gleamed in a secret triumph.

"I wish you would post me up a bit," he carelessly rejoined. "My brother is half crazy on those Tombstone and Bisbee mines. He wants me to go in with him, but I dropped some money through him at Harqua Hala five years ago, and I would not take his single judgment. I'm going to send him out some goods and a man. I've got to go to Cincinnati for a week or ten days, and then, I'll be back. I'd like to have a further talk with you. *Could you go out there?*"

"I'd have to have an outfit," ruefully said Ryley. "I got laid out here in Wall Street a few years ago and I've been trying to get even with the street. I hate to leave here a loser. I'm not fit for rough work, but I know Southern Arizona. I sold a lot of Tombstone properties in London in eighty-two and eighty-three." The arrival of the drinks tuned up Ryley, who eagerly attacked the breakfast when it was served, with the drunkard's false appetite.

"I wish that you were a strong man," said Dalman, at the end of a half hour's gradually growing intimacy.

The lawyer and his dupe were now alone, for Yakey, with a beautiful sense of social propriety, had lounged away to "get shaved," and to have a shine. "But there's one thing you can do—and that is to post me well," continued the imitative member of the tribe of Levi. "I'll pay you well, and I'd like to see you on my return. If I don't get another man, I may send you out, if we can agree on terms. Where can I meet you and have a good talk with you?"

The outcast dropped his eyes. "Better here, I guess. I'm staying at the Empire Lodging House down here on the Bowery, and it's a devilish rough place at night," rejoined Ryley, "sizing up " Dalman's plain business exterior.

The counselor had "dressed down" with care to a Grand Street standard. But, he could not conceal his prosperity.

"All right! I'll meet you here to-night," rejoined Dalman. "What is the show to sell any Tombstone property over in London now?" He affected to flatter Ryley with the glittering pretense that he was still cognizant of the speculations in "Western mining properties."

"It would take mighty good handling," slowly replied Ryley. "You see, I was flush when I went over to London. I was well fixcd. I had very good letters, and I worked with a rich London promoter, a stock broker, 'Chandos Brandon.' Of course, *you* have to 'give up' a good share, but it's the only way to make money. An American speculator can hang around London a whole year, and spend half the price of a mine, and not get inside the ring unless he 'gives up,' to a cool insider."

"If I were to fit you out in good shape, what could you get this fellow Brandon to do with a good mine, now?" eagerly said Dalman.

The third round of drinks came on as Ryley calmly said: "He has thrown up the game forever. Poor Brandon died last year a suicide and insolvent! The Barings worked him into the Argentines, and, then he went all to smash. *There are others*"—dreamily babbled Ryley, as Dalman hastily interjected:

"What sort of properties did you sell through him?"

"Let me see," mused Ryley, his memory stimulated with the food and drink. He dreamed over a cigar a few moments. "There was the 'Copper Glance,' a good copper lead; an interest in an Arizona onyx lead, and some gold mines, *The Live Oak and Magnolia.*"

"How did they turn out as investments?" said Dalman, carefully trimming his cigar.

"*I don't know!*" sadly replied Ryley. "I made money on the copper and onyx, and I had a big race over the Continent for a year! *I lived high,*" he sighed, "and came on here then with my old friend Harper. I started a broker's office, and we were turned down, finally, for all we were worth, and more! So I'm done up, and out of the game."

"And the gold mines?" carelessly questioned Dalman.

"I don't know," said Ryley. "I had sold my own half in Arizona, and I sold out the other half for a friend of mine named Hugh Dalton. I let them slide cheaper than I should, for poor Dalton got in trouble in Tucson. He was mixed up in a row there, and killed a deputy sheriff who was drunk and trying to coldly butcher him. But, the deputy was in with the government crowd, and so, poor Dalton skipped the State. I sent his money to him, for he wired me from San Antonio, Texas, to let her go. The 'sports' paid Dalton's lawyers, and got him out on bail, and away he scooted. He has never dared to go back, and I was laid out here, busted. I can't go back, and all the money I sent Dalton went to the gamblers who had saved his life. I never knew how the mines turned out. There has been some big money made in Tombstone," mused Ryley, "but, the mines are only very rich pockets, enormously rich; but when you've worked one out, the whole mine may say 'good-bye.'"

"*And, your old partner, Dalton?*" slowly said Dalman, whose heart fluttered as he saw a cunning look creep into Ryley's eyes. "If you went out for me you might drop into a good thing through him."

Ryley fixed his eyes firmly on Dalman's startled face. "I tell you he is dead, too. *Knifed at El Paso*, over on the Mexican side, by a damned greaser, and he lies buried there. I would never want for a dollar if he was alive. Besides, if he had ever tried to go back, that blood-thirsty Earp gang were all in power. They would have killed him. The deputy sheriff Hugh shot was just as bad as the James boys, the Youngers, or the Daltons. No, poor Hugh Dalton was driven out, and he is dead, I tell you—*dead!*" The voice grew irritable.

"And you never even heard *from him*, how the mines turned out?" said Dalman.

"No! For Brandon sold the thing out to a private investor, and I suppose that the Arizona half-owners got away with the Englishman. I never knew who it was, but it's all the same—the Englishman gets soaked, every time. Bless you, down there, the one Territorial Court is owned by the local gang, and this fellow Morris Blum that I sold my interest to is in with the whole Pacific coast gang—Senators, Judges, and Territorial Governor. The Johnny Bull would have no show there. It's a close game to run up against!"

"You left no enemies there, with this gang," said Dalman, in a brown study.

"Oh, not a bit!" eagerly cried Ryley. "I was solid enough with all of them. *I'm not a 'gun man',*" he said, simply. "But, poor Hugh Dalton, was a high roller. The 'mad Englishman,' they always called him. Nobody could bluff him for an inch, and *that's why* the gang hated him, for *he had seen better days!* No!" amicably remarked Ryley, when the fourth round of drinks came in, on Yakey's return. "They tried to follow Hugh with an extradition, but he slid out of Texas, and went up into the Pan Handle to the old home of the Bender gang, and he laid low for a while.

"He was a game sport and a square gambler, was poor Hugh. And, when the thing blew over, Hugh worked the western trains and made his headquarters at El Paso. I'd like to get down there and find out all about the poor lad's wind up. It was the same old story. *Woman business, you know!* Hugh was a devilish handsome fellow in those days. He had another gang of enemies, too, for he ran off a mighty handsome Mexican girl from Magdalena called Pepita. She was a crack-a-jack for beauty, only seventeen then, and the daughter of the Jèfe Politico at that town, and that's a big man in Sonora. Those fellows may have killed Hugh over at El Paso—to even up. *They never forget nor forgive.*"

"Well, I'll come in to-night at eight, and have a good talk with you," said Dalman rising, as Yakey strolled out for his secret orders. He shook hands warmly, and handed Ryley a twenty-dollar bill. "Don't fail me, for I've got to take the midnight train for Cincinnati. I think that we can fix up a deal. If my brother has a good mine down there, he had better hold it, and work it cheaply if it turns out well."

"Right you are Mr. Levy," said Ryley, eager to be off on a secret cruise and "break the twenty." "You couldn't get a dollar a basket for the best Arizona mining stock now, in either *London* or *New York.*"

The first use that William Ryley made of his windfall was to hospitably tender the "usual courtesies" which Moses Dalman most gracefully declined.

While Ryley was hobnobbing with "Billy Schwartz," who mentally dedicated the twenty-dollar bill to himself, Dalman was whispering sternly his very last orders to Yakey in the private room.

"*This fellow is slyer than he looks!* He has been adroitly lying to me. I'll bet a hat *the other chap is not dead!* Just find out what he says in his drunken moments. Note every muttering, and he is not to leave you for a moment. I'll be on hand at eight to-night. You'll get your pay *then*," smiled Dalman. "For, I want him half sober, *at any rate.* Keep your eyes about you!"

The rounder's greedy eyes lightened as Dalman gave him a ten-dollar bill "for expenses."

"*Are we to lose him to-night, Boss?*" hoarsely said Yakey.

"*That depends,*" gloomily muttered Dalman. "If he won't talk he is better *out of the way!*"

"Ye see, I want to put the right crowd on him, and fix him with a little loose money in his clothes," was Yakey's last ominous remark as Dalman slipped out of the side-door. "Ye can bet on me to the last gasp," was the last seal of Yakey's devotion, for he was bound to earn the judiciously withheld reward.

It was three o'clock in the afternoon when Counselor Dalman was interrupted in his study of a projected brief by the imposing apparation of Isidor Blum. The Hebrew "operator" was visibly perspiring in that inner Semitic excitement which always tells of precious "gelt" endangered. Locking the door, the chief of the Blums grasped the lawyer's arm nervously: "Vot you find oud? Nodings? By God! Ve must vork quick! Old Bend has chust mailed a letter in the 'drop' to-day to 'Carstairs, Lyon & Carstairs,' of Sheffield, dem English lawyers. An' he dond tole me of id. *De old rasgal!* It gost me fifty dollars do have a look at id. De boy begged id of de bostal garrier. I vas afraid to steal it. He vould gable over to them. Now, I have god on de drack of old Gurnel Harper, who vas de bardner of dis Ryley. A merchand vot I know from Texas knows vere he hangs oud. Gan you not dake the next steamer und go over to London? I give you deventy dousand dollars, Dalman, if you throw off dem English fellers, und you gan buy dem oud—for Blum Broders. I'll give you a name of my agend in London, und he gan pay the money dere, und dransfer the hallf inderesd *lader* to us."

Moses Dalman's square jaws shut like a steel trap as he bowed his head in a secret alarm. "To-day is Tuesday; I'll quietly take Saturday's steamer and go, unknown to any living soul! But, you must keep quiet! Don't go near old Harper! He might sell us out to Bent! You'll put up the money, sure, for I miss some good practice in going two weeks earlier!"

"Boses!" sententiously replied Isidor Blum, "*I'm a man of my vord!* I redain you, *brivately*, now! Here's a check fur two dousand dollars fur de exbenses, und I meet you on the steamer wid my brivate instructions und a cerdified check fur de dwendy dousand dollars. My agend vill gash it *in London.* Und, now, nod a single vord do old Bend! *You vas owned by Blum Broders!*"

"*It's a go!*" said Dalman, snapping the lock of his roll-top desk. "Give me your word that you'll not go near old Harper and I'll clean out and play sick a day and make all my private preparations. When I leave here Friday night, the Sunday papers will register me at the 'Grand Union Hotel,' in Saratoga. I'll be in London before even the office-boy here knows I have left New York!"

Moses Dalman's heart beat like a trip-hammer.

"Glorious! *Glorious!*" cried Isidor. "Gome up to my house any evening after den o'clock. I'll be on de vatch. I bromise to led the ding alone here. You gan do de business, und, if you vellers find Ryley—den—keep him dark, dill you gome back." The happy client rolled away to the elevator, and left Moses Dalman pacing his office, like a caged tiger.

"I think I will lose Mr. Walter Ryley *to-night*, or *to-morrow night!*" grimly said Dalman. "I'll either make him talk, or else relieve him permanently *from babbling!* He lied to me about this fellow, Hugh Dalton. The gambler, I swear, is somewhere in hiding. He must not turn up! I will make a clean job of this! I'll begin with Ryley—do up Bent, and finish off with '*Blum Broders.*' But there'll be no damned meddling of Gambler Dalton. If he is really dead, then the sooner I lose Ryley *the better!* If *not*, Ryley cannot go into eclipse *a moment too soon!* I must post Yakey." And so, with a snaky smile, Counselor Dalman stepped out and cashed the two-thousand-dollar check. "This is the real sinews of war," laughed Dalman. "*The good, long green!* It opens the way to man's domination, and looses the greedy devil of passion, always *slumbering in woman's heart!*"

Moses Dalman lost no time in reaching Einstein's Empire Lodging House. He found Ben Solomon, the robust "bouncer," and ex-officio night clerk, about to "go on duty," the simple ceremonies of which performance consisted in hanging up his Bowery promenade coat, donning a cardigan jacket, and laying out his "black jack" and revolver.

"*Glad you've come,*" growled Ben. "Yakey's had a devil of a time with that damned fool, Ryley! They are now behind the scenes, next door, at the 'Victoria Loftus's Highkickers'! Some way or another the gang has got on the idea that Ryley has struck 'flush times' once more. De kids, de gals, and de blokes is all onto him! Out for de 'long green,' see! 'Money talks,' even on the Bowery."

"Is the man drunk already?" formally questioned Moses. "L couldn't trust him with a plain job, then!"

"He'd never get out of the city limits *with a two-dollar bill!*" frankly replied Ben. "He's all square enough, but he's an awful 'lush.' De drink would turn him down, and he'll be back on your hands, busted! He's square enough, poor devil! A gentleman once! It's the old thing! *Stocks, women,* and '*booze!*' No! He's a candidate for the Potter's Field, or *de table!*" Ben Solomon's significant gesture indicated the probable inroad of the dissecting knife upon poor Ryley's cadaver.

"*Can't he be cured?*" perfunctorily asked Dalman, desirous of playing his part.

"Cured *be damned!*" vigorously replied the "bouncer." "All dese Bowery suckers lasts only t'ree or four years! De young gals wear out and cave in! Dese 'rounders' can't stop their lushing! *Dey won't*, see? Dey've all got dere tickets fur de dead wagon! Now, dere was an old jay wid a Burnside hat, and one of dem copper G. A. R. buttons, up here lookin' for Ryley *to-day*. I give him *de straight steer*, see? Told him we'd fired Ryley out, and sent him over to Hagan's, on First Avenue. Den I made Yakey cheese it with the ole boy! Dey was having a quiet booze up in de room. *It wasn't safe*, see?"

"Go over to the theater, and send Yakey at once over to me! *I'll make it all right! Hurry up!*" said Dalman, as he significantly tapped his pocket.

"Don't keep him long," said Ben. "*De evenin' trade is comin' in!*"

"All right," sharply answered the lawyer, whose nerves now tingled with the necessity of instant action. "Bent on the hunt for Ryley—old Harper fumbling around—he might soon know of me, and Isidor Blum will be writing to '*Simon*,' '*Max*,' '*Jacob*,' '*Isaac*,' and several other 'Blums' in Texas, Europe, and Arizona—these fellows may get a cinch! It has got to be pushed now, *the losing of our friend Ryley!*"

Dalman's breath came short and quick as he waited. While he cogitated, Yakey dashed in.

"*There's hell to pay!*" he eagerly cried. "Ryley seems to have been sharpened up by the good liquor we put into him, and a few square meals. I held him upstairs until the afternoon theaters would open, feeding up with some good medical brandy that I got at the drug store. He suddenly dove under his cot and then commenced to fool with his valise and began to look over the papers. I played off the sleep act! He threw out the old clothes and turned over his papers. '*Robbed, by God!*' he cried, as he ran to the door that I had locked. 'I wonder if I ever sent those mining papers back to Arizona Jack?' he murmured, and then he began to gibber under the excitement, which brought the liquor into his brain. 'They'll never find him. Never! *Jack is all right!* I'll write to Pepita, *and post her!* Yes! *The Pinkertons are after him!* The damned blood-sucker detectives! There's a thousand dollars reward for Hugh Dalton! But *they'll never find Arizona Jack!* I'll fix that!' Now, Boss, I laid low, and then he came and shook me up. '*I want to go out,*' he said. '*What for?*' sez I.

" 'To get a drink and *write a letter!*' sez he. '*Ye can have all that here,*' sez I, and I hollered for Ben, who brought up the drinks, a couple of rounds. Now, Ben got him an envelope and paper and ink, and he scrawled off a letter. '*Got any stamps,*' sez he, after the second round. '*Fix her up! I'll post it,*' says Ben, '*when I go for de oder drinks!*' I give Ben de wink, an' so he flim-flammed the letter. See? Sent her away with a piece of blank paper, and Ben's got de copy of de envelope and de real letter locked up in the safe! We'll give her up—*on shares.* See?" Yakey winked in a hungry manner.

" *All right, my boy!*" said Dalman. "Now, this fellow is really playing a fluke on us. I'll tell you what I'll do! You go back and jolly him along till I come in at eight! I won't mention this Hugh Dalton. There's fifty each, for you and Ben for those papers. Now, you pump him about this 'Arizona Jack.' *I shall not even mention his name!* To prevent his clearing out I'll show up, and I'll give you my orders *to-night.* You can tell him that you can make me give him the job, and advance him fifty dollars for a first outfit. That will put you solid with him, and, so *he'll talk* to you freely. Find out if he really wants to go down there, and see if he wants to stop *at El Paso.* After to-night, you can load him for good! Ben gets *his* fifty when he gives me the paper; *you* will have *yours* to-night, and, if you get him good and confidential, I'll double it!"

"*I'm on, Guv'nor!*" joyously cried Yakey, as he darted away in time to witness "the Golden Palace Cave" scene, wherein Queen Stalacta (Miss Rosie Reckless) appeared gracefully denuded of all clothes, save some shreds of silk and sundry meretricious gems of suspicious luster.   Before the plaudits had ceased, Mr. Ben Solomon had thrown open "Mr. Einstein's" safe, and handed to Moses Dalman a letter, with a slip of paper, indorsed "*Señora Pepita Morales, El Paso, Texas.*"

Dalman counted out fifty dollars, and then, with an unmoved face, read the few lines.   The warning was significant, and showed Ryley's sudden alarm.

"Tell Jack that the Pinkerton's men are looking for Hugh Dalton *up here!*   He must keep shady, watch all the trains, both from the *East* and *Arizona!*   I would run to Rincon, Albuquerque, and Denver.   He is a gone man if he goes inside the Arizona line, but *they don't know who* "*Arizona Jack*" *is.*   I'll write again.   *Trust nobody but the sports,*" and, it was signed "Walter Ryley."

Dalman turned to Ben.   "Did he make any row with you to-day?" he queried.

"Yes, he said he had lost some valuable papers," replied Ben.   "I told him that his old valise had been laying around here unlocked for a whole year, and I told him *I'd bust his crust if he said I took 'em.*"

Ben Solomon grinned a murderous leer as he loafed away.

"*I'll have Yakey close him out to-night,*" mused Dalman, as he slowly descended the stairway and went home to a quiet dinner in his apartments.   "*Ryley is ugly* and *on the downward path,*" reflected Dalman over his cigar, not knowing that the pet name for Einstein's Empire Lodging House was "Hell's Slide," a vigorous, if not graceful rendering of "*Facilis Decensus Averno.*"

CHAPTER III.

On his way down to Billy Schwartz's saloon that evening, Mr. Moses Dalman's crafty movements illustrated his intimate knowledge of New York City topography. He had varied his route on every occasion of his visits to the Bowery, and he also cheerfully reflected upon his old axiom that "a lawer can be seen anywhere and everywhere." Still he did not ambitiously court public notice on this especial occasion, and so, he chose the front platform of a car, dropping off a block or two away from the side-door of Schwartz's saloon.

"What more can I get out of this fellow?" he mused. "Nothing effective; and I must hoodwink old Bent and the good Isidor. No! There's no use in delaying now!" And having bestowed the Pepita Morales letter in his safe, he was now ready for action. "Once this human waif is lost from sight forever," he reflected, "I can tie up the whole thing, and I am easily master of the situation. I now hold old Bent and the whole Blum gang in my hand. For, I can soon hunt up this Arizona Jack if I wish to." He chuckled over the foresight with which he had written on to a legal chum at Tucson for a careful report of the present whereabouts of Andrew Hanson, the Notary Public of Tucson, whose "hand and seal" attested the General Power of Attorney, under which the Live Oak and Magnolia interest of Hugh Dalton had been sold in London by Ryley. "If the notary's books are reachable, it may pay me to have the entry destroyed, or not, as this game breaks," thought the cool schemer. "If the notary's records are '*non est*,' then, I should know it, and I can keep the thing in law for twenty years." He was unusually cheerful as he slipped into Schwartz's saloon; especially so, as Isidor Blum's ready money was now being used to betray this rediscovered clan of the "Ten Tribes."

"Well, I'm not practicing law *for my health*," laughed Dalman, as he nodded to Billy Schwartz, now in his "coign of vantage" behind his own bar. "He also practices at the bar," cheerfully ruminated Dalman, "only, *on the other side of it.*" And yet, for all his sins of omission and commission, the best of the two practitioners was the burly German who had worked his way up from a saloon "slavey" to a possible "Assemblyman," by the grace of the people of New York, free and independent. For, Schwartz had killed none, nor had he compassed their sudden destruction; he only allowed them to slowly poison themselves "on general principles," wholesale or retail.

"In there," laconically answered the saloonkeeper, who was a man of huge girth, large watch-chain, and few guttural words. His dazzling bosom diamond, real, proved that the house of Schwartz was solidly founded upon a rock—*Rock and Rye!* Schwartz was a model "saloonkeeper" on safe lines, and he smiled broadly on friend and foe in an unctuous welcome.

Dalman scented the half defiant social atmosphere, as he approached the excited Ryley and the good-humored Yakey. The ex-broker had re-collared himself; wristbands, a gaudy tie, and a pair of twenty-five-cent glass onyx cuff-buttons gave him an "air of distinction," and the comparatively new derby, with a pair of "job-lot" shoes, proved that Yakey had dressed his man up to the flush times "standard." He was a "new man" to all intents and purposes. While Dalman unobtrusively ordered the drinks and cigars, Yakey found time to whisper in Dalman's ears, "I've got the whole thing out of him! He's beginning to be a bit ugly, and the gang is all onto his 'heaps of style.' Don't trust him. *He may skip out!*"

"You're sure that you have pumped him dry?" whispered Dalman, with a glance at Ryley, who had wandered out, and was "showing off" in "treating" Schwartz.

"*Everything!*" said Yakey. "He will take your money advance, and I think that his idea is to get down there, and so, warn this Arizona Jack himself. I can see that. Look out for him! He's no fool, not a little bit."

"See here, Yakey!" said Dalman. "We will go right in, and load him up for good, to-night. I'll stay till

he's well on the way   *You must lose him to-night!*   I'll
do the handsome thing.   I have brought down fifty
dollars in one- and two-dollar bills.   When I go home,
you must dump him, far away, *over on the East Side*,
where he'll never come back.   Then, bring all the
papers in his valise, *every single scrap*, up to me at my
rooms.   I'll be waiting there, and my own man will be
on the lookout.   I'll tell him that you are a process-
server, coming to report.   Here's your fifty now.   Ben
has already got his."

"All right," carelessly said Yakey.   *"It's de night
of all nights!*   For de gang is well on to him, and de
women over there will set their men on his trail—when
I leave him.   He's a walkin' wonder to de gang, and
a two-dollar bill or two will soon touch 'em all off."

The return of Walter Ryley was the signal for a
veiled duel of wits between Ryley and the man now
coldly plotting his betrayal.

Yakey yawned over a copy of the *Police Gazette*,
while the two men wandered away Arizonawards, in
the useless talk.

"I have put off my Cincinnati trip for a day to see
how you like the idea of going down below.   I've had
some more telegrams to-day.   I have half a notion
now to join my brother in sinking a hundred feet on
this mine, and perhaps it will save us both money by
finding out if it's a ledge or not."

"When would you want me to go?" guardedly
queried Ryley, trying to be still master of a mind befogged with alcohol, and excited with his afternoon's
return to "high life" on the Bowery.

He dimly wondered at Mr. Levy's dropping all reference to the Hugh Dalton transactions.   The proximity
of a "cash advance," however, lulled his suspicions,
and he glowed amiably under a couple of drinks, while
Mr. Levy discussed the pros and cons.   Yakey, in an
adjoining "cabinet particular," was busied in a gay,
convivial conference with several flathatted, gaudily
dressed young women of brazen and socially defiant
countenances.   From a rear music-room, the sound of
a woman's uncertain voice rose, with here and there an
uncracked note, to the piano accompaniment of that

mysterious individual always called in saloons, "the
Professor." The appealing words rang out in a rum-
mellowed strain

"And when you've done with pride and anger,"
I know you'll call me back again."

The prima donna had finished a second song about
the folly of taking "the horseshoe from the door," and
then drifted into an encore, "Write Me a Letter from
Home," at the urgent call of certain Jack Tars of the
United States battleship *Pompono*, before Mr. Levy
and Walter Ryley had "fixed it all up." It was a gay
scene of easy abandon there in this shrine of Melpo-
mone, Bacchus, and Venus!

"You see, I'm very uncertain in my movements,"
said Dalman, who was already wearied of the useless
by-play and the simmering of this Hell's Kitchen. He
took out a package of bills. "Call in your friend as a
witness now. *I'll give you now, fifty dollars for expenses*
and for the very good pointers which you've given me.
If I'm not back from Cincinnati in a fortnight to offer
you the job down there, you're perfectly free and you
can keep the money. We'll have no trouble in agreeing, however, I think," concluded Dalman, who observed that the bright-eyed Bowery kestrels had crowded
in, following in Yakey's wake. Moses Dalman did not
wait to be formally presented to Miss Gussy Montmo-
rency, Miss Tillie Effingham, and Miss Florence Vane,
whose turns in the dime theaters came on between ten
and twelve, but he gracefully included the whole circle
in his comprehensive invitation. "*And now, what'll
you take*, for I must be leaving!"

"Then, everything is all fixed?" growled Yakey.

"I want your postoffice address," thickly muttered
Ryley as he lifted his glass, saying, "*Here's luck.*"
His stowing away of his windfall of money in various
pockets had not escaped the aforesaid kestrels, and it
was duly "piped off" to a trinity of east side "ladies,"
who had dropped in "*on their way home*," at Yakey's
secret suggestion.

"You'll always have Yakey to post you," carelessly
answered Dalman as he stepped out and modestly settled for the party's stirrup cup. Such a bonanza prince

seldom visited Schwartz's Hester Street corner, and Dalman, shaking hands with Ryley, was a hero of romance as he sauntered off to the music room under the safe conduct of Billy Schwartz.

In ten minutes, Yakey glided back into the card-room. "Stay here ten minutes, and then *get out for your life!*" he whispered. "We are starting him off now *for the East Side.* There's one or two who have gone on ahead to rally the gang. 'Beer Glass Annie' has taken charge of him, with her running mate, 'Mollie Malloy,' and you must get the first car at the corner—and—*don't ever show up here* again! They're already fighting over him, even now, like sharks over the body of a dead sailor! I'll come to you to-night, sure!—with all the papers!"

"Lose him to-night, then, *for good and all!* And then you must give Einstein's house the shake—*as soon as it is over*," said Dalman. "I'll pay you right off—*the very moment I see it in the papers.* Not a word to Ben Solomon! He must not know. For your own sake, we want no third party in this little secret."

"How could Ben know? De last act will go on *over dere*," softly whispered Yakey, pointing a dirty thumb toward the far off East Side, where the rushing tide from Hell Gate streams under the gloomy, deep-shadowed, deserted warehouses of the East River. "Dere's no hope for a duck wot's got de mob after him *over dere. It's hell's own stamping ground!*"

With a sickening smile, Moses Dalman listened to the volunteer prima donna's last song, "*See That My Grave's Kept Green*," as Walter Ryley's voice rose up high over the departing clamor of the revellers headed by Yakey, "Come along, Annie; we're all going over to the East Side; *I'll bring you back safe!*" Dalman remained for a few minutes watching an impromptu waltz to the strains of the "Beautiful Blue Danube," and then with the "usual music hall courtesies," effusively thanked the singer. As he wandered out of the side-door he nodded gayly to Billy Schwartz, but after a glimpse at the vacant rooms whence Walter Ryley had departed, in the stupor of his maudlin jollity, he was haunted all the way home by that stern old legal maxim, "*qui facit per alium, facit per se.*"

"Damn it all ! What difference does it make what happens to this battered old wreck ?" impatiently ejaculated Dalman, as he lay that night tossing on his bed, until long after two o'clock, when a sharp ring at his bell brought him to his feet, with the cold sweat standing out on his brow. "*That's Yakey!*" he shiveringly murmured, as his valet admitted a burly man with a bundle. "*Well?*" gasped Dalman, as the newcomer tossed down his package.

"There's the stuff—all of it. *He's gone for good, now—he'll never turn up!* He was rotten drunk when I left him—an' *a deadly gang was onto him!*" growled Yakey.

"How will I know ?" murmured Dalman, affecting an air of unconcern.

"*Watch the mornin' papers!*" bluntly said Yakey, "If he goes in de East River, it's always a week or ten days before dey catches the floaters—*see?*

"If he caves in anywhere around town, I'll post you myself. I'll watch out *at de Morgue!*"

Yakey felt a bank bill crumpled into his hand and was hastily pushed out as Dalman hoarsely murmured : "Come here after ten, *any night up to Saturday.* I'm *off for the country* then. Clear out of Einstein's, and only let *me* know if Ben Solomon has any news."

"*He won't!*" expostulated Yakey, anxious to prevent a useless division of the future spoils. "If he crawled back, Ben would fire him for 'a played-out bum.' I'm solid wid all de cops, and you'll have de only intelligence from yours truly. I've already moved back home. You'll find me down at Bryce's ready for special duty. So long !"

"All right, Yakey! I'll need you on other matters, by and by!" was Dalman's softened reply as he slammed the door, and, tossing the bundle of papers into the opened trunk, locked it, and threw the keys on his dressing table, with his moneyroll, watch, and revolver. He breathed a shuddering sigh of relief. "*It's all over* by this time!"

"I'll need you in *de near future*, as de society reporters say," mused Yakey, who despised his fellow Hebrew's chattering fear of the culmination of his murderous plot. "De Counselor's got a long head but, *no sand,*" he mused, as he sped away to an all-night joint, where he verified the figures (100) on the bill so hastily thrust on him. "*Dis isn't de last, my boy,*" cheerfully pledged Yakey, as he renewed an old acquaintance with a young lady of vivacious manners, who was gayly finishing a night begun in a Turkish smoking parlor, by "taking in the town."

"She's a mighty good looking 'alibi,'" grinned Yakey, "I'll freeze to dis gal, and show myself to the cops as her 'Armand,' while she does de great 'Camille' act. It will prevent remark, if de boys should make any 'misfit' with poor old Ryley."

Counselor Dalman found little sleep after the visit of his "process server," and he was up early next morning and ready for the labors of the day. Sauntering out before the fashionables had opened their jaded eyes, he was once more the carefully groomed young star of Judah, whose solid prosperity was always manifest in his dress. Costly was his apparel as his clients' purses could buy, but not rising above the sober lines of a prosperous follower of Kent and Story. His breakfast at the Imperial, was punctuated by a cursory examination of the morning journals. "*Nothing,* yet" he sighed, as he stepped into the pay telephone station, and arranged for a morning meeting with Max Rosendahl, his open legal foe and secret professional "collaborateur." The interests of opposing clients were judiciously "see sawed" by these Dromios, who mouthed fiercely at each other in the battlegrounds of the courts. It was the secret association of a solemn pledge made in their school intimacy to "milk the coin" from different sides, and, to pool the resulting creamy spoils!

"I must have free hands and plenty of swing," murmured Moses, "to dodge Bent and the Senator, as well as Blum Brothers. The already secured pointers on Brandon, Gladwyn, the notary, and this will-o'-the-wisp Arizona Jack, give me easily the first game of the rubber. But, I must find a sure way to keep 'Carstairs, Lyon & Carstairs' out of the whole thing. '*Principals only,*' as the *Herald's* Personals say, in the 'matrimonial announcements' of '*shapely blondes*' and '*foreign noblemen.*'   *I don't* want to fight a blundering firm of **foreign** lawyers."

On this sunshiny morning Counselor Dalman patronized the Café Savarin's famed restorative cocktail, before he "showed a smiling Providence " behind his " frowning face " at the office.   Things were decidedly running his way!

During the day, he started uneasily at each unfamiliar incident of the going and coming of the callers at the office.   He had, in a two hours' conference with Max Rosendahl at this gentleman's "law mill," at No. 16 Wall, arranged to furnish friend Max with a list of court appearances during the vacation months, and to send on his own private instructions from London, leaving the details to Managing Clerk Abram Levy.

"You can come in for an hour every morning.   I'll give Levy his orders, and when all is ' O. K.' in London I'll cable over to Levy.   In the mean time you are to take my mail, and the only tip is ' *Gone into the country for a two weeks' absolute rest.*'   Not a soul but Isidor Blum will know that I have sailed, and even him *I will post personally.*   You are to know nothing of my address.   I give it to you and to Blum alone, as *the* ' *Langham,*' *London.*   Between you and I, *I will not be there,* but I'll keep a room there, so as to get my letters and cables."

" *Going over on a ' dark horse ' expedition,*" laughed Max.

Dalman nodded.   "Do you want any money, Max ?" he volunteered.

" *Square it when you get back.*   I've got plenty— *some lying idle,*" was the good-humored reply.   "Then, Saturday afternoon, you can look in and watch Abram Levy a bit.   Abe's all right—*if he doesn't get drunk.*"

"And, *should he do so?*" anxiously said Max, "I don't wish anything to go wrong while you're away."

"Then put one of your own clerks in to sit at my desk there *on watch.*   Charge his salary to me.   *That'll bring Levy* at once up to the notch.   He is afraid I will dismiss him.   *He's a better lawyer than I am,* if he would only give up the beer barrel and his extended women acquaintances," justly remarked Dalman.

It was four o'clock when Dalman suddenly bethought him that he had forgotten to record Yakey's extended recollections of Ryley's maunderings and his disjointed remarks, "*in vino veritas.*" Sending a boy on the run up to Bryce's to bid "Yakey, the process server," to attend him at once, Moses Dalman arranged in his mind the conference with Isidor of the evening. "It's clear that we both must throw off old Bent—before I can successfully fool Isidor. I'll just go around and post Isidor by and by."

An hour later, Mr. Dalman left his office in an exceeding good humor. Yakey's detailed report of Ryley's mutterings proved that "Arizona Jack" still had a "local habitation and a name," having substituted that free and easy appellation for the high-sounding "Hugh Dalton," and El Paso, as a safe headquarters, in lieu of that nest of his foes, Tucson.

"I suppose its the thrall of the Mexican beauty," mused the Hebrew lawyer. "He is a damned fool to linger near by, in the very jaws of the sleeping lion of the law. I wouldn't run the same risk for all the senoritas of the Cordilleras." Dalman forgot that only a gentleman at heart will utterly throw himself away in a mad lover's constancy. Moses was eminently practical in his dealings with the fair sex, and he was already carefully making a note of all available Jewish-American heiresses in his "cabinet reservata." "Time enough to fool with marriage when I have reached my professional mark and made a fortune," he laughed. "If I pull off a half-interest in the Condor Mine I'll need no 'shatchen.' None—*unless Morris Blum has lied to Isidor!*"

"I think that I can depend on Blum Brothers keeping faith with each other. They reserve their lies *for Christians and their customers,*" and as Yakey turned to go away, Dalman had paused after locking up his safe, with the entombed memoranda covering some new points of Ryley's career. "*Any news yet?*" Yakey shook his head. "*Watch the journals, and wait for me,*" he whispered, as Dalman gave him a handful of the Perfectos which had excited Abram Levy's wrath.

Dining at Delmonico's after a half hour spent with

Isidor Blum in planning their "arranged interview" with the stern old miser Bent, Moses Dalman smoked his post-prandial cigar in a calm content.

"*We have spiked old Bent's guns forever, if the East Side gang has done its work well!* I leave nothing behind me to be raked up, for old Harper's babble would be but a drunkard's hearsay chatter. *Only to know that Ryley's lips are sealed,* then I will defy the world to rob me of this half of the Condor Mine. If I don't slice the cake on *one* side, I will *on the other!*"

Moses Dalman's professional gravity was never more marked than when he briskly seated himself between the gray-headed old wolf of finance, Bent, and the secretly exulting Blum, at the table in Bent's splendid corner suite at the Fifth Avenue Hotel.

"*I will just let them make the game,*" he mused, contrasting the cold, clammy secretiveness of Bent with the bustling self-assertion of Isidor Blum.

The rich Hebrew was redolent of business prosperity, good living, finest Havana cigars, and rich Tokayer and "Liebfrauenmilch!" Rubicund, with curved red lips pursed out with the pride of life, his face was a blazing sun, the exuberant vitality of the Americanized Hebrew showing out in every line. The cold, slaty face of Bent was the crafty visage of the successful monopolist, for the waiting game of Life had been his. The straight, cruel slit of a month, the hooked beak of the bird of prey, the round, steady bluish, pitiless eyes, all marked him as one sure to be in at the death. And, how many financial funerals had he attended as chief mourner and residuary legatee!

"*Well, what's your report, Mr. Lawyer?*" said Bent, after waving his hand at the sideboard, where the "spirit" was conveniently near. The others bowed a declination. Isidor lived "kosher" at home, and only drank at his meals or between deals.

Dalman watched Bent grudgingly sip his white wheat whisky grog, and then answered: "*I have not found this man Ryley!* He may have drifted back, westwardly. Have you learned anything?"

William Bent's long nights of gigantic "poker" battle against men like the California bonanza magnates had taught him the acme of the art of "scientific lying." Screwing his cigar around in his teeth, he silently shook his head, while Dalman and Blum secretly swore a vengeance against the treacherous man who was furtively running down Harper and tapping the English solicitors, "on the quiet."

"I have looked over the whole matter professionally," authoritatively said Dalman. "As my clients, you two men, must now both agree on a line of business action, and, also, upon a legal policy. *Your own business action is clear.* To keep the probabilities of the Condor Mine's richness hidden. Any public excitement would bring some emissary down upon you *at once!* These 'finds' are taken advantage of at once to bull the market abroad, and to revive the ghosts of moribund old deals—half forgotten. The safest legal policy is, for me to investigate—over there —and so to find out all I can. If we rake up this fellow Ryley, you must remember, that he is a veteran 'mining sharp'! He will be a thorn in your side! A blackmailer—treating between the lines—*with both parties.* He has parted with whatever interest he had. Let him be kept in the dark! Let Morris Blum shut the mine down, and hold it. Any local boom would be reported on the London Exchange at once. *You* and *your silent partner,*" Dalman smiled as Bent winced under the thrust, "can control the courts, the departments, and the Territorial Governor. *We* can then easily bluff off any foreign litigant. I've got to go to the country for a couple of weeks for my old father is very ill, and I must see him. Let me see, Mr. Bent, you leave for Portland, Oregon ?——"

"*To-morrow morning!*" snapped out Bent. "And I must be in London July 15," said Dalman. "If I sail the eighth, I am safe. There's a great annual conference of my insurance clients over there. . So I've two weeks left for family affairs, and then I'll get at the matter at once in London. There are two courses: the one is to befog and delay them; the other—*the wiser*—to beat them down, buy them out, or fool the title out of them. You must act as the circumstances warrant."

Isidor Blum was beaming upon the lawyer when Bent coldly said: "I've watched a good many of these distant negotiations. They fail usually with stolid Johnny Bull. Our best fight is to fight them at home, *out of the courts*, and *on our own ground*. It must be under the blanket. If you can get this thing into any one man's hands, why, *get him to come over to Arizona. Morris Blum can handle him then!* There's more than one way to skin a cat. Chances are ten to one they will send a paid expert. We'll put men on him the moment he strikes New York, jolly him up, fool him, buy his report, or get the surveyors to lay off the lines of the claims wrong. We can divide the British interest with them. Give them all "horse" quartz and porphyry, and keep the whole mine to ourselves. If it's a *principal* who comes, and he won't be handled, then there's a dozen 'frontier accidents,' that can always happen. Should they sue, then play the old game: keep them waiting five years, *while we gut the mine*, get the stock off our hands, and then leave them only—*a hole full of water!*" Old Bent chuckled grimly at his own neat plan.

Bent paused and emptied his glass. "You'll be here all summer, Blum?" he queried.

"Oh, yas! De ladies go to Saradoga; I hang oud at Long Branch and worg de stog marged a bid just for fun, und some oder leetle 'brivade deals.'"

Dalman winked salaciously. He had settled up the aftermath of one or two of Isidor's little private deals, for Isidor was vain and weak, as regarded "dimity." Always an expensive luxury, *a la longue.*

"Then you can keep up a look-out, a judicious one, mind you, for this fellow Ryley, while I am away, and Dalman is abroad. If you find him, then telegraph to me at the Union Club, San Francisco. We will get him up to my Montana mines on some fancied deal, that'll only cost us a few hundred dollars. Once there, *he'll not bother us again.*" The old scoundrel's face was as pitiless as a Sioux Indian brave creeping up to scalp a wounded and helpless foe!

"*So it's all fixed!* Morris and Dalman will act under your orders. My side of the house will wait for the news to come from you. One thing—I would not hesitate to buy out this English cloud on the title, if it can be done inside of safe lines, from first hands."

"Vot do you gall a safe sum?" said Isidor.

"Oh, twenty-five thousand dollars!" carelessly said Bent, ringing for a cold bottle of Pommery Sec. "Anything over that, I would fight on. *We are all safe now*, as long as this fellow Ryley is not flourishing around New York. Dalman, you need no points! You know just what to do. Now, Moses, the whole thing hangs on you, and Morris; I don't think that you will coldly stand by, and see yourself robbed. There's Bill Murfee down there—the superintendent. He'll fix the thing *just for devilment*. Bill is the fellow who sawed a bridge in Idaho, and let the stage and 'three adverse holders,' go down two hundred feet into the Devil's Cañon. That settled the case of the 'Python vs. the Anaconda, No. 6.' Bill will stick at nothing!" Dalman shuddered, and rose to go. Here was a possible deadly foe—this cold-eyed old brute.

Bent smiled grimly, and dismissed his guests; after a few whispered words to Isidor Blum, and when the two men walked out of the Fifth Avenue, Isidor Blum grasped his companion's arm gayly. "We haf now god a regular bic-nic mid Bent. He bud all in mine hants, and yours. Now ged your dicked, for the *Umbria*. I meed you dere on board mid de check. Ole Bend was chust a leedle doo schmard. You vork for Blum Broders *on de quied*. All ve vand is de didle in another name, so ole Bend dond suspegd us." The lawyer's eyes gleamed steely blue as he mused for a moment.

"*It will be in another name, count on me for that*," calmly rejoined Dalman. "Now, I've got to work like mad to get away from New York, with no one knowing it. You can keep an eye on Bend. See that he does leave town—he may be lying. Watch out for ole Harper and this Ryley chap, and let them alone. Give me two weeks *alone*, in England, and I'll quickly solve the mystery. If any strange thing happens before I sail, come around to my rooms between ten at night and five in the morning, and my man will let you in. And *no one else!* Don't send anyone. Be sure to certify that check." said the prudent Dalman, anxious to prevent any "change of heart" as to the payment of the twenty-thousand-dollar fee, for robbing one set of his robber clients, in the interest of himself, and preventing the robbery of Bent and the silent Senator by those energetic merchants, "Blum Brothers," of Tucson, Arizona, and elsewhere. "*It's a breddy neat game we blay on de ole man,*" chuckled Isidor, and his lawyer squeezed his fat diamond-sprinkled hand.

"*Pretty slick,*" cheerfully replied Moses Dalman, as he went away to join a poker party which reunited the cream of the Semitic jeunesse dorée of New York City at a supper party following an alleged meeting of a riding club. "The whole town will know of my whereabouts—and—my departure for the country to-morrow morning. These fellows will spread it everywhere. It's a good 'safety play' for me, if Ryley should be found derelict. They are only a pack of society jackals!"

Two o'clock found Moses Dalman with a sparkling eye and a flushed face, bravely backing a tremendous run of luck at the poker table. He was the envy of the crowd of hawk-eyed young sons of Mammon, who watched the reckless plunging of the man whom they all secretly envied and openly admired. For, Moses Dalman, sure of his success, had early lost the pained servility of the Americanized Hebrew, who so often "fights up hill," socially. He knew no reason to apologize for his keen intellect, his dubious tricks, his shameless and corrupt heart, for in dealing with man, woman, client, the bar, or courts, he had found that his "Christian Brothers" could match the daring Israelite, and often "go him one better" in calculating villainy! He was but a bright Knave of Diamonds in the particolored pack shuffled a million times a day, in great New York, where diamonds always take hearts, and clubs sometimes wins, the spades covering the dark work of the clubs!

Three o'clock found the Bowery deserted by all but the occasional drowsy policeman, the furtive footpad, the lynx-eyed women ghouls, and the drunken flotsam and jetsam of a great city. The electric lights flared out in a lonely glare, while the yellow gas blinked below a few all-night lodging-house entrances. The side streets were dark and silent, and prone in many a dark hallway, lay the victims of three-cent schooner beer and "five-cent" tumblers of whisky.

A fly by night hackney carriage now and then rattled along with its freight of "light flesh and corrupt blood." The heavy roll of early butcher wagons and gigantic beer vans alternated with the rattle of the Italian two-horse vegetable wagons, each dying sound accentuating deeper the despairing lethargy of the dead ebb tide of the ghastly wee sma' hours *"on the Bowery!"* Even Vice had crawled off to its lair, satiate of its nightly prey. The blear-eyed drunkards, in a dull coma, lay waiting for the dawn, till the fiery revival of the morning "eye opener" should weld one day of sentient debauchery into another. For even the Bowery must snatch the four hours of rest between two and six, for sheer want of human food to feed upon. Over his night desk at Einstein's "Empire," the burly Ben Solomon nodded by his empty flask. The house was full and, so was its managing major domo, the vilest bully of the debased Bowery haunts. Near at hand hung his loaded blackjack, and the kerosene lamp, burning low, smelled vilely of the crusted wick. Trade was dull, for harridan and thug slept!

With a start, the half-drunken bully awoke as a tottering, wretched form darkened the door. Club in hand, the hulking rough sprang to his feet. There was the swing of a loaded club, as the fleeing form paused at the head of the narrow darkened stair, then a half smothered cry as the heavy club descended, a sickening crash, and all was still, for something lay there below huddled into a shapeless mass! The burly loafer's heart blood froze in one gasp! "*The cops! This is a settler.*" His brain cleared of its first phantom vision, Ben Solomon crept down the stairway, candle in hand, for, the falling man had clutched at the street door, closing it with a loud clang.

"*Good God! It's poor old 'bum' Ryley!*" groaned Solomon, the flaring candle dropping from his hand, and leaving him there in the silent darkness alone with the dead.   He had seen the horribly twisted neck, the prone form lying distorted there, and a horrible fear now possessed the brute.   "*Out of here!*" he gasped, and so, with one mighty effort, he dragged the attenuated form of the dead waif of misery along the pavement leaving it sprawled out upon the stones of a dark corner near by, but, half hidden by the black shadows of the night."

"*De cops 'll soon find it*, and *ring in de ambulance*," whispered the brute, as he fled back into the hallway of the Empire, quickly double locking the door.   Then, opening his safe, he took out an extra whisky flask, and, swallowing a huge dram, waited for the finger of chance to arouse the sleepy guardians of the night.

In ten minutes, the clang, clang, of an ambulance wagon aroused the sleepy brute.   He sprang up in the ecstasy of his relief.   He was safe now.   Poor old Ryley!   *Dere he goes, a dead stiff; I didn't go fur to do it, nohow;* I thought it was a strange gonoph, or some dead smart sneak thief; *I must hold de jaw*, and *let him rip*.   Poor old boy!   He wuz wanderin' back for a place to lay his head!   But, dey done him up awful, *over dere*, on the East side!"

Ben had seen in the battered face, the stripped form, and the bruised and bleeding hands, the claw marks of the vampires who had fought and struggled over the "small bills" which led poor Walter Ryley to death's door.

Moses Dalman was three thousand dollars winner, in cash and good checks, when the Perennial Riding Club coterie broke up that night.   "Sorry for you, boys!" he cried.   "I'll give you all your revenge at our first fall séance.   I'm off to the country, for a two-weeks' run, to-morrow, and I may cross the water later.   You'll always find me ready to chip in."   After a parting salute of magnums of "Iron Head Irroy," to the favoring goddess Fortuna, Dalman drove slowly down from the Park to his apartment.

"If I only knew—" he muttered, as he swung the door of his little safe, and stowed away his poker winnings. "They will all remember *seeing me*, to-night, for they paid for the pleasure of my company," he grimly smiled, as he glanced at his watch. "By Jove! Four o'clock! *I need rest,*" and then, he betook himself hastily to his slumbers. The face of Walter Ryley was ever present in his excited dreams. It was six o'clock in the morning when he realized that his valet was vigorously shaking him.

"Here's that process-server again," timidly began the valet, "and he *insisted on seeing you;* would take no denial."

"*Let him in, you fool!* Don't you see that I'm awake now," gruffly cried Dalman. "Get out, and have me some coffee sent in at once. I'll dress myself. Stay, and come back with the coffee. *Hurry it up!*"

As the street door closed on the valet, glad to avoid his master's wrath, Yakey stood beside Dalman's bed. The lawyer affected a nonchalance, which did not for a moment, deceive the bearer of the grave tidings.

"You'll see it all in the evening papers; *the damdest thing,*" began Yakey. "It's awful cold! Got a drink here?" He followed Dalman's pointing finger and refreshed himself copiously from a bottle on the sideboard. "Ye see, poor ole Ryley was done up for good, but, he crawled back from where they had left him for a real stiff, and made his way over to de Bowery, tryin' to get back to the Empire. *It wuz mere old habit, ye see.* An' on de corner, near de ole joint, he was sandbagged by de mugs, and his skull smashed *like a busted cocoanut!*"

"De pockets wuz all turned inside out, de scarf and wris'bands gone, and all his 'roll' was took. *See?*"

"*Where is he?*" shortly said Dalman, with an averted face. His voice seemed strangely far off to him, and he pointed to the bottle, which Yakey handed over with the democracy of villainy. The coward drank a stiff horn, in a gloomy silence. "Ben sent down a boy to wait for me, and bring me up dere. De 'cop' recognized the poor old boy, and Ben showed him the room marked off the day before. He's over to the Morgue now! *It's all on de level, now!* What'll I do! *De reporters is on to it!* De ambulance came in from de Fourteenth Precinct Station, First Avenue and Fifth Street. Ben wants all kept on de quiet, fur de good name of de house, and so he'll manage all. I told him it wuz none of my funeral, and he's locked up the valise. *What'll I do, now?*"

"First," said Dalman, springing up, and giving Yakey a ten dollar bill, "Get over there to the foot of Twenty-sixth Street and *see him really dead!* Then, get your breakfast, and meet me at Mulholland's saloon down in South William Street.

"*De Harp of Erin?*" grinned Yakey.

"Yes! I have a job for you; and you are not to go near the 'Empire' again, till this whole thing is forgotten. I'll be downtown long before nine o'clock. Do you know old Harper?"

"That's de ole Grand Army consort of 'de late departed,'" vulgarly replied Yakey. "I'm solid wid him. Ben made me steer him away, and I gave him a few rounds of drinks. I got his whole story."

"*Then, we're all right,*" cheerfully remarked Dalman. "Get out now. I'll give you your last orders down there. I suppose this thing happened too late for the morning papers to get it?"

"Ben says it was three o'clock when de poor old bloke fell down the stairs *and killed hisself,*" stupidly muttered Yakey, whose head was turned by the gigantic dram he had taken.

"Well, go ahead," calmly answered Dalman, as the valet's key turned in the lock, and Yakey ambled away in silence.

"You scoundrel! *You lying scoundrel!*" mused Dalman as Yakey shuffled down stairs. "The two of you may have throttled him for the balance of the money and then, hurled him downstairs to break his neck. I do not fear either of you after that slip of a whisky-loosened tongue."

The lawyer rattled away Batteryward in high glee two hours later, as he contemplated the gulf now yawning between William Bent and any possible disclosures. "Harper, even this Arizona Jack, all of them, are powerless to reach Ryley now! Neither Blum nor Bent can ever *play me false.*" And then a horrible misgiving smote him. "*If Yakey had lied! I'll go and see for myself,*" he cried. It is the only way, for where can I trust a man, or a woman either, in God's world, *when money stands in the way!*"

It was nine o'clock when Yakey strolled into Mulholland's, where Dalman awaited him. The fortunes of war favored the Counselor, for Colonel Harper was already practicing at the bar, and vociferous in query as to the continued absence of Ryley. "I have a business matter of considerable importance awaiting him," said Colonel Harper, who had entirely forgotten his whilom entertainer. A nod to the active Mulholland kept the Colonel still oblivious. "Ryley is there, sure enough, No. 3 in the row from the door; entered as ' *Unknown man;* ' *no effects*, save the ragged clothes that the gang put on him, when they robbed him, and *a piece of tobacker!*" murmured Yakey.

"How long will they keep him there?" whispered Dalman.

"*Seventy-two hours!*" said Yakey, finishing his drink.

"Ah!" quickly remarked the lawyer. "You see this old fellow? Scrape acquaintance with him, and keep him drunk *till that seventy-two hours is over!* Don't let him get above Canal Street! Here's a hundred dollars for you, and twenty for the drinks! I'm going out to the country to-night! I've got a detective watching this old fellow now! He'll see you around with him! Call at my office late Saturday afternoon, and Levy will give you another hundred! I won't be back here till September 15. Then, I'll make you a royal present. Are you satisfied? Remember, I'm always your friend! I'll see you later!"

"*Perfectly,*" said Yakey. "I'll jolly the old fellow, and keep him off the track! He'll be drunk till Sunday, and I'll warrant that he never sees a paper!

"It's as much *to you and Ben*, as to *me*," menacingly, said Dalman. "The detective has an idea as to how Ryley was done up." He walked out leaving "Yakey" quivering under the spell of fear. "*He's a cool scoundrel!*" shivered Yakey.

Leaping into a passing hansom, Counselor Dalman cried: "To the Yacht Landing, foot of Twenty-sixth Street. Get over the ground, *I'll pay double*. In thirty minutes the lawyer gazed blankly at the vacant wharf. "Too late; the yacht has gone!" he murmured. "*Wait here!*" And then stepping rapidly into the little one-story house in Bellevue Hospital grounds, he passed down the room, with its glass partitions. A single glance at No. 3 on the marble slab sufficed. Ryley lay there under the icy shower. "*What becomes of the unknown dead?*" said the lawyer, slipping a two-dollar bill into the hand of an attendant. "*Dead House, Registered Grave, Potter's Field*, that means *dissection*," winked the official. "*No. 3, there, has already passed the inquest!* Classed as "*Unknown, skull fractured by fall, or blow of heavy instrument.* "He goes out to-night! Got no friends, *see?* Photograph kept, clothes exhibited for thirty days, and then, stowed away for a year! That's all. "*Thank you, sir!*"

The coward visitor fled away stealthily, and dismissed his driver a block from his own sumptuous apartments. "So, they did not lie! I am all safe now!" mused Moses. That afternoon, after a raffiné Turkish bath and toilet, Moses Dalman drove to Blum's office.

"De ole man is gone for good," chirped Isidor. "Now *for piziness!* I meeds you on de *Umbria!*"

"*I'm all ready to slip off!*" replied Moses. A cheerful private-room dinner at Clarke's, with "one fayre nameless mayde," and a study of all the evening journals, put Counselor Dalman in splendid shape. The account of the little event on the Bowery in that cyclone sheet, the " New York Whirled," was the spiciest item, and caused Dalman a huge internal satisfaction. "I am sorry, Maud, that I cannot take you with me to the country. Back in two weeks," laughed Dalman, as he sent the "young lady" away in a hansom. Two days later, he buttoned Isidor Blum's certified check for twenty thousand dollars under his steamer jacket, and gripped the old schemer's hand, when he cried, as the *Umbria* whistled, warningly, "*Don't forget.*" "Now for my little deal on private account!" laughed the villain who had sealed up all the avenues of the past. He paced the deck murmuring:

" I will skin the whole lot. Half the Condor is to be mine !"

CHAPTER IV

" THE HANDSOMEST WOMAN I EVER SAW."

COUNSELOR DALMAN watched the irregular sky line of New York City fade behind him, with a singular feeling of personal relief. He kept his stateroom closely, and gazed out alone on the panorama of New York Bay. He vainly tried to persuade himself that he had taken a whole stateroom merely for his personal comfort. He turned away from a last glimpse at the Statue of Liberty, rising grandly out of the old star fort on Bedloe's Island, for the rushing rivers meeting off the Battery continually recalled Walter Ryley's doom. "Why did they not strip him and then toss him in the East River. There are five hundred of these nameless wrecks of life dredged out of the dark meeting waters annually," he mused.

"Ah! Then, *I would not have known the truth!*" He recalled the grim interior of the Morgue—those awful prone statues in dead clay—with the anguished searchers for the lost, driven on by undying affection to reclaim the tenantless shell of the departed spirits. He saw again the callous attendants, the morbid loungers, the ferret-eyed human ghouls who traffic in a nameless merchandise of which no man can be the architect! "I am glad that I have used the clerk's name, Abram Levy, for my ticket," he mused as he carefully locked up the pile of journals over which he had pored in search of further light upon the fracas which led Ryley to his death. "*Thank Heaven! It was none of my doing!* Morris Blum's report of Ryley's death to the Sheffield solicitors will stand unchallenged till doomsday. It's all right, but, I must keep shady. Some friend of old Bent's might telegraph me as being over there under an assumed name. A pair of green glasses, taking my exercise only at night, eating my meals in my room, and so I am proof against all. I am really traveling in the interest of the Blums."

And, with all this special pleading, the acute lawyer knew that he lied to himself—that he was a fugitive murderer at heart, a smug villain betraying his trusting, if greedy, fellow Hebrews, and false to his oath of office.   He was gloomy and morose when the mists arose and the waters swelled around the laboring ship. He sought surcease of sorrow in the flask and craftily enacted the *rôle* of a sufferer from *mal de mer*.   The permission for a light, and sundry nocturnal visits of the attending stewards broke up the gloom of his first night at sea.   For the sullen plunges of the laboring ship, the lonely waste of trackless waters, recalled to him the dark outward voyage on the Sea of Death of the broken man, who merely stood between him and the proposed theft of a half interest in the Condor Mine!

But the morning brought him all the reinforcement of a vigorous nature, and his scheming brain returned to the weaving of plans destined to ripen into a golden future harvest.   He grimly laughed at the peculiar method which he had devised of following up "Arizona Jack's" trail.

"It is the longest way round, but the shortest way home," pondered Dalman.   "Here are two horns, in case I am forced into a dilemma, and I can work either to win or lose on the English, as well as the Blum Brothers' title, to the mine.   It is clear that this criminal, Arizona Jack, dare not go back openly to Tucson.   He would fall a victim to the machinery of the law set in motion by the artful Morris Blum, or else be assassinated by such of the Earp gang as have not yet yielded up the ghost *with their boots on*.   For, the border vendetta is undying.   The 'gun man' never forgets nor forgives.   '*Semper paratus, with the shooting apparatus,*' is the law of Tombstone District, where this gruesome ledge of gold ore is very appropriately named the 'Condor.'"

"None of the 'star actors' in the drama to come can ever reach *Arizona Jack* but myself.   I can either rebuild his fortune, use him to pull down the Blum Brothers' case, or bring him forward to break down the British case.   *He is my heavy gun in reserve!*

Strange game of cross purposes. Moses Blum goes into this swindling scheme believing Arizona Jack to be dead, and that Ryley is alive. I play the game with *Jack alive* and *Ryley dead*—dead and forgotten!"

The long days on the ocean drifted by, with Dalman closely studying all the permutatives possible in his search for a fortune "*en bloc.*" He had long passed the period when a few thousand dollars seemed to be "ready money" to him. He knew the wealth of New York's millionaires, congested with vast riches, and he aspired to be one of them, one of the flinty-hearted plutocrats who deny themselves nothing that can be bought with money—or knocked down with a golden club!

Vitellian feasts, Borgian voluptuousness, the moral abasement of a Tiberius, the merciless craft of a Nero, all these human excrescences can be silently grafted on the modern plutocrat, securing riding, *en mâitre*, the Golden Calf! The blue-spectacled man was avoided by parasite and gambler, by adventurer and 'ladies with a past,' on the voyage, and so Dalman passed undiscovered.

For, stealing on deck only at night, and busied by day, in his note-making and studies, Dalman was ignored. He was classed as merely a timorous member of that strange people who, however successful on land, have not taken very keenly to the sea.

The modern Hebrew waits at the shores for the waters to be piled up, so that he may pass dry-shod, in emulation of his singularly fortunate ancestry in their comforable passage of the Red Sea. A Jewish navy is probably only a bright chimera of the future! The very first man, on the dock at Liverpool, valise in hand. Moses Dalman skimmed past the customs, and thus caught the first London train. A part of his artful schemes was to be the presentment of himself in ultra London guise, on this distant bend of the shadowy trail of Arizona Jack's transferred fortune.

"I suppose the poor devil only got a few thousand dollars to cover his escape from the fangs of the law. Ryley seems to have been square with him, and to have dealt with him on the level. Probably he would do anything in this matter, for half the sum which old Isidor has given me to come over here and fool him." So ruminated Dalman, as he folded up his blue goggles on arriving in Lud's town. "He must be my very last card to play, for, an American gambler, a sport par excellence, may be fantastic, romantically generous, and, if he harked back on Ryley's death, he might choose to follow me up. But, pshaw! Harper, the only one who could have taken the alarm, was kept sodden drunk. Ryley's name was not mentioned in the journals, and Yakey and Ben Solomon would both have to swear the death to have been 'strictly accidental.'"

Counselor Dalman, with his bit of a valise, was eyed askance at the little "Prince's Hotel," on the Strand, but his decisive manner and promptly-displayed ready money soon won him a standing of the best. Flying visits to swell tailors and outfitters caused a stream of purchases soon to set toward his cosy apartment, while, in a hansom, the busy American measured London's endless miles.

"I don't want them to think that I've just come over. I will affect the air of the Anglicized American operator," laughed Moses.

Before the three days needed for the confection of a handsome wardrobe had elapsed, Isidor Blum, in New York, received a cablegram dated at the Langham.

"It's just like that old scoundrel to put his London agents on to dog me, so I'll have a quiet week to myself," laughed Dalman as he penned his dispatch: "Called away to Frankfort for a week; all right so far; address Langham." "My banking and insurance clientage will fool the old man, and it will make him swallow that fairy story," genially decided Moses.

The acute schemer had decided to trust no underlings on his quest for the real owner of the half-interest in the Condor, and, already familiar with London, he personally reconnoitered the vicinity of Chandos Brandon's office. His morning spent with a legal correspondent of some years' standing resulted in the detailing of a smart young clerk to attend the "American solicitor" in some supposed secret investigations as to the marketing of certain stolen railway and government securities. The legal records, the Stock Exchange list, and a dozen simulated inquiries befogged the smart clerk, who was only too eager to escape to the delights of the music halls with Moses Dalman's handsome daily tip. Two days of dredging in the deep seas of the past, brought to the surface the managing clerk of Chandos Brandon, who had been in business in a considerably large way. And Moses Dalman deftly gathered up the facts of the past history of the dead broker.

Moses Dalman's note-book was soon filling up with various details of the history of the bankrupt and deceased Brandon, and he saw at once how time, death, and ill fortune had swamped the Brandon business bark. It had been whelmed under the seas of financial misfortune. Dalman had judiciously veiled the real object of his queries, and his smart young "conductor" was searching over London, with certain marked lists of "missing or stolen securities," while Dalman cosily dined at the Cannon Street Hotel, with Edgar Allen, late managing clerk for the unfortunate broker, and now, the chief accountant of the Lanarkshire Fire Insurance Company.

The mellowing influence of good port and fine beeswing sherry opened the heart of the Briton, as they watched the stolid butler remove all but the wines, spirits, and the coffee and cigars.

"I don't suppose there would be any way to reach the books of the late Mr. Brandon. He must have kept a regular list of all the valuable American securities which he handled," purringly remarked the stranger.

Allen was not as yet sure whether "Abram Levy" was lawyer, detective, banker, or police agent, but he realized the keen ability of the querist. "A right up and up fellow, toned up to money matters, change, and all the movements of capital," mused the accountant, as Dalman deftly loaded his man.

"I don't see as how the Commissioners of Bankruptcy would let any one open a dead insolvent's records, save on a high tip from Scotland Yard, or an order through the Home Office.   There's always your Hambassador, you know," said the cockney clerk. Dalman smiled.

"True, but *this is a private inquiry*," candidly admitted Dalman, with the unabashed front of a peerless liar.   "If I can only get the description of the American securities that Brandon marketed abroad, I have all the numbers and description of the ones I seek, and so, we may trace out a possible means of recovery for the great company which I represent," modestly said Dalman.   "Mr. Brandon's insolvency and death is a sore blow to me.   He handled 'Americans' and railways, very largely.   I have obtained tips at home leading up to him here.   I find him dead and, his records unavailable."

"*It is hard*," wailed Allen, after Dalman had carelessly referred to a fifty pound fee for a list of the members of the missing securities and the customers.   "I entered them by the thousands of pounds, of course, but, mere memory would be useless."   He was gazing into the fire gloomily, when "Abram Levy" said "We heard of a letter regarding these securities from one of Mr. Brandon's clients, a country investor, but he did not give his own address.   He seemed to be very dissatisfied with the fall in Americans, a Mr. St. John Stanhope or Gladwyck, or some such name.   I would have copied it, but I expected to find Brandon here alive.   My mission is, of course, secret and I came away in great haste."

Dalman was standing lighting his cigar with his face turned to the window, as he cast out his ground bait. His heart beat quickly as the accountant energetically said "St. John Gladwyn is the name !   But that puzzles me ! what year was the letter written in ? "

"*Eighty-five, I think*," slowly said Dalman, setting himself in a chair, after refilling Allen's glass.   "Oh ! Come now ! *There's some error !*" cried the clerk.   "I never knew of old St. John buying any Americans or railways, and eighty-five must be a mistake. *I'll tell you why.* For, the old gentleman was just crazy on gold reefs and mining shares.   Brandon had made a good bit of brass in organizing and promoting them

here, the ' Western stocks ' as you call them.   This old
gentleman used to come down the line from the North,
I forget just where from, but I do remember that the
name of his place was Leigh Hurst.   He was a nice
old cove, had been in the foreign service, some way,
in his youth—and always dabbled a bit.   He parted
friends forever, with Brandon, *in eighty-four*, and he
was not reconciled to him when he died, three years
ago, but, it was about an American mining property
they quarreled.   I always kept the stock and share
ledger—and I am sure I never charged up or listed
one to Gladwyn.   *No! It was the Live Oak and Magnolia affair that killed the poor old boy!*   He even served
papers on Brandon fof the recovery of the twenty
thousand pounds which he paid for that property."

"It was a tidy sum," craftily said Dalman.   "Did
Brandon drop him in a hole?   *Was it worthless?*"   His
heart was beating rapidly now.

"*Hardly that*," answered Allen.   "Poor Brandon
took the property off the hands of a very showy American named Ryley.   Yes! Walter Riley, or Ryley!   I
think it was a 'y.'   They had some joint dealings.   I
believe that Brandon intended to float and market the
property.   He had taken the twenty thousand pounds
from Gladwyn to secure a block interest in a good
mine.   He found out too late that Ryley had sold him
only an undivided half interest, and that the mines could
not be legally exploited, organized, or floated.   Ryley
became soon mixed up with a fast set, went to Paris,
thence home to America, and I wrote to him dunning
letters till we were assured he was dead, or had fled,
or disappeared in the wild West.   Then, the crash
came!   Brandon had nothing to recoup Gladwyn with,
and I, myself, during the liquidation, had frequent
visits from the old gentleman, who would not even
speak to Brandon.   *Poor old boys!*   Their feud is done.
This old boy Gladwyn really worried himself to death
over this thing.   He only survived Brandon a short
year, and died but two years ago.   I well remember
seeing the note of his will, quite a decent little personality, also; but, I have forgotten all the rest.   I was
glad to drop it, for I tried to cheer poor Brandon after

his trouble, but he sank like a stone, weighed down by his troubles. As for Gladwyn, it was useless to talk to him, and when I got my present inside position he could not follow me up. So the whole thing is now well out of mind."

"You could suggest no way of my finding out his representatives?" seriously said Dalman.

"Oh! For that matter there's always the '*Agony Column of the Times.*' 'Wanted—Heirs of St. John Gladwyn. Principals only. Will hear of matters to their advantage by calling on or addressing X. Y Z., Charing Cross Hotel. You see you can keep dark and find out just what you wish. It'll only cost you a few pounds. It stirs up nearly every one if you make it to their advantage."

"*See here, Allen,*" said Dalman, "I'll give you the fifty pounds if you'll find out where 'Leigh Hurst' is for me. I'm far too busy to run around, and besides I might be imposed on with false pretenders. Drop me a line or a shilling telegram, and I'll call at once," said Dalman, giving his address as "Abram Levy, Prince's Hotel, Strand, London."

"There's just a long shot," said Allen, smiling. "I sorely want your fifty pounds, and I mean to have it. The cabbies all knew the old boy. I never knew him to have any friend in London but Brandon. My late employer, too, was proverbially close-mouthed. The cabbies know all the railway guards and porters. I can describe the old fellow, and, perhaps, they may have sometimes attended to his parcels and little commissions. I know that he used to come and go by St. Pancras. I'll use all my odd time. So do you put in your advertisement. Keep it up for a week, and *between you and me*, we'll find out Leigh Hurst, and the heirs of the late St. John Gladwyn. You might do a shrewd business turn, if you could loosen the deadlock of that title. The only trouble was the English laws. It was awkward that the property could not be organized and put in the market. The old gentleman was too old to go off to the wilds of Arizona himself to see the property, and I fear that something has happened to Ryley. *He was rather a fair sort of a chap*, and I believe women and wine broke him down

" In fact, Brandon himself told me once that Ryley had been cleaned out in Paris. Such a fellow, hardy and bold, was very likely to seek his fortune again in the West, and he never got the letters, likely. It could easily have then been fixed up to buy or sell to the others interested, for then, *at the flood tide*, we could have then sold all the mine, and so, *cleared a fortune*. Now, if you could only find this Ryley."

The clerk was eager, as Dalman sadly faced him. " Poor Ryley! He will never answer any letters. He is dead and buried, for one of my bond principals knew him well in his better days. He drank himself to death—and friendless and alone—*somewhere out on the frontier*. Well, *all this is a sad disappointment*," sighed the disguised lawyer. " A trip for nothing, I fear. The whole thing shows only the wear and tear of speculation. Here are three more fallen by the wayside, and the unsubstantial fortunes heaped up have vanished. It seems to be the old rule. The honest sheep are always sheared, and the 'operators' themselves, falling into dissipation and becoming reckless, are trodden down under the wheels of the Stock Exchange Juggernaut."

Abram Levy prepared to dismiss his stool pigeon, " *Mind you, I don't care a single rap* about the mining speculation. I fear that Brandon loaded poor Gladwyn to the extent of his purse, with the interest, which he found a drug on his hands. I must be going. Let me hear by a note to Prince's Hotel if you get the location of Leigh Hurst. I will be running all over France and the Low Countries for the next fortnight. Should you succeed, just send *me* the address of Leigh Hurst. I'll send *you* a P. O. order for the fifty pounds, there, *at once*. Any other points of interest would be an outside matter. Above all, *work quickly!* Time is money nowadays!"

"A right proper smart chap that," mused Allen as he took the " underground," homeward to his little nest at Brixton. " I hope to win his fifty. It would be a Godsend now." And then, Allen dimly remembered that Carstairs, Lyon & Carstairs, of Sheffield, solicitors, had once looked up the accountant's little home, and vainly queried for news of the absent Walter Ryley. "*Shall I warn them?*" he pondered. "*Better not!* They would get the fifty pounds *probably*, and I— *only a vote of thanks.* I will just write to the Sheffield agents of the Lanarkshire. If there's any considerable place named Leigh Hurst down in the West Riding, I'll soon know it, and there may be some future commissions in this man Levy. He is an out-and-out 'un, *that he is.*"

Counselor Moses Dalman, jogging up Fleet Street to the Prince's Hotel, enjoyed his evening cigar.

"I will harass this fellow with letters about the bond transactions. I must ignore the mine. He is very shrewd, and he might draw down Carstairs, Lyon & Carstairs on me. That would complicate my task. I opine that English 'solicitors' are just as greedy of profit as their American brothers of the New York bar. And, Mr. Edgar Allen, you must not follow me to my real abode. But, I'll try the '*Agony Column,*' and by to-morrow, too, I shall burgeon and blossom in a new English binding as a work of British art. And I've a fair show to throw them off as an "American cockney."

Like the smartest of men, often overshooting the mark, busied with all his stealthy precautions, Moses Dalman did not realize that he later owed his "open sesame" to the desire of the overburdened family man to pay up some little bills. For, Edgar Allen slept not till he had written the Sheffield agent, with directions to instantly telegraph the location and ownership of Leigh Hurst, if it should be found in picturesque Yorkshire.

On the morrow, Abram Levy "made his trunks," as the sprightly Gaul has it, and departed in the splendor of his "up-to-date" London "good form," bag and baggage, for the Euston Square Station. "I shall, perhaps, have letters arriving here, and shall return to you later. Please send my letters down to Low's Exchange!" he grandly remarked, with a royal tip all around. That very evening, Moses Dalman slept at the Langham Hotel, under his true name, having selected a proper apartment for a stay of a fortnight. His day had been a busy one until he re-transferred his ample belongings from the waiting-rooms at Euston Square. The tide of fortune seemed to bear his argosy bravely on. At Low's Exchange, he had received a bundle of American letters addressed to "Abram Levy." He passed over the vigorous appeals of Isidor Blum, and rejoiced over a letter from his agent in Tucson, while he cosily breakfasted at a snug little chop-house.

"*This is glorious*," chuckled Dalman, as he read the Tucson missive of his trusted friend. "I shall always bless the inventor of incendiary fires—revere the Emperor Nero, the Chicago widow's cow, and the 'aspiring youth who fired the Ephesian Dome.'" He read, with a positive delight, the news apparently of sore disappointment. "I regret to say," wrote his legal confrère, "that Andrew Hanson, late notary public, did not possess a constitution rugged enough to resist the combined effects of 'mescal' and frontier whisky. He lost his office building and entire records in the great fire of eighty-eight, and there is no way of legally reproducing any documents bearing his seal. This is very awkward, but, many other correspondents of mine are in the same fix. Hanson lies out on the hillside peacefully sleeping among his old clients, many of whose lives ended suddenly, as a testimonial to the unerring pistol and bowie-knife practice of our accomplished fellow citizens. If it's a real estate matter I may, however, be able to find you what you want. The stone court house, with its records, was saved 'from the devouring element,' as the Tucson *Clarion* neatly put it."

The schemer danced for joy. "*This is splendid!*" He enjoyed the humorous letter. "Funny, but valuable. *I* am the sole arbiter of the future of the Condor Mine now," gleefully ruminated Dalman, with memories of Morris Blum's Yiddish scrawl: "There's a million easily in sight in the pocket of rotten gold ore. We have drifted around and bored through with the diamond drills, and I've let that part of the mine fill up with water, for I broke the pump valves myself."

"*All right, Brother Morris*," murmured Dalman, "*you* are working in *my* interest while *I* toil for brother

Isidor." He sped away and inserted the suggested advertisement in the famed "agony column" of the *Times*. "*Now*," he mused, as he walked briskly from the cashier's office, "If I find Leigh Hurst, I am armed at all points. Whom will I dig up? Some pig-headed Yorkshire tyke, I suppose plump with beef, pudding, and 'homebrewed.' As old Bent says, these chaps are often doltishly stolid, and very shy of Yankee smartness. But, *I'll play my fish warily.*"

That evening, the counselor extended his social studies as far as the Alhambra and the Burlington Arcade. "I shall soon have the real London manners," he smiled, as he returned to the Langham, stimulated with unusual potations, and yet, anxious at heart, for in all the "woven paces and waving hands" of the glittering ballet, high over the strident music hall chorus, he saw the departing face of the unfortunate Ryley going blindly to his doom, and heard that whisper of accusing conscience "*qui facit per alium, facit per se.*" "*Hang it all!* I didn't think this dead chap would take a European tour with me." He finished off a jolly night at the Langham, drinking heavily and fell asleep dreaming of *Arizona Jack, Leigh Hurst*, and the *Agony Column of the Times*.

The first duty of the anxious schemer on waking was to pore over the "Agony Column" till he found the desired announcement.

"HEIRS WANTED."—A personal conference is desired with the legal heir or heirs of the late St. John Gladwyn, Esq., of Leigh Hurst. Principals only. Address
"HONESTY," care Low's Exchange, Charing Cross.

"I think a week of that, will do the business, at least *I hope so*," said the joyous lawyer as he made his morning toilet. "I think now I will follow out my assumed character of a sight-seer, and do the jovial, a little."

He arrayed himself in Piccadilly style and sauntered out to his apparent pleasures. But, before giving himself up to enjoyment, he visited his whilom headquarters at the Prince's Hotel. He received a cheery welcome.

"Right glad you came in, sir," said the pretty office girl. "Here's a telegram just arrived for you."

Moses Dalman could not conceal his satisfaction as he tore it open and read:

"Leigh Hurst is three miles from Pately Bridge, Nidderdale, Yorkshire. The party owned it. Send P O. Order. Further information when desired. Edgar Allen."

"I think I will take a little run out of town to-night," mused Moses Dalman, after he had consulted a Bradshaw, and hastened away to send a money order for fifty pounds, in the name of Abram Levy, to the fortunate accountant. He supplemented it with a brief note addressed to the Lanarkshire Insurance office, in which he thanked his humble friend, closing with the words, "*Off to Berlin, for two weeks. See you on my return.*" He had struggled with the geography of the North, East, and West Ridings, and decided to move by York, to Knaresborough, and down the valley of the River Nidd, to Pately Bridge. "*Just a rover, in search of the picturesque,*" laughed Dalman, "*and, any other little artistic effects I can pick up.*'

He was now buoyed up by success. "Thank heaven, this seems to be a good bit away from Shef-field," he mused. "They can't run over in an hour and plant the family solicitors on me. It seems that Messrs. Carstairs, Lyon & Carstairs are a good hun-dred miles from Brimham Crags."

Over his luncheon, Dalman skimmed a handbook of Yorkshire, and began to orient himself. "I can be back in two days, and, unless I need Mr. Edgar Allen, he shall never hear of me, nor *see me again.* I can probably narrow down the field of inquiry and come to the struggle of wits forearmed." And then he craftily laid his plans for his Yorkshire *début.*

It was an hour before sunset the next day when the entrance of a fashionable stranger convulsed the knot of yokels and drovers, draining their mugs of home-brewed in the little village inn, not far from Pately Bridge. "*This must be on the enemy's very line,*" re-flected Dalman, eyeing the huge old Druidical ruins overlooking Nidderdale. "That's Brimham Crags, sure enough, and the Hurst is within a mile." He had gazed on the weather-beaten sign flapping upon an antique hammered iron standard, dating back to the wars of the Roses. The diamonded panes, heavy masonry walls, and time-honored oaken beams, with the antique dressers and quaint display of pewter, gave an air of faded respectability to the hostlery, which still sported its stable-yard, and attendant hostlers. The car of Progress seemed to have rolled past on other highways, for the villainous railway alone disturbed the quiet of these dreamy Yorkshire vales. Noting a man in a smart livery, Dalman decided to accost him.

"Could you direct me to Leigh Hurst?" cautiously demanded the secret spy of Blum Brothers.

"*Only a stone's throw from here to the Porter's Lodge, sir,*" said the coachman, arresting his hand in an involuntary salute, for beneath the splendor of Moses Dalman's raiment, the shaven servitor smelled "the man of business."

"Is there any way that I could see the premises? I am a traveler, and, I am told, the old place is picturesque," replied Dalman.

"Aha!" instantly sniffed out the servitor. "*An artist, perhaps;* he looks a bit foreignlike—a bit Germanish!" he decided, as Dalman, seating himself at a white-scoured table, called for a pint of port after suitable query.

He bade the maid serve his casual conversationalist, and, appreciatively sighed when the smart coachman continued: "I've no doubt that Miss Lisbeth and Master Cyril would have you shown over the house, but, they went down to London on the four-fifty. I drove them over. This is the Leigh Arms, and on the estate." He quaffed his bitter and lit a cigar.

"I am sorry that you can't see the house, sir, but since Mr. Gladwyn's death, there's no one shown over the grounds. Now, *there was an antiquary for you*, sir, and a man always ready to show off Leigh Hurst to artists and *gentlemen traveling.*"

The personal valuation of Moses Dalman, Esq., had risen with his proffered hospitality. In half an hour, the acute lawyer had found the sunny side of the Yorkshire servant, and was in high favor with the bustling landlady, for he had ordered a dinner of the best, in a private room, and this, alone, lifted him up above the strolling artist or the ambitious commercial "bagman."

"*It pays to play the gentleman in England*," cogitated Dalman, "and, *it costs something to sustain the character!*" But, as he was spending Isidor Blum's money to further a plan of robbing him, he felt that the end justified the means. Long after the now voluble coachman had abandoned ale and taken to a "drop of good spirits," telling all that he knew of the modern family history, and much that he surmised, Dalman delved into the general career of the late St. John Gladwyn, and, at last, dismissed his now jocund friend to an easy homeward jog, for the wagonette was at the door, drawn by a pair of spanking bays. "I am sorry, but I must go on to York to-night, on the eleven o'clock train," said Dalman, at parting.

He finished his dinner in solitary grandeur, and strolled out alone to where he saw the old Elizabethan mansion gleaming out silvery in the fair moonlight!

"They went down in haste to London. Morley's is always their headquarters. I must not risk lingering here! Probable absence, several days. Will telegraph for their carriage to come to train. My cue is to get back to London, and to see that the advertisement reaches the interested parties—at once.

"For, I think the few shillings, that I paid out on that self-sufficient youth, were well expended. I can meet them, forearmed and forewarned. This fellow is a walking family history. I will keep out of the way of 'Carstairs, Lyon & Carstairs,' and Mr. Edgar Allen shall see me no more. This situation may need delicate handling. *Le jeu est fait! I am ready now to act*," mused Moses Dalman, as he returned with a contented air to the delights of the Leigh Arms. He left behind him the reputation of a 'sweet-spoken, pleasant gentleman' with buxom Molly, the pretty maid who long treasured two shining half-crowns, as the patents of Moses Dalman's nobility.

With a rush, a screech, and a roar, the train dashed into St. Pancras Station the next morning, bringing back the Hebrew knight-errant thoroughly armed, *cap-à-pie*, to the projected personal meeting with the heir or heirs of the late St. John Gladwyn. "Looks as if they had a bit of money, and, so, they may be devilish tough customers to starve out. It appears the ancient Leighs stood out a good siege there in bold Noll Cromwell's time. The blood may be fiery yet. Here is the fox's skin needed to piece out the lion's hide. I must bamboozle them, for if the thing once drifts out of my hands, *I am a dead duck.* I can only fleece the Blums right and left. *But, my God, it shall not drift out of my hands!*" swore Dalman, as he remembered the pale, accusing face of the dead Ryley. "*I'll have my share of the Condor!*" and the human vulture drove away to the Langham, sending a special telegram, unsigned, to each of the visitors at Morley's, couched in plain words, bidding them read advertisement in *Times*, headed "*Heirs of St. John Gladwyn.*" "They will have that by noon—*surely*," chuckled Dalman, as he leisurely breakfasted, with the air of a "grand personage," in the salon of the Langham. "To prevent them tracking me, I will hang round the Charing Cross Hotel, and watch Low's Exchange *from hour to hour*," decided Dalman, as he called a four-wheeler, and departed to pick the closing threads of his crafty intrigue.

Suddenly a professional "snag" loomed up before Dalman's prosperous bark on the flood-tide of fortune. "There is some old game of 'catch, as catch can,' or 'devil take the hindmost,' in this thing. Brandon was a good business man. Such a transfer as Ryley's would be utterly valueless unless the papers were executed so as to be legal in America. No one of these principals has ever visited America, or Arizona. There is the Legation and the Consulate General. If the power of attorney and bill of sale are spread on the books of record there, and the bill of sale bears the Legation or Consulate seal, my hands are tied." Even before he paused' at Low's Exchange, the schemer drove down to the confidential lawyer, with whom he had a considerable banking and trust business to look over. Dashing off a memorandum of names, he dispatched an office assistant to trace down the books of

Legation and Consulate for any transfer of property in America, from Walter Ryley to Chandos Brandon, in the years eighty-three, four, and five. "Here's a five-pound note! If you find anything, get a certified copy at once! And, do not leave the offices till you have personally searched both sets of books! Take your employer's office card! Do not mention my name!" significantly said Dalman. "And come to me the moment you are done, at the Charing Cross Hotel; you'll find me there until six o'clock, and you'll find a good dinner waiting for you, and—something else. Bring a rough pencil-copy of the document."

Moses Dalman, ever sly, jovially gave his legal correspondent a personal tip, after the assistant hurried away on this quest.

"I am desirous of keeping under cover, in London, on this visit." mysteriously said Dalman, with a self-satisfied wink. "The fact is a 'society lady,' whose name has been linked with mine, in New York, *has arrived in London!* It's a case of *noblesse oblige!* You must reverse the song '*Just Tell Them That You Saw Me!*' I authorize you *to say you didn't!* A note to me at Low's Exchange, to 'Abram Levy,' you know, will bring me at once, or a postal telegraph message. I have borrowed my own head clerk's name 'for this occasion only,' as the play bills say."

And so, the London lawyer, who had a neat little assortment of skeletons in his own closet, smiled and sympathetically stroked his glossy oriental beard. "*Depend on me, Moses!* I'll not give you away I hope that you will have a good time while 'lost in London.'"

"*I intend to,*" emphatically remarked Dalman, as he darted down the stairs. He was now ready for the "heirs of St. John Gladwyn."

Ten minutes later he walked into Low's Exchange and received a letter and a telegram addressed to "*Honesty.*" With a grim smile, he entered the nearest public and opened his missives.

"The trout seem to have risen to the fly at once," he mused, "and they are wary enough too, *it seems.*" For the letter and dispatch were the same in their tenor,

"Name place and time of meeting as soon as possible.   Send answer, by telegraph, to L. L., Morley's Hotel."

Leaving his port unfinished, and tossing the waiter a half-crown, Moses Dalman sought the nearest telegraph station.

The words, "Four o'clock to-day, drawing-room, Charing Cross Hotel.   Answer there to A. L.," were flashed along the wires to "L. L., Morley's."

With a glow of satisfaction on his face, the intrigant dallied over his breakfast at the Charing Cross.   He was happy, for he had burned all his bridges behind him.   On receiving an answer from "*L. L.*," he recognized a business-like snap in the promptness and decision of the movement of the "Heir or Heirs of St. John Gladwyn."   "There is no foolishness in this," ruminated Dalman, as he read: "*Will be there at four sharp; will ask for A. L. at office.*"

"I should say that 'L. L.' knows his business," was the complimentary verdict of the lawyer, who, with a sudden forethought, dropped a note to the London *Times* to discontinue the publication of the notice in its "Agony Column."   Seated watching the grand entrance of the Charing Cross Hotel from a convenient nook in the smoking-room, Moses Dalman's hawk eyes never left the broad doorway.   He felt that he was on the eve of the crucial struggle of his scheme.   Something in the sharp brevity of the answer jarred upon him.   "I must hurry slowly, now that I have fenced off every avenue to the past," he decided, and it seemed to be impossible to decide upon a definite course of action.   "I have my limit from Isidor.   Five thousand pounds for the transfer of their interest.   Yes, *their interest* to another.   If I am successful, and the thing goes into the hands of Isidor's secret trustee here, the man he has named, then I will have a keen London spy at my back, and I must fight Blum Brothers, facing both ways.   Delay, yes, delay is easy for me to manipulate, but *it brings me no nearer to the buried 'chispas,'* the yellow, rotten gold ore bonanza of the Condor.   If I knew whether that power was recorded—*I d——   There he comes,*" he gasped, as the office assistant, with a glowing face, dashed into the hotel, making his way to the smoking-room rendezvous. "I have been over all the records of both offices. They are splendidly indexed. No deeds, no powers of attorney, no conveyances; only this bill of sale of *an undivided half interest* in some mining ground from Walter Ryley, attorney in fact for Hugh Dalton, to Chandos Brandon, in July, '83. I went carefully over the whole records of the Powers of Attorney, in fact, *twice.* The name of Ryley or Hugh Dalton does not appear. Very loose way of doing business! I'll have the certified copy to-morrow. But, the transfer's worthless without the Power of Attorney."

"*Thanks,*" said Moses Dalman, holding out a ten-pound note. "I'm called away on a little business. Keep the certified document and we'll have our jolly dinner when I come back. Go down again to-morrow and carefully go over the whole subject again This is worthless to me. I'm afraid that what I sought is not there. But, *no matter!*"

Moses Dalman watched the clock in the main hall nervously, as the hands crawled on toward four.

"I have *now* my foot on Blum Brothers' necks, for the original Power of Attorney is valueless, and I can use both barrels of my legal gun. I may join 'Arizona Jack,' and perhaps present him with the half a fortune, or else *grab the whole* for *myself.* Now for the heirs or heir, *Mr. L. L.*"

Dalman drew out his Jurgensen repeater as the hall clock chimed four, and murmured: "*Right to five seconds. Now for Mr L. L.*" He fixed his eyes on the office counter, where three singularly self-satisfied young women clerks gazed with a mute disdain upon all comers across the marble slab.

Suddenly, a carriage stopped before the door, and a rosy, yellow-haired youth of twenty escorted a lady across the sidewalk.

A convulsive movement of two gigantic flunkies throwing open the glass doors, attracted Dalman's eager eyes, and as a graceful woman glided past him toward the drawing-room, the lawyer dropped into superlatives as his eyes followed her tall and stately form.

"*The very handsomest woman I ever saw in my life!*" declared the startled schemer, springing to his feet as a little page, efflorescent in silver buttons, timidly indicated the stalwart British youth, whose frank, handsome face had brought a melting glow to the visages of the supercilious "lady clerks."

"*Gentleman to see A. L., Sir!*"

CHAPTER V

"I WILL SEND CYRIL!"

MOSES DALMAN was suddenly thrown off his guard by the apparition of beauty which had flashed past him, sweeping along with the confident stride of a conquering goddess. The lines of an old song returned to him:

> "She came and passed with footsteps fleet,
> A shining wonder in the air——"

He was utterly unprepared, with his professional mantle of gravity, as the young Englishman advanced, simply saying: "If you are A. L. then we have come to meet you!"

"*I am A. L.*," ejaculated Dalman, "but are you *L. L.?* You use the word '*we*,' I observe! Let us step into the writing-room a moment!"

As they crossed its threshold, the American's sweeping glance told him that they were alone. He keenly "sized up" the frank-faced young collegian, a model of manliness in his simple tweeds, so deceptive as to the bulging brawn beneath.

"*I am Squire Leigh*, Cyril," began the youth, "and my sister Lisbeth is the *L. L.* whom you seek. For, while I am heir to Leigh Hurst, my half-sister, Lisbeth, is the sole heiress of my poor uncle, St. John Gladwyn. Our place is down at Brimham Crags, near Pately Bridge. *Do you know England?*"

Moses Dalman's safety play of a nod, was his only answer as Cyril Leigh continued.

"We came down at once on seeing the *Times* two days ago. Did you telegraph to us at Morley's to look at the *Times* advertisements?"

"*Certainly not*," calmly said Dalman. "I should have called in person had I known of your identity. I answered your letter and the telegram signed L. L. I see that my business then is with your sister. *Shall we go in to her?*"

"*First*," said the young man, with some hauteur, as "his sister" drifted into the conversation on the other man's lips, "*Whom have I the honor to address?*"

"Arthur Lemon, of the Chicago Land, Mining, and Stock Exchange," promptly replied Dalman, who felt that he was dealing with a couple far above him in the golden book of society. He felt a strong desire to isolate these people from all his immediate surroundings.

"I am at a loss to know what you wish to see my sister about," hesitated Leigh. "My poor uncle only left her a few thousands in the funds. I take the family lands, and right sorry am I, too, that Leigh Hurst is entailed. I know of no American property of my uncle save an unfortunate mining investment in Arizona, or some such wild State."

"It is precisely with regard to that matter that I wish to see Miss—or Mrs. Leigh?" queried Dalman.

"Yes, *Miss Lisbeth Leigh*, my half-sister, and my elder *by some years*," stiffly remarked the young squire. "But, I don't know what we can do here about this matter. The papers are all down at Leigh Hurst. We never valued the property as much. It would be useless to pay succession tax on a mere shadow, only representing twenty thousand good pounds of good money thrown away. Of course you'll meet our family solicitors? *Are you a legal man?*"

Moses Dalman assumed an air of deprecating gravity. "No! I am not," he firmly replied, "but I was an old business associate of Walter Ryley, who sold the property to Chandos Brandon. Poor Ryley is dead and gone—died alone, out West—and he always felt that he had brought trouble and loss upon an innocent party through Brandon, for he received several letters from the late Mr. Gladwyn!"

"Why did he not answer them, *then?*" fiercely said young Cyril. "The whole affair was a beastly fluke. Whether Ryley or Brandon robbed my poor uncle, I do not know, but *I do know* that the loss aided to carry the old gentleman off."

Moses Dalman now drew on his stock of professional patience. "I think, Squire Leigh," he said gravely, "that only Ryley's ignorance of law led him into unintentionally deceiving Brandon. Brandon's bankruptcy and trouble, of course, prevented him recouping Mr. Gladwyn, for, after his failure, he had neither the means nor the power. I have all the letters of Brandon and Mr. Gladwyn to my poor friend, Ryley, and I may, in a measure, aid to recover some portion of the loss. But, I will deal with no solicitors," he firmly said. "I can explain myself briefly to your sister. The whole affair is confidentially in my hands. If I drop it you will never get anything!"

"Oh! *Come, now,* that's rather hard lines!" said the high-spirited young man, flushing crimson. "*Your words imply a threat!*"

"Nothing of the kind, my dear sir," blandly, said Dalman. "To show you that I feel the whole matter, I will go at my own expense to your home. You can confer with your sister. Let me see such documents and papers as you have there. I will examine them in your own presence, or your sister's, and give you such advice, or make you such a proposition, as is fair. Ryley and Brandon are both dead. *Blood pays all debts!* Death releases every debtor, great and small, certainly as far as human pressure goes. I buried Ryley, and *he left no estate.* His poverty alone prevented him from answering Brandon's recriminations and St. John Gladwyn's appeals. For Ryley, was an uneducated prospector—a man of fair address, a miner, a broker, a successful speculator, and later, one who drifted down in despair to drink, and the unconscious suicide of the bottle.

"*There's the whole situation.* Let us see what we can do. I have pressing business on the Continent. I must return to Chicago soon—and a friendly glance at the papers can hurt no one,"

"*But, my lawyers?*" said the agnostic youth, leading the way to the drawing-room.

"They are powerless to influence my offer, or that of the principals whom I represent. I have nothing to divulge to them. It will be a practical business offer that I will make to you, and one not dependent on your 'solicitors,' as I believe you call them. Their slow methods, their many formal conditions, do not suit us busy Americans. I think that you can easily understand my offer when I make it, after finding out what you have; if you decline it, then I am free to go about my business, without complicating my principals."

In the drawing-room Mr. Arthur Lemon, of Chicago, bore himself with a most respectful deference as Cyril Leigh presented the American stranger. He was conscious of the power of a pair of steady, earnest, dark eyes as the Lady of Leigh Hurst greeted him with inquiring interest.

Lisbeth Leigh's rich, steady voice, her earnest manner, her perfect mental poise, impressed the self-conscious charlatan at once. "This is the guardian angel of the young Squire," he mused. "*Twenty-five* or *twenty-eight;*" he could not guess the age of the splendid woman—too warm in nature for a Juno, too serene for a Venus, and with the face and figure of a goddess. The North County never bred a sweeter lass than Lisbeth Leigh, whose dark hair swept in splendid curves over the noble forehead. Her beautiful face was lit up with an eager interest as she watched the impassive visage of "Mr. Arthur Lemon of Chicago."

"Your strange summons calls up my dear uncle's chiefest sorrow," said the lady, after Cyril Leigh, in ardent whispers, had taken his sister aside for a few private words. "I can hardly understand your reluctance to conferring with our solicitors."

"It is my habit, Madame," respectfully said Dalman, "*to deal directly*, and in this case the strict orders of my principals bind me. Are you familiar with the story of the Live Oak and Magnolia purchase?"

"*Too much so, sir*," rejoined the lovely English woman, "I *divided* my dear uncle's *sorrows* as well as *shared* his *joys*. In fact, my brother being absent at school and Cambridge for the last ten years, I was my uncle's sole companion, and often his volunteer secretary." Her dark beauty lit up under the tender smile of grateful recollection, the memories of a loving heart.

"God! I would like to bring that look once—*just once*—into that woman's face," mused the would-be swindler. He was now absolutely positive that she was the handsomest woman he had ever met! "I will not master her in any by-play of juggling words," he quickly decided, as he weighed the resolute bearing of this splendid daughter of Eve, and noted her perfect self-possession, without haste and without rest. "*What do you then definitely propose?*" she searchingly said. "You surely must have had an object in seeking us out. Before we unveil our family history, and show our private papers, it is but just that we should know wherefore and *to whom*. Our solicitors, bankers, and business agents usually exhaust the usual prudent inquirers before we became confidential,—*with strangers*," she steadily continued, gazing at the disguised lawyer, as if she would read his innermost thoughts. In his own heart, he knew that she was weighing him in the balance; he writhed in the presumptuous over-dress of the Pall Mall lounger, and recognized the unassuming fitness in attire of brother and sister. "She might be one of Murillo's women, *with a little more brains*," decided Dalman, who had the Semitic love for art, music, and form.

He decided upon that tacit flattery which often disarms even the ablest women. "*Let it be as you wish, Miss Leigh*," he simply said. "If I should visit Leigh Hurst to examine the documents and papers to which your brother has referred, let me be considered only as a *stranger coming upon business*. You probably can intrust such family papers of your own selection, as you may wish me to see, to him. He will be near you to advise you, and I have nothing to propose until I know that the title to this shadowy property lies in some one who is capable of contracting, alienating it, or selling it either now or in the future. I feel assured that you will be enabled to decide without technical legal assistance. I shall so arrange my affairs that if you decline to entertain business relations with me I will go over to Hull, thence to the continent, and at once catch a homeward steamer, for as I have briefly said, I am a man of business." He was modestly deferential and downcast.

"Pray, do not misunderstand me, Mr. Lemon," simply said the lady. "A Yorkshire welcome is a warm one. I have no doubt that my brother would be glad to show you Leigh Hurst."

"Certainly, *certainly*," murmured the young Squire, whose brow was clouded. He was not as quick in his intellectual operations as his serene and stately sister. He had shunted all the resposibilities of this affair upon his beloved Lisbeth, and, in fact, his thoughts were far away, for he was at the period when a young man's fancy lightly turns to thoughts of love. Impervious to the charms of his own beautiful sister, whom he accepted as an accomplished fact, an all-round Diana of mystic wealth of wisdom, he was sorely troubled now about another man's sister, a bright fay who had easily turned the head of the handsome young Yorkshire son of Anak. "*We had better go home to-night, Lisbeth,*" said Cyril. "There's nothing more to be done *here*." The lawyer's eyes met the lady's in a sudden surprise at her merry glance of helplessness.

"If you leave it to me, Cyril," she said, softly, "*let us go home by all means.* Mr.—Mr.—"

"*Lemon,*" suggested the American, anxious not to forget his assumed name.

"*Mr. Lemon can follow to-morrow, I presume.* We can send a carriage over to meet him at Pately Bridge," she said, flushing slightly, as Dalman respectfully said:

"And I would be thankful to Squire Leigh if he would bespeak me rooms at the nearest inn. If you will give me the hour and the route, I will arrive and meet Mr. Leigh at Pately Bridge to-morrow evening."

"You must come to us," said the squire, but Dalman's manner was perfect as he met the lady's gaze.

"*I am a plain man of business, Squire Leigh,*" he said.

"I will be happy to see an old English place, though, under the guidance of its master."

The lady rose, when Cyril, tearing out a leaf from his betting-book, jotted down a few notes of travel. "If you will telegraph your departure I will meet you myself," said the young Squire, with winning courtesy.

"And *I*, will have all the papers ready for you," said the Lady of Leigh Hurst, with a slight inclination of her head, "*so, that you may lose no time.*"

Moses Dalman stood with bent head as the young beauty of the North Countree passed out guarded by her blond Apollo. "I have not imposed on that clear-eyed woman *one whit*," mused Dalman, pulling himself together; "the brother, I could handle with a trout line, and I don't know if I could land her *with a net!* *Sweetness* and *strength!* She looked me through and through."

As the carriage rolled away, Lisbeth Leigh's carved lips were resolutely silent.

"He is either *more* or *less* of a gentleman than he pretends to be," she mused. "There is something uneasy, something uncertain, something *unsafe* about that man. There are several natures wrapped up in him, and why he seeks us out is a mystery; but for *his* profit, not *ours*, that *I will warrant!*" And Miss Lisbeth Leigh planted her colors firmly on a sudden mountain of distrust.

"Take me home! I am tired! *I must think this all over, Cyril!*" said the serene sister, noting the lively Cyril's microscopic eye "taking in" all the varied forms of passing beauty.

"Queer lot, that fellow," briefly summed up Cyril. "*Looks to me like a deep kind of a party!* Sort of a *business cad*, but *cunning!*

"*There are two of us to watch him, Cyril*," said Lisbeth, gravely. "And this old matter has been dropped as valueless already by the solicitors," said the young woman, who was her uncle's sole heiress and executrix. Her fair face was now shaded, for she remembered St. John Gladwyn's dying regrets, "Cyril's only a rash boy, Lisbeth, darling. *He will, of course, marry!* You know what other women are! You will have to leave the Hurst. I had hoped to leave you a handsome dowry, but now there's only a packet of worthless papers to show for twenty thousand good pounds! Whether the American betrayed Brandon or not, poor fellow, he *ruined himself, crippled me*, and *has robbed you* of your *marriage dowry!*"

It had not eased the broken old man's regrets when dark-eyed Lisbeth Leigh turned her frank, womanly face toward him, serene and steady.

"Marriage portions are no thought of mine, you know!" she said, with a sigh—the mocking echo of laughter fled in happy years. But, on this evening, when the brother and sister drove back to Morley's, Lisbeth Leigh was startled at Cyril's explosive remark: "Remember, Beth, what I tell you! *That's a sharp chap!* Whatever that thing, or mine, or hole in the ground is worth, it's worth *more to us* than what *he will offer!* That chap has a beak like a bird of prey. He is here to make money—for *himself*, not *for us*, nor for these principals he speaks of—like a cockney Hebrew money-lender. I have a year before I go up for my 'Army Exams.' If the property has a value, let me just *run over* and take a look at it." Cyril closed with a triumphant, "So, there you are, all safe!"

Lisbeth Leigh gazed admiringly at the eager face of the young fellow, and clasped his hand fondly as Cyril said: "*It's only for you, Beth, dearest.* You should have been born the heir of Leigh Hurst; I'm only fit to go and have a shy at the Dervishes, or, perhaps, the Cossacks, *by and by!*"

Moses Dalman's one scoring shot had been his quiet declination of the perfunctory invitation to be a formal guest at Leigh Hurst. Accustomed to the easy-going methods of an unclassified American society, in his brief business visits to England, he had not fathomed the sturdy guardianship of the British home. True, he knew that a New Yorker now entertains at his club, a Parisian at a café or restaurant, and that only slapdash Americans in these days threw their homes open to Tom, Dick, and Harry, but, he had not fathomed the *noli me tangere* icy disdain of the well-planted Briton, for strangers, however glib in manner, or "slick" in appearance. He had seen scores of Americans fail in "impressing" John Bull at home, by their arduous forwardness, and restless nervous familiarity of approach.

He recognized a powerful nature in the queenly poise of Lisbeth Leigh. "I will never fool that woman into the tossing of this embryo fortune over to me, *without due reflection.* Young and beautiful as she is, she bears the record of some strange life experience on her noble face. Not the kind of woman, perhaps, who knows all men, but, some one man has entered into her life, to cause her to man all the walls of her defenses. *No 'chateau qui parle' there!* And, this same resolute, clear-eyed woman is likely to turn upon my tracks—and investigate me. I will cut off the lights, and, Miss Lisbeth, if you grope, you shall grope in the dark." Dalman was on the defensive.

A council of war with his wits at the Langham, led him to decide upon a decisive course of action. "I will be called at six o'clock. I will direct all my mail to be sent from Low's Exchange to Blum's secret agent. *'Off to the Continent'* is the word at Prince's Hotel, here, and also at Low's Exchange. 'I shall not return to London!' will be a good 'stop off,' for I can take the earliest train, take all my belongings to York, and from that convenient hiding-place watch Miss Lisbeth. For if she does not consult her solicitors and put them privately on my track—then, I'm a fool. *There is distrust in that woman's eye.*"

Counselor Dalman was correct in his estimate of Miss Lisbeth Leigh's agnosticism. His refusal to go through the clammy hands of a firm of English solicitors had marked him as a Yankee schemer. And as the train rushed away in the night, Miss Leigh, brooding over her uncle's losses and Cyril's jerked-out snap judgment, decided to know more of the matter before giving any faith and credence to "Mr. Arthur Lemon, of the Chicago Stock Exchange." "This Pandora-box gift of poor uncle St. John's, a useless dowry of which he dreamed, is mine alone. *There is no need of hurry,*" she sighed, "for my life lies bleak and bare before me. There is only one last heart-wrench to come, the day when Cyril brings the Lady of Leigh Hurst to rule in my place. *And then——*" she resolutely put aside all her memories, hopes, and fears with the proud consciousness that she was "equal to either fortune," even if left alone among the raging waves of life's tempestuous sea! "*We come and go— alone,*" she sighed. "Hands that clasp, loosen—those who go on the way with us soon fall off or disappear, and 'the kingdom of a quiet mind is man's only inheritance from the gods!'" Ashen and sober reflections for a young beauty still in her flower!

As Mr. Arthur Lemon stepped out of the train at York, the next day at two o'clock, he consigned his extensive luggage to the care of the intelligent baggage porter. A half hour's tour of the vicinity enabled him to select rooms in a quiet hotel and install his belongings.

"I shall look over the country for a week or so," he remarked as he registered his name and paid for his room in advance.

"Now, I can defy the bright-eyed Miss Lisbeth," laughed Dalman as he hastened back to the station to catch the Pately train. He had plainly marked his luggage with the initials "*A. L.*" "That will either do for 'Abram Levy' or 'Arthur Lemon,' he chuckled, "should either Allen or Miss Leigh try to dog my movements. Now for the duel of wits!"

He was busied in weaving his plans as the train left the historic Eboracum, and speeding away from the junction of the three Ridings, rushed on to Knaresborough and Pately.

He was jocund in covering his tracks so neatly.

"Letters, my secret movements, and all my steps are arranged so that Bent and Blum cannot fall on these people without great loss of time, and even Allen is ignorant of the real object of my quest. The only people whom I have to fear are 'Carstairs, Lyon & Carstairs.' I must *not* face them, for some professional guarantees of good faith would be demanded."

With all his *sangfroid*, he was startled to see the waiting wagonette at Pately Bridge, in charge of the impassive-faced groom whom he had so jovially entertained at the Leigh Arms

"*Here is a fatal break!*" he instantly reflected, but he trusted to the disguise of his demure dark attire, and his future use of an odd five-pound note.

"*Thank Heaven!* The fellow does not recognize me," mused Dalman, as Cyril Leigh advanced to meet him with an embarrassed sense of the "half-arm" policy of holding off his strange visitor.

"I've put you up at the Leigh Arms, Mr. Lemon," said Cyril. "They will treat you nicely, and I hope you'll consider yourself my personal guest there. We live a very retired life," added Cyril, blushing crimson. "I've been away for years, and my sister has been secluded since my poor uncle's death."

"I am in your hands, Squire Leigh," courteously answered Dalman. "Time is of value and you naturally wish to confer over the situation. I'll be ready to pay my respects after dinner. I might perhaps look over the papers with you this evening, and to-morrow we can meet in the afternoon for a discussion."

"*That's just our ideas,*" cried Cyril, in an evident relief. "In fact, my sister bade me suggest that you should breakfast with us to-morrow and we can show you over the old place." Mr. Arthur Lemon courteously bowed in silence.

Twenty minutes' drive at a spanking pace, brought the party to the door of the Leigh Arms, where Dalman was led by the young squire to a pretty apartment.

"They'll serve you a fairish dinner here, and I'll send over for you at eight," said the young man, leaving Moses Dalman to his own devices.

Though the Yorkshire cheer was of the best, Moses Dalman was disturbed at heart when he saw the flash of the coachman's eye, proving that he had been recognized. In an irresolute moment, he placed his finger on his lip while the footman was removing his "light marching order" luggage. The shaven servitor winked impassively while Squire Leigh was giving the landlady his last orders.

The beautiful Nidderdale was spread out before the American's restless eyes, as he smoked his after-dinner cigar in solitary grandeur. He had wondered at the stately solidity of his "fair upper rooms'" garnishing.

The exquisite cleanliness of the old roadside inn, with its heavy carved oak furniture, told him of the inherited renown of the Leigh Arms. A huge four-poster bed in his sleeping apartment, draped in purple and yellow; the lavender-scented linen; the quaint old silver service, and the dreamy beauty of the landscape, brought him a drowsy sense of well-being. It was a fair and peaceful country side, the Yorkshire valley.

"Pretty considerable people, *these Leighs*," he murmured. "The Squire's modest marking out of his boundaries here, indicates a substantial wealth. The sleepy village, too, is on their grounds, and yonder is the castle of the fair antagonist—by no means a 'Sleeping Beauty.'"

A quarter of a mile away the old bell tower of Leigh Hurst rose above the irregular sky line of the long gray-walled Elizabethan mansion, framed in its sturdy English oaks. The last sun rays lingered on the beetling Brimham Crags, whence a fair Norma might have once stolen away from Druidic rites to meet a handsome Roman Pollio.

"*I must be wary*," he decided, "in the showing off of the old place. I will gain a bit of the family history. Here's the pretty maid servant, a few shillings will fix her. The coachman I can tip handsomely and, so, get all the future pointers I need. And, of course, his mouth will be closed with the seal of the 'sovereign.'" In the pleasant evening hour, he saw the historic home of the Leighs as he was driven through the splendid lodge gates. There had been no chance for a word of warning to the coachman, as the officious people of the inn escorted him to the wagonette.

But, ignoring the beauties of park and glade, of the dreaming dells and the fair meadows of Nidderdale, he casually addressed his conductor. The footman was providentially absent. "I wish to have a few private words with you," began Dalman. "I want to visit the surrounding country a bit. And you can keep my first visit here *private*," carelessly added Dalman.

"All right, sir," cheerily rejoined the driver. "To-night, when I drive you home! I understand."

"Any one visiting at the Hurst?" continued Dalman, with a lingering fear of "Carstairs, Lyon & Carstairs." "Only Miss Powning, of the Hall. Fine old place, sir! There you see the tower, through the trees, on the other side of the cliff. Leigh Hurst is a rare old place, but, Powning Hall is one of the jewels of Yorkshire. Pity, too, there's no one to succeed her now. Ah! The Pownings were always a mad lot!"

With a splendid sweep through the graveled walks of an old Dutch garden, the wagonette dashed up to the great arched entrance of the Hurst, where handsome Cyril Leigh, with a great Irish deerhound at his side, gravely welcomed "Mr. Arthur Lemon, of Chicago." The duel of wits was on at last, now!

Passing through a superb hall, dividing the east and west wings, Dalman was ushered into the great library, where pictures of the greatest heroes of literature and art occupied places of honor between the recessed alcoves.

A rare old oaken ceiling threw back the gleam of a dozen wax sconces, and a rich bronze railing with the arms of Leigh interworked, guarded the upper book galleries. Around the great hall, in glass cases, the spoils of generations of traveled Leighs were proudly exhibited. It was the life record of their Wanderjahre.

Before the great mantel at a long table, covered with papers, sat Miss Lisbeth Leigh, her chosen battleground being the unrolled maps of the Live Oak and Magnolia claims of Tombstone District, Arizona.

"I wonder if this possible Venus is *merely a cold-hearted Minerva*," mused Dalman, as the steady glances of her moonlight eyes—serious, not sweet—were fixed upon him.

"We will defer any social welcome, Mr. Lemon, until to-morrow," said the Lady of Leigh. "I have here all my uncle's journals, the letters from Brandon and Ryley, the accounts, and all his personal memoranda. I will leave them here now, in charge of my brother, and you can examine such of them as I have thought fit to meet your eyes. Here is a certified copy of my uncle's will, and of the papers constituting me his sole executrix. *Of course*, I do not expect that you will copy or remove any of these documents. I shall also expect that you will permit me to read the original letters from my uncle to Ryley, and all letters from Brandon to Ryley. My uncle's letters were mostly written by me, and I am quite familiar with their general tenor. *You have brought them with you?*" She fixed her eyes earnestly upon him.

Dalman bowed his assent. "Then you would oblige me if you would allow my brother to take a memorandum of their *number, dates,* and *general description.*" Dalman was astounded at the lady's business-like manner, but he calmly replied: "I see no objection, Miss Leigh." With a last glance of warning instruction to Cyril, the stately beauty moved away, leaving the two men to a study of the papers.

"Of course," stiffly said Cyril, "you can see the maps, title and will papers, and the letters from Ryley, at once. As to Brandon, we will talk later. We can easily compare the handwritings of each series."

"I will begin in such way as you deem best," politely rejoined Dalman, determined to "sweeten" upon the young man whose frank bonhomie could be trusted to disarm him. "Here are all the packages of the Brandon and Gladwyn letters. You can make your own schedule, while I look over these maps and legal papers. Pray don't let the tone of them influence you. It is easy to divide success, and always a bitter thing to shoulder the results of disaster from one old friend to another. The whole thing fell out wrong. I believe that Ryley was honestly deceived in the mines. I also think that Brandon was forced into a corner and 'unloaded' upon his old friend, your uncle."

"How did you know Brandon was an old friend of my uncle's?" suspiciously demanded young Leigh.

"I think the last letter shows that," quietly answered the schemer. "The last letter in which Gladwyn threatens to sue Brandon for foisting off an unavailable property on him."

"That woman suspects the usual *Yankee trick!* I have a trump card to play which will paralyze Miss Mischief's resentment. I think that I can show her a real home 'British swindle,'" reflected the New York attorney. "But, she has prejudiced young Leigh against me *already!*" And then and there, he decided that the hostile young Diana might congeal into a callous Minerva, but never warm into a glowing, open-armed Venus.

"I'll let my Lady of Leigh take a first trick or two. *I come in on the rubber.* If I could only get this boy off alone with me in America, I could easily 'bamboozle' him! He is *rich, liberal,* and *will probably make it up* to his beloved half-sister."

"When you are ready, I will call my sister," gloomily said Cyril, as he ran down the yellowed leaves of the papers handed him by Dalman.

"Mr. Lemon" briefly exclaimed, "*All right!*" for with a mind of photographic accuracy, he was gleaning every detail of the maps and topography on the pretentious plats, pompously lettered, "Property of St. John Gladwyn, Esquire." "I can draw a rough sketch of this from memory," he jubilantly thought, as he furtively transferred to his cuff the surveyor's name and note of filing at Tucson, the county seat of Pima County, Arizona, and a similar indorsement in Cochise County.

Ten minutes showed him that Miss Lisbeth Leigh was really the one person whose signature was needed to convey to him the undivided one-half of the hidden million of the Condor. The will, succession, and estate papers were all in due order.

"Your sister seems to be a famous hand at business," remarked Dalman, as he laid down the red-tape-fastened bundles of legal documents.

"She has had practical charge of Leigh Hurst for ten years," answered Cyril. "She was of age already when my parents were both lost at sea. My uncle's death gave me another guardian, and Mr. Carstairs, who is my trustee, allows her to handle the whole estate. She is a wonder. Uncle St. John relied absolutely on her judgment, poor old boy."

Moses Dalman paled slightly.

"*I have to work quickly here* now," he decided. "This resolute young woman will bar my way out, and per-

haps pop Brother Carstairs in on me *at once.* I have
no doubt that my lady is at her tricks now. But, I'll
fool her—*to the top of her bent!*"

And so he plunged into the perusal of the letters of
Walter Ryley and the unfortunate broker, Brandon.

"These letters, you will observe, are addressed to
Chandos Brandon—the Ryley letters," said Cyril.
"Poor old Brandon turned them all over to my uncle
as a poor means of trying to get something back out
of the sharp Yankee."

Cyril Leigh glanced at Dalman's reddened face.

"I beg your pardon, Mr. Lemon," he said, "but I
do feel a bit hot about the trick that cajoled twenty
thousand pounds out of my uncle's pocket. I intend
later to make this thing up to my sister Beth, and
when I am twenty-one I shall cut down the timber on
Leigh Hurst and put that sum in the funds for her,
whether she will have it or not. For, I'm going in the
army, and I cannot leave her the old place. *There's
the blamed entail,* and a distant cormorant waiting for
me to be knocked over. There's a Leigh or two always laid out in all our wars. Vane Leigh at Corunna,
Colonel Gerald at Waterloo, my Uncle Cyril in the
Crimea, Arthur Leigh, his son, at Ulundi, and two or
three navy men were buried under the salt sea waves.
Poor old navy chaps. We have their pictures and
swords here; that's the Leigh inheritance, with a few
hard-earned medals, orders, and ribbons."

"Please let me see the bill of sale from Brandon to
your uncle—the original," quietly answered the specu-
lating scoundrel. "Do not speak harshly of the dead.
I honor you for your noble intentions to your sister,
and respect your regard for the family honor; so when
we have finished with this document you may call Miss
Leigh in, and I will perhaps astonish you both! For
whoever sinned against St. John Gladwyn's peace of
mind, whoever defrauded your sister of the substantial
dowry, it was another than the dead man whom you so
rashly blame. *I can prove it,* and Miss Leigh herself
will be the first to acknowledge it."

Cyril Leigh gazed in astonishment at the confident
American, and rose when Dalman at length said, "*I
am ready.*"

The American paced the great hall, gazing upon the world spoils reverently treasured there, the serried columns of rare old books, companions of vanished midnight hours, and cast his eyes over the riches loading the table. "A rare old house—it must be an anticipated agony for her to yield it up to another, even the bright-eyed wife to come, of this dashing young fellow. She would be a rare queen in one of our American palaces." He was awed by the venerable reality of the splendid old home from whose barricaded doors, and out of whose diamond-paned windows the loyal Leighs had poured a galling fire on the cropped-haired Roundheads. "Damn the law of entail! *It's a cold barbarity*," he mused. "The death of family love, the crucifixion in poverty of the *many* that the *one* may roll in luxury!"

While he was contrasting the magnificent conservatism of the grand old English home, with the varnish-smelling rawness of the mushroom American palaces, quickly rushed up after a tidal wave in stocks, the door opened, and Lisbeth Leigh, on her brother's arm, entered the library hall. Some clinging robe of fleecy white gave to her noble form a goddess air, and the white roses of Plantagenet, clustered at her breast, lent this daughter of York the graces of a dark-eyed Galatea. Dalman dropped his eyes in an admiring awe.

With her brother at her side, Miss Leigh narrowly watched the American's face as he gravely said:

"Your brother has now seen all the letters which I possess, Miss Leigh, and I have gone into the matter as far as I care to before consulting you. I am ready to prove now to you, however, that my dead friend, Ryley, was *not* the cause of your uncle's considerable loss, but that *another* took advantage of his confidence. I will leave all the papers with you to-night, and make you the following proposition, which is personal and strictly between ourselves. The two mining claims are really worthless, and only valuable for a vein of water struck in their depths, which is available to work some other mines adjoining, in which my principals are interested. The two claims have been carefully opened and explored. They have yielded nothing. There

has been no charge whatever against the estate of
Brandon, or Gladwyn, for capital, taxes, or the peri-
odical work required by the American law to hold
them.   Now, *I* will give you, in *cash*, for a complete
transfer to me of all your interests, *just what Ryley
really sold the claims for*—their true value as a specu-
lative purchase then, and not the huge sum extorted
by Brandon from his confiding friend."

The brother and sister gazed doubtfully at each
other.

"Then, you mean to say that Brandon used the opportunity of trusting friendship to get my uncle's
twenty thousand pounds into his hands, and to give
him a comparatively worthless property?" doubtfully,
said Miss Leigh.

"*Precisely so!*" calmly replied Dalman.   "Brandon
was the swindler, if any.   He never laid out a single
dollar on the property, and he turned it over to his
friend at a vastly increased valuation, and also after
he knew that he could give *no legal title* and *proper
possession.* In the last ten years, your side has forfeited all
its rights, and under the American laws you must pay
your one-half of all the past expenses, or else abandon
the property.   *You have no power to reclaim it!*"   A
pair of dark eyes met his own in grave surprise.

"If so, *why do you seek us out here?*" steadily, said
Miss Leigh, exploring his face with a firm glance of
inquiry.

"Because we wish a legal title to the water, and are
anxious to increase and extend the works upon our adjoining properties.   If you receive the original sum
paid to Ryley, without interest, you are fortunate in
escaping the burden of the ten years' unsuccessful
work.   You could not regain possession of the mine,
without paying these considerable sums, in any case!"

"I cannot believe Chandos Brandon to have robbed
and deluded my uncle," said the splendid woman, after
a pause.

"*I will prove it to you, to-morrow, Madam,*" gravely said Dalman, "and, I will thank you to send me to
the inn, for I must telegraph to London for a paper.
I will be ready to-morrow to prove the facts which I

have stated, and, if you decline my offer, I am then ready to leave for the Continent, and return to America." He was careful to conceal his eager anxiety.

Cyril Leigh's face flushed. "*May I not offer you some refreshments?*" he began, with a glance at his sister.

"*Thanks. No,*" soberly replied Dalman, rising. "We have shown our minds to each other, and I must be about my business. You see, we could easily use and enjoy the coveted water, without seeking your title—and even against your protest—but my principals are men of honor!" To which unmerited compliment, the hovering shade of the great founder of the house of Blum Brothers would have made a visible return of glowing gratitude, were it possible.

With a bow to the woman, seated now, the prey of her warring emotions, "Mr. Arthur Lemon, of Chicago," quitted the home of the Leighs, when the butler announced the wagonette.

"I shall listen to your proofs to-morrow, sir, and then, be ready with an answer—*as soon as possible!*" said Lisbeth Leigh, inclining her stately head. "I must have counsel," she murmured. "There's only Miss Powning left to me in the world, for Cyril has no lights to guide," she sighed. "His headlong generosity would repair the wrong." Looking out after the vanishing wagonette, she marked the sturdy trees of Leigh Hurst. "They shall never fall if I can prevent it," she fondly vowed, as she went silently up the great stair, past the trophies of the chase, the dented armor, and the proud banners of her ancestors. "*Leigh must be always Leigh!* It matters not for me, *now!*" she sighed. There was the burden of an old sorrow resting on her this night.

As she laid her hand on the door of her guest's room a hand was laid upon her own.

"*It is the anniversary,*" gently said old Harriet, "and she is on her knees, praying *for the loved and lost one.* I will call you."

Lisbeth Leigh turned and went softly down the stair.

"*A vigil of undying love,*" she murmured. And,

standing, gazing out at the moonlit groves of Leigh, she bowed her stately head in sudden tears.

"Not a *word*, not a *sign*, not a *ray of hope*. My God! Where on earth is *that nameless grave ?*" And she lingered until she was called, forgetting the crafty schemer until the morning, for two loving woman hearts wcre soon beating close, in one hopeless sorrow —one wave of fond regret. The beautiful vales of Nidderdale are as open to care and sorrow as the bleakest moor.

The young Squire of Leigh sauntered back alone from the lodge gates.

"*I don't more than half like this fellow.* He won't see Carstairs; he seems to be cold and sly. As Beth says, 'why does he seek us out if our title is worthless ?' I'll turn the whole thing over with Beth after he makes his offer. And she shall not jump at it either in a hurry! While an oak stands she is the Lady of Leigh Hurst, and while I do not marry. But, *I'll fix that !*"

The Squire smoked several meditative pipes, and then, made the rounds with Dermot, the great Irish hound, stalking at his heels.

"There they are, *Aunt Cornelia* and *Beth*," he fondly said, gazing on the light alone in the Blue Chamber. "Always the same old sorrow, the vain regret. My God, if we only knew he was dead—Beth might then—" but, he broke off his soliloquy, knocked the ashes out of his pipe, and went up to his lair in the shadow of an old sorrow.

Far away, Moses Dalman was returning from the nearest railway telegraph station. He had succeeded in transferring a five-pound note to the pockets of the shaven coachman, and in the hour's jaunt had deftly extracted a very fair history of the houses of Powning and Leigh from the watchful driver. "*I'm not anxious to have my movements chattered about.* You can post the maid and the landlady to keep dark," said Dalman, "and I'll be back soon, and *you shall lose nothing.*"

Driving past the splendid gardens where Powning Hall shone out as one of the gems of picturesque and storied Yorkshire, Dalman wondered at the driver's tales of the mad Pownings. "There's no one now, for the old lady's the last of the line. There was a nephew, a splendid fellow too, but some blight came over him. He's been dead and gone these ten years, leastways Miss Powning wears black for him! I don't know who the hall goes to, but, Miss Lisbeth will surely get the old lady's money. And she's an angel on earth, is the old lady."

Moses Dalman was bitterly morose over his last cigar. "With such prospects, the slaty-hearted Minerva may laugh at my modest offer. I must clear out and work by letter, if she refuses, for Solicitor Carstairs may be on the way. Damn it, *I'll throw her over!* I will bully Blum into a contract, perfect their title, and take a hundred-thousand-dollar-fee. The coachman's all right, he won't blow on me. Money talks, even in Yorkshire!"

Mr. Arthur Lemon was puzzled at the cheerful smile which reigned upon Miss Leigh's face when they assembled in the library at four o'clock the day following. He had verified the glories of the old mansion, and was fairly on his way into the good graces of Cyril Leigh, while Miss Lisbeth sat in deep counsel with the lonely mistress of Powning Hall.

"*I will not delay you,*" gravely said the American, as he received his bundles of letters. "You have now examined all the papers in existence. *There*, Miss Leigh, is the certified copy of the original bill of sale of Walter Ryley to Chandos Brandon. You will observe that Brandon paid *five thousand pounds* to my dead friend for this property—*all that he asked*—and then sold it *to his friend*, without a clear title, for *twenty thousand!* The letters prove that Brandon and Ryley were to handle it together. They were to be made partners with the other people at home. Now Brandon pocketed fifteen thousand pounds, and left Mr. St. John Gladwyn in the lurch."

There was a silence until the brother and sister, in a single voice, demanded, "*And what do you now propose?*"

"I will give just five thousand pounds in cash for your interest in full, and I then defy any one to attack the memory of my dead friend. *This is a first and last proposal!* I will leave here in an hour, if you are willing. You have that hour to decide, and, if you say '*No*,' I then withdraw my offer, and depart, *as I came.*"

The brother and sister exchanged glances.

"*Stay*," said Miss Leigh, "I will make you a counter proposition. *I am ready now!* I will send my brother Cyril to Arizona to inspect this property." Dalman's sudden start did not escape the gleaming eyes of the Lady of Leigh. "*It will cost five hundred pounds to make the voyage and an examination of the truth. Pay down that sum.* I will then sign an agreement that if the matters are found to be *as you relate*, you shall have the property for *five thousand pounds*, paid down in New York City, or in Tucson, Arizona, *as you may prefer.* Cyril will take all the original papers with him, and a legal power of attorney to execute the sale in my name. There is a United States Consul in Sheffield. *He can prepare the papers.* You add the sum of five hundred pounds to the price if the sale goes on—if you have misrepresented the facts *you forfeit the sum.* I will give you an hour to consider my proposition. Stay and be our guest at dinner."

"*I will accept the offer now, on the spot,*" said Dalman, smilingly. "He can verify the thing in two months. But, I do not wish to lose my dinner. I will agree with your brother on the details of the papers. He can bring them. I'll pay over the money to-night, slip over to Hull, and *meet him later at New York.* So, we will shake hands and call it *Westward Ho!*"

Miss Lisbeth Leigh bowed her head as the two men clasped hands.

BOOK II.

PERSONALLY CONDUCTED.

CHAPTER VI.

THE COACHMAN'S WARNING.—AT EL PASO.

MORRIS DALMAN wandered around the superb demesne of Leigh Hurst under the guidance of the young Squire until the first dinner-bell clanged out. His keen eye noted all the homelike glories of the English gardens—the velvet lawns, the superb stables, and the model farmhouses, and he duly admired in turn, horses, sheep, the blue-blooded North Country cattle, and all the substantial adjuncts of an English manor. A casual chatter on business punctuated the young master's local explanations. He was fired with the romance of this trip.

"I say, Mr. Lemon, you must coach me a bit about the road, you know. When do you sail ? It would be a bit unhandy for me to leave here before a month."

"That suits me, Squire Leigh," said Dalman. "I have a couple of valuable patents to secure in France and England. When we are done I'll run over to York, cross the channel from Hull, run on past Paris and Berlin, and then take the first available steamer homeward in point of time from Bremen, Hamburg, Rotterdam, Antwerp, Cherbourg, or Havre. I will be back at Chicago long before you arrive in New York; and my lawyer will meet you there. If I am not near New York I will join you at Fort Worth, Dallas or

Denning.   Here is the card of my confidential attorney and New York business manager."

He handed the Squire a professional card.

MAX ROSENDAHL,
ATTORNEY AND COUNSELOR-AT-LAW,

16 Wall Street,

New York City.

"Be sure to register that in several places, so that you do not lose the card. Rosendahl is always in daily telegraphic and long distance telephone communication with me. He will take care of you in New York, buy your railway ticket for you, notify me, and forward anything at once. He will give you my location on your arrival." The careless boy was well pleased with "Lemon's" thoughtfulness.

"And the trip, itself, how long will I be?"

"*Oh, call it a month!*" easily, said Dalman. "A week to go and another to return, and say two weeks in Arizona. That, with the two weeks on the ocean, makes six weeks' absence in all." The heir of Leigh Hurst was, in his heart, calculating how he could bear the exile from two haunting blue eyes.

"I see the whole thing; but about those papers? I'd *really* like to have Carstairs's opinion on them," mused Cyril Leigh, as they mounted the great bell tower for a view of the surpassing landscape.

"That is an easy matter. I will write out a contract for the sale of the interest to *me* for five thousand five hundred pounds, upon your countersigned approval at Tucson. This can be signed here, in duplicate, to-night, and the receipt of five hundred pounds, on account, acknowledged. To-morrow, you can run down to Sheffield and see your lawyer, Carstairs; he can then prepare the full General Power of Attorney from Miss Leigh to yourself, approve the executory contract, and have her Power regularly verified and recorded at the United States Consulate at Sheffield. I will go on about my own business. Should there be any little break in the proceedings, you can telegraph to me,

'*care Thomas Cook & Son, Ludgate Circus, London.*' lf
your solicitors find all to be correct, please simply
cable to 'Rosendahl,' 16 Wall Street, New York—
'Coming, Leigh,' and when you are ready to sail,
name the boat on which you engage your passage,
which, by the way, *do at once*, as the rush home soon
begins." There seemed to be a friendly provision in
all these well-considered details.

"*That's all perfectly proper*," said the Master of
Leigh, whose frank mind recognized his perfect safety
in the countersigning of the contract at Tucson, the
right of notification, and the apparent open dealing of
the whole proposition.

"It's a small matter, after all, and so I cannot do
anything more for you," said Dalman, as his eye
rested admiringly on the Englishman's superb birthright. "If this were mine, I would not leave it even
for the army," said the enraptured Dalman.

"Ah, my dear fellow! *Comfort is not a career !*" cried
Leigh. "We Englishmen always reach out from
these homes and so, manage to govern a good bit of
the world. You see the property always remains in
the family by our conservative laws of entail and pri-
mogeniture."

"It seems strange, and even coldly harsh, *to us*,"
mused Dalman. "*There's a case in point !*" He pointed
to the splendid tower of Powning Hall. "They tell
me that fine place goes without a direct succession."

"*Not so*," answered Cyril Leigh. "It's true that
the direct heir disappeared nearly ten years ago. Miss
Cornelia Powning would take no steps after seven years
to declare her nephew legally dead. The next of kin,
though distant, is of the old blood, and has several
years to attain his majority. It will be honestly settled in time. *Of course*, when the lady dies, and the
heir-at-law is of age, he will have to push those settlement proceedings. He will then step in and claim his
own. The individual often perishes, but the race, as
a rule, survives. You will meet the lady at dinner,
and do not be astonished if she asks you any peculiar
questions," concluded Leigh, "for she still insists
that she has clairvoyant glimpses of the man whom

she still fondly cherishes as living, and always sees him as she would wish him—still alive—in the light of an unfading and undying love. He was a fine fellow, already a marked man in the army, and I fear that he was in some cowardly way made away with! *I never met him!'* I was a lad at school, and he was on foreign duty. Only a couple of years after his return to England he dropped out of the ken of the living as silently as a plummet sinks in the sea. *It's a very sad story*, and *we never refer to it."* As they descended, Cyril Leigh said: "After dinner I will have the butler show you all over the old house, while my sister and I conclude the papers, which you can sketch out. Then, as you say, you take the morning train to York and Hull. I will get away to Sheffield and telegraph you if all is right to the care of Cook, so that you can go ahead homeward. I've no doubt that all will suit my people, especially if you leave me the certified bill of sale from Ryley to Brandon. I'm afraid the poor old broker got in a close corner, and—so squeezed my poor uncle. I see clearly Ryley's innocence of any intentional fraud. He made *no* personal representations, and he certainly raised no price. That was Brandon's own work!"

There was a shade of disappointment on Dalman's brow as he sat alone with Cyril Leigh through the elaborate ceremony of the seven o'clock dinner in the great dining-hall. "Has 'Miss Minerva' flown the track?" was the schemer's startled first thought, as the mellow light streamed in through the great stained-glass west window, where the coat of arms of the Leighs was blazoned, with their ancestral motto, "*Loyal à la mort*," shining out in pride.

"I am sorry that my sister is obliged to remain with 'Aunt Cornelia,'" said the Squire, "but the dear old soul has just had a severe, sudden attack. We will arrange all the papers, however, so that you may not be delayed."

Seated in the chair of state at the head of the table, Cyril Leigh gave his guest a few sketchy stories of the proud old county, the heir of brave Saxon traditions, twice as large as its fellows, once the seat of old Roman Empire, the battle-ground of Dane, Pict, Scot, and Saxon; its hills and dales studded with castles, abbeys, and priories, Druid-peopled groves, feudal holds, splendid rivers, romantic waterfalls, and the hero-hunted fields of Stamford Brig, Wakefield, Towton, and unhappy Marston Moor, recalled the vanished days of old romance. Lemon listened entranced as the boy told these olden fables. Fairy, brownie, and imps of the fell still linger around Caldron Snout, foaming High Force, Aysgarth, and Hardraw. Wordsworth's dreamy genius has immortalized the Strid. Gordale Scar and Malham Cove tower to the quiet skies, and the fountains and rivulets of Bolton, Roche, St. Mary's, and Whitby murmur yet requiems for the cowled monks.

Moonlight and sunlight linger in silver and golden floods on the splendid holds of Conisborough, Skipton, and Pontefract; Richmond's old crumbling Norman keep; grim Warwick's hold at Middleham; Bolton Castle, the prison of the fairest and unhappiest of queens; Wressle Castle, Percy's home; and Clifford's stern tower at York; all these speak of the mighty barons who couched their lances for the love of bright eyes, long dulled in death.

The central jewel of the fair county of Deira, magnificent York Minster, overlooks the crumbled dust of Saxons, Brigantes, Romans, and haughty Normans. Hadrian's feet wandered once by the Ouse and Foss! Severus breathed his last here in Eboracum, and the glory of the vanished ages clings around York, the hallowed site of the first metropolitan Christian church in England, the first English monarch's Wittenagemote, and the first English Parliament. Truly a magnificent scroll of history !

"I would like to show you our brave old Yorkshire," said Leigh proudly, when the wine and walnuts alone remained.

"*Yes; but I must hasten to America—to make ready for your coming,*" regretfully said Dalman, when they adjourned to the library.

In a half hour, the acute Dalman had finished drawing the simple papers of contract, and then quietly said: "I am ready now to hand over the five hundred pounds, *to sign the contract*, and to deliver to you the Ryley bill of sale."

He was face to face with his destiny, and he trembled in an exciting suspense. "Will she sign?" he mused. "If she does, my fortune is made!"

While the dissimilar companions waited for the Lady of Leigh Hurst, above them in the Blue Room, Lisbeth Leigh was bending over a silver-haired woman, who had watched the last rays of the golden sun glimmer and slowly die away on the beautiful scars of the Nidd. Pale, with a transparent complexion, her glassy, blue eyes aimlessly fixed upon vacancy, she murmured, opening her arms and waving her thin, bloodless hand: "He came back to me! *I saw him again!* He stood by my side, his finger on his lips, silent, but, with the other hand, he beckoned—beckoned onward—always *onward!*"

Then Lisbeth Leigh softly said: "It was only the anniversary—the coming of the sad day—which tells us both again the story of the past, and opens the wounds of the heart once more. The time when we both stand by the grave of our hopes. I, too, dreamed a strange dream, Aunt Cornelia. He came to me and touched my ring as a signal of his presence. I could not see his face, but I heard his voice, and the words were: '*Loyal à la mort.*' I seemed then to see him far, far away, but still waving his hand, and I could hear his voice, '*Loyal à la mort, loyal toujours!*' I had prayed last night for a sign—for my own heart was full of Cyril's going away—and, it seemed that the one who came to me, whispered: '*Come! Come!*' Are these signs and wonders?" the beautiful woman whispered, "or, only fond delusions of the heart?"

"And so you have decided, my child, that Cyril shall go out into that wild, western land?" tremulously faltered the lady of Powning Hall. "Remember, we are then left alone—*you and I!*" The maid had entered with the Squire's message that the papers were ready for signature. "*He will have it so!*" sighed Lisbeth. "And, it is true that a few weeks will bring him back. It all seems fair enough—the final decision is left in Cyril's hands—and yet, with all these precautions, *I distrust that strange man!* He is not what he seems! I feel that he knows more of this than even he has told us. But, Cyril vows that if I do not let him try and reclaim my lost inheritance, he will cut the timber—and that shall never be! Leigh Hurst shall never lose its bearded hallowed oaks!"

"My dear child, you will have my savings—*all my savings!*" tenderly said Cornelia Powning, "even if I cannot give you Powning Hall; but, we are only two weak women. *Let Cyril go!* The Leighs were always masterful men. You shall go down with me and see Mr. Carstairs. There is the British Minister, and the Consuls, too, to guard him. Good old Carstairs will find a way to watch over our Cyril. Besides, remember, it is only your final signature that transfers the property. After all is over, he can sign at the city of Tucson, and then, three days' travel brings him back to New York. Go down, my child, and *sign the papers!* May God prosper you."

While Moses Dalman wandered over the great house, through picture gallery, tapestried passages, old state chambers, and pondered over the visages of departed Leighs, in steel cap and cuirass, brave lads who died in the Low Countries, red-coated heroes of the Peninsula, and men of mark in gown and surplice, he marked also the fair galaxy of departed stars of beauty, whose light shone again in Lisbeth Leigh's eyes.

"*One woman for a man to lay down his life for!*" he muttered. "I cannot read the riddle. That she is not yet wedded is a Yorkshire mystery, but *a riddle only to be read by others!*" he sighed. "My motto is now '*Patience!*' for if I get him over to America, *the game is mine!* I will have either the whole or a part. Not a soul in England can trace me. Two words to Isidor Blum, by cable—'*Coming home*'—will silence him. I have the key of the whole situation in my hands, thanks to Ryley's valise, and I am now a later Warwick. I can make or unmake the king of the Condor mine. This boy, once out there, can be handled by me *as I will!* For he will never get out of the clutches of Morris Blum, Bill Murfee, and myself till I get that title.

"If I can only get hold of this fellow, Arizona Jack, I will be easily master of the Blums, Bent, and the Senator. I will know all the facts before the little game comes on, down there, and, at the last, we can all turn in, and 'bamboozle him.' I can work secretly on him, and if he will not sell down there, I can find a way to bluff him, *in my own interest.* He shall never meet Isidor Blum, the sly old Bent, or any of them till I have traced out Arizona Jack. He shall be 'personally conducted.'"

There were tears in Lisbeth Leigh's beautiful eyes, as she stood by the table, pen in hand, listening to Dalman's wandering footsteps above, as her brother urged her to sign the contract.

"Cyril," she softly said, "we are the last of the house of Leigh, for the next of kin are all practically strangers to us. I fear this man's future influence over you. I know how easy your nature is. Will you take me down to see Carstairs on this matter, and then agree to be strictly guided by me, in your quest, to act as I decide for you, after conferring with my old friend? Then, *I shall always feel safe,* for when I yielded to your pleading last night, when I adopted your plan, it was only to save the grand old oaks of Leigh Hurst—the trees that sheltered both of us in childhood. *Do you promise?*"

"*I do*, most heartily, dear Beth," said the young man. "So you can sign, with a happy heart. I'll follow all your injunctions to the letter," he earnestly said. With a firm hand, she then traced the words "Lisbeth Leigh" upon the duplicate contents, and sealed them, in silence. The young squire was standing at her side, gazing fondly at her splendid face lit up with a glowing love, as she picked up her seal ring. And she sealed it with that tender old motto, "*Loyal à la mort.*"

"Here is a token of our compact," she said, "wear this other ring for me until you return. It also has our family motto graven within it, and while you wear it you owe to me *obedience*, remember. Whenever you see it let it recall your pledge, with its words '*Loyal à la mort.*'" And she smiled brightly through her tears as her brother kissed her trembling lips.

"You are simply worn out with dear old Cornelia," he soberly said. "It was her anniversary of sorrow, but I take this to be your happy omen," he brightly cried, clasping her to his breast, "*two true hearts of adamant.*"

It was a little ring of two hearts joined, and set in sparkling diamonds.

"There, I will call in this stranger and get rid of him now," briskly said Cyril. "I suppose we will want a couple of witnesses." He sent for the butler and the gamekeeper, and, in their presence, "Mr. Arthur Lemon, of Chicago," also gravely signed the papers.

"I believe that the witnesses should also see the money paid over," remarked Dalman, as he laid down the certified copy of Ryley's bill of sale and a packet of Bank of England notes. "You will find the sum of five hundred pounds there, I believe."

When the signatures were all affixed Dalman gravely observed, "Miss Leigh will see that I am to designate the person to whom the interest is to be finally transferred at Tucson. This is a contract for a deed to myself or my assigns. I have no doubt your solicitor will approve all. The memorandums as to your Power of Attorney are to be strictly observed. Otherwise, *your trip would be a fruitless one.*"

"*I understand all,*" gayly said Cyril.

"Then I will take my leave," said the bustling American with a bow to Miss Leigh. "To-morrow night must see me well over the Channel."

"*I have depended upon your honor, sir,*" said Miss Leigh extending her hand in adieu.

"Your brother will find the facts exactly as I have represented them, Madam," said the keen-eyed American. "And *if he does not,* he holds all your title in his hands until he is perfectly satisfied. Your trust, therefore, is really *in him,* and as to me, *you can be perfectly reassured.*"

"I will drive you over, myself, Mr. Lemon," courteously said Squire Leigh, "and hasten your departure."

"Thanks!" said the stranger. "I will take the midnight train for York."

The beautiful woman watched him go, with a strangely agitated heart.

Dalman turned his head as he passed on out of the great hall door, and saw Lisbeth Leigh standing there at the foot of the old stairway, down which the cavaliers of her race had marched, to go out and die at Marston Moor.

"*A royal woman*," he mused. "*One worthy of all that Life can give!* The man who wakes that woman's heart to love will drink of the chalice of Happiness! But the untold story of her face baffles me. There's neither pride nor passion, no carven life-record, but the shade of a stifled longing—*the shadow of some unavailing sorrow is there*." And Dalman was soon lost in the shadows of the night.

The young squire was hardly on his way to Sheffield on the sunny morning following Dalman's departure, before Isidor Blum, at New York City, had received a brief cablegram, with those decisive words, "*Coming home.*" The old Hebrew schemer chafed in vain, unable to read therein the outcome of the negotiations, until his hawk-eyed negotiator should steam up the Narrows.

"It's a damned vunny despatch for a lawyer vot god dwenty dousand dollars to do the vork vid," mused the disgruntled Isidor.

But a gleeful man was now Counselor Moses Dalman, who had slipped back to London and waited two days in hiding, hastily concluding all the fragmentary business left over in London. He was not seen of the local men who knew him, but he quickly obtained the dispatch for Mr. Arthur Lemon, care Thos. Cook & Son, Regent's circus. The words "Solicitor approves, papers all correct, power of attorney properly registered, sail in three weeks from Liverpool on *Umbria*, will cable to Rosendahl," told him that Squire Leigh was disarmed of all suspicion. The game was now in his *own able hands*.

Dalman gayly bought his ticket via Southampton, meeting a fast German boat homeward. "Once on the water, cut off from Carstairs and Miss Lisbeth, the boy will be a mere plaything in my hands," laughed Dalman. And when he steamed past the Lizard, he laughed in glee at the skillful manner in which he had buried the dead past of the Condor mine. "No one but myself can roll the stone of silence away," he chuckled. "I am, at any rate, already twenty thousand dollars to the good, and I hold the future of the mine in my hands."

A horrible fear lest the Blums should secretly gut it, and hollow out the bonanza hidden there, now alarmed him.

"Ah, no! They would never dare! Old Bent and the Senator would be on the watch to smash their scheme. Now *for a fine double play at home*." He smiled at Cyril Leigh's easily given intelligence. "I'll have the first news soon sent to Rosendahl of his sailing. And I think that I now have both ends of the loop securely knotted in my hands. But what shall I tell the eager old Isidor Blum? He will demand an account of my stewardship. My only point is to keep Cyril Leigh out of their hands. *I must trust to Rosendahl for that*, for I dare not let any one face Arizona Jack but *myself*." There was food for reflection in the "Mugby Junction," wherefrom all the roads diverged. "One single false step on my part," thought Dalman, in alarm, "and the control of Cyril Leigh drops out of my hands forever, for Bent and Blum would overbid each other, and then Miss Lisbeth might get her twenty thousand pounds back. I would be left *with only my fee*. There would be nothing to hide, and if I am caught in playing them false, there is *a possible disbarment before me*, and that *I could not afford*," mused the greedy lawyer. "I must hoodwink old Blum— but *how?* He is no weakling boy."

So impressed with these dangers was Moses Dalman that he landed in New York unknown to his friends, having used the fancy cognomen, on the voyage, of "Arthur Lemon."

"It may seem to be a proof of good faith *later*, and old Carstairs may investigate me a little through the Cook agency. I will have a night with Max. If Rosendahl can't help me, *who can?*"

And so it fell out that Busch's Hotel at Hoboken had the honor of entertaining "Arthur Lemon" on his arrival.

Max Rosendahl, summoned by telegram, made a "night of it" with his returned college mate.

"Things are all in splendid trim down at the office," said Max, "only, old Blum sends daily demands now for your whereabouts, and that big fellow, Yakey, has looked in once or twice to see you. Blum will take it strange that you arrive so mysteriously. We must blind him."

"Bah! I can tell the old boy that I was dogged around England and just gave the other fellows the slip. *He has got to be resigned*, for *he can't prove that I am lying*. And now *to business*."

The wily practitioners turned the matter of hood-winking Cyril Leigh and fooling Blum over in many different ways.

"As to Leigh, you must rush him out of New York. I don't mind the expense of a man to secretly follow him on to El Paso. But *whom can we trust?*" said Dalman. "I'll handle Blum myself. He's afraid of me. And I'll quietly steal off down to Arizona, I think, and see Morris. I'll make them pay well for the trip later."

"Moses," said Max, joyously, "I've got a sickly brother Jacob, who is just out of college. He is *one of us*. I'll let him follow Squire Leigh down to where your friends meet him, and he can post us *at both ends*, if there's any monkey business. *The boy is a bright one*."

"*Bravo!*" cried Dalman.

"Then I can handle Blum. I will fool him with the idea that the agent will only talk on the ground, and, *to me!*"

"That's the scheme!" laughed Dalman, and several silver-necked bottles were emptied gayly as the ferret-eyed schemers knotted up, link by link, the chains to bind that Samson of Judaic finance, Mr. Isidor Blum. "The old boy has too much money; we will bleed him a little," laughed Rosendahl.

Mr. Isidor Blum hastily abandoned his *dolce far niente* at the West End Hotel, Long Branch, when an early morning telegram reached him, while he was enjoying a sumptuous breakfast "by the sad sea waves."

There was a twinkle of triumph in his eye as he read Moses Dalman's telegram: "*Come at once; waiting here for you; most important. Must go South to-morrow on our business; keep my arrival quiet.*" The signature, "*Moses D.*," stirred him like a bugle blast. And, yet, a shade of gloom settled upon his brow, for while his better half, Madam Blum, was making herself socially and physically large at queenly Saratoga, her lord had a special engagement to drive "far down the road" that very afternoon with a dashing, golden-haired beauty, *whose name was not Blum*, and who could never be mistaken for a "dark-eyed daughter of Jephtha." This same lady pouted somewhat when she received a large bouquet, a brief note, and an apologetic, carefully calculated, check from her truant Isidor. "*Money talks,*" remarked the professional exponent of womanly naughtiness "in several advanced stages," as she tore the letter of her Hebraic Armand up, and carefully hid the undamaged check in her swelling corsage.

"*Pizness before bleasure!*" had very wisely decided Isidor, as he arrayed himself to visit "Moses D., Room 42, Taylor's Hotel, Jersey City." "He's an exbensive lugsury, is Moses Dalman," growled Isidor, "and I must see vod I get for my dwenty dousand dollars. De gurl gan vait; *dere's lots of gurls*, bud only *von Condor Mine!* I can see de gurl do-morrow, all righdt. *She vill vait for me!*" which enunciated an indisputable social truth, and proved old Isidor's acumen!

Moses Dalman was a stunning picture of "Londonized New York" as to garb, when old Isidor Blum puffed up to his room at noon.

Nothing escaped the keen-eyed old Hebrew, not even the *A. L.*, conspicuously disfiguring his London luggage. "*Hello! You vas oud for a masquerade ball, Moses?*" cheerfully puffed Isidor, as he ordered the mint juleps, and gazed on his returning dove sent out from the ark of Blum Brothers. "*Vell, vod's de report?*"

Dalman coolly settled himself. "We've got a pretty cool party behind this interest over there, Isidor," said Dalman. "Whether it is your enemies at Tucson, and every great house has its business enemies, you know, or, whether old Bent has played you false (which I suspect), I can't decide. I worked througn the sharpest friend I had in London, and soon found that old Carstairs demanded all the names of all the principals, and the usual truck-load of powers, and papers, and bank references, and official documents. This would be fatal, and soon give us all away. I have succeeded, however, in advancing five hundred pounds for the expenses of a confidential agent, who will come on, *at once*, with full powers, and all the original papers. He will meet me, or my representative at Deming, New Mexico, and then go on unknown, *to inspect the mine*. He will examine the situation at the Condor mine itself, and then be ready at Tucson to sell, *if he finds that I've not lied to him*. I dared not come out in the open, and betray us all, *so* my own legal friend has the contract locked up in London. But the man will follow on, at any moment, and he will meet me at Deming. The final sale is to be made at Tucson, or, *at the mine*. I had to put up this advance money to prevent old Carstairs telegraphing out to some British bank in New York or San Francisco to send an expert or an agent down there. If they did this thing, *then* old Bent would surely fool both of us. You know that he and the senator are devils at that sort of thing. I gave my own man over there a thousand pounds for his secret work for us," Dalman paused, and waited for Isidor, whose fat hands were stretched out as if clutching at "a diamond in the sky."

"You vasn't fool enough to give them your *real name*," almost yelled Isidor.

"Not for a moment," coldly said Dalman. "*What do you take me for?*"

"And you say that he brings de reel babers, *all of dem*, and *de vull powers* do act?" hoarsely said Isidor, "and no one knows *who he vas*, till he gets do *El Baso* and Deming?"

"*That was my game*," said Dalman. "I had to do something. I've got the contract over there that holds them till we get done with this fellow who comes. But we must work *on the quiet*," gravely said Dalman.

"*See here*," cried Isidor, "I've been at work here vatching ole Bent und de Senador. Dey vas drying do be underhanded. Dey haf hunded up old Harper *here*, und dey sbend blendy of money on de old fool. And von good bit of luck ve got. Dad vellow Ryley vas found dead *here*. He vas sandbagged und killed down *in de Bowery*. Und *so* dese vellows vas fooled, und haf *drowed away all dere money*. I had a brivade vatch on dere tracks."

"*That's a good thing for us*," calmly said Dalman, "if Ryley is out of the way."

The lawyer cheerfully finished his mint julep.

"I know it," replied Isidor. "Dere vas a row at the lodging-house. Old Harper dried to make drubble, but de beople broved by the bolice the death was accidental. Und I god old Harper's story for a few ten-dollar bills. So *dad's all right*."

Isidor arose and walked the floor excitedly for a quarter of an hour, while Dalman calmly smoked and "let the goose cook itself in its own fat."

"*I dell you vad I do*," decisively said Isidor. "I giv you a check for de money you have laid oud. Ged ride away down to Tucson and see Morris. I write to him my whole blan, and *I will give him my orders*."

The dark face was glowing with energy, greed, and fierce sinister light.

"You can drust Morris for life und death. All you must do is do get dat fellow easy und quied into Arizona. Keep your mouth shud aboud *vere you go to*. You are shust to make a little drip around by Colorado Springs *vor your health*. *Led us leave id all to Morris und Bill Murfee*. Dey vill put up a job on this fellow. Perhaps before he geds to the mine, perhaps later, dey vill have the *title*, de money *back*, *too*, if we must pay it, and *all the papers*. Chust you do *vat Morris tells you*. It's no case to make papers. I can debend on Morris. *He's de smartest broder I haf got*. Und I give him my brivade orders, so you don't get gompligated. *You understand me?*"

"Tell me just what I am to do, and just what I am to get," said Dalman.

"Nobody knows, so far, you are back in New York?" demanded Blum, anxiously.

"*Not a soul*," emphatically answered the lawyer.

"Then get out without any one knowing that you are on this side of the Atlantic. I will give you ten thousand dollars to hook de English fellow on to Morris Blum's agent, what he sends. You get that money there, *from Morris.* I give you a draft for it, and ten more—if the deal goes through—when you come back *to me.*"

"And if the fellow should fight shy, and want me to go along, or send a man?" said Dalman. "Sometimes these Englishmen are not such fools as they look."

He thought of Leigh's dark-eyed guardian angel.

"I allow you dwendy-five hundred dollars *now*, for expenses," said Isidor, drawing out his check-book. "Pick up some damn fool at El Paso and send him along—any one. You can go yourself for de trip. Nothing vill happen *to you. You vas safe.*"

"And *the Englishman?*" queried Moses Dalman, to whom a lightning thought had come. *He burned to be on the road now.*

"*I leev that to Morris and Murfee*," doggedly said Blum. "I chust don't vand to know dese details. Id's always ugly to know details. *You* gan bet your sweet life Morris vill get de babers *all right.* He knows how to but up a job!"

"And, I've nothing to do but to turn this greenhorn over to them?" said Dalman, paling slightly.

"You vill have a good time wid Morris—and you chust leev all details to him—and *be dam'd careful to forget all about the whole proceeding!* You lay low down dere! You hav used anoder name in England—and you've god no responsibilidy—*you see!* Dis ding is our pudding now, *ve vill cut it up!*

"Here's my check for de expenses. I wride und delegraf to-night. You chust telegraph me here from Deming: '*All right, M.D.,*' ven de Englishman starts for the mine. Aftervards, all is in the hands of Morris. You can help, if you wish, *vid your legal advice*, but, *you must mix up in nodings else.* Dat's my wishes, und *Morris* vill look out for *all de details.*"

Isidor Blum shook hands, and puffed away, anxious to escape the eyes of his tool and deceiver.

"*That old scoundrel already knows more of the mine*

than he has told me !" growled Dalman. "Max will be here at seven, for a last word; and, at nine I'm off to find Arizona Jack. If he's alive, then, I will show Mr. Morris Blum a neat little turn before I am done; but, I'll be out of Arizona, 'before *he knows de dedails,'*" mimicked the schemer.

"I'll take good care to keep out of these cruel rascals' hands," mused Dalman, as he finished his cosy dinner. "They might apply the '*facit per alium, facit per se,*' principle to me. But, I'll play Arizona Jack, against Morris Blum, every time, if he is in the land of the living. I hold the balance of power. The fools will all drift into my hands *at last.*" The arrival of Max Rosendahl brought a new surprise.

"Here is a cablegram that I have just received," excitedly said Max: '*Sail a week sooner; Aurania; ask at Astor House for Robert Ross. Notify Lemon.'*"

"By Jove! there is some undercurrent!" mused Dalman. "I'll warrant now that Miss Lisbeth's '*fine perceptions'* are at work. Well! *I'm off to-night—* and you see he is coming over also—under an incognito," said the departing trickster. "You are to do but one thing—to rush him out of New York, follow him on, and then telegraph to *me!* Let your brother telegraph daily to 'Arthur Lemon, Deming, New Mexico,' and I will also wire to you from there. Should Blum or Bent follow on the track, you are simply to ignore the whole thing."

Over their wine, with their heads close together, the two conspirators laughed gayly at Dalman's last inspiration. "Some one, either here or in England, has probably been meddling with this agent, who has jumped off a week in advance, and under an assumed name. I shall go first to St. Louis, Wichita, and La Junta; then run along down by Albuquerque and Rincon, to El Paso and Deming. So, I will 'throw off' everyone on my trail. Let your brother telegraph me always to the Planters' Hotel, El Paso, under name of 'A. Levy,' the date of his arrival.

"How will I know him?" Dalman's keen wit was working now on the defensive.

"*Just look at me !"* grinned Rosendahl. "Jacob is

a 'second edition.' I'll give him your photograph.
You don't need his!

" And if you should need any help out there, run up
from 'La Junta' and see my cousin, Simon Rosendahl.
I write to him before I go over to-night. I'll telegraph that a friend is coming, and that my letter
is on the way. He has grown up with Denver, and is
a rich fellow, a banker and a keen speculator, and he
knows everybody in Colorado, New Mexico, and Arizona of note. Gay devil, too; had to skip out of here
when a boy of twenty. It was a little '*woman* scrape,'
but it made his fortune later. Look out for Simon,
he's a high roller at cards. Don't stand up against his
game."

" He may be just the man I need to post me. I'll
run up and see him *surely*. Write him so. As for you
and I, we'll square up when I come back, Max," said
Moses, glancing at his watch. " Now remember, rush
this ' Robert Ross ' out of New York by New Orleans,
Fort Worth, and El Paso to Deming. Tell him that
I will wait at Deming to meet him. You must say to
him that you have forwarded the cable and had my answer back. Now remember, Planters' Hotel, El Paso,
and use my *carte blanche*. No one in New York is to
know I've returned. Rule the office with a rod of iron.
Just say nothing if any one corners you, and *post me*."

In a half an hour Moses Dalman was on his way to
the " field of operations " for the ownership of that red,
rusty, gold bonanza lying unreaped under the gray cac-
tus-fringed rocks of the Condor Mine.

There was a thoughtful trinity seated around the
dinner table at Leigh Hurst on the eve of Cyril Leigh's
departure, while Moses Dalman was whirling away to
be the first on the ground.

The young Squire's cheerfulness, at parting, was
bravely assumed. " I should feel different, Beth, in
leaving you, if Aunt Cornelia had not promised me to
remain here with you *until my return*. You will not be
lonely, for each week you will know of my safety by
the cabled words, '*All right!*' And, you remember,
I have pledged myself to follow all your injunctions!"
He turned on his finger the quaint little ring which his

sister had given him. Two hearts joined, whose surfaces of bright, sparkling, tiny diamonds gleamed under the mellow wax light.

Lisbeth Leigh's eyes rested fondly on the frank-faced blond young Squire. "Remember, *you are to obey* me *in all*, and never forget it! Let the sign of our compact teach you that. Cyril, we are the last of the Leighs! And, remember, also, that you take my heart away with you—our joined hearts!"

Before the beautiful white-haired mistress of Powning Hall left the brother and sister together, she called Cyril aside: "Remember, my boy," she tenderly said, "*we are all mortal!* It is always the unexpected which happens. Neither you nor I can leave Lisbeth, either the lands of Leigh Hurst, or Powning, but she shall have all my personal property. And you must not rashly risk yourself in that wild land. I only beg you to be prudent, *for a Leigh needs no other counsel.* If anything should happen to you, remember it would break *two* hearts, Cyril, not *one*." And then she stooped and kissed him on the brow with a modest kiss, as he half knelt at her side.

Cyril Leigh felt the silence of the great library, while Miss Leigh led her dear companion away. It was the first foreign venture of his life, this strange, sudden going away.

"*Poor Beth*," he murmured. "With all her beauty—the splendid talents fit to rule a kingdom—she will insist and live on here in shadowland alone with Aunt Cornelia. How strange that she will not even lift her eyes to all the men who have tried to find the way to her heart. I will ask Cornelia some day. When I return, *I will know wherein this shadow lies*, for next year I will be of age and master of Leigh, and then if Cornelia Powning will not tell me, down goes the timber, and Beth shall have her twenty thousand pounds in the funds. Nature cruelly robbed her of a fortune in making her a girl. Robbed her of all these grand old acres sweeping down the Nidd. Let Nature's own treasury pay her back. If I go in the army, she shall not be left to sit here in the shade. Marry or not, she shall be Miss Leigh of Leigh Hurst, and be at least

free of all the meaner cares of a woman's helplessness." While he mused, his sister, entering, laid her
white hand on his brow.

"*Cyril,*" she gravely said, "here are your last
marching orders. I have kept a copy. It may seem
strange to you that I wish you to travel as 'Robert
Ross,' but you must yield. Carstairs has already
written to the British Consul at New York, and to the
agents of our bankers. There is but one thing for
you to do: If there is any chicanery or deception, you
must turn and come home *at once.* Sign nothing—*say
nothing!* Keep your own counsel, and in case of any
trouble, telegraph to the British Consul at New York."

"*Why these gloomy ideas?*" tenderly said Cyril.

"Because you are inexperienced; because I know
what it is to lose the beloved; because I am haunted
with the sense of this strange man's insincerity," replied Lisbeth Leigh, and then she hastily added:
"You were so young when you lost your parents, and
when your own dear mother died in that ocean horror,
I lost a mother *for the second time.*"

She had noted the questioning glance of her broth-
er's eyes, and a crimson glow rushed over her cheeks.
With womanly art she would hide the story which even
Cyril never had guessed.

It was midnight before the brother and sister separated, and as Cyril folded her to his breast he whispered with his good-night kiss: "Is there *nothing else*
you would tell me, dearest Beth?"

She clung to him, sobbing.

"*Nothing,* but that I love you, only *you alone* in the
wide world. You must always be Leigh of Leigh, and
the stranger's foot must not cross our threshold as
master."

The Squire bounded from his bed when the larks began to tower over the fragrant velvet meadows of the
Nidd, and with youth's eager unrest hastened his preparations for departure. One cloud alone had hung over
his rosy dreams. "I might ask dear old Cornelia before I go. It might make a difference, but I have no
right to steal upon darling Beth's heart-confidence. She
will herself tell me all—*in her own time!*"

Lisbeth Leigh stood in the morning sunlight on the great stone steps where many a brave-hearted woman of her race had "girded her warrior's sash" in the brave old days. The parting moment came, and bright, brave, serene, and tender she kissed her brother's lips, and whispered: "Go now, Cyril! and, *for God's sake*, remember all your promises to me!"

A last blessing from Cornelia Powning rested on the brave young fellow's brow, and then straining Lisbeth to his heart once more, he turned his steps away from the great vaulted doorway.

Down the lawn the wagonette rattled merrily away, while waving handkerchiefs, love's last signal, greeted him, and loving eyes, tear-laden, saw the last salute as Cyril waved his "Good-bye" back from the lodge gates. The long quest for the lost inheritance had begun!

The fresh morning breeze moved the perfume-laden air, and Cyril had caught the last glimpse of the old Hall before Brackett, the coachman, ventured upon a halting confession of a servant's imprudence.

"I'd not ha' spoken, Squire," said the shame-faced Brackett, "for I'd hoped to the last you would take *me* over the sea *with you*. But you're a young man, after all, begging your pardon, and my father died out there in the Crimea with your brave uncle. You know the American gentleman who came here on this business?"

"*Yes! yes! What of him?*" hastily said the Squire, with a secret misgiving.

"He made out as if he came here *for the first time* to meet you and Miss Beth, but he was down here *two days before*, and staid a day, and had a good look, too, at the old place. It ain't much *in itself*, but he's a sharp enough party in business, and he also made *all kinds of inquiries*, so they tell me over at the Leigh Arms."

The conscience of Brackett was too seared on the subject of "tips" to admit the truth about the ten-pound bonus of Moses Dalman.

"I supposed he was a kind of artist fellow or newspaper chap, a sketchin' or writin' up the 'Homes of

England,' and that sort." Brackett coughed. "But, as I'm bold to believe you've business with him, look out, Squire! *He's werry artful an' sly.*"

The man had now eased his alarmed conscience.

"Lisbeth!" thought Cyril, instinctively, as he gave the repentant coachman an undeserved five-pound note. "*Not a word of this to Miss Lisbeth,*" he sternly cried. "If you break my positive orders I'll discharge you *on my return.* But I give you my thanks, *all the same.* I'm up to his tricks; and *keep silence, now.* Remember, that's my last word!"

With an inspiration of tenderness, Cyril dashed off a few last words to the Queen Regent of Leigh Hurst, and then lightly sprang into the mail train as it rattled along.

"I see the whole little business scheme! The mine is probably a good buy at the money. I'll watch Mr. Yankee, and perhaps catch him at his tricks. *He shall double that five thousand, or I'm a beggar!*"

Squire Leigh, youthful and reckless, was all unaware of the future attention to all details even now animating the not guileless Morris Blum and Mr. William Murfee, superintendent of the Condor Mine. They were making ready for the coming guest.

But, after cabling his departure from Liverpool, he mused long upon Lisbeth Leigh's premonitions and this first proof of Mr. Arthur Lemon's Chicago slyness. "I'll give that fellow an ugly Yorkshire backfall yet to offset his mean Yankee trick," he glowered, as he walked the decks of the *Aurania,* or lingered in his smoking-room corner. Mr. Robert Ross had become a plotter in his own way in defense of Lisbeth Leigh's lost dowry. "Poor girl," he sighed. "If it is pride in going out empty handed to her bridal that keeps her single, I'll lay every oak low. And Cornelia shall tell me the truth. *It is a woman's pride and a sister's love that keeps her silent.*"

A week later a hawk-nosed, gray-eyed man sauntered down the dusty, unpaved, sandy streets of El Paso and eyed the struggling efforts of sporadic business to vivify the sleepy Texan town, whose one-story adobes stretched far over the cheerless burning plain.

A fringe of cottonwood marked the course of the sluggish Rio Grande near by, beyond which the faint blue lines of the Mexican Sierras rose sharply cut in the clear skies. "Take away the railroad and this thing would die of inanition," scornfully sneered Moses Dalman. He leisurely followed a copper-skinned Mexican boy and dawdled carelessly along in the glaring heat, looking like any pawn of the frontier business world, in his slouchy suit of gray "store clothes" and a four-shilling straw hat, for Abram Levy was dressed up to his modest *rôle*.

"*Señorita Morales' casa*," mumbled the little Mexican boy, catching Dalman's half-dollar and speeding away in delight. There were trees and flowers around the comfortable adobe. A hammock was slung upon the varanda, where a row of red earthen water jars shone out in the shade. The sound of a guitar was heard tinkling within. It ceased abruptly as Dalman let the gate swing with a resounding clash. When Dalman reached the veranda a white-robed form stood in the door, a singularly beautiful Spanish girl of twenty-four, with her hands crossed in sudden alarm upon her breast. "It is the Señorita Morales," said Dalman, lifting his hat. "*I must see Arizona Jack at once. I have a letter for him from Denver from his best friends!*"

CHAPTER VII.

MR. ROBERT ROSS, BRITISH TOURIST.

WITH a timid gesture of entreaty, Pepita Morales retreated like a startled fawn, and begged her visitor to wait a moment at the opened door. Dalman was touched by the woman's plaintive beauty, and her soft voice fell musically on his ear as she called to her hidden retainers. "*José!*" "*Panchita!*" In a few moments she returned, having caught up a light black shawl which draped her thoughtful face as she held its folds shyly under her chin. With a gesture of simple dignity she said "*Enter, Señor.*"

Dalman's quick eye had noted the flashing diamonds and emeralds on her taper rosy fingers, and the golden chain and cross of rare Guaymas pearls at her bosom. "*The fellow has devilish good taste*," muttered Dalman, as he stepped into the large room where a scarred faced old man servant of fifty stood glowering fiercely at the "gentlemanly visitor." Even in his studied "business apparel," Mr. Moses Dalman was an Adonis compared to the slouching Texans and mongrel denizens of El Paso. In the open doorway of the dining room a stout yellow faced meztizo woman of forty stood, gazing at him in semi-hostile pose.

"*The home guard*," thought Dalman. "I am not '*persona grata*' yet."

"It is strange that your friends did not tell you *where Juan is!*" suspiciously remarked the sad-eyed señora, as she extended her hand for the letter from Simon Rosendahl, which Dalman tendered with his frankest manner. His keen eye noted the machête hanging ready for use in José's cowhide belt, and he felt that any assumption of frontier gallantry would bring about a termination of all parley. If aught of passion lingered in the beautiful Spanish woman's wistful black eyes, it was only alarm for the absent Juan and a re-awakened tenderness.

The quick-witted lawyer hastened to allay her evident fears. "They did not know, but they sent me here to you. You can send the letter to 'Arizona Jack.' *He will understand!* I, *too*, am to be *a friend!*"

The young señora, holding the letter out at arm's length, as if it were of an explosive nature, murmured a few words to José, whose glittering black eyes never left the audacious stranger's aristocratic person. José was a fighting Yaqui, and he was the 'grand inside and outside guard' of the comfortable nest, in which the fugitive outcast had installed the daughter of the Jefe Politico of Magdalena.

While mistress and man conferred in Spanish, Dalman gazed around upon the evidences of comparative wealth and taste. The room was a palace drawing-room compared to the bleak ranch houses of many of the millionaire Texans who had tens of thousands of cattle on hundreds of thousands of acres.

Dalman saw, a quarter of a mile away, the huge iron skeleton of the railway bridge over the Rio Grande. "Jack is a good strategist," he mused. "Here, at the corner post of New Mexico, Texas, and old Mexico, he can evade all legal pursuit easily. A masterly spot for a sudden change of base. And with a night's run, he can reach the soil of either Arizona or Colorado." He smiled at Arizona Jack's smartness, for Simon Rosendahl, at Denver, had told him of his friend Jack's neat habit of slipping over the bridge and sleeping on the Mexican side, when any trouble threatened, leaving his house in the hands of the stolid José. "Smuggler, gambler, associate of horse thieves and 'off color' frontier heroes, this pretty woman can easily placate her fellow-countrymen on the other side, while Arizona Jack's title to life on the hither bank, is the two Colt's frontier six-shooters, which are his personal jewelry. Four railways meeting here, will take him in a jiffy out of any impending trouble. He seems to be an intelligent devil!"

Months of enforced patience in the exasperating scenes of the New York courts had taught Moses Dalman a rare patience, and so, he only smiled gravely and bowed when Pepita Morales, in her prettily accented English, said: "Señor Juan has gone down the Mexican Central to Chihuahua, and you can perhaps see him *in four or five days*, but *only on the Mexican side!* I will send him the letter, and then, if you come, José will take you over to El Paso del Norte, where you can see my husband."

Dalman was frankly respectful as he said: "That will be very good. If the señora will send the letter, I will be here in five days, and I will gladly go with José. It is only to help your husband that I come."

A faint crimson glow tinged the clear olive cheek of the Mexican beauty.

The reassured woman conferred with her watchful retainer, who slowly relaxed his grip on his *machête* handle.

"Are you the señor who wrote him the letter from Nueva York, which was sent to me?"

"*I am his dearest friend*," soberly said Dalman.

"Then the thieves, or some one, surely *stole the letter*, for there was only a piece of blank paper in it when it came. And, *Juan was so angry! Madre de Dios! So angry!*"

"He will understand all when he gets my letter, señora," said Dalman. "He must be here to meet me. Tell him I am working for him and I put myself in his hands. He will understand all when I see him. *I am alone*," said Dalman, stretching out his empty hands, "and, I go over to Mexico, unarmed, *with two brave men.* You can see that I am his friend."

"*Bueno!*" said the Mexican beauty. "Come back, then, on the fifth day, and at sunset, José shall take you over the river to him. But, Señor Estrangéro, make no mistake. *Juan is muy bravo!*"

Her lips trembled as she turned away, and at a sign, José escorted the visitor to the front gate.

"*No place for fooling is El Paso,*" mused Dalman, as he walked unconcernedly away.

Gazing back, he saw José leaning over the gate, still viewing the suspicious stranger's retreat. And, with a judicious haste, he leaped on the west-bound train, having hastily telegraphed to Max Rosendahl in New York, and bought a ticket to Tucson. Dalman breathed freely when from Deming late that night, he sent a warning dispatch to Morris Blum at the Palatial Golden Rule Bazaar. The simple words, "*Coming. A. L.,*" were a talisman to the resident partner. The lawyer eyed askance the dreary gray rocky sand wastes of that "arid zone," which stretches in one gray "stony lonesome," twenty-five hundred miles from Point Isabel, Texas, to San Diego, California.

"*The devil's own land!*" muttered Dalman, "and, barring this 'svelte' Castilian beauty, Pepita Morales, the inhabitants seem to be the devil's chickens. There should be gold under the surface, for, as to its exterior, this waste might well be called '*Hell's Delight!*'"

Sliding along easily on the steel rails, Dalman pictured the olden horrors of the time when the fierce Comanches harassed the weary emigrant wagon trains crawling slowly westward from San Antonio, Texas, only to turn the resolute defenders over to the tender mercies of the murderous Apaches, whose reign of blood and realm of death swept eastward as far as Stein's Pass, and stout old Ben Ewell's Dragoon Springs. Dalman chuckled over his "easy job" at Tucson. "I am only to placate Brother Morris, take my ten thousand dollars, and turn this fat-witted Yorkshire sheep over to Morris Blum for the shearing. It is lucky that I am not cast for a star part."

From Simon Rosendahl's descriptions of Arizona Jack, Dalman had resolved not to make any mistake in a gingerly handling of that mysterious individual.

"*Arizona Jack is no common 'gun man,'*" said the Denver Israelite with bated breath. "He has been a man of mark in some brighter social field before, and he has in addition picked up all the local deviltry of the last ten years here. Suspected of a close intimacy with the most dangerous characters west of Kansas City and south of Denver, he is habitually taciturn and peaceable, but when roused he is as fierce as a lion at bay."

"Several citizens, '*not lost but gone before,*' have made fatal mistakes of judgment in regard to Arizona Jack's amount of nerve. *Sand!* Why! There's a whole Sahara desert of 'sand' in that fellow's cool character. He moves among these rough fellows as thoroughly apart, as a particle of oil in a spray of dancing rain drops. And *he's always on top! Don't fool with him, Moses!*" expostulated Rosendahl. "But he's a game 'sport,' and 'on the dead square,' if he fancied that you had even a distant speaking acquaintance with the police authorities, you would not be alive in five minutes afterward. And so, remember, I have warned you! I've done all I could to start you out right."

"You don't think that I am damned fool enough to come down here to engage in a gladiatorial combat with this crazy fellow," resentfully said Dalman. "*I want to do him a good turn.*"

"And, incidentally—*yourself,*" sneered the Denverite.

"*Well, I'm not in business for my health only,*" laughed the lawyer.

The two new-made friends were both devotees of the Golden Calf.

Mr. Moses Dalman, Counselor-at-Law, was, however, possessed of considerable moral nerve, and he confidently counted upon self-interest, and a desire for a future revenge on the part of "Arizona Jack."

"If he is frank with me, and *sensibly admits that he is not dead*," mused Dalman, "I think that we two will get our claws pretty deep into the Condor mine."

Dalman, in the fifty hours of his journey to Tucson, carefully avoided the unctuous familiarities of the commercial travelers; the whisky-flask courtesies of the "one-lung" tourists; the prying attentions of that "booby" who is ever at hand on a Western train, and the mild flirtations of a dozen dusty and touseled women of more or less iniquitous social records.

At eleven o'clock at night, he stepped into Morris Blum's "ambulance," and ensconced in that gentleman's private residence den, an adjunct of the "great emporium," was soon growing confidential over a good supper with the boldest of the Blum tribe. Morris, a bully and coward, affected the "slap-dash" style of the bold frontiersman, which smeared the only judiciousness of the "trading Hebrew" into an unlovely compound. Round-shouldered, swarthy, with budding sensual lips, and a prematurely blasé air, the young financial bully of thirty-eight was a vulgar master, and alfamiliar companion. For, Tucson had spoiled even his plain Hebraic manners, by an easy commercial success. The cigars and "Cutter whisky" coarsely furnished forth the table, after the meal served by an insolent-looking, handsome Mexican slattern, whose *diablerie* plainly indicated a woman's crafty contempt for her supposed physical master, although he was the slave of her daily caprices. The "damaged beauty" having retired, Morris Blum's self-sufficient "previousness" gave Dalman himself, no chance to blunder.

"This thing is all now blocked out between Isidor and myself," he frankly said. "I have his letters, your check on New Orleans for ten thousand dollars is ready. Isidor telegraphs me to beware of Bill Murfee. Bent has been combing New York to find that fellow

Ryley, and he has also been privately writing and telegraphing to Bill Murfee.   Now, I've got a little plan of my own!   I will call Bill up here to Tucson.   He is always ready for a drunk and a fandango.   Under my eye he won't bother me.   As Isidor said, all that *you* have to do is *know nothing!*   Now, Bent's spies may be here even now and already on the watch!   The old man may try to buy the interest out and out before I get to this fellow *Robert Ross.   I've thought it all over!*   Instead of you remaining here I want you to take the noon train out of town, and *get back at once to Deming!* I will get Murfee here and then send him away up to Prescott, to stay a week or ten days on some easily fixed up business.   *He's about the only man that old Bent would trust down here!*   As to Robert Ross, I will be down at the mine *myself* to receive *him.*   But, I do not wish him to come on by the railroad through Benson to Fairbank and go up to the Condor Mine, *as usual.*   Let him get off at Bowie, and come round *to the south of the range,* and cross the mountain between Bisbee and Camp Huachuca.   I will send over an ambulance and light wagon with my own men to meet him at Bowie.   You can get him well ' jollied up ' at Deming, and come on to Bowie *with him.*   You can there give him a letter to me, signed ' *Arthur Lemon,*' and tell him that I am all ready and waiting for him at the mine.   My men will treat him splendidly.   All that you have to do is to telegraph me to Tucson when he starts, and then, *get back to New York City, as if the devil was after you!* "

" *See here, Blum,*" said Dalman, " I have seen this young fellow in England.   I don't want anything to happen to him.   It might be traced to me, and *I do not propose to hang for your crafty firm!*" Morris Blum dropped his easy swagger, and showed the cold, bloody, greedy coward in his sudden rage.

" Remember, Mr. Lawyer, *all the details were to be left to me.*   Do you think the firm of Blum Brothers has given you thirty thousand dollars just for a *song and dance!*   I want you now to take your money, and get over the line to El Paso and New Orleans.   If you want to play a lawyer's ' safety game,' then register at the St. Charles Hotel in New Orleans under your own name.   The banker's there will give you an alibi.   I'm going to have *the fellow's title* or *the papers*, and I wouldn't hurt a hair of his head.   *I'm too smart!*"

"And, *if I refuse?*" growled Dalman.

"Then I'll tear up the check, just give you a thousand dollars *to go home on*, and you can tell Isidor that you have betrayed your best clients.   He will fix your goose for you *in New York*.   No, sir, you can't afford to fight Blum Brothers."

"*And, if I choose to warn this man?*" doggedly said Dalman, who saw the chance of perfecting the title to the Condor mines now slowly slipping from his grasp.

"*Then, blast you, you won't get back to El Paso alive!*" growled Morris Blum, as he poured himself out a drink of whisky.   "You're on *my ground now*, and *I am King of Tucson* here!   Why, if I told old Bent that you were playing false, he and the Senator would have you disbarred.   We are too strong a team for you to fight.   No, Mr. Dalman, *take your pay* and *go along home*, and so *keep out of trouble*.   I will run this thing now.   If you do the right thing you get your *other ten thousand* on your return, if *not*, you surely will *lose the ten here*, and we may as well now play with our cards on the top of the table.   I can stop your check on New Orleans *by telegraph*.   So, unless you want to lose twenty thousand dollars, all you can do is to turn that fellow over to me.   I'm accustomed to have my own way, and *I will have it!*"

"But if he fights shy?   He may not want to go out on the desert with strangers," artfully said Dalman, restraining his wrath with difficulty.

"*Pick up some fellow at Deming*," relentingly said Morris Blum.   "Some one who knows the trail.   Give him a couple of hundred dollars to bring the man down to the Condor, *by Bisbee*.   You can say that all is ready, and that you will meet him yourself at El Paso on his return.   Give him the Planters' Hotel address. *You need not be there*, of course.   That's your little joke," guffawed Morris.

Moses Dalman caught at a last floating straw.

"*There are no large towns on this route?*" he said.

"*No!*   And the Mexican border's only a few miles

off, *all the way along*. The fellow whom you send can get the train at Nogales, and either run down to Guaymas or go back to Deming. I'll see that he is well taken care of. No one will know that you have sent a man along with him. *Leave the whole thing to me. I'll fix it.*"

"When do I start back to Deming?" said Dalman who was evolving a plan of his own. "*If I had only seen Bill Murfee,*" he mused, and he then began to see that he was being quietly hoodwinked by the great "Blum" combination. "*Can Yakey have blabbed?*" he fearfully thought.

And yet, the twenty thousand dollars in the wavering balances decided him!

"*Let the Englishman look out for himself,*" he decided when Blum said:

"You must take the noon train back, and *you are not to leave the house.* We might all get into serious trouble. I'll have a good breakfast ready for you at ten, fix up your money, give you a first-class send-off, and you can do your work at Deming, and get home. Old Bent's private orders to Bill Murfee have reached me. The devil of a Mexican woman that he has got at the mine is a sister of my pretty Carmencita here, and so I am posted by her, on all the cur's sly tricks. I'll keep a man after him and let Carmencita's sister go up to Prescott with him. Bill Murfee will never leave the Territory *if he blows on us.* I get all old Bent's communications. A man's always sure to be a fool with the woman he lives with! And both these girls were educated in the Convent School here. *They are as smart and wicked as they make 'em.*"

The coarse lover roared at his own low wit.

Dalman curtly said, "All right! *I'll go to bed now.* Get me out at Tucson, and *the game goes; as you lay it out.*" The half-enemies at heart accordingly sampled a bottle of champagne, and Dalman, with evident relief, saw the morning sun at last light up the Picacho hills. He was a very thoughtful Eastern passenger the next day, having omitted doing the "lions" of that strange town, old Tucson, so hopefully planted in fifteen hundred and sixty, where the mail-clad Conquistadores of Spain guarded the white-robed priests, when San Xavier del Bac was founded with bell, book, and candle.

Spain, Mexico, and the United States have successively flaunted their diverse flags over the sandy vales, now beginning to blossom with the vine and orange under the protecting guardianship of the Iron Horse. For, the swart Apache to-day cowers in his mountain reservations, and modern "business rascality" replaces the old gold-seeking crusade of the bloody Spaniard. Only a hasty glimpse of the dusty plaza, with the strange medley of soldiers, tourists, Indians, Mexicans, and mongrel traders, was vouchsafed to Dalman, as he settled himself back in his Pullman car, with Morris Blum's ten-thousand dollar check neatly buttoned up under his vest.

Dalman had been driven alone to the station, and he regretted not his brief acquaintance with the bluff and insolent Morris Blum.

"What a brutal loafer," mused the angry lawyer. "I would like to give that fellow a neatly devised '*roast*' of some kind, but I can't afford to give up twenty thousand good dollars. If I could hit it off with this cool devil Arizona Jack, and get hold of the title papers, or else run the frightened Englishman over to Mexico, and speculate later, on Blum Brothers, it would be *a neat revenge.* But, alone down here, I would simply be butchered if I made any row." He chewed the bitter cud as far as Deming, when a telegram, addressed to Arthur Lemon, informed him that Robert Ross would arrive the following day at New Orleans. "*That gives me but two days to work on Arizona Jack's cupidity!*" mused Dalman. "Thank, Heaven! To-morrow morning finds me back again at the *Planters' Hotel, El Paso.*"

It was with feelings of a keen anxiety that Moses Dalman again sought the shaded veranda of Señorita Pepita Morales' substantial adobe mansion on the sandy El Paso plain. The lawyer had sent on his warning dispatch to the spy, luring Robert Ross on to the artful embraces of Mr. Morris Blum. "*What a loafer,*" snarled Dalman, who remembered with disgust, the huge, blatant prosperity of the Blum Emporium, now swollen into gigantic proportions at Tucson. "*A simple, overfed, cowardly robber!*"

There was neither welcome nor aversion on the pale face of the lustrous-eyed Señorita Pepita Morales, when Dalman looked once more into her sadly lustrous eyes.

"*He awaits you over there,*" said the graceful Mexican. "Come back here alone—*at nightfall.* José will conduct you, and *you must surely come alone, Señor Americano,*" said the woman, with a sudden, mournful energy. "*If you would work Juan ill, then turn back now, for death awaits his enemies.* Remember, he is wild when aroused, and *muy bravo !*"

"Do I not put my life in his hands ?" boldly pleaded Dalman. "And I go open handed and unarmed, to him."

"*Then it is well,*" said the woman, simply, standing embarrassed before him, while José looked mutely on from the open door of a sleeping room. Moses Dalman noted, carelessly cast down in a corner, a Winchester rifle and a broad silver-mounted belt with a pair of heavy revolvers, with two carved eagles on their white ivory handles.

"*Argumentum ad hominem,*" bitterly murmured Dalman. "The whole frontier seems to be engaged in a border passion play of murder as a fine art." But he simply said, "*I will be here at dark !*" and, wandering back to the Planters' Hotel, devoted the afternoon to billiards with the "gentlemanly" barkeeper, and varying his quotations with perfunctory listening to the usual "horrifying tales," related to the "tenderfoot," who furnishes the grist to the mill of Bacchus.

"I think I will be glad to get a glimpse of the Battery once more," mused the frightened New Yorker.

It seemed strange to Dalman that night, when he descended from the tram car on the Mexican side of the river, that he should, with no misgivings, leave the highway and plunge into the darkness of the mud-walled straggling Mexican adobes under the guidance of the taciturn José, who was a walking arsenal in himself.

"*Muchos ladrones !*" sententiously remarked José, tapping his Winchester rifle significantly.

The sly Moses Dalman had prudently divested himself of all his valuables save a few dollars in silver change, his own personal possessions being all locked in the safe at the Planters' Hotel.

"I don't suppose that he will begin by ' *holding me up*,'" mused the cowardly man, who had sent Arizona Jack's old partner to a nameless grave.

"*Acqui estamos!*" grunted José, as he led Dalman into the back room of a little Mexican drinking "estanco."

On the bare earthen floor of the front room of the tienda, a dozen scoundrels were playing monte upon an old horseblanket stretched on the ground, while sundry prototypes of Venus, Messalina, Phryne, and other "social celebrities" were awaiting their coveted tribute of "mescal and cigaritos." It was a "go as you please" tienda.

As Moses Dalman bowed his head to enter the dimly lit back room, he started back, when a stalwart man sprang forward and seized him firmly by the right wrist with his left hand.

"*Here I am! What the devil do you want of me?*" said the speaker in a rich ringing voice.

Mr. Dalman observed that the right hand of his interlocutor held a formidable-looking pistol, and that the aforesaid pistol was cocked and ready for use!

"I came here on a peaceful errand to see you if you are the man known as Arizona Jack, once Hugh Dalton, of Tombstone."

"Who gave you that last as my name?" cried Jack, not relaxing his hold.

"Your best friend, Walter Ryley, now *dead and gone!*" firmly remarked Dalman. "I am perfectly unarmed, so *you need not stand on your guard!*" said Dalman, as the outlaw heavily dropped the imprisoned wrist.

"If you had been chased for years over four States, you would understand me," bitterly said Jack. "Now, sir, we will start fair. Sit right down there before me and tell me *why* you seek me! Let me have a clear, straight story, or there will be trouble *for some one!* What'll you drink? There is fairish good Hennessy brandy and good soda here!"

"*I'll follow you,*" coolly said Dalman, pulling out his cigar case and calmly offering it to the agnostic host.

José, at the door, his rifle at a poise, kept his eyes glued on the two men, who now faced each other with an eager curiosity. Arizona Jack was a kingly figure as he gazed at his unknown visitor. Moses Dalman found an instant reason for the sad fidelity of Señorita Pepita Morales to the man who had borne her to this strange land, far away from the sound of the convent bells of Magdalena.

"It would be a mere waste of time to dally," said the lawyer. "I have all Ryley and Brandon's letters about that mining interest which you sold through him over in London. If *you* are the man whom I seek, Hugh Dalton, then, *I have a fortune awaiting your grasp.* If you are *not*, I have only thrown away a month and some thousands of dollars in hunting you up. The whole Denver gang of your friends will back my faith, and *I've put my own life here at your mercy to prove it.*"

Arizona Jack was now gazing intently at Dalman. He had sprung to his feet. "*It's not for myself* I care, *but for Pepita.* For her! she shall see Sonora again, and *a little ready money would make her welcome. The one who comes home full-handed is always forgiven!* I *am* the man whom you seek. *Arizona Jack, Hugh Dalton,* the discoverer of the Live Oak and Magnolia mine. Don't seek now to fool or betray me! By God! we would die together *right here!* I swear it!"

Dalman eyed his man steadily. "*I am risking my life to help you out here,* Dalton," he said. "I am a lawyer. *I have money. I want more,* for reasons *of my own.* I live where *money is power* and 'six-shooters' *don't go!* We fight with check-books, not Winchester rifles, *on my chosen battlefields! You can trust me!*" he coolly concluded.

"What guaranties can you give me that you are not a Pinkerton agent, or the spy of the authorities?" sternly said Jack, dropping his head on his hands.

"The word of your Denver friend, whom you always trust *your life to.* The fact that we *both* must risk our lives in this deal. *My* enemies are *yours,* and we cannot afford to betray each other. It would be only a mutual ruin. I will back my faith with the two things that all men value—*money* and *life*—both *my own!* I am not a fighting man, Dalton, but you will find that I am not afraid of anything. I have just come back from Tucson, and I have been in the hands of Morris Blum, Bill Murfee, old Bent, and all that 'outfit,' as you call them down here." "Arizona Jack" growled with an oath: "*A mighty fine gang of thieves.*"

"How will you guarantee your faith *if I tell you all?*" suddenly demanded Dalton.

"I will deposit ten thousand dollars in cash in any bank in New Orleans that you may name, and remain *here*, hidden in El Paso, under José's guard, until you have gone to the mine and back, *if you dare to make the trip!*"

"I dare do anything *now*, for I'm *desperate*," said Dalton. "Now, what name shall I use in talking to you?"

"Arthur Lemon, business and mining agent, Chicago," said Dalman. "That's the 'official name' down here; of course *not my real one!* I'll meet you half way all the while."

"Let me have a good square look at you," said Dalton, standing close to his visitor. The two men eyed each other in silence. Dalman observed the splendid symmetry of the outlaw. Five feet ten, with a noble head well set on powerful shoulders; close, curly brown hair, a steady, dark brown eye, a sweeping, unkempt beard, a firm aquiline nose, and a broad, square brow. Above the shade line of the sombrero the forehead was white and smooth as a woman's, while the exposed face was burned to the red tan of the prairie. His well-shaped hands were brown as coffee, and a pair of riding boots sheathed his shapely legs to the knee. Even with all the abandon of the frontier costume, there was a nameless air of ease and elegance in the young man's bearing.

"You have lasted out well your ten years here," soberly said Dalman.

"*I let whisky alone*, for a man can't afford to drink

when he has either to *shoot* or *gamble*," simply said Arizona Jack. "And, my friend, you are in this deal for money only. *Your face tells me that*," said the outlaw.

"*I admit it*," frankly replied Dalman. "You are not an American," he hazarded.

"*I'm here ; that's enough*," mused Hugh Dalton.

"And, out of place here," steadily answered the lawyer.

"*The world's all the same to me now*," bitterly closed the gambler. "But we're losing time. I'll accept your guaranty, if we make a deal," he resumed. "You would never get away alive from José if you fooled me once."

"I would not wish to; you would only lose your life in the quest," replied Dalman, "and *I* would take *my sentence of death* north with me. You know the gang we've got to fight."

"*You bet I do*," sternly said Dalton. "I put one of them out of the way in old times because they wanted that mine, and I had to skip the country."

A ray of light of the past illumined Dalman's mind. "I suppose that they used Ryley as a stool-pigeon, and then swindled both principal and agent. They must have soon found out that there was a mine in the two claims."

"See here, Lemon," said Dalton, "I'll not beat about the bush ! I was bred a soldier, it matters not *where!* A bad woman ruined my life, and sent me to the frontier for hiding. And, when the Tombstone gang decided to kill me—to get that mine—a good woman saved my life ! *You've seen Pepita Morales?* She is my lawful wife ! Even if I did not use my own name, *she is still my lawful wife!* I was an Ishmael when I drifted to Arizona, ten years ago, and, at twenty-eight, I could not withstand the pleading of her girlish eyes; for she loved me ! I had helped to drive some Apaches to bay, and our party wound up after the chase, at Magdalena."

"The old Jefe Politico down there hated us Americaños, and the risk was the temptation. I ran that girl off from the Convent School, where they had placed her in a pleasant prison. She loves me more tenderly to-day than then. But Mr. Lemon, mad love always bears its own sentence of death, either to the love or the lovers! She is a child yet, in the ways of the hard world. I cannot protect her here. I've surrounded her with some comforts. José and Panchita would be ready to die for her. But, my roving life takes me away; the officers may be on my track; a chance knife thrust, or pistol-ball, may cut my career short. *I do not care a damn* now, *for myself!* My past life lies behind me. I have long had a presentiment of some coming trouble. The four cross railroads here are traveled more and more daily. It's touch and go with me. I've sworn never to wear a handcuff. They wanted to lynch me, if I killed my man, over in Tombstone, and I ran up against one of their best fighters. Pepita saved my life *then.* The second jailer was a Mexican. She brought a horse under my window, with a pair of pistols and a Winchester rifle— money, too, for *she sold her pearls.* But I bought them back, soon afterward, *at five prices!* The Mexican sawed my window-bars, and here I am! I only got *three* thousand dollars from Ryley for the half-interest in the mines. He got *five*—but one thousand went to him, and one for expenses. Now, if I can get a block of money—say *your ten thousand dollars*—I'll send Pepita on home to her mother in Magdalena. Old Don Gregorio is dead. Panchita can take her on, and José can stay with you. With that, she is a rich woman in Magdalena. Sonora is a garden of fertility and cheapness. There are no children. I've been led to this by the attempts of the sporting fraternity, at El Paso, to get at that defenseless girl. By Heaven! she is as pure as the Mater Dolorosa! If I live I can get over there from Chihuahua, any time. The Mexicans are all true to me, *just for her sake*—poor girl! In any event, she's better off than here; I am less exposed, and the damned gang of jackals are baffled, for her name is her protection at Magdalena. She would be a queen in Sonora with that money. I've had to kill *two* of these love-making fellows here, in fair fight, mind you, in eight years, and, José *one.* *It's only* the *whisky's work!* They are all afraid enough of me to let her alone, when they are sober." His face hardened. "*I've no place to take her to!* As for myself, I don't care. I'm strapped now. I've lost my last dollar, and I'm desperate.

> "Cut off by the land that bore us,
> Betrayed by the land we find,"

he dreamily repeated.

"Yes, the old song we used to sing in India is true."

"Then, you were in Her Majesty's service," quietly said Dalman.

"Don't be *too mighty inquisitive*, Lemon !" roughly said Dalton. "*I must make this girl safe!* If I could get her safely to Magdalena, I would then run up to Denver and Ogden—go out to Salt Lake and San Francisco, and later work down to Guaymas, by steamer. As a 'gentleman traveler,' I think I could raise fifty thousand dollars in a good season, at square card playing. Over on the Pacific Coast these fellows would not hound me down, and I would do the 'heavy swell' act ! There is no chance for a change of character down here. And I've no money to work with here."

"*Dalton !*" earnestly said Dalman, "*I can see that you owe the world nothing !*"

"Not a damned thing !" fiercely cried Dalton. "I was trapped, betrayed, ruined, in my foolish youth—to suit a corrupt woman's damned caprices ! Here I am, at thirty-eight a mauvais sujet, a human wolf !"

"I will guarantee you the success of *both* your plans," boldly said Dalman, "If you will only act with me *now !* And—I will tell you the honest truth! I will ! Not the *whole* truth—for that would be suicide for me, and *do you no good !* But all that I can tell you now will be the truth, and you can place your girl wife in a place of safety, and—then operate where your surroundings will be those of a *man,* not a *beast.*"

"That's what I want," gloomily said Dalton. "The first killing on the frontier dooms a man to always be ready to shoot at sight, in self-defense, and Wild Bill, Jesse James, Billy the Kid, John Wesley Hardin, and all the boys, finally run up against a 'cold deck' at last ! *I'll trust you! I dare anything*—only, there must be *no risk to Pepita!* That's my *one* stipulation ! "

"Do you know the country from Bowie to the Condor mine by Bisbee?" said Dalman.

"*That's the way I rode out*," said Dalton. "I would have gone into Mexico, but Pepita's father had a hundred 'rurales' in waiting, ready to butcher me. I kept out simply so she should have a protector. Poor girl ! She's as lovely and as useless as a lily. To say her rosary, and play a few love songs on her guitar, is all she knows. But, she has the heart of an angel, the devotion of a true woman, and, strangely enough, the courage of a lion."

"Suppose that you send Pepita right on to Nogales with Panchita, and so be free to act. She might help you there," said Dalman.

"*The money?*" dubiously said Arizona Jack. "I've been playing to hard luck for a year."

"I've got five thousand dollars of my own in the safe at the Planters' Hotel," said the lawyer. "I can give you that at Bowie if you go on with me, and then have *five thousand more* sent on by Blum to meet me there, for I have to show up there for a day. *Have you any friends there?*"

"I have a dozen who would die for me. Game sports, too. I don't lack for men friends, but they are all '*declassés*,' like *me*, and will die with their boots on, *as I will!*"

"Could you alter your appearance so as to be safe from detection?" demanded Dalman. Dalton laughed. "*With a close crop, a clean shave*, a deep stain of Mexican Yaqui brown, and a *Chihuahua rig*, even Morris Blum wouldn't know me," replied Dalton. "Now, go ahead! *What's your reward?*"

"I will be flatfooted," said Dalman. "I go on to Bowie with you, and come back here with José, and stay till you telegraph to him, '*all right.*' Do you know that Ryley swindled you in the interest of the Blums to give them control of that mine ?"

"*How can you prove it*," fiercely demanded Jack. "*He is dead, you told Pepita.* Dead men can't talk. It's easy to defame the dead."

" *Yes!* But he sold your mining interest for twenty thousand pounds, your half alone to Chandos Brandon. I have the papers.   Brandon sold it in two weeks for that sum, and more.   They made a ' wash sale ' between themselves for five thousand pounds to cover the swindle ' on you.' "

" *The robbing scoundrel!* He told me ' *dollars,*' not *pounds,*" yelled Dalton, "and then, took two of the five, for trouble and expense."

" Yes, and the two divided twenty thousand pounds in good British gold.   Ryley spent his half on ' Selina Lorraine, the Queen of the Air,' a Parisian circus beauty, and, cast off later, sank lower and lower, and at last died *in the gutter* in New York.   Now, Blum Brothers, old Bent, and the Senator——"

" *Stone! that old scoundrel?* " interpolated Dalton.

" *Yes, Stone*—are all playing traitor to each other. Each side wants to buy the interest—a clean half of the mine—from a secret agent of the outsider who bought it from Brandon.   Brandon, too, is dead—a bankrupt —and the title is still covered by the papers which the secret agent is bringing on from London."

" *Who is he?*" cried Arizona Jack, springing up with an oath.

"*Robert Ross*—a raw boy of twenty," replied Dalman, " *and, he is to arrive at New Orleans to-morrow.*   I saw him in London.   He will bring every paper, all the titles and originals.   Blum sends an ambulance over to Bowie to take him to the Condor Mine.   They mean to trick him into selling for a moderate sum, or, perhaps, to *overawe him.*"

"And, *you will go on with me?*" said Arizona Jack. " You are sure of the title being tied up ?"

" *If the papers which he has are destroyed,* then the real title is in you," said Dalman.   " I will furnish all the money—*fight the case,* and *take your title to it,* for *one-half of the proceeds.* You must outwit them.   The Ryley sale can be set aside for fraud.   They will not know that you have stripped him.   You can send Pepita on first— *to-morrow. We can follow on the next day.* I am just to cajole him, and to send a man on with him, so as to allay the agent's natural suspicions.   I made all these arrangements in England for old Isidor Blum. If you proved to be dead, I was going to have a shy myself at this young fool. But, *Morris Blum has made all his own arrangements down here.* He has sent Bill Murfee up to Prescott out of the way, and——"

"That means that Robert Ross will be met atthe mine by Morris and his gang. I know the brute's hand! See here, Lemon! It's you and I, now, *for a fortune—to the death.* Half and half. If I get this whole thing into my hands—but how can I trust your legal knowledge ?"

"My practice is twenty-five thousand dollars a year," said Dalman. "When you sign your deed to me of an undivided quarter interest in the mine, and you have my five thousand dollars to-night, with your security of my body for the *other* five, I will tell you *what there is in the mine!* We take our risk together."

"And you will remain at El Paso," said Jack, "*with José?*"

"*Certainly*," said Dalman. "If you strike first, or get the fellow over the Mexican line, Morris Blum will not dare to squeal, for I will tell you all to-night after we sign the papers."

It was a long time till the outlaw found his voice.

Arizona Jack was standing, quivering in every limb with rage.

"*I will fix him myself!* I owe *England* and *English blood*, and *English cant*, and *hypocrisy* a debt, only to be wiped out with some one's blood! I was sent to hell by a baby-faced English beauty; my prime of life has been stolen to please their crafty stock-jobbers, and so I'll strike back—*like a blind rattlesnake!* It's the vengeance of the gods! Let's get out now! Come over to my house. José will go on ahead. I take a boat at the river. He will escort you to the hotel. You can get your money, and then the papers can be signed to-night. Then Pepita and Panchita take the noon train and go on through to Nogales. José will be back when we get there, and you can telegraph to Morris Blum. *Caught in their own trap!* And I can stay on the Mexican side, and go up to San Francisco later by steamer."

The sad-eyed José was astounded when the three

men together made their way down to the Rio Grande where Arizona Jack's ferryman landed them in the garden of the gambler's domain.

"I'll be here in half an hour, Dalton," said Dalman, "with the money, and we can find a notary to-morrow when you go to the train with your wife."

That night, Dalman slept in peace under the outlaw's roof, for the money had passed, the papers were all signed, and Arizona Jack's strange ally closed his eyes listening to the murmurs of the excited and over-joyed Mexican exile whose heart yearned for the pleasant valleys of Sonora and the open arms of her simple-hearted mother.

The stolid José awoke with the mocking birds of the sedgy Rio Grande, and had already convoyed a swarthy family of Mexicans from "*el otro lado*," who aided in Señora Pepita's simple preparations for departure. José, carefully rolling a huge store of papelitos and cleaning his rifle and belt arms, was the Honorary Captain of the chattering crew, who were really directed by the energetic Panchita.

"*I shall remove nothing but a few valuables*," said Hugh Dalton. "This establishment really belongs to a wealthy Mexican who deals in horses, 'dexterously transferred' from Texas to Mexico, and vice versa. I have long been the trusted messenger of this '*horse trust.*' Besides, it allays all suspicions. The people in charge are the keepers of the 'tienda,' where we meet on the other side. Poor as that adobe hovel seems, I have seen two hundred thousand dollars in Mexican eagle dollar pieces stacked up there in raw-hide bags ready for smuggling over. Eight per cent. duty saved, made a profit for a single night's run of sixteen thousand dollars. But, the glut of silver has ruined the fine art of 'money smuggling,'" grimly said Hugh Dalton, "and Othello's occupation's gone," he growled.

With rare tact, Dalman wandered away to the hotel for his breakfast, and then purchased two railway tickets to Bowie, Arizona, a first-class for himself, and a second for his Mexican servant. His work was done when he had telegraphed to Morris Blum to send five thousand dollars in currency, and a check for five thousand to his business agent at the straggling town of Bowie, with orders to take up the first ten-thousand-dollar check on New Orleans.

The cheering words: "Robert Ross arrives in three days at Bowie. I will be with him. I came on here to meet him," brought great joy to the heart of the bullying capitalist at Tucson.

Under the directions of the wary outlaw, Dalman remained absent until Señorita Pepita Morales, with her two attendants, had been whirled away westward over the cheerless and dreary El Paso plains.

The night's revelations had lent the color of the rose to Pepita's fair cheeks, and from a distance Dalman only noted that her springing step was as light as a fawn's as she tripped through the station to a Pullman car, swathed in the black "*manta*" of the middle-class Mexican woman.

When the train went screeching away westward, Dalman awaited Arizona Jack in a saloon hard by the hotel. Hidden in the card-room he remained, while Hugh Dalton easily had the documents of transfer verified by the seal of the County Court Clerk, and a half-interest in the outlaw's share of the future bonanza had passed to the lawyer.

Pepita Morales wondered at the five-thousand-dollar windfall hidden now in her bosom, and she had kissed her generous husband with childlike impetuosity when he whispered at parting: "*You shall have as much more, querida, when we meet, and so, your mother's heart will be opened to you.*"

Confident of Pepita's safe arrival in Nogales, Arizona Jack led his new confidant to the deserted house by the river bank. "I'm all free now, Lemon," said Jack, "to change my character! We cannot talk on the train. Let us go over the whole thing to-night! There's no time to *argue cases* when we bring our little drama on in the Tombstone District! I will thoroughly disguise myself to-night. To-morrow morning Arizona Jack says '*Adios*' to this beastly hole, El Paso. The other fellows will close things up. I'll send José back to do that and *to protect you*, for I've telegraphed on to

Pepita's mother to send a couple of the 'compadres' up to Nogales to meet her. And she will be a little queen at Magdalena when they have killed the fatted calf." He stooped and picked up a blue ribbon which the vanished beauty had dropped, and hid it over his heart. "Now, *for our plans!*" he resolutely cried. "Pablo, here, is on guard! We are safe! As you say, we are both going to play a game—for life or death, for fortune or a crushing loss! What's your news to-day?"

"Tickets ready. I've a telegram from the Louisiana State line. Ross will be on to-morrow's train. I telegraphed back, 'Waiting at Deming for you.' You will run right on to Bowie and be at the station when we come in. I'll tell him I've engaged a good guide, one recommended by private confidential friends, a man who speaks English well and on whom I can depend to the last gasp."

"*Good enough!*" said Arizona Jack, sternly. "Lemon," he said, "I have given up ten years on account of this mine. I was not an outlaw till they tried to rob me of it and run me out of the country. They set their bravest bully on me! Since the flash of my pistol on that fatal night my whole course has been downward. Blum, Ryley, and the whole lot have swindled me. I will cut my way back to this fortune! For Pepita's sake, poor child, I've cast away the last scruple! *They shall repay with interest!* I'll defeat them, even if this fellow Ross finds his Condor mine to be the sand waste mirage desert of death down there 'and the mountain vultures pick his bones.'"

"How about Morris Blum and Bill Murfee? Dare you face them?" anxiously said Dalman.

"Ah! Pepita will send a dozen fellows over the line to hover around and wait for me. *I will have help!* I know the brutes I must fight. My fellows will hang around Camp Huachuca. I'll be over the border like a frightened coyote when I get the papers."

"*I will leave all to you, Jack,*" frankly said Dalman. "Now that we are partners, I can tell you that Morris Blum has explored the mines in secret and cross-cut and drilled a million dollars' worth of bonanza ore now covered up!"

"*Well, it shall be ours!*" cried Jack, while the clicking wheels bore along over the Texan prairie a brave, bright-faced lad going blindly alone into the trap.

And yet, the white wings of Love were spread to guard and guide him. On her knees at Leigh Hurst beautiful Lisbeth Leigh this night, was praying for her brother's safety. For she waited for the dawn and for answers to her belated warning. But the repeated cablegrams to "Robert Ross, British Tourist, Astor House, New York," were undelivered. He had gone and his eyes rested on the words, "Our agent will meet you at Deming."

CHAPTER VIII.

OVER THE ARID ZONE.

COUNSELOR MOSES DALMAN, of New York, was thoroughly happy at heart, as he sat at ease in the hideously over-ornamented Pullman car next day, which bore the schemer and his "*Mexican servant*" out of El Paso. So perfect was Arizona Jack's metamorphosis that Dalman himself in the morning, had taken him for one of José's murderous looking replicas from "over the Rio Bravo."

In their long vigil of the night, in vain Dalman had tried to draw Jack out further upon his stormy past. "I have dropped like a plummet; here I am; that's all, my friend," he resolutely said. "What future I had was irretrievably ruined when I left the other side. I wish to God that I had been born a loafer," bitterly burst out the outlaw. "*Why?*" calmly queried Dalman. "Because I would then have been spared years of bitter *remorse*," shouted Jack. "Regret *of my own*, I have long buried, but *remorse* for the sorrows of an innocent heart that has withered slowly to its breaking after my disgrace, *that is the living hell on earth*. Besides, I have Pepita's lonely miseries to answer for."

The specious lawyer murmured some platitudes about

"all men being more or less the victims of circumstance."

"*Rot, all rot, Lemon!*" vigorously replied Arizona Jack. "*I was a gentleman once—I'm only a vagabond now*, I know it. And neither the code of '*heavy swell*' or '*bad man*,' have I lived up to. In either line of life a little more of the sneak in me would have made me, perhaps, a successful hypocrite. Now, here I am going out calmly and knowingly to break several of the commandments, and the proof of my brutality is that *I don't care a damn*. You are in this game only for *money*, but I am in it *for revenge*, and to shelter the head of that defenseless child whom my own stupid vanity has led into a life of misery. By God! If she'd only murmur, or drink, or be untrue to me, or play the sleek Jezebel, like the woman who sent me to augment the army of loafers out here, I would be, perhaps, happier. But she is a child-hearted, trusting one, and she even yet thinks me—(Yes, even now!) —something of a man!"

Arizona Jack filled up an unfrequent glass of brandy and went away to his sleep, roughly saying, "*I am ready for the iron game. A little fight to the grim finish!*"

Without a word of adieu, unnoticed, and unregretted, Hugh Dalton turned his steps westward, among his enemies, to follow the dark, wistful eyes of the passionate young beauty who had nestled in his heart. And, having stifled the still, small voice of conscience, the undaunted adventurer, playing his "lone hand" in life, felt his spirits rise as he carefully examined his frontier revolvers and recharged the magazine of his Winchester. The wild thrill of the desert life was on him again. The yearning for the vast, lonely reaches of the silent cactus plains. He thought of that wild ride years before under the sparkling stars, when Pepita Morales pointed to the silver moon sailing over the towering, far off Mexican mountains.

"*There is my home, Juan!*" she had cried, as the fleet horses dashed away, leaving the avengers baffled, "*but, all the world is my home when you are by my side!*"

A tender light dawned in Jack's eyes as he mut

tered: "It's the only reparation I can make—a bold dash to do the *right* thing *in the wrong way!*" And he blithely hummed his old freebooter song,

> " And it was on the sandy
> Banks of the Rio Grande
> Where we lay,"

as he crossed the New Mexican line.

Dalman, dreaming of the outcome of the intrigue for the control of the " Condor," was supremely indifferent. He cared not which side he ultimately championed, as long as he crossed the final scoring line, *a winner.* "It's a pretty tangle," he mused. " The Blum crowd, old Bent and his veiled backers, this daring outlaw, and *myself!* I think that I hold the 'high hand,' for Cyril Leigh and his sister, for all old Carstair's smartness, do not know the fatal break in their chain of title. That *'power of attorney'* from Dalton to Ryley was *never recorded* at the American Consulate General or Legation. *I have the original* locked up, thank God, safe in New York, and the notary is *dead* and the *books burned.* The title bought by St. John Gladwyn, in England, is **not** worth a rap, with no proof of power of attorney from Dalton to Ryley spread on the records. *There never can be another! Ryley is dead!* And this game fellow, Arizona Jack, may die *also.* For there'll be several parties on the 'war trail' soon *down here. His life is held only at a pin's fee.* I am legally sure of *half* his interest now, for the El Paso bill of sale to me is good, both in fact and law, and, should Señora Pepita Morales Dalton become a fascinating widow, *I can then hold the balance of power*, and control the Condor mine by legally acting for her. *As far as I go*, if the Blums work their will on ' Robert Ross,' I have them ' on the hip,' for they would be in my power. *The game is mine*, and I'll make that old blunderhead, Isidor Blum, *pay me well* for fighting myself. For when I get back to El Paso I will transfer my half of Hugh Dalton's interest to *Moses Dalman*, of New York City, and I can sign the transfer there as *Arthur Lemon.* The seal of the court at El Paso is good *all over the world. No* notary-public nonsense about that!"

While the lawyer and the disguised outlaw were sweeping along on the "Southern Pacific," over the cheerless New Mexican mésas, and Cyril Leigh vainly gazed around for the "fortifications," at Fort Worth, there was a sorely puzzled man seated in the official chair, at the British Consulate, New York City. Angus Brummel Featherstone, Esq., Her British Majesty's Consul-General, grew redder and swelled more visibly than his official toga warranted, as he wearily cast a letter and several unanswered cablegrams over to Vice-Consul Walsingham; the even parting of whose Hyperion curls, was a prototype of the balance of the scales of justice.

"*Here's another one of the Lost Pleiad cases !*" the Consul sighed. "Mad boys, spendthrift heirs, missing partners, recreant husbands, faithless lovers, decamping defaulters, hair-brained 'younger sons,' and long-haired 'elder sisters'—all these undesirable social lunatics of the four kingdoms—are supposed to be my official game ! I am supposed to hunt them all up—with an outlying war party or two of Irish agitators, Fenian generals, escaped dynamiters, and other heirs of Robert Emmet's treason—but not, of his respectability ! This correspondent seems to be a woman of position,' for her friend, Miss Cornelia Powning, is the head of an old Yorkshire family—these Leighs are of the Squirearchy, dating back to Alfred's time, and the Bank of British North America, and Bank of British Columbia, have already sent confidentially to me about this young Cyril Leigh. They have even telegraphed to their San Francisco houses. I don't see what we can do, Walsingham, save to write to the British Consuls at New Orleans, San Francisco, and Guaymas, Mexico, to afford him all needful aid and protection.

"I suppose that means *money; it usually does!*" gloomily concluded the official, "And, *yet*, the young madcap is rich, and the only heir to a splendid Yorkshire property. I wish to heaven there wasn't an orange grove, a cattle ranch, a buffalo herd, a grizzly bear, or a pretty American heiress *in the wide world.* Our young fellows act like mad fools, *over here.* Here's this young chap, sailing around as 'Robert Ross,' a name fit for a bagman, when he is Squire Cyril Leigh, of Leigh Hurst. Better telegraph to the Consul at Guaymas, for our letter might be caught in a local Mexican revolution, and, so, be 'hung up' there till the millennium. He is not here, that's certain; for I went into the 'Hastor 'Ouse,' myself, and found, from the head 'clark,' that a British youngster, Robert Ross, had arrived on the *Aurania*, stayed only a day, received a sort of Jew-fellow, who outfitted him and bought his tickets for El Paso, wherever that is, and then left town, after twenty-four hours. Write and telegraph, and mark all '*Confidential.*' They are to report here any happenings. The banks have given me *carte blanche*. Whether marriage, ambling scrape, speculation, love affair—anything up to murder—*I want to know it*. It's strange," growled the old man, as he reached for the London *Times*, "that nothing of a satisfactory nature ever seems to happen to our young fellows over here! They are helpless as lambs unless they are out-and-out '*bad lots*,' and, *then*, my Gawd, I'm supposed to square all their bills, and to placate the angry mothers, fathers, brothers, and even *the Yankee girls themselves*, who fall into the hands of our 'castaways.' I wish to Gawd the escaped valets of the British Isles would not stream over here to play the 'Lord-Algernon-Fitz-Percy-Clinton' game, on the whole circuit from Hoboken to Waukesha! And, yet, every marrying Yankee mamma has the latest copy of the Peerage."

The Consul dropped his eyes on the *Times*, slowed down his engines of wrath, and then indulged in a soothing nap while the disgusted Walsingham executed "Lord Marmion's high behests." "There should be a Home asylum for the British noodle," ejaculated the angry Vice-Consul, who carefully passed "the labors" over to "a squire of low degree," and resumed his own official occupation of looking bored, and keeping his hair split exactly on the "median line." The mere responsibility was toil enough for the young V C.

Neither the Consul-General, nor that civil-service exquisite, Walsingham, ever knew of the real reasons of the "danger signals" sounded from Leigh Hurst.

Cyril Leigh, on his way, jealously eyeing every one trying "to scrape acquaintance," had already cabled twice back to Pately Bridge, and he now only awaited his arrival at Deming to send the third message: *"All right!"* And yet, he was not satisfied with the scant ceremony of his New York reception. The insincerity of Arthur Lemon's prowling around Leigh Hurst, before he met them, and the fact of the advertisement in the "Agony Column," both these things had impressed him as *"suspicious."*

Cyril Leigh reflected when wandering around New Orleans, where he phlegmatically "rested over," a day, that Max Rosendahl's civilities in New York City had been unceasing, almost even pressed to the point of a " polite surveillance."

He had noted on the long stretch from New York City to New Orleans a young Hebrew-American of a startling family resemblance to the agent of "Mr. Arthur Lemon."

"All that sort of chaps look alike !" growled the Squire, but his patience was exhausted in the Crescent City when he became confident that the Hebraic youth was secretly following him. He doubled around a square or two, and, at last meeting the shadow face to face, he broke out: *"What the devil are you after anyway, my lad ?"*

But the impassive youth only politely raised his hat and murmured some words of a foreign language, perfectiy unintelligible to the frank-faced squire. On the ferry steamer at Algiers, once later in a crowd at Fort Worth, and, lastly, in the eating-house at El Paso, Cyril Leigh had wrathfully observed the haunting form of the stranger. In his clumsy British fashion he " tipped the guard," as he termed the lordly conductor, who grinned broadly when the Englishman communicated his suspicions.

"Oh! *That young fellow !* He is only a student going out to Colorado Springs for his health. He only speaks German and Polish. Why, I had to get a man to interpret for me in speaking with him!"

This was apparently a "clincher," but Robert Ross,

as he left El Paso for Deming, saw again the unwelcome face of the haunting shadow glaring at him from the crowd.

Mr. Jacob Rosendahl laughed slyly as he sent in a final warning dispatch to Deming, addressed to Abram Levy, and concluded: "*Wait for you here—Planters' Hotel.*"

The frolicsome spirit of Love had also been playing its pranks at the "Leigh Arms," to the future discomfort of the British Consul at New York. Brackett, the coachman, for two years the bond slave of pretty Mollie, the head maid of the Leigh Arms, had confided to her the story of Arthur Lemon's "business," and his own sage suspicions of that prying first visit. The intention to start a "public" of their own "after marriage," had swept away all reserve between the two lovers.

"*Did you tell Miss Lisbeth of this, Joe?*" said the maid.

"I gave the young master a little tip, but I'm afraid to bother Miss Leigh. She might give me the sack. You know how high-spirited she is!"

Pretty Mollie dissembled, but before she mustered her courage to warn Miss Leigh, Robert Ross had left New York City. Then, urged on by a guilty conscience, Mollie finally made a "clean breast" of it all. She had buried her head in her apron several times before she told of Arthur Lemon's first flying visit; of his catechism of Joe Brackett; of the artful "boring process" applied to Mollie—in return for a princely tip.

"You see, Miss Leigh, I only thought he was an artist gentleman, or some writer, looking up the old families. And Joe Brackett, too, he's just that stupid he just told the young master that the man had run down here and inquired for the family, and—gone away. And the Squire is—so unsuspicious, so used to home folks. But it all comes back over me *now!* That American man is so artful and deep. He went over the whole family history, and learned all about Squire Gladwyn, and the family lawyers, and all. There's some trap set for Squire Cyril, and *so, I made bold to come and tell you all.*"

Resolute Lisbeth Leigh sent for Joe Brackett, who was soon placed in the pillory of cross-examination under his mistress's frown and his sweetheart's bright eyes. With a pallid face, Miss Cornelia Powning also listened to the confessions of the garrulous servants. When the frightened lovers were dismissed, Miss Powning in vain tried to calm her excited hostess.

"I know *now* that all this is to be used in some way against Cyril," Lisbeth mourned. "I have had a presentiment of coming sorrow since my strange dream—when I saw——" She stopped abruptly. "I urged Cyril to let me demand the full names of all the principals in this matter—or to extend the price, here, to the full twenty thousand pounds!"

"So," soliloquized Miss Leigh, "and he *would go*, and *see for himself!* He seemed to be possessed of the idea that some good would come of it. 'If it is valuable enough for them to come over *here* to buy it, then we should go *there*, to see it,' he said. Fatal haste," cried Lisbeth, "Either we should have sent a good man with Cyril, or have arranged with the New York bank to send down a representative with him, *from there*. But, there's no reasoning with a Leigh, *once his blood is up!*"

Cornelia Powning pointed to the faraway tower of the Manor church. "There they lie, my darling Beth! Generations of Leighs and Pownings who went out to roam over the world and left loving women behind at home, to weep in silence as you and I do today! It's the doom of woman to sit with folded hands —and, *wait*. You should see Solicitor Carstairs at once! I would go down *to-morrow*." And then the pale-faced old patrician went back to the seclusion of a room haunted by one beloved unreturning face, the bright-hearted, generous-souled young soldier, who was the last of the "mad Pownings."

Miss Lisbeth Leigh's executive energy astounded the parchment-faced old Solicitor Carstairs, next day. "My very dear young lady," he smoothly said, deprecating all emotion, "I will, of course, send the telegrams to the Consul. You have already once written to him. I will telegraph to the banks. *You may dismiss all fears*—this fellow is only a Yankee sharper driving a close bargain. Suppose you do lose a few thousand pounds? *Squire Cyril would have his way!* He was wildly El Dorado mad—to make this trip. The Yankee naturally did not wish *to face me*," Carstairs grimly smiled, "for, *I* would have got the *whole worth of the property out of him*. But it's too late, *too late to talk!* You are as resolute in your own quiet way, as your dashing brother. After all, what matters it, you know that Miss Powning will leave you all her personalty; and you will be pleasantly astonished—*astonished*, my dear young lady," said Carstairs, rubbing his hands, softly. "I drew her will. Poor Powning, what a blow to the dear old lady. Bless my soul, it's nigh on ten years now, since the Captain disappeared like a thief in the night." The splendid woman's pallor was unnoticed by the old babbler, but her lips trembled as she murmured, "Was there never any sign, not a rumor, not even a conjecture?"

The old solicitor jingled his bunch of golden seals. "Not even a guess has been hazarded. And, strangest of all, never a charge, never a discreditable rumor, never a bill or a *post obit* turned up. I knew Lieutenant Colonel Granville Leger and his wife, too. Neither of them would ever mention his name. The Lieutenant Colonel simply ignored the affair 'for the good of the regiment.' He kept all the journals quiet for the sake of the service. Of course, we all expected to hear of some frightful gambling losses or some hidden delinquency, but even the splendid personal outfit of Powning—his horses, furniture, art treasures, library —the whole thing remained unclaimed, as well as some bank balances left at Grindlay's, and in the army agent's hands."

"*No, he's surely dead.* On the honor of a family solicitor, I can say, Miss Leigh, that there has never been a single trace of him discovered, and Cornelia Powning has spared no money in trying to trace him. I always feared some coming disclosure for the first year or so, some strange story of hidden folly, or worse; but I've long set him down as an innocent victim. Victim of some dark plot, some dastardly revenge, perhaps *a woman's.* Who knows? *My heavens!*" The old Polonius broke off his relation in a wild alarm as Lisbeth Leigh's head fell back in a sudden swoon.

It was only after the Lady of Leigh had been escorted to her homeward train, that Carstairs's wits returned to warn him of an inadvertence. He had absent-mindedly jotted down in his fee-book, under the heading "Leigh":

"1. Consultation as to American matters, 21s.

"2. Office work, telegrams, and expenses, do., £3 5s.," when he suddenly remembered an old story. "Bless me, they were fond of each other, *so the story ran.* Yes, yes, *yes!* I'm just an old stupid, and what's worse, apologies are out of order. When I go down to London, I'll see Granville Leger's solicitors. He is dead, and Madame Marie D'Orsay Leger also. There's no endangered military career now to interfere with professional confidence. The ——— Hussars have long forgotten their dashing troop captain. But it is my duty toward the finest estate in the North Country to look up the thing. It may be there is a loose string left hanging out *somewheres.*" And the old man sighed as he drove homeward in his neat little brougham to nod over his port after dinner. For, twenty old families of the grade of the Leighs and the Pownings regarded the bald cranium of Solicitor Carstairs as the sacred depository of their family confidences, all neatly entered in the immaculate fee-book at 21s., for Carstairs despised a "sovereign" in accounts and clung to the good old-fashioned "guinea," for the potent reason, dear to "a gentleman of a certain age," that it contains twenty-one shillings in its invisible round to the vulgar twenty of the coined sovereign. And he had softly gotten far along in the way of life.

His imprudent gossip had brought on a new storm of sorrow sweeping over the womanly heart of Lisbeth Leigh. She could not but listen, as the old man babbled on, and long after gentle Cornelia Powning slept that night, under the gray-mossed roof of Leigh Hurst, Lisbeth Leigh, her startled heart throbbing with a new sorrow, mourned for one who had gone out of her life. "*I was only a girl, then,*" she murmured, gazing at her imperial form, as she stood before the great cheval glass. "*I did not go out into the fierce, restless life of hot-hearted London,*" she said. "*There was perhaps a woman—a woman's treason, a woman's vengeance.*"

The splendid beauty gazed through her tears long, that night, upon the face of the man who had brought the sting of sorrow to her bright young life. The winds were wailing in the old forest of the manor, as she dropped the picture, and burst into bitter tears. "After all these years," she sobbed, "a new sorrow! *Is all the world false?*" And she whispered, as she gazed upon the face of the vanished heir of Powning Hall. "*What woman?* Whose hand sent you out to the ignominy of a fugitive, or doomed you to death. Thank God, that *Cyril does not know.* He *never shall know*, for this is my own sacred sorrow. Cornelia, herself, *shall never know. It shall die with me!* Cyril was but a boy in school. And *he—he* was in India. It was only five months from the time he came back, in honor, with wounds and medals to attest his soldierly faith, that he left me without even one last word." She sobbed herself into a sad and dreamless sleep!

The shadow of this new sorrow lingered on Lisbeth Leigh's face the next day, so that even Cornelia Powning feared some new danger for the heir of Leigh wandering in unfamiliar lands. She did not know how proud a heart beat in Lisbeth's breast, for the shadow of the newer sorrow darkened the soul of the Lady of Leigh. There was a gnawing suspicion of a wrong done to her innocent girlhood by one who had waked the sweetness of her Harp of Life, thrilling with the rich strains of a golden youth. But the receipt of Cyril Leigh's dispatch, "*All right. El Paso, going west,*" brought back the happy light to Lisbeth Leigh's eyes, and she waited for the signal of her envoy's meeting with the agent of the purchasers at Deming. "Dare I telegraph openly him to beware of this strange bargainer?" she tormented herself. And at last she was fain to be content with old Carstairs's well-formed general judgment, for, at twenty-eight, even in her calm retreat, Lisbeth Leigh had learned that men love the jingling of yellow gold more than aught else on earth! "*A sharp bargainer,*" she mused. "And after all it seems that I shall have money enough. For the strange past is a sealed book forever. The blow that struck at Cornelia Powning's last hopes has withered my heart before its time! *What will I do with this easy-gotten wealth,* even if it shortly comes?"

Unconsciously, the splendid woman was keeping watch and ward by the grave of a dead love, still true to her own self, still true to the ideal of her young heart, whose gentle garrison of loving thoughts had been summoned in the old happy days by the ringing bugle call of a brave Lancelot who had strangely passed out of her life. And only a womanly pride now stood as the faithful warder of her troubled heart." She flushed under Cornelia Powning's clear glances. "*No one shall ever know. The past is mine alone,*" she proudly avowed. And so, in the narrow empire of her burning heart she clung to the love which had been to her only a cross, where all seeming hope of a golden crown had long ago vanished!

Counselor Moses Dalman was fretting in a secret excitement foreign to his usual well-balanced temperament as he gazed up and down the straggling streets of Deming, while waiting for the train bearing Robert Ross to the hospitalities of the owners of the Condor.

He had carefully given to Arizona Jack all the orders needed to play his humble part at Bowie.

"You will find Morris Blum's ambulance and party waiting there, and you can leisurely spy out the whole surroundings. I must leave all the methods to your wits and nerve now."

"Arizona Jack" himself was in high glee, for he had received a telegram bearing the words of cheer: "*All right! Nogales!*" and he knew now that Pepita Morales was safe in her mother's arms once more!

Moses Dalman had so far kept faith with the man he secretly feared, for while the train tarried for a scanty meal at the bleak town of Deming, Dalman, at the telegraph office, obtained Morris Blum's last secret orders: "The money and check have been sent on to you by our agent, as requested. Telegraph to me instantly the arrival at Deming of your friend. New York partner very anxious."

In the gray of the evening the cheerless, sandy streets of Deming, New Mexico, wind-swept and bordered with shabby "stores" and low drinking booths, were even more dreary than usual.

Jostled by burly teamsters, drunken loafers, and wandering human wrecks, Dalman was at last relieved from his vigil when the long, lumbering train rattled in. There was no mistaking the rosy face and stalwart proportions of the expected "Robert Ross," whose Kharkee suit and knickerbockers were the cynosure of all eyes.

Dalman, passing down the line of Pullman cars, eagerly scrutinized the little knots of jaded travelers going west in search of wealth, health, or a varied note of languid pleasure. He was, however, not prepared for the evident coldness of Cyril Leigh's greeting.

"*How long do we stay here?*" abruptly said the English youth. "I want to have a bit of a plain talk with you before I go on a step further."

There was a decided dissatisfaction lurking in Leigh's eye, and he gazed at Dalman with a frankly inquisitive air.

"We can easily take the morning train down to Bowie; the town is just over the Arizona line," said Dalman. "I've made all the arrangements to send you down to the mine from there, by a frontier stage coach, and our principal will meet you at the Condor mine, but three days' easy march from Bowie. The party and ambulance, as they call the coach, are all now waiting there for you, and I've sent my own guide and representative down this very morning to see that all is ready for you."

Dalman bustled around, and in half an hour the young squire's luggage was piled up in the corners of a roughly partitioned room in the "Palace Hotel," whose tawdry "bar," devoted to cards and killdevil whisky, left little room for the culinary and sleeping arrangements. The "good entertainment for man," was assorted whisky ; for beast, a run over the straggling pastures thinly sprinkled with gramma grass.

Dalman left his semi-hostile guest to discuss a solitary dinner of fried bacon, beans, and "alleged" coffee, while he sauntered out to send the expected news of Robert Ross' arrival over to Morris Blum at Tucson. The head barkeeper watched the crafty lawyer disappear.

"There's the head robber, I suppose. The young English fellow is probably some capitalistic noodle brought out here to be swindled. I've never seen this fellow's face before, but, Arizona Jack is the head devil, evidently, and here *in disguise.* He was with this fellow and went off *alone,* west. There is a sharp little game in all this, and one played for high stakes, for the gang down at Tucson will fill ' Jack ' full of holes, if he ever lands there. The young Englishman is just a pudding—' a jack pudding ' for these two!"

Dalman's grave face had marked no internal anger as he disappeared, but he muttered, "*Damned snob,*" as he wrote the words, "Party here seems quite dissatisfied, handle him with care. Will report his departure from Bowie. *Look out for all outsiders.*"

"I'll just let this young upstart now *make his own game,*" mused Dalman, as he wandered back and offered his services to "Mr. Robert Ross."

"I'll have a serious talk with you in an hour," gruffly said the Squire. "I want to go to the telegraph office myself, now," and, in charge of a hotel "runner," he stalked away.

"*Damn his impertinence,*" growled Dalman. "He wants to keep me in the dark."

He was exactly right in this conclusion, for the broadshouldered young Squire had really stolen away to send a home cablegram. He was satisfied when he had traced these words :

" Shall go to the mine to-morrow. Determined to raise my price to the full sum paid. Answer to Tucson. Will arrive there in one week. Lemon is here!"

While Dalman anxiously awaited the Englishman's return, Morris Blum was striding up and down his sanctum in Tucson. He had ruminated long over the warning note sounded by Moses Dalman from Deming.

"There is some dirty deviltry on foot! Perhaps old Bent has posted this boy! Here is Isidor, too, worrying me from New York. He telegraphs, 'Raise price to the full twenty thousand pounds, if necessary! Be sure that the papers are original. Don't let the man get away. You can give him our exchange on New York!'"

A sudden fear possessed Blum. "*We must control this mine!* If Bent buys that title, and we should incorporate, he will have three-quarters of the mine, and our grip is lost forever!"

The slouchy Venus who presided over Blum's den entered, saying: "*Some one is here from the mine!*"

The frowsy face of a hangdog-looking frontiersman appeared at the door.

"*I wuz late, boss,*" he drawled, "but I had to wait for the three Injuns. They was out 'a horse huntin',' " he guffawed, "in the hills."

"*Who've you got ?*" demanded Blum, hastily.

"Wall! There's 'White Heron,' 'Lame Wolf,' and 'Standing Bear,' three of the biggest renegade cutthroats between here and the White Mountains."

"*Here's fifty dollars!* Get what you want for yourself in the store. And, remember the train leaves in an hour! Get down to Bowie with these fellows, and you must turn the three Indians over there to Jim Willetts. Did you get the three he wanted ?"

"*Yaas,*" drawled the red-bearded Missourian.

"Well, be sure to get your party off. Jim Willetts will tell you what you are to do, and I'll meet you later at the mine. Jim will telegraph to me from Bisbee. If you want any more money, Jim will give you all you want."

As the frontiersman disappeared, Morris Blum grinned in the satisfaction of a coming security. "With Jim Willetts and his party in one gang, and this brute, Lem White and these three Indians in another, I will warrant that 'Mr. Robert Ross' will not get away *very far*, not if my plan works. And the fellow is as green as grass. If he had been allowed to come here to Tucson *first*, some gossiping fool might have put him on his guard, and I guess I'll take all the money down to the mine and pay him there. I'll get the papers away from him, and have a legal contract quickly signed. If he is ugly, then, *well—he will run up against something hard.* He must be fixed before he gets to Tucson, for there are *Bent's spies*, and *our own enemies* to fear. There would then be no chance to buy this thing without him seeing the bottom of the mine *first.* Down at the mine or near there the trick must be worked. But nothing to give us away. *Some natural* happening! I must see him first, and then we must *part as the best of friends*, to meet at Tucson. *By God! I have it. Yes, I have it!"* joyously cried Morris Blum, as he went off to sleep over an inspiration—after he had heard the whistle of the train taking Lem White and his three "friendly Apaches" out of town. "They'll still be at Bowie at three o'clock. *Time enough!"* laughed the great Morris, to whom "the details" now appeared somewhat easier of arrangement.

By a couple of tallow candles reinforcing a shilling kerosene lamp in this dingy chamber of the Palace Hotel, at Deming, Cyril Leigh sat facing Moses Dalman, on the eve of their final separation. The American furtively eyed the young Squire, as he said guardedly:

"I have put myself out to arrange all this business for you, in good shape, and I've tried to make your trip here as pleasant as possible. I am now going on up to Denver, to examine some mines, and when I see you off to-morrow, Mr. Ross," said Dalman, "*my work is done,* both as regards you and *my principals!* Now, *what can I say to you?"*

Cyril Leigh said, bluntly: "Lemon, I have dealt fairly with you, and only after your departure from Pately, I learned that you had been down at Leigh Hurst, *incognito,* spying around my house, before we met. You took advantage of the simplicity of my Yorkshire servants, to pry into all our affairs. And you have, so far, concealed the name of your principals. This whole thing carries an air of mystery that I don't like. Why don't you go along with me *yourself?* You *are* the man I really am dealing with!"

Dalman felt his "castle in Spain" crumbling very rapidly, but he had learned in court to quickly control his too intelligent face.

"*There are several reasons*," he calmly said, lighting his cigar. "I had learned, by mere hazard, of your family-seat after the insertion of the advertisement. I ran down there, hoping to meet you. I was not sure I was on the right track. I learned at once that both of you had gone up to London, and a mere chance word of a servant referred to your brilliant sister as being the real directing mind of the family. Now, my dear sir, *I have had a vast experience of business with women!* It has been *a very unsatisfactory one*, for they always see a rat behind the arras, or, else, they think that *they hear him!* I learned that you stayed at Morley's, usually, and I went up to London. I saw, at first sight, that—(excuse me) your sister rather distrusted me! Now, I kept silent as to my first visit, for that sole reason. Women are women, *all the world over*, and to get a woman to sign any business-paper, *even at its double value*, is a herculean labor. As for this affair of yours, it's after all, a trifling one. You will see for yourself! You will find the thing to be just as I have represented. My principal, who will meet you there, has your contract to sell the interest for five thousand five hundred pounds. The amplest opportunity will be given you to investigate, and I cannot further aid you. You are safe in every way, and your money will be there to meet you."

"I will give you a letter to the manager of the Condor Mine," concluded Dalman. "I did not care to spend a month with the English solicitors, and as for the whole affair, I am glad to wash my hands of it. You can soon judge for yourself. I have sold a mine for a million with less bother and with far less running around. We work quickly in *America!*"

"*All right, Lemon!*" doggedly said Cyril Leigh. "I'll keep to my pledged word and to our bargain, *but* if I'm not satisfied as to all the facts down there, why I'll have further opinion and guaranty, or *I won't sell*, that's all. I tell you this *right here*, for I don't like double dealing in any way. We Englishmen are not as *cute* as you Yankees, but *we're not blind fools !*"

"I'll be ready at seven to take my train," said Dalman, a little wearily, "and I prophesy that you'll find all perfectly satisfactory *down at the Condor !*"

The two men separated for the night and Moses Dalman walked the plaza of Deming for an hour after the young Englishman's light was extinguished.

"Pig-headed, suspicious, and a greenhorn," he mused. If any scruples had ever existed in his mind as to the proposed operations of "Arizona Jack" in "removing an obstacle" he now angrily dismissed them. "It's that dark-eyed divinity of Leigh Hurst who has frightened this raw boy. *She saw through me.* Jack must get at these papers *by hook* or *crook.* Once destroyed, some 'fortuitous happening' removing him forever, then *we are all right. The other fellows will probably make sure of it.* Jack, of course, gets safely over to Magdalena and I get his dispatch at El Paso. I will tie up the whole thing in law and *he will be* perfectly *safe* as long as he keeps over the line in Mexico. I can handle the legal fight and *I'm sure of a fortune.* And I'm glad to get away *from the danger line here !*"

It was four o'clock in the afternoon when the taciturn travelers dismounted at the little railway station at Bowie. A white canvas-covered roadwagon, drawn by four singularly unattractive-looking mules, was drawn up at the platform, and a knot of curious loungers marked, with "sweet wonder in their eyes," Mr. Robert Ross's Anglican external decorations. The fact of his being the only unarmed man in the party of half a dozen crowding to meet him, stamped him as a "tenderfoot" agent or principal of high degree.

Big Jim Willetts, lurching up to Arthur Lemon, lazily remarked: "*We make our headquarters over to Levy's store.* They'll put the gentleman's traps in. And, as my men are liable to get drunk and commence a shootin' here, if he's all ready for the road we kin pull out now. *The goin's good!* The baggage wagon's all ready, and *we kin make fifteen miles* on our way to-night."

"I'm game for anything," said Cyril Leigh, eyeing the black, gray, stony hillside settlement with ill-concealed disgust.

"Then, dinner's all ready over there," said Willetts. "*Let's go over.* There's a Mexican fellow here askin' *for you.*"

"*Oh*, yes!" carelessly said Dalman, as he noted Arizona Jack leaning quietly against a post of the Levy establishment, and eyeing a superb red roan horse, whose braided horse hair lariat he held in his hand.

The frontier moss trooper's usual outfit decorated the uncouth but convenient Texan saddle. Mr. Sigismund Levy escorted his guests into the messroom of the business house, where Robert Ross unconcernedly took his seat, his leather dispatch box at his side.

"*I have a few little details to attend to,*" said Dalman, "and, so you'll excuse me, as I stay, and you go on."

Closeted in the business office, Moses Dalman hastily scrawled his last telegram to Morris Blum. Delivering up his ten-thousand-dollar check, and receiving the bundle of notes and a five-thousand-dollar check from Levy, Dalman walked across the road to where Arizona Jack was standing beside the returned José, in front of a Mexican "posada."

"*Quick! Come inside,* Jack!" whispered Dalman, "I've got your money now, ready for you, and, this fellow is strangely suspicious!"

In five minutes, Arizona Jack had received his last payment, and the parting words were spoken.

"Do you know these other fellows who are of the party?" anxiously cried Dalman.

"*All about them!* I've good friends here! The sports, and they have watched them! I've got a clear field, for they do not know me! But they are *a cutthroat lot!* Now, the east train goes back at seven; José will go on with you to El Paso—as we have agreed. I've got my own plan, and a dozen good fellows near Camp Huachuca are waiting to help me. You'll get my telegram from Nogales or Magdalena in a week. *If you don't,* then you may know *that I'm dead*—and, *also that fellow* who's going to sell my stolen property.

"Now, José will get on the train, and, *you be sure to do the same! Don't make any foolish mistake,* Lemon," said Arizona Jack. "I've staked *my* life—and, *José holds you, in gage*—to prove fair play till I get over the line! After that, I'll come when you need me, for, we will open out on this gang of thieves. *Come along, now*, and *introduce me to my man!*"

A few last words, in Spanish, to José, and the two conspirators joined the group in front of Levy's store, where the ambulance—now all loaded up—stood ready for departure. Only "Big Jim Willetts" and the young Briton were to be passengers, the remaining escort having ridden on with the loaded baggage wagon bearing the tent and stores.

Moses Dalman sat in the private office of S. Levy, facing the young squire, after he had duly presented to him "*Vittorio,*" *his own guide!* "This man speaks English very well, and he thoroughly knows the country," said Dalman, after Arizona Jack had acknowledged Cyril Leigh's careless nod with a jerk of his head, as he stood rolling a cigarette. "He will bring me back any message you may wish to send. *You can trust him to the death*," remarked Dalman.

"Here is a full letter to the superintendent of the 'Condor mine,' who will entertain you. There will be an agent there from Tucson to meet you, and the papers and documents we signed will be in their hands. They have a letter of credentials from me to you. From the mine you can go down to Tucson with the officers. This is the easiest way to reach the Condor, as the other side of the range is very rough. I may come back from Denver to El Paso to visit my cattle-ranch, to which Vittorio returns. I would be glad to see you later in Chicago," said the counterfeit Arthur Lemon.

"Thanks for your kindness," stiffly said the young squire. "But, I'll hasten back directly to New York the very moment I have finished this business."

"And then there's nothing more I can do for you. Remember, *Vittorio is to look out specially for you*," said Dalman. "These other people I don't know, but Willetts is an old frontiersman, and he knows every inch of the road."

Dalman bit his lip as the Squire promptly rose and

climbed into the "ambulance" on Willetts' hailing signal. The Englishman had never even offered his hand in adieu! The driver gathered up his reins, and in a cloud of whirling dust, the light wagon rolled away down toward the vast silent valley sweeping off, in a double swell, for a sheer fifty miles to the bald, basalt crags, beyond which the blue crests of the Tombstone Range rose.

Arizona Jack had lingered, a graceful figure, lightly poised on his sinewy red roan charger. Under his knee, his Winchester rifle-sheath peeped out ominously, and the two Colts frontier pistols hung from the broad belt, where gleaning cartridges encircled the rider's waist. Knife, poncho, canteen, and picket-pin, with the lariat coiled on the saddle-horn, proved the disguised outlaw ready for the road. Under his broad sombrero, the dark-brown eyes gleamed with a curious fire. The Mexican costume and coffee-colored Yaqui stain had proved so far impregnable. He leaned down over his saddle-bow for a last hand-shake. "*Pepita is over there;* my friends are already near Huachuca. I've also got word to some old cronies at Bisbee and Tombstone. *Out on the desert, yonder,* I'm good for any half-dozen of these fellows; and, now, *that man is mine, dead or alive !* He's got the papers that will never see Tucson! *Leave it to me,* and, *remember, dead or alive, the Condor is mine !*"

With a light touch of the spur, the splendid steed bounded lightly away, and Dalman stood there spellbound, watching the two wagons now trotting along a half mile away on the downward slope, the straggling riders closing in around the unconscious dupe of Morris Blum. After them, the sunlight glittering upon his braided sombrero, rode the undaunted outlaw, who had taken his life in his hand, to rob the spoilers of his lost mine.

"*I'll be glad to be once more over the Texas line,*" mused Dalman, "*before the lightning strikes,*" and he wandered back to join José and purchase the tickets for the return.

As the sun went slowly down, and the black shadows crept down into the great arid zone below, sweeping far to the east and west, and silver stars twinkled out upon the Mexican mountains, walling in the south, Moses Dalman breathed a sigh of relief when he leaped aboard the eastbound train. José had stoically entered the second-class car forward and resigned himself to the never-absent cigarito.

"I am safe, at any rate, for a fortune out of this intrigue *sooner or later*," mused Dalman, "and the very moment these thieves down here despoil that Yorkshire lubber, I will put a pin into the fine cog-wheels of Messrs. Blum & Co. From the looks of that escort party, I think that I may perhaps fall heir to *the whole interest* of my brave friend Arizona Jack. If he does not work slyly they will surely find him out and kill him, and *then* make way later with young Leigh! *In which case* I am the king of the Condor. But I will not grace these sandy *mèsas* again. I can work my upheaval from New York, with Max to help me."

Arizona Jack, riding carefully on after the two wagons now trundling merrily along in the dusk, was suddenly brought face to face with a most unwelcome personage.

They had made five miles from Bowie when he observed a horseman ride out sneakingly from behind a chapparal grove, wherefrom he had evidently been observing the ambulance in which Robert Ross was now idly chatting with his conductor, the unlovely big Jim Willetts.

Retracing his path carelessly toward Bowie, after the outfit had been lost to sight, the strange horseman met Arizona Jack suddenly and awkwardly at a bend of the road sharply turning around a sand dune.

With a careless "*Buenas tardes, amigo,*" the rider passed on.

Jack's lightning hand was all ready to drop on his pistol butt, but the stranger only nodded his head and gruffly returned the salutation in Spanish.

"*My 'make-up' is pretty good,*" the outlaw growled, "*when even Bill Murfee does not know me when we meet face to face!* There is some sneaking treachery here. *This fellow is after no good.* He was supposed to be three hundred miles away, *at Prescott.* It is Bent's work probably, keeping his own tab on his scoundrelly partners."

And Arizona Jack's face clouded deeply when Lem White and the three Indians rode in at midnight and joined the circle around the campfire.

"More thugs and murderers," mused the embarrassed guide. "*My job is a tough one!*"

CHAPTER IX.

"WE WILL GO DOWN ALONE!"

ARIZONA JACK was keenly conscious of the dangers now besetting him and the almost inevitable failure of his cherished plan as he, with all an old frontiersman's craft, aided to make "Mr. Robert Ross" comfortable for the night. The long southwesterly slope of cactus covered sandy plain which they had traversed was dotted with the whitening skeletons of horses and cattle. The night wind fiercely drove the sharp alkali dust into their faces and the four hours' march was made in a sullen silence.

Big Jim Willetts, a central figure of authority, "bossed" the erection of the light wall tent, the location of the camp fire, the setting up of a fly to cover the mess chest and improvised table, and sent his animals out to a mournful cropping at the scanty salty grass by the spring, under the guard of Lem White and his Indians. Far away below them, the moonlight shone on the desert "swale," whose clinging vapors had tantalized them in the rays of the setting sun with the mocking mirage of lakes as blue as Como, studded with unsubstantial fog islands of fantastic shapes. The night winds whistled in the mesquit groves and drove the lodged sand from the sage brush and cactus into their faces ; and a few straggling willows alone marked the little spring.

Seated on a camp-stool, Robert Ross gazed around the dreary scene, turning his eyes to the far-off buttressed crags of the Dragoon Mountains, barring their way to the Condor Mine. A tin cup of "preliminary coffee" in his hand, he accepted the silent services of "Arizona Jack," who arranged his convoy's camp bed with a plainsman's sagacious prevision.

"Anything is better than the squalid shabbiness of Deming and Bowie," mused Cyril Leigh. "This is, at least, the storehouse of Nature's elements. A desert as lonely as if no man had been here since the making of the world, but it is unpolluted by frontier loafers. Its dreamy death in life has a fascination all its own!"

He was now on his guard and alert in all his faculties. The young Squire was filled with a secret distrust of all his human surroundings, and his callous good-bye to "Arthur Lemon" had left him tranquil, preferring to be alone among the rude strangers.

"*These are only rough fellows*," mused the frank-hearted boy, "while he, is a dangerous, smooth scoundrel. But if I see any peg to properly hang a refusal on, *they'll not hoodwink me!*"

He was disgusted with the vanishing glimpses of American prosperity.

The whirling dash through New York's Babel to the hills of the middle States, the glimpses of the piney mountains of the south, the dismal lean gulf plantations, the bleak lonely Texan waste, the burning arid zone, the sandy New Mexican *mèsas*, and this last sinking into the desert of death, impressed him with a dull aversion.

"And so, all I will see of far-famed America ends in a hole in the ground up in those mountains," he gloomily concluded, as he handed "Vittorio" his tin cup. "Not a single prospect pleases and every man is vile," he paraphrased.

He had observed the mental inertia of big Jim Willetts, whose sottish life was only punctuated with pay days, fandangoes, gambling bouts, and "whisky jamborees." "Big Jim," whose sandy beard flowed over his brawny blue-shirted breast, felt that he "had done the polite thing" when he lazily pointed out the bearings of Bisbee, Tombstone, Camp Huachuca, and the lonely Condor Mine, and then roughly sketched the itinerary of the three-days' trip.

"We will camp just outside of Bisbee, and then, make a long march the third day, and so, get to the Condor at night."

Cyril Leigh caught at the idea of an extra communication with the dear, dark-eyed Lady of Leigh.

"That's a bit of a town. I can surely send some telegrams on from there!" demanded the tourist.

"*Certainly*," gruffly replied Jim Willetts. "I'll halt a half hour *for you*, but I'll take my men out of town, and leave but one man behind with you. My fellows would just go on a 'rip-tearing spree there if I didn't 'round 'em up' and get them out of the town limits."

The deftness and quiet dignity of "Vittorio" impressed "Robert Ross," as the pseudo-Mexican wandered around the lonely camp after his self-elected master. His slightly accented English was a grateful sound, compared with the hoarse profanity of the rough crowd of frontiersmen.

"I'd give you a man of mine, Mr. Ross, to wait on you," bluntly said Jim Willetts, "but *that big greaser there* has nothing to do but to wait on you. *Make him useful!*" And so, Arizona Jack fell into the monopoly of all personal attendance upon the English visitor. With an amused interest Cyril Leigh watched 'Vittorio" perform the evening toilet of his big red-roan charger, and then, arrange his own simple couch on the lee side of the stranger's tent. The saddle and saddle-blanket, the "poncho," *voila tout!* a lodging at discretion, under the white prairie stars, coldly shining down, while the coyotes bayed the pale moon in shrill defiance.

When Arizona Jack returned, after a stroll around the camp, he was easier in his mind. "Not a single face that I know, except 'Big Jim,' and whisky and 'monte' have long ago rubbed me out of his mind! There seems to be the parts of two different parties here. Can it be that Bill Murfee is playing a double game? He is by this time probably out of Bowie! I suppose that his duty was only to dog this poor boy into the hands of the others. He undoubtedly telegraphs his sly backers all the moves! Probably he has some one spy here in the gang! *But, who is it?*

Those scoundrels will only be left to fight each other *later!* The Blums, and Stone, and old Bent! This fellow with the three Indians may, perhaps, be Bill Murfee's chum!" And Arizona Jack so rightly decided next day, when he overheard the fact that Lem White was an assistant foreman of the Condor. Big Jim Willetts, the leading transportation master for Blum Bros., was, of course, the man in official charge of the "whole outfit." The big bully was always ready to enforce his orders with fist, knife, or pistol, and Cyril Leigh had been sickened at heart already with his frequent fiery potations, his proffers of Blum's best "red eye," and his over-accentuated bestiality! It was "an inspiration" that caused Leigh to walk up to Jim Willetts, standing grandly before the fire, and say, quietly, "*I'd like to have a horse to-morrow. I am fond of riding.*"

"*Why, certainly!*" growled big Jim. "Lem White can give you his, and he can ride in here with me. Your Mexican chap can pilot you, and pick you out if you get drowned in those big lakes that you asked me about to-day."

Leigh put up with the coarse joke, and simply said: "*All right.*"

And so, after a good night's rest, in the morning the young Squire cantered gaily on ahead of the lumbering wagons, with Arizona Jack at his side. The slinking coyotes fled away before them; the nimble hares scuttled out of their path, and many a bit of prairie lore did Cyril Leigh extract from his watchful guide. The mysteries of the "horned toad," the Gila monster, the clammy, green scorpion, and loathsome black tarantula, the bloated rattler, and the deadly "side-wiper," were all explained in Vittorio's broken English. Nature's delightful desert offerings!

"*Singular fellow!*" mused Arizona Jack. "*Unarmed, frank, and unsuspicious,* and *Englishman like,* that dispatch satchel slung under his Kharkee tunic probably carries all the papers, his letter of credit, and *God knows what beside!* It would be a blessing to run him off, over there to Nogales, *and so, save him.*"

Mindful of the stake that he played for, Arizona

Jack now eyed every human being in the party with a keen suspicion. And his seemingly listless hands were always ready to drop on the pistol butt at a moment's notice.

"I think that I'll stay pretty close to big Jim Willetts. In any 'little trouble,' he will be the *'first to cross over,'* and then, the rest I could handle pretty easily, only *those damned renegade Apaches!* What their 'allotted task' is seems to be as yet *'in the gloaming' of doubt.* But, I'll be sure to have that satchel yet! There are two courses: one *to steal it* before he gets to the Condor, and *the other* to take it by force afterward. This fellow will never give up his signature till he gets the money at Tucson. And *with Pepita in reach* on the other side, I'll just let them wake up some morning and find the satchel gone, and then—*good-bye to 'Vittorio!'* I can reappear at Magdalena as 'Arizona Jack.' It's the surest, the safest, the *only* plan. I should have had my gang over here. They fooled me!"

Careful to make no reference to the Condor mine, Blum Brothers, or the object of the quest, Vittorio easily accounted for his marvelous knowledge of the frontier.

"Used to drive horses here—caballos—from Sonora, Señor," he said, "*long time ago.*"

The safe ground of Apache stories was reached, and it afforded a theme for the long days' conversations, as Cyril Leigh watched the three shock-headed, stunted redmen silently trotting along, cutting off all detours of the road, and so easily keeping up with the wagons dragging along in the heated gray desert sands.

"Big Jim Willetts" improved the two hours' noon-day halt to establish a lien on Lem White's next month's pay at poker, and to increase the "spiritual influences" guiding him by plying the whisky bottle marked "*Cutter, private stock,*" which was Blum Brother's especial pride.

Robert Ross, British tourist, found both Lem White and Willetts singularly devoid of information about the Condor Mine.

"*What the hell's the use to talk about it?*" sagely ob-

served Willetts.   "You'll see *the thing for yourself, in
a couple of days!   And it ain't much to see!*"

Lem White's guffaw supported the teamster's statement.   "*All Tombstone is played out,*" he curtly observed.   "Mines shut down, men laid off—going to
hell as fast as it can!"

"*Why?*" flatly demanded Robert Ross.   "Only a few
little pockets of rich ore—*that's all!*   In the big excitement of ten years ago, they plastered the whole
mountain sides with worthless locations.   Some was
sold in Frisco and New York, or over *on the other side*,
but the only money now here is what's been put into
these damned holes!   You can buy a hatful of Tombstone mining stock for a drink now!   It's a mighty
good place to get away from."

Mr. Robert Ross, British tourist, having duly refreshed his inner man, stuffed his short pipe and
wandered away to sit down on a bleached skull, the remains of a gaunt Texas steer, and to think this charming prospect over.   The young Squire was no business
man, but the eagerness of the two frowsy rascals to
persuade him of the worthlessness of the Condor
Mining Company's neighbor locations was too evidently
suggested.

"*Arcades ambo,*" he murmured, stealing a glance at
the taciturn Vittorio, seated a few rods apart calmly
discussing his bacon and beans, and after a pint of
coffee, lighting the "corn shuck" papelito.   He is a
gentleman compared with these same *American Sover-
eigns,*" wrathfully said the Briton.   His dogged nature
arose in a mute resistance to the schemes of the would-
be purchasers.   "It's a far cry to Lochaber!" he
mused.   "When these chaps nosed us out in Yorkshire and sent their glib agent, Lemon, over there to
buy this worthless half-interest for fifty-five hundred
pound, the thing is surely worth enough for me to keep,
or else to get *more for it.   I'll get nearer to the truth*
than the mouth of a hold filled with water.   Suppose
that I buy it *myself* from Beth, I may tie these fellows up in a little sly game."   And then determining
to wire his whereabouts from Bisbee, and to negotiate
at Tucson only, he lapsed into a cheerful insouciance.

"They've probably been put on to pump me a bit, and *load me up with these stories.*"

Cyril Leigh was no genius, but, Briton-like, he determined to stay till the last gun was fired. And so he cheerfully betook himself to studying plain craft under Vittorio's skillful guidance, the triumph of the afternoon being the neat dropping of an antelope at four. hundred yards with Vittorio's borrowed Winchester rifle. This first head of game, and the nucleus of a collection of horned toads, rattlesnakes' rattles, and other curiosities put the young Squire in good humor. He had arrived at a mental conculsion to absolutely ignore the subject of the Condor Mine, and the evening found him deeply interesting the Apache Indians by his questioning of them all under the tutelage of Vittorio.

"*Lem !*" said "Big Jim" Willetts, as they took their last good-night nip, "that young chap is either a simple child, or else *a damn sight smarter than we take him for !* He's a blamed good rider! Your broncho couldn't buck him off, and he dropped that antelope as neat as Buffalo Bill would 'a done! *A man that can ride and shoot is not all a damn fool*, not, *by a long shot !* The only thing is *he don't drink no whisky !*"

This last severe censure was sagely explained by Lem White, who cut off a chew of plug tobacco and expounded his experience.

"Them English fellers are raised in satin-lined baby carriages, *an' all that*, but *get 'em out here*, an' *turned loose*, and they're holy terrors! I oncet knowd an English fellow at Virginia City in the flush days. He split his hair in the middle like a gurl, an', *damme*, if he didn't git to be '*an out-and-out killer !*' He even stood off ole Sam Brown, and he soon could wax a monte-card, pinch a faro deck, empty a bottle, or yank a gun with any son-of-a-thief on the whole Comstock."

"Now, *there was Arizona Jack*," the speaker continued, as Vittorio within hearing calmly busied himself with making Robert Ross's praire bed. "Jack was as game as Wild Bill. He wuz English, *I always allowed.*"

"Right you are," said Big Jim. "Pore fellow! The

damned greasers butchered him, *down to El Paso.*   I know'd a fellow that was there and see it.   *Jack was always dead game!*"

As Vittorio moved calmly away, Lem White said, lazily, "That there greaser has something of Jack's walk and quiet way."

" *Yas,*" answered Big Jim. "He's one of them Chihuahua fellows, an' some on 'em are nearly white, and *mighty tough customers to tackle.*   I killed one of 'em down to Fort Yuma one time, an *it was just touch and go!*"

With a last pull at the bottle, the two wiseacres lay down within five yards of the dauntless refugee whose finger had been ready to drop on the trigger of his pistol as they "spoke lighly of the spirit that's gone."

" *A close call,*" murmured Arizona Jack, rolling himself up in his poncho, and gazing at the elegant figure of the young Squire seated by the red campfire with the three Apache Indians amused at his inspection of their debonnair aboriginal cookery of some cast-off beef bones.   Fox and wolf slept peaceably side by side in that desert camp, while the frank-faced English lad puffed his "bit of baccy," and thought of the dear woman far away in the green valley of Nidderdale!

"*It takes all kinds of people to make up a world,*" laughed Cyril Leigh, as he generously emptied his tobacco pouch among the stolid Indians, and calmly lay down to rest without a fear though surrounded by plotting thieves and would-be murderers.

" Lem," said Big Jim Willetts the next evening as Red Rock Peak rose frowing over them to the south, "Thar's bigger fools in *Cochise County, A-ri-zo-na, at Bisbee,* than this here young English dude."   Willetts accentuated his remarks with a "giraffe" drink. They were now nearing Bisbee, and, Mr. Robert Ross was proving an out-and-out good plainsman.   "Vittorio" had given him sundry practical lessons in frontier riding, with the loose knee and the swinging leg, and, at the noon halts, the Squire had practiced with rifle, revolver and, even the Indian bow and arrow. He vastly amused himself with the Apache's tricks of knife-throwing and shooting at dimes at twenty paces.   There was a quiet dignity in the "close mouthed" Englishman which caused Lem White to say: "Oh! He's only a damned human clam—*dead stuck on himself*, and he has a growing case of the 'big head!' *Let him alone.*" "*It's just as well*," growled Willetts, "I've pumped him on his home, his family, his business backers, and he just don't hear, and turns off to the Injins and to that damned 'greaser,' who is teaching him cowboy tricks.'

It was true that Robert Ross was mute as to the Condor Mine. He was eager to hear all the stories of "Bigfoot" Cochise, the Apache chieftain, the terror of the olden days of the "Regency," when King Death reigned with a bloody scepter, from the fastnesses of the fierce Hualipais and the White Mountain fortresses of the Apaches to the dark defiles of the Comorabi Range, the Santa Atoscos gorges, the Santa Rita, and that grim charnel-house, "the Picacho."

From Peloncillo to Pinalero, from Santa Catalina to Tortilla hills, every defile was an olden death-trap, and cruel Cochise, from his natural bastion of the Whetstone Mountains, the Canille, and the Huachuca, fell upon all the straggling emigrant trains, unarmed freighters, and weak escort parties, paving his road with skulls and dressing his rude warriors in fringed scalps. A reign of blood and terror!

Vittorio, riding with the Squire, was a living itinerary. He led the party dexterously on over the Fort Bowie Military Reservations, down past Alkali Flat, Sulphur Spring, Cochise Spring, and under the shadows of Mule Pass Mountains, to where Bisbee's smoke arose in the distance.

The Englishman had conceived a quiet liking for the silent Mexican, who, like himself, ignored the ruffianly crew, and rode well apart from the card playing, the drinking, and foul jests of the two men, now the sole occupants of the ambulance.

"How far is it to the Condor mine from Bisbee," said Robert Ross to his guide.

"A good long day's march, señor," said the guide. "We first cross the railroad pass, then strike down across the valley to the Huachuca Mountains, and the mine is on the west side, about twenty-five miles from Elgin. From there, you can take the railroad to Tucson, or even from Bisbee, which is at the end of the track in the mountains."

Cyril Leigh wheeled and faced the impassive relator. "And *so*, I could have come within twenty-five miles of the mine *by rail?*" he said, mystified.

"*Yes, señor!* By either Benson and Fairbank to Elgin, or up here to Bisbee. *Certainly!*"

Mr. Robert Ross was quietly thoughtful as they approached the straggling mining settlement of Bisbee.

"Where do you leave me?" he asked of Vittorio. "*I want you to go on to Tucson with me.*"

"*Excuse me, señor!*" said Vittorio. "I will see you through the whole thing—as far as Benson, and then go back to my master at El Paso. From there, you are on the main Southern Pacific to Tucson."

In vain the guide tried to ward off the Englishman's entreaties.

"*I will pay you well, and go on back East with you,*" urged Robert Ross.

"*He will have it so!*" darkly glowered the disguised outlaw. "*It is fate! Dare I go on into the trap at Tucson? There is Pepita—first and last!*" And, so after much cogitation and many cigarettes, he said: "I will telegraph on to El Paso from Benson or Elgin. If Señor Lemon says '*Si!*' then *I go to Tucson*; if *not*—if he is in a hurry—*I leave you there*, but *I would like to stay.*"

Big Jim Willetts was true to his word as they neared the "jumping off place" at Bisbee. He stopped the ambulance near the straggling town, and lazily called out, "Mr. Ross, if you have anything to do here at Bisbee, you can either stop now, or else ride back, after we go into camp. I'm going to camp over at Soda Springs, two miles out. For we'll have to start at four o'clock to-morrow morning to reach the Condor by night, and it'll be late enough, even then."

"*All right!* I'll stop as we go through, if Vittorio knows your camp," replied Squire Leigh, reining up Lem White's "bronco."

"*I want the whole party to get out of town first, Vit-*

torio," said "Mr. Robert Ross," with a quiet air of decision. "You can ride on and find out where the telegraph and postoffice is, for me. *Let no one of our party see you! Remember!*"

The Master of Leigh Hurst looked on in quiet amusement from a distance, when Lem White descended "for supplies," at the "Blue Wing Saloon," and was soon followed by Big Jim Willetts. Vittorio was calmly ambling his big roan through the few streets of the sparsely inhabited mountain mining resort, in search of the blue sign, "*Wells, Fargo & Co.*," "*Postoffice*," "*Western Union Telegraph*," telling of the "end of civilization," in these uplands of Cochise County.

While Lem White, returning, adjusted a box filled with a dozen whisky bottles on the "boot" of the ambulance, lashing the "precious goods," with much superfluity of cords, "Big Jim" wandered to the end of the saloon porch with two wanderers who had closed up on him, and the three began an eager discussion. Cyril Leigh moved his horse a few rods away as the sound of oaths and obscenity rent the peaceful evening air. Suddenly, "Big Jim" smote the smaller of the twain a fearful blow with his huge red fist, and was in another moment wrestling wildly with the other combatant, who suddenly bent and pitched his opponent clear over his head with a dexterous twist.

"*That was a proper Cornish hoist!*" cried Cyril, approvingly, while Lem White and a couple of loungers separated the scufflers, and "Big Jim" was at last pulled, cursing and raving, to his "ambulance."

"*Take him along, Lem,*" called out the saloonkeeper, who had quickly appeared at the door, pistol in hand, "*you fellows can do your own killing over at the Condor. Now, get a move on!*" and in a few moments, the ambulance followed the crawling baggage-wagon, which had already passed the imperial limits of Bisbee.

Cyril Leigh anxiously eyed the victorious pair of miners as Vittorio came cantering out of a side street. The two fighting friends followed on and noted the stopping of "Mr. Robert Ross" and his escort at the telegraph office.

"*Thank heaven!   That's a relief!*" murmured Cyril Leigh, as he saw his letters deposited in the mail-bag, and cheerfully paid his bill for a cablegram addressed to the Pately Bridge address, which his careful sister had laid down.

"*Poor darling! She will be anxious!*   But in a few days I will be at Tucson.   She will know all, and I will be off on my homeward way."

He was studying the "broncho," with a view to mounting him with the least possible exhibition of deviltry, and had whispered to Vittorio: "*Not a word as to where we went!*" when the victorious wrestler approached him.

"*Cornish to the heels!*" thought the young Briton.

"*Be you the London man that's come away here to see the Condor Mine?*" the stranger said, anxiously.

"*Yes, I am!   What can I do for you?*" kindly answered the young Squire.

"*Ride around the corner into the dark alley,* and then *me and my mate will tell you!*" earnestly answered the man who had laid out "Big Jim."

The evening shades were drawing down, and the "saloons" began to glitter with the fitful kerosene, as Cyril Leigh handed the reins of the "broncho," to the mute Vittorio.   "*Wait here for a moment,*" he said, with his pulses tingling with a strange excitement.   In the side street he eyed the two men as they crouched back out of sight.

"I'm Tom Faison," began the wrestler, "a Cornish pick drifter, laid off from the Condor mine two months ago.   My mate, Barney Farley, 'Red-head Barney,' ran the diamond drill up there for that son-of-a-gun Bill Murfee, this fellow Willetts's boss.   I want to get a stake so as to get back to the old country. *Damn Arizona and everybody in it!*   I can make fair wage as a Liverpool longshoreman, and live among my own kind.   Barney Farley, too, wants to get away to Pennsylvania.   The 'gang' from over there will surely kill him now if he hangs around here."

"What for?" queried the astounded squire.

"*It'll cost you just five hundred apiece to know,* and *make or save you many a dollar.*   Ye're a young gentleman, I can see it, *the old stock*, and *you've run up against a low bad gang.* Are ye on the buy or the sell ?"

Cyril Leigh gazed at the blue eyed Cornish giant and decided to trust him "on the general chances." "*On the sell, is the idea,*" he said, "but, *where do I come into your plans ?*"

"Barney darsent talk, *for his life*, till he knows he can clear out on to-night's train, and I go with him, on guard. They docked our wages, kicked us out, and we're too poor to even buy a pistol between us. *We can prove what you need to know!* Can ye come back here alone *to-night?* You get the money for us and *you'll make a fortune. I swear it by my dead mother's grave.* But then, we've got to skin out at once if we give these scoundrels away."

"I can ride in at eight o'clock. What were you fighting for?" said Leigh.

"We only asked a few dollars to get to Benson, from there *we could steal our way over to El Paso* anyway. *You see Big Jim's bloody mark on Barney's face?* If 'Redhead' had got to his knife, *there'd been a killing*, and a *lynching, to-night*," gloomily added the big Cornishman.

"I've got it, half in American money, half in Bank of England notes," said Cyril Leigh. "I tell you what I'll do now. Here's fifty dollars apiece. You can easily get to El Paso with that. Tell me fifty dollars' worth each, and *the rest you'll have to-night.*"

The Cornishman gasped out: "*They're humbugging you as to the value of the mine. Don't sell out to them.* They've waited ten long years to fool you. *Now, I'll prove it to-night. Will you come?* For God's sake, take chance luck and *once trust to a stranger. Not a word to a living soul.*" In five minutes, Leigh and his guardian were cantering away to Soda Springs. It was after the camp supper, supplemented by dainties from Bisbee, that the young Englishman announced his desire to look over Bisbee by lamplight.

"*Don't be late*," growled Big Jim. "There's a hard march to-morrow before us," he said. "*To-morrow is a very hard pull.* And you better have your man with you and handy with his shooting irons, for *Bisbee's a hell-raking place at night.*"

Cyril Leigh cast his glances back at Big Jim and Lem White drinking by the campfire, the red light flashing out on the white tent, with its background of the Soda Spring willows and the closely parked wagons. Not a follower was allowed to straggle, and the wearied animals were all rejoicing in double rations.

"*It may be foolish*," mused Cyril Leigh as Lem White's broncho sprang lightly over the flinty road. "But I'll have a shy at it, just for luck! A countryman would not betray me here, a stranger, in a strange land. *If he does*, why, I can just enter 'Experience, £200 to Profit and Loss.' Perhaps it will be a good investment."

"Mr. Robert Ross" rode directly to the postoffice, and then bade his squire of horse await him there.

"*I will only take a little look*," he said. "I've never seen one of these mining places at night." And then he slipped around the corner, leaving "Arizona Jack" burdened with the two horses.

"I suppose the youngster will have a peep at the dance houses and saloons," mused Jack. "*I ought to have given him a pistol.*" And then, he blushed in conscious shame at his own future design to rob the youth who so frankly trusted him.

"*It must be*," growled the outlaw lurking on guard in the darkness at the corner of the general store. "*Any one recognizing my face—then, it would be boxes for two—I risk my life to get this title to the mine. And if the others have swindled me, he must yield it up !*" He was ashamed of his own cowardly part.

Not a hundred yards away, Cyril Leigh faced Faison and Barney Farley.

"*Be brief*," he said. "*We must march at four o'clock. Now tell me all, and, if you convince me, I've the money with me.*"

The young man's simple manner touched the big Cornishman.

"We have each bought a good second-hand revolver down here of a Jew, and we make the break for El Paso to-night. With a little more, Barney can get to Pennsylvania, and there fall into a good job at oil or coal drilling, and as for myself, I can ship at New Orleans on a cotton boat and easily make Liverpool."

"*I'll see that you get home anyway, never fear!* Now, *out with it!*" said Cyril Leigh.

"Tell him, Barney," said Faison, "*we'll trust an Englishman's honor for the money.*"

"Redhead" Barney Farley said: "Then, *here goes!* These two mines, Live Oak and Magnolia, lie side by side, only six hundred feet apart, and overlapping each other a quarter of a mile. There's a deep shaft sunk down on each, but both are full of water now and all the men are knocked off.

"Between the two mines lies a bonanza of rich rusty red rotten quartz seamed with gold. *There's a million dollars in sight there* and more to follow. They have drifted in to *the right* from the *one* mine, and *to the left* from *the other*, and have sent the diamond drills in ahead from the end of the drifts in both mines, on the one, two, three, and four hundred foot levels. One drift from each mine is drifted clear across, so as to meet, and I bored test holes ahead at Bill Murfee's orders at every vital spot.

"There's an ore body there six to eight hundred feet long, four hundred feet deep, and three to seven hundred feet wide. *They are very sly!* The dumps outside show only *bastard white glance quartz*, and all the pay ore has been stacked up in the galleries. We struck a vein of underground water sometime ago, and at first bulkheaded it."

Cyril Leigh listened with a beating heart as the miner resumed.

"After Morris Blum and Bill Murfee had carefully sketched and measured all the drift and ore bodies, Bill (who's the very best miner in all Arizona), stood by my side with a revolver and took away the borings as I did the exploring drilling—and kept me under his own eye for three long weeks. This same son-of-a-gun, Lem White, slept with me on watch and I was regularly searched daily. But, when they were all off their guard a moment, I hid some of the borings. I've got them *here* in Bisbee, for I got a teamster to bring me over four coal oil cans full of them—he's an old chum of mine."

"*To make a long story short*," said Barney, "when they had explored this whole thing, then the bulkhead was busted and the mines were filled up with water; *both of them!* The two claims is shut down '*waiting for a pump*,'" grinned Barney, "and the men they have kept on half pay are just loafing around, '*doing assessment work*' and making a show on the North and South Condor, where there's only blank quartz as white as milk. They are just waiting to fool you and buy a fortune *for a song*."

"*Can I believe this?*" said the astonished Yorkshireman. "What must I do?"

"Talk fair to them, but slip down to Tucson as soon as you can. Keep your own mouth shut as to what you mean to do. *You're perfectly safe, once you are down there*, at Tucson," said Tom Faison. "I heard Bill Murfee and Morris Blum talking when I was stealing a nap in a little side drift. They have waited and covered all up so as to get this English title all right, for all of them knowed that Hugh Dalton, '*English Hugh*,' that was killed at El Paso, really owned half the mine, and if you've got that half, *hold on to it, for God's sake!* Speak them fair! Get in, *at once*, with the decent people at Tucson. The Blums are cutthroats! I always believe that they had Hugh Dalton murdered over at El Paso. Then, *get a good, honest lawyer!* Demand the mine to be pumped out and *carefully examined*. Make them give you, in advance, a map of it, and then *open out on them*. Have the diamond drills run through again from the Live Oak to the Magnolia, and, by Heavens, *you'll find this bonanza there!* But *get some true, brave friends around you, first. Tell your lawyer all! And do not sell out to them, at any price! Now, if you believe us*, Barney and I will give you these borings, and you can leave them here with the teamster, who has a little house down here on the road. *We'll follow you on*, and *meet you secretly, down there! Morris Blum is the one dangerous fellow you've got to fight!* There's a great fortune in your hands! There's no cost now but just *to chamber out the ore!*"

In the darkness of the night, Cyril Leigh gazed into the men's eyes with a wildly beating heart. The whole secret of Arthur Lemon's sly visit to England was plain *at last*. "*Not a word to a living soul of all this!*" pleaded the two men, "*or you might never get alive to Tucson!*"

Squire Leigh's wits were about him. "I'll play the gentle stupid," he mused. "Take Vittorio, then, and steal away, politely, to Tucson, and, when safe at Tucson, I can find out some respectable people, and then boldly give them my ultimatum!" he decided. "*Not a word to a soul! That's my salvation! I've fallen among a den of thieves!*" He faced the anxious comrades. "*See here, men,*" he gravely said, "*I'll trust to you! We might be followed!* Give me your word of honor that you'll leave the four cases of borings with your friend, to my order. '*Robert Ross,' here's your money! Look it over now,* and *get out of here,* and *so, save your lives.* And all I ask is, *keep my secret! I know now all that I want to!*"

Barney Farley grasped the Englishman's hand. "*I'll send you Andy Faxon's receipt for the four cases of ore samples. Where shall I send it to?*"

"'*Robert Ross,' General Postoffice, Tucson,*" said Cyril Leigh. "I'll get it there, and he shall have a hundred dollars *for 'storage.'*"

"*Then,*" said the big Cornishman, "*what else can we do? Is there nothing else?*"

"*Yes,*" said Cyril Leigh, "When you get to New Orleans go to a notary and make oath to the fact of your two stories, and send the two depositions to the *British Consul* at *New Orleans,* 'to be called for by *Robert Ross,* of Pately Bridge, Yorkshire, England,' and here's a fifty-dollar bill for your layover. Send your address there also, each of you, when you get home, for I can see I'll probably have to come over here *again.*"

"You've saved two men's lives!" cried Tom Faison. "*And, you have made your own fortune,* God bless you," added Farley.

"Then we're *all* satisfied!" cordially said Leigh. "Get away now, at once, men; for I can see you're in danger! *It's high time that I am off for the camp!*"

Without another word to Vittorio, Cyril Leigh mounted the broncho, and rode swiftly out into the dark night. "*Beth! Darling Beth!*" he murmured. "If I'm a fool in this, I'm only a fool *for your own dear sake!* At any rate, I'm on my guard." And then he laid his head on the rough camp pillow and dreamed of the far-off one whose dark eyes followed him into the wild desert with the loving glances of a tenderness never to be met again.

"*I'll soon be at the bottom of the mystery!*" he murmured, as the distant coyotes sang him to sleep. Vittorio was left wondering at Cyril Leigh's strange nocturnal expedition, but he bided his coming time.

Cyril Leigh was dreaming of the green reaches of Niddesdale, when he was rudely aroused at four o'clock, and mechanically bolted his morning coffee.

"Don't you want to ride in the ambulance *to-day?*" demanded Big Jim. "*It's a long pull!*"

"Thanks," quietly said the Squire, "*I prefer the horse!*"

And it so fell out at five o'clock in the morning, that the Englishman could see Andy Faxon's honest face, when Willetts held up his train at the teamster's, just long enough to buy a few bags of grain. Cyril Leigh himself lingered long enough after the wagons to hear the honest teamster's whispered confidence.

"The boys got away all safe *last night!* I'll hold the stuff safe here for you! I've buried the four cans of borings under my stable floor here, first stall. Look out for all those people at the Condor, they're a bad lot. Get to a place of safety as soon as you can, and I'll express to you the positive proof of their rascality. Count on Andy Faxon to the death, but *don't you give me away. They would butcher me*, and I've got a little family here."

Cyril Leigh's hand-grasp at parting was his pledge of honor and he rode silently on, watching the morning light gilding the gashed sides of the lonely gray Arizona mountains. Vittorio was grave and preoccupied on the march, while at the ambulance "Lem White" and "Big Jim" laughed over their "cut-throat euchre." By ten o'clock, the little train had crossed the railroad track and was rattling smartly down toward the wide, sandy valley, where Fort Huachuca lay thirty miles to the north. Cyril Leigh's chance-met disclosure of the night before led him to realize when he crossed the railway all the covert duplicity of Arthur Lemon and his principals.

"Of course, they did all this just to prevent me meeting *any one who would undeceive me.* The long detour, the rushing through Bisbee, there'll of course be the companion swindler waiting for me at the mine."

And so, while the two loafers in the ambulance wondered at Robert Ross's moody air, the young man thanked God for the chance *rencontre* at Bisbee.

"*Do you know, Lem,*" said Big Jim, when they had reached the bottom of the sweltering sandy valley and the three hours' "dry camp" rest was being given to the animals, "*I think this young booby is plotting some mischief ?*"

"*Ah, Morris Blüm will do him up in good shape. It's none of our pie !*" roughly answered Lem, as he reached for the bottle.

The young squire, having stuffed his pipe, was standing on a sand dune overlooking the vast dreary waste of sage brush, straggling mesquit, with the spectral "nopales," and the fierce-fanged Spanish bayonet cactus and thorn, as final adornments. "*A land of gold and blood, a land of liars and thieves,*" mused Cyril Leigh. "There's no one I can trust. *Vittorio,* a nameless frontier Mexican rover, with perhaps a dozen notches on his revolver butt. *I must make it only a duel of wits.* Once at Tucson I am safe, for I will at once see the United States authorities, if there are any. There's an army post at Camp Lowell. I would *surely* be safe there." While they toiled five hours over the merciless gray desert sands, Cyril Leigh turned over the whole problem.

"*I'll keep this* Mexican man Vittorio. He surely is not in their game. *He, poor devil, has some other game of his own in life.* He will be at least a witness. *Once on the railroad,* I am out of the hands of these sharpers."

Vittorio's steady eyes were fixed on the southern spur of the Huachuca Mountains as they drew near at four o'clock. "*My God,*" he muttered, gazing at the brown leather strap of the Squire's dispatch satchel, "*Only two or three nights more!* If I can only get him *alone,* anywhere away from *them.* There, within three hours' gallop to-morrow is Pepita, the true-hearted child, in waiting, and Pablo already hidden at Mc-Laughlin's Peak. Once in touch with these two, I could make a neat turn at night, then *cut* and *run for it.* But *it must be after he leaves the Condor,* and, by Heavens, he may sign all these *like a fool.* Dare I warn him?" and the bold outlaw eyed the ruffians in advance. "*I must be sly.* Once recognized here and *I'm a dead man.* Pepita must first have the other five thousand. I'll take no chances *for her sake.*

"They would have killed this poor boy *before now,*" mused Arizona Jack, "*if they did not want his signature to that Bill of Sale.* If he gives it, then *his life is not worth a sixpence.* I might warn him to sign *only at Tucson.*"

And when they reached the Point of Rocks at seven o'clock, and the fierce red glaring sun had dropped behind the Canille range, the puzzled Hugh Dalton had fiercely determined to "*trust to luck.*" "There's always a way out of everything—*in time,*" mused Hugh, as his thoughts returned to Pepita, when they resumed the march due north over a firm red jaspery road.

The star of Love swung its lamp far up *above him* and gleamed out white in the clear blue heavens now braided with jeweled planets. Other days and other scenes returned to harass the desperate wanderer. "*He* goes back to life and love—to home—to all that makes England—England, and *I* must wander over the earth like an Ishmael!" With a groan, he murmured, "*Where is the promise of my youth, once written on my brow?*" as he rode on in lonely silence. It was eleven o'clock at night, when Vittorio at last turned to Cyril Leigh, and pointed to a half dozen lights twinkling on a spur of the western slopes of the Huachuca Range, a half mile away. and a few hundred feet above them.

"*Señor,*" he quietly said, "*there is the Condor Mine— your journey's end.*"

The young Squire stopped his horse. "*See here, my man!*" he said. "I want you to promise me to stay with me. I may have need of your help! *Let no one know of this.* I will pay you well! *You* must stay with me, take me down to *Elgin*, and go on later *as far as Benson*, with me. I'll also pay your fare and your horse's transportation. But, *not a word to these men!* I want you ready to leave when I am, and to keep away from me, while here, at the mine."

"*How long do you stay?*" said the seeming Mexican.

"*Two days*, and *then* I'll strike for Elgin *by day or night*. You must somewhere get me a horse. *You have your own*. I'll pay all—*liberally.*"

"I must go down to Miller's Station then to-morrow. It's half way to Elgin. I can get a horse there, and come up on the night after. I'll then picket out my horses, and come in to the mine at sundown, the second day. You can say that I've gone over to Nogales, *that's all*," answered Vittorio, his voice strangely agitated. "*I'll go with you*, Señor, and take you to Elgin, but remember *none of these fellows must know where we go to*. There's Calabasas—Sanford's—and Crittenden—all are stopping stations. *We can give them the slip*. Trust to me. *But, I must keep out of their sight.* I'll be here, and come to you at sundown on the second day."

"*It's a bargain, Vittorio!*" said young Leigh, reaching out his hand. The outlaw's hand was as cold as a stone, for in his heart, the thrill of a coming vengeance on Fortune had congealed his blood. "*Alone at last with me!* I will see Pepita and Pablo to-morrow, and then *the mine is my own!* For, he is afraid, and means now *to run away.*"

When they rode up to the rough porch of the Condor office-house, the Mexican guide whispered, "*You can depend on me in life and death, Señor!*" Cyril Leigh sternly said, "*Remember, now! Keep your faith! You shall have your reward!*" "*I mean to, I will!*" grimly soliloquized Arizona Jack, turning away to seek a night's camp with some Mexican teamsters who had sheltered in a hill-side hollow from the mountain breezes. For he was only a fellow of the baser sort and not worthy of the hospitality of the Condor Mine. He had nothing to be robbed of now!

Mr. Robert Ross, of England, was effusively welcomed at the door of the rough shed house by a boisterously polite man who pompously announced himself as "*Morris Blum, Managing Partner of the Condor Mine!*"

The young Squire threw himself into a chair and stretched his stiffened limbs. "Seventeen hours on the road is a fairish bit—even in your rough country. *I'm a little done up*," said Leigh, accepting the stiff "toddy" which Morris brewed as an earnest of welcome. The two "high contracting parties" now faced each other in a secret "sizing up," while Blum led the young man away to the Superintendent's room. A table set for two was in readiness, a sleek Chinese cook already watching his master's signal. Cyril Leigh heaved a grateful sigh for the relegation of "White" and "Willetts" to the men's boarding-house. The Master of Leigh Hurst smiled at his strangely decorated sleeping-room which was quaintly papered with alluring cuts from the "weekly illustrated journals." "High kickers" on tip-toe, and décôlletée soubrettes, attested the absent Bill Murfee's devotion to the "fairest of the fair." The Squire's luggage being duly deposited, he silently seated himself at table, his eyes roving over the pretentious wall-maps of the Condor Mining Company's "properties," with a few skeleton working sketches of the explorations, a desk, an admirable assortment of guns and pistols, a well-stocked drinking beauffet, and a few rough chairs, with rawhide laced bottoms, made up the decorations. A dreary enough social outlook!

The memory of his strange advisers at Bisbee guided Mr. Robert Ross in keeping up a judicious reticence, while burly Morris Blum effusively "did the honors."

The British tourist noted Blum's blazing finger diamond, his dandified semi-frontier dress, ill according with that smug Semitic trading visage.

"*He has dropped nothing of the peddling Jew, but his civility*," mused Leigh, who had heard the praises of Morris Blum sounded for two hundred miles by those worthy satellites "Big Jim," and Lem White.

The Squire entrenched himself in his immobile British hauteur, while Blum "flowed on like a river,"

alternately tempting, leading, and teasing his tired
guest. The usual effort of jollying the stranger along
into a loose-tongued intoxication failed, and the baffled
managing partner at last left his guest to himself.

"*I'll be ready to go on with the business to-morrow,*"
remarked Robert Ross, "*and to see what you have to
show me. Will it take us long to go through the mines?*"

"I shall call you at eight, Mr. Ross," said Blum. "I
think we can finish all by to-morrow night, and then
I'll take you down to Tucson with me. I'll go and have a
talk with my men now."

Cyril Leigh cheerfully submitted to the ministrations
of the moon-eyed Soyer of the Condor, and with some
little private precautions as to barricading his bed-room
door and examining the window fastenings, locked up
his papers and lay down to a dreamless sleep.

No inhabitant of the Condor camp was astir earlier
the next morning than the tourist, when the impatient
neighing of hungry horses and mules announced the
coming dawn. Standing on the porch of the shed,
Cyril Leigh saw the morning mists roll away, and the
great blue cone of McLaughlin's Peak rise up between
his westward glances and the far-off range in the hazy
west, at whose northern foot lay Elgin. Far to the
north and south swept the rugged Huachuca Mountains, shutting off the eastern morning view, and a
few straggling pines feebly clung to the rocky knolls,
whence the sharp-voiced coyotes barked in the rosy
dawn. The dreary valley lay five hundred feet below, opening, fan-like, out toward the Mexican border-
line, beyond which the piled-up peaks of Sonora were
flushing rosy in the coming day. A few rough sheds
and huts were clustered around the office-house, a
couple of corrals inclosing the score of draught and
riding animals, and a blacksmith-shop seemed to be
the only evidence of the actual operations of the Condor Company.

Ah Sam, the cook, early astir, offered the Englishman a cup of coffee, which he drank, and then, lighting
a cigar, Cyril Leigh wandered out alone along the bleak,
rolling hill sides. As the light gleamed over the bald
knolls, the stranger could see, stretching in an irregu-

lar line, the gleaming white quartz heaps from a score of excavations.

"*There should be gold here in plenty to tempt anyone to this God-forsaken wilderness !*" he mused, as he braced himself for an hour's wandering along the lines of the irregular croppings.

Before he returned he had stood beside the shed-covered shafts of the Live Oak and Magnolia, where a portable engine and rude hoisting gearing showed the points of attack of the hidden bonanza. The considerable rock-dumps at the mouths of the two main shafts, separated from each other a thousand feet or more, proved by their great mass that they represented many hundreds of yards of shafts, galleries, and levels. The rough description of Tom Faison and Barney Farley was confirmed, for he could see the water rising to within twenty feet of one shaft's mouth and forty of the other, the flood being evidently on the same level. The silent desolation of the whole scene, the straggling camp, and the shiftless appearance of the workings, was an apparent confirmation of "Mr. Arthur Lemon's" statement of the valueless character of the two claims. Below, on a terraced shelf, a few hundred yards away, were the red surface heaps, indicating a half dozen projected new workings.

"*There's nothing to show anything of value here !*" energetically decided Leigh; "I must bring it out of this smug trader *by a quiet refusal to sell.* I can only get at the truth *from my enemy's lips !*" And, so, with one longing look at far-away Elgin, Cyril Leigh returned to begin his battle of wits.

He had been paraded all over the unpromising hillside before noon, and had listened for hours to the specious propositions of the now offensively familiar Morris Blum.

"*You see, Mr. Ross,*" said the glittering-eyed Hebrew merchant, after they had finished the noontide meal and had sat down on the porch to enjoy their cigars, "*There's really very little to see here !* All that we have to do is to talk things over and examine our respective papers and authorities. I have had a dispatch from Mr. Lemon, at El Paso, that he has explained matters thoroughly to you, and so I came down here prepared to sign the papers and make you the payment here under instructions of my partners. So, if you will kindly get out all your title papers and authorities, we can go over the whole matter. I wish to leave for Benson to-night. We can sign all the papers here, and I can have them witnessed. There's a notary at Fair-banks, and I will pay you the whole sum when you de-liver up the bill-of-sale of Chandos Brandon to St. John Gladwyn." Mr. Morris Blum paused. "I have brought all the money down in United States notes, so that you can see we are ready to fulfill our contract. I shall, of course, wish to have a certified copy made at Tucson or Benson of your power of attorney from the present owner to sell! I have a document, duly certi-fied by Arthur Lemon, designating me as the person to take the title. *And*, here it is! You might then go on East, from Benson, and save the trip to Tucson."

"*There is but one obstacle in the way*, Mr. Blum," quietly said the young Briton. "*The mine is full of water*, and you have not as yet shown to me *the interior workings!*"

Blum's glittering black eyes were fixed with a grow-ing interest upon the Squire.

"You don't mean to wait here till *all the water is pumped out of that mine?* Why, it will be next season before our machinery will be set up below or we drive a tunnel so as to drain these mines and then use the water below for our reduction works."

"*It's very awkward for me and perhaps for you*," gravely said Robert Ross, "but my *positive instruc-tions* do not permit me to sell the half interest in these two claims unless I personally verify the statements of your agent sent over to England."

"Why, *the thing's impossible!*" angrily cried Blum. "*I am not here to perform impossibilities!*"

"Neither am *I* to break my *principal's positive or-ders!*" firmly said the unconscious-looking young man, turning his calm blue eyes pleasantly upon the schemer.

"I am afraid, then, that *the whole thing must wait* either until you drain this mine or else open it by a drainage tunnel, so that an expert, agreed on by both of us, can examine and then report upon the truth of Mr. Lemon's statements."

Morris Blum sprung to his feet in a sudden rage.

"*Do you mean to jump your contract, sir?*" he cried, with rising wrath.

"*Not a bit of it!*" calmly said Cyril Leigh. "You will observe that your privilege to buy at the figure agreed upon lapses *now!* For *I am ready to examine the mine.* You *have nothing* whatever to show me."

"And *then* you will refuse the *money if I tender it?*" cried the exasperated intriguer.

"*I shall most certainly refuse it until I see the mine* or have it properly *examined.* And now I warn you that I shall not show you my papers or go into any further details."

Morris Blum glared at the calm-faced Briton.

"*This is dishonorable!*" he cried.

"*Now stop right there!*" firmly said the young man. "*Our side of this mine knows its legal rights* and you *had better consult your other partners.* There's no use to bully, *for it won't change my purpose.* I'll give you a day to think it over. *Otherwise, I will leave here to-morrow night!*"

"*And go home!*" roared Blum.

"*Go where I please,*" politely said Cyril Leigh, taking out his pipe and cutting up some tobacco. "I shall report the contract of purchase as forfeited to my principals."

"*And you get nothing for your dead-horse interest,* then?" said the baffled Israelite.

"*We will let it stand idle, as it is,*" smoothly re-marked Leigh. "When I leave here you lose your right to purchase! You should have had the mine ready for my inspection."

The afternoon sun was sinking when Morris Blum at last found out that he had met more than his match in this rosy-faced English boy. A horseman was soon galloping away to Elgin with an alarm dispatch ad-dressed, "*Isidor Blum, New York City.*"

At night, when the two men separated, Mr. Robert Ross had come out of his shell far enough to say, "If you will go over to Tucson with me, and agree to pump the mines out, *at your own expense*, and have them examined by an expert, whom I will name and pay, on his report agreeing with your own contract statement, I will then agree to sell the mine on the first-named terms. If the facts *are not as stated*, then you lose all your chance to buy, and must pay all the expenses. *You know that you dare not sell us out*, and *you have no right* to make any debts on our account. *The bill of sale guarantees that.* We own an *undivided half-interest*, remember. And you cannot incorporate or sell without our permission. *My lawyers are good ones!*"

"*I shall make you a new proposition in the morning, Mr. Ross*," gloomily said Blum. "I have sent an express rider down to Elgin with a telegram to my partners. I propose now *to end this game of cross purposes.*"

"I am willing *to do the right thing at the right time!*" politely remarked Cyril Leigh, as he declined a fiery "night cap" of the Old Private Stock brandy.

"Thank God, Vittorio will be back to-morrow night, and then, *I'll have a horse of my own*," was the sturdy young Squire's last thought when he kissed Beth Leigh's picture, and fearlessly slept among his foes.

But until very late that night, Morris Blum, Lem White, and "Big Jim" sat in a dark-lantern council. "I've telegraphed to Benson to Bill Murfee," grimly said Morris Blum. "He will stop off the north end of the valley, and your party the south. By God! He can't fly, and *I think we have him! He must never get away with those papers!*"

Mr. Morris Blum's face paled as he read Isidor's dispatch, when the pony-express rider galloped up, at eleven the next morning. Mr. Robert Ross was calmly smoking his cutty pipe, and adding to his stock of natural curiosities, when the now ferocious Morris Blum strode up to him: "*We'll end all haggling over this thing!* Your English party is in the thing, so I'm told, for twenty thousand pounds—*first and last!* If you'll give me now, a quit-claim deed—*a bill of sale*—and relinquish all the papers, I'll give you the five thousand pounds cash down, and accepted exchange or telegraphic transfers on New York, by Wells, Fargo & Co., *for the other fifteen thousand pounds!*"

The frontier merchant's face grew livid as Cyril Leigh politely said: "*On the same terms*, pump the mine, and *have it examined by two experts!* I'll pay half the pumping, as well as half the experts' fees—*if you are right!* If you are wrong we will keep one share of the mine."

"*You are a damned robber!*" cried Blum, striding up to his unruffled opponent.

"And you are *a great hulking bully!*" said Cyril Leigh, turning away to whisper to himself, "*The two starving miners were right!*"

As he gazed down the dusty road, Vittorio sauntered over from the corral, smoking his ceaseless papelito.

"*Damned if I wasn't right!*" growled Lem White, after Morris Blum had ordered his own ambulance. "*Thar's but one chance! That's to lose him on the way back!*"

But the three thugs were astounded when Robert Ross calmly said, as Morris Blum offered him a ride to the railroad: "*I will come down to Tucson in a few days. I want to look over the country a little!*"

And it was early candle light, and Morris Blum, was already ten miles away, when Cyril Leigh strolled over to the teamster's camp.

"Saddle up, Vittorio, *we will go down alone!*" quietly said the imperturbable Briton.

"*Your luggage, Señor?*" whispered the astonished guide.

"*They can send it after me,*" coolly said Leigh, "*I may be a month at Tucson.* Say not a word to any one that I am going away." And then, with a glance at the hang-dog faces of the loungers around the Condor, he said, sternly, "*I don't care to be followed!* Get me to the railroad at any point, just as you choose. *I trust to you alone!*"

"They'll not get you *away from me, Señor!*" grimly answered the guide. "See that bunch of willows there? *Be down there in half an hour!* Say nothing. But, *I've got friends waiting at Miller's Station*, and we will go across the *mèsa*."

It was the second surprise, for Morris Blum had left without a word of his intentions.

The astounded Chinese major-domo was speechless when he found the superintendent's house deserted that night at eleven o'clock. Mr. Robert Ross's room was, however, locked, and that gentleman was smartly galloping along over the jaspery bottoms a half-dozen miles away, before Ah Sam had at last peeped into the windows and discovered the bed to be empty.

Cyril Leigh's blood was up, and his fair hair was blown back by the wind as he rode lightly the big red roan of "Vittorio." It was a silen ride, for "Robert Ross" had now vowed to save the golden, unreaped harvest of the Condor for sweet Lisbeth Leigh, who now waited in vain for answers to her cablegrams. "*On! on!*" he pointed. "*Only get me to the railroad!*" And Arizona Jack waited, *now secure of his prey!* For they were out on the desert alone together at last!

Mr. Morris Blum's face was dark as he thought over Isidor's last brutal dispatch: "Go to limit of twenty thousand pounds; if refused then, *close out other party; details left to you.*" The managing partner was now well on his way to Fairbank.

"*Who the hell has given him a tip?*" growled Blum. "Has Murfee piped the game off to Bent and Stone? Are they behind this seeming fool?" He turned now fiercely to the "*details of his plan,*" with the two scoundrels at his side. "*Are the Indians on the trail?*" he huskily whispered. "*Yes, and our men, hiding near Miller's, waiting for you to send us back! It would never do* to have anything happen to him until you are well along on the railroad *toward Benson,*" said Big Jim.

"*Damn it! He's got no horse! How can he get away?*" queried Lem White. "With Bill Murfee's party and ours to watch him, *he is a trapped coon!*"

"Well! '*Make it a road-agent job*' or '*an Indian depredation,*' just *as you choose, boys,*" cried Morris Blum. "*I'll post Bill Murfee!* Only, remember, *every damned scrap of paper that he has, I want;* and it would be just as well to mutilate him! It will look more like *Apache work!*"

As the wretches drank to their success, Arizona Jack, riding at the side of the brave boy whom he was bent on betraying, mused: "*Why can I not take him over to Mexico*, at Nogales, and rob him there? *But, the mine is my own now!* He is in my power!"

And, all unconscious, Cyril Leigh rode on to his doom!

CHAPTER X.

TRUST TO PEPITA!

MORRIS BLUM'S eyes were eagerly strained to see the lights of the little railroad station at Elgin when Lem White grasped his arm.

"*There's some one following us. Hold up!*" And both "Big Jim" and "Lem," springing out, Winchester rifle in hand, with the wagon swung squarely across the road, stood on guard at either flank as a horseman dashed up at full speed.

Blum had grasped his ready revolver and prepared for defense, for the rich merchant was surely a golden prize for the bold "road-agents," who reigned from Nogales to Tucson.

"*My God! It's White Heron!*" cried Big Jim as the slim young Apache warrior dashed up to the side of the wagon.

His pony staggered and reeled, for the messenger of grave tidings had mercilessly urged the swiftest horse in camp, under only the weight of a bridle and girthed blanket. "White Heron" himself was clad only in breech-clout and moccasins, and the sole weight that he carried was the two revolvers and knife slung to his buckskin girdle. A quiver of arrows and short Apache bow completed his "*costume de rigueur.*"

"Here's hell to pay now," shouted "Big Jim," after a brief colloquy in Spanish.

"I always told you he was not such a soft fool after all! Ross sneaked out of the camp at dusk, and was quietly picked up in the bushes by that greaser fellow, Vittorio, who bought him a fresh horse, and now he's making off for Miller's Station."

Blum threw down his revolver with a curse.

"By Heavens! *That same greaser may be a spy of*

old Bent and the Senator. He will never show up at Tucson! I see it all now. They can get to the railroad at Crittenden, to the south of Elgin here, and then go on to Nogales, and so safely make Mexico! *Once over that line he is lost to us* forever. The booby now smells a rat. *Who in hell could have posted him?* Where are your damned Injuns, Lem, who were to watch him and head him off if he made any break?"

Blum was raving in his murderous rage.

"*Don't get riled, Morris,*" said Big Jim, taking a pull at his flask. "Lame Wolf and Standing Bear have followed along on the trail. One of them will wait at Miller's for my party, and the other will follow on and leave a good trail for us to pick up." While the three scoundrels hastily parleyed the Indian had got his breathless horse in shape and was walking him gently around.

"Let this fellow get over across country to 'Miller's' on the dead run as soon as he can, and tell the other Indian there to help him slyly run off all the horses in the corral. Ross and Vittorio may be resting overnight there. They will think we all went off deceived, and that they have quietly given us the slip."

"Lem, you can take the Indian's horse. You can get to Miller's in two hours, but, ride him lightly."

Morris paused in his orders as the Indian reported the horse getting over his exhaustion. The Indian was racing away out of sight on the keen run before Blum said to White: "*Make a mix up of it!* If they've started for the railroad, follow them and shoot them down for horse stealing. Of course all the horses must be run off first and this fellow will appear to have been killed *by mistake. Get all his papers!* And there's a cool thousand in twenty dollar pieces for each. We will be at Elgin in half an hour. I'll jump Big Jim and a good fellow back to you on a buckboard with fresh horses. So you'll have men enough for the job, and Bill Murfee too, will be down before six o'clock and he will make for Miller's. Leave one Indian there to bring the gang on. Just get old Miller drunk and tell him you're out after these same horse thieves—ladrones. His Mexican woman won't give anything away Now, be *off with you.*"

The ambulance then dashed off with its four horses on a dead run, while Lem White, with a careful glance at the stars, struck smartly out across the *mèsa*, for Miller's station.

"Morris," said Big Jim, as the light wagon dashed along under the impulse of the four galloping "bronchos." "There's a man down here at Elgin, 'Dynamite Dick,' who was a terror with the Doolin and Dalton gang. He's in close hiding, for he was run out of the Panhandle by the Pinkertons. He was with the James boys, Cole Younger, and all that outfit, and he helped to butcher those Chicago fools, the Pinkertons, who were sent down to unearth the Benders, and to capture Frank and Jesse James. He's my man. He's a bold-hearted wretch. He must go, too."

"*All right,*" cried the breathless financier. "Pay him well. I'll make it right. Give him the same fairy story about horse thieves. Take him back to the mine, and Bill Murfee will soon square it all up."

They dashed up along side the platform as the train swept up from Nogales and, in ten minutes, Morris Blum was rushing on to Fairbank.

"*Two hours more,*" he groaned in impatience, "but after I pass Fairbank I am clearly out of this job, and Jim and Lem will perhaps fix the thing *before Bill can get down. But, Murfee can cover it all up,* and the horse-stealing trick is a good one." And so, the coward rejoiced that his "*public reputation*" was safe!

Two smart horses sprang away from the little Mexican hovel at Elgin station, where Lem White had found his trusty tool, and the light buckboard swiftly sped along back over the level desert road toward Miller's station. Lem White had delayed but half an hour and Mr. Morris Blum's little army of scoundrels was converging upon Miller's station long before Blum had whispered his last orders to the excited Bill Murfee at Fairbank.

The two men met at the junction of the Bisbee and Nogales railroads with no outward sign of the nameless deed to be engineered and covered up under Bill Murfee's directions.

"*I've got three good fellows here with me,*" curtly said

Bill Murfee, "and the down train is coming along in half an hour. Your team will be fed and rested, and we can be at Miller's in four hours. You surely told your driver to be all ready when the train gets to Elgin?"

"Yes," said Blum, as they wandered away out of hearing of the few passengers hanging around the board platform with its rough ticket-office shed.

"*Can you depend on your men?*"

"*I should smile!*" roughly said Bill Murfee. "One of them was head devil of the Button gang, who killed Frank Chavez at Santa Fé; another, was for years with the Earp gang and the Stage Robbers here; and the last fellow was Ike Clanton's best man in the Rustlers. Now, these fellows know every single pot-hole in Pima and Cochise counties, and we will *mix it up* so that nobody will ever get on our trail. The only thing you've got to do is to put up the money, and *plenty of it!*"

Morris Blum turned fiercely. "Come up to Tucson *the moment all is over*, and *I'll fix you*. Lem and Big Jim are all right."

"You had better invest about a thousand dollars *now*, Morris, *in a little special tip*," said Bill Murfee, lazily. "You'll regret it *if you don't!*"

"*I've not got it with me*," retorted Blum.

"*Your check* is good! I can cash it in here. Hurry up! *The train's coming!*"

"All right," snapped out Blum. "Talk quick! I'll give you a check at the station. I've got my check-book with me!"

Bill Murfee leaned his burly form against a post; his bushy black beard and long hair gave him a ferocious appearance as he stood with one hand on his revolver butt.

"*Old Bent is playing to fool you and your brother!* He may even have bought your lawyer in New York; but he's evidently followed up this English chap and the man who brought him to Deming, and there was a gang from Bowie that followed your outfit all the way down to Bisbee. It's my opinion they've now got this Englishman into their hands, and, so, *run him off!* If they buy him safely out, you and Isidor will have to play second fiddle in the Condor mine. Now, Bent and Stone would follow me to the death if they knew I gave this away. You've got to take care of me—*you and your brother*—now. If this Englishman ever gets to the railroad, then, the only way is to run up against him somewheres, with a row and *have him* 'accidentally' killed in a mix-up! Then, *we can easily get all his papers!* After that, you don't care a damn for Bent!"

Murfee grinned at his own smartness.

"How did you find all this out ?" cried Morris Blum, turning pale with impotent rage.

"Fellows from Bowie told me, who saw the other fellows dogging after your outfit. But, the Injuns and Lem White kept so close a lookout, there was no chance for a dash on the camp. *Case of dog eat dog !* The fact is, old Bent has been watching you at Tucson and Isidor in New York. *Somebody's sold you out.* And, if that English chap ever lives to get out of the Territory, the title will surely turn up in the hands of these two cold-hearted skin-flints. *Damn all you rich men !* You're not square with each other, and, besides, nobody gets a dollar out of any of you unless the eagle squeals with pinching!"

"Come on, *come on !*" cried Morris Blum, in a panic. "I'll give you now your check. I've got to telegraph from Benson to Isidor. I must not be seen around here. Bent might get a hold on us."

"*That's just the way.* You rich fellows are all cowards, and *we* do the dirty work and *you* get all the pudding. Now, if *I* pull this off, *you've* got to take care of me for life !"

"*So I will, Bill, my boy !*" cried Morris, his teeth chattering. "There comes the train. Get all your fellows aboard. I'll soon bring you the check."

He rushed away, while Bill Murfee lounged up to the single passenger car. *I'll go on and milk both sides of this affair*," growled the burly mine superintendent. You only sent me away to hoodwink me, Mr. Morris," mused the ruffian. "And but for these three sneaky Injuns and that Mexican fellow, I'd 'a' run Mr. Robert Ross away *on my own account.* Who can that rascal greaser be ? He just stuck to the boy's side as if he was a leech."

Mr. Morris Blum, the redoubtable chief of the Golden Rule Bazaar, never knew that Bill Murfee himself had followed on and traced his skillfully-conducted party as far as Bisbee!

"*Pretty neatly done in Morris,*" laughed Bill Murfee, as he pocketed the check when the train drew out, and the excited "managing partner" made his own alibi sure.

"It was a very neat trick to keep *me* out of the way and to bring this boy, roundabout, into the Condor. He has evidently not been 'loaded up' with Tucson gossip, but whoever posted the boy *knew more than I do.* At any rate I'm in both parties' pay now, and *neither dares to squeal on me.* The English lad doesn't seem to be a little bit of a fool. If they've really frightened him *he may get away,* and *then——*" Mr. Bill Murfee applied himself to the bottle with the comforting conclusion that whoever got the mine at last, there was a fat slice of the "golden bonanza" waiting for Bill Murfee.

"And *I'll keep both sides carving at it,*" chuckled the blackmailer.

He knew alone that Senator Stone, in San Francisco, and William Bent, in New York, were now silently and secretly undermining the agglomerated Blums whose interesting family chain stretched from New York to Fort Worth.

"*What a damned lot of rascals,*" remarked Bill Murfee in the interests of morality, as he dreamed over the most effective manner of "rubbing out" the representative of the English half-interest. "Of course, when the thing gets blown abroad, *after the job,* should it fail, the lawyers will *eat up* most of the mine, for there's no fair and open way to defeat poor Hugh Dalton's interest. He's got a cinch on the title if he lives."

The essentially practical nature of Bill Murfee was shown in the laconic remark he made when the four men climbed into the waiting ambulance at Elgin. He pointed in the direction of Miller's Station, and then sternly cried, "*Drive like the wind!*"

The three ruffians, whose "personal baggage" of

Winchesters and revolvers was supplemented only with well-filled ammunition belts and whisky bottles curled up in their corners, while Bill fiercely dreamed of the job on hand.

The stars were gleaming down from the clearest skies on earth as Cyril Leigh rode silently along over the lonely desert, side by side with Arizona Jack. When the serrated range of the Huachuca Mountains had faded away behind them, and one by one the lights at the Condor camp dropped out of view, the Squire dropped into a moody silence. There was no sound but the ringing of the horses' hoofs on the flinty *mèsa*, and the Briton dropped behind his guide, who led the way lightly along between the gaps of the mesquit groves, the cactus patches, and the clustering clumps of tall nopales. The wail of a distant coyote, the boom of the mountain owl, the scurrying dash of a frightened prairie wolf rudely roused from its lair alone broke the silence of the balmy night of late July.

"*Lisbeth, darling! Your dowry is now secure!*" fondly mused Leigh, "*and the old oaks of Leigh Hurst shall not come down!*"

Half afraid that he had erred in refusing Morris Blum's highest offer, the Squire mused over his future course.

"*It will be safer at Tucson!* There, I will have the lawyers and public officials to aid me, and respectable witnesses of my movements. I can remain a week there till the New York bank announces the payment of the price, *if I decide to sell.* And I need not conceal my true name and station, *now.* For *the mask is off.* These fellows only wish to hoodwink me, and buy us out as cheap as possible. They shall pay for the fortune that they have covered up!"

He revolved in his mind all his sister's instructions, and a glow of pride warmed his heart. "I have followed out her plans and wise suspicions. *What a clear-eyed darling one is my Beth.* She distrusted that smug fellow Lemon, whose whole game was to trap us into selling a fortune at less than a shilling in the pound. I wonder if he will turn up Jack-in-the-box at Tucson, now?"

It was eleven o'clock when the silent Vittorio turned his head. "*There, Señor, is Miller's Station, only a half mile ahead of us, now.*" He slowly added, "There you can rest and I can bait the horses. There is no train up the road till noon to-morrow. The night train has already gone up."

"We can ride into Elgin from here in three hours," Leigh impatiently cried. "Why not push on *now—to-night ?*"

"Because the horses are worn out with being hidden in the bushes, and are knocked up by this quick ride. The little station over there at Elgin is full of thieves and robbers, and the men whom you must avoid may be on watch for you there. *It might not be safe.* They parted with you in no good humor, you say! Better rest at Miller's to-night, and I'll rouse you at seven, and so we'll be safe in Elgin at ten o'clock. Then the station will be open, and you will not be interrupted by any one. You can send on all your dispatches from the telegraph office there, and then keep right on to Benson and Tucson. The Nogales day train brings up a full load of respectable passengers. Elgin station is no place for you at night. But in the daytime you are perfectly safe." And Arizona Jack blushed, under cover of the night, at his own lying scheme.

"*All right,*" drowsily murmured Cyril Leigh. "If it's best, let it be as you will. *Is this station a safe place ?*"

"There's only the keeper, an old man, and his Mexican wife," answered Vittorio. "They watch the hay pile of the stage company, and there's only an old mud wall corral and a few bags of grain. Nothing for the ladrones to steal, Señor."

"Very good! *Then we'll stop !*" carefully said the unruffled Briton. "I don't mind a bit of hardship. It's my last night on the desert!"

"*So it is,*" mused Jack. "*I could get the papers now.*" But he waited for his own pals at the station.

The guide was strangely moody and quiet as they plodded up to the one-story adobe, where a single room was walled off for the companion of Station-keeper

Miller's dreary desert watch.   A blinking light glimmered in the outer room where old Miller, a castaway German, slumbered, half drunk, with his arms and hands resting on the low counter of the little store. A dozen black bottles, a few cans of "tinned goods," a bit of coffee, and panoche sugar was the simple stock of the station.

A few dogs, pigs, and gamecocks were mixed up around the little hovel, where a "lean-to" shed afforded outside storage for Señora Miller's rude *batterie de cuisine*.   The outlines of the corral loomed up dimly a couple of hundred yards away, with the mud walls surmounted by a row of palisades, and ten miles to the west, McLaughlin's Peak, a huge shadow, hovered in the thin air, with one bright star clinging to its topmost crag.   Vittorio's hail soon brought out the sad-faced Mexican woman, whom Miller had "annexed" by the loose tenure of Arizona "go-as-you-please" matrimony, a blessed state, "*de facto*," not "*de jure.*" The frightened woman dropped her eyes as Vittorio spoke earnestly to her in her own tongue.   She led the wearied stranger into the one refuge room, where a curtained alcove hid a rough bed.

"I'll first *see that the horses are all safe, Señor !*" curtly said Arizona Jack, as he trotted off to the corral.

The silent woman placed a jug of water and a black bottle on the table beside the lonely man, who eyed the squalid interior suspiciously by the light of the one kerosene lamp.

"*I think I'll not sleep,*" he mentally decided, as the slatternly woman bestowed herself in a hammock, under the back porch of thatched boughs. ·Miller snored on still unconscious, while Cyril Leigh listened to the sharp snapping bark of the distant coyotes, their song now and then merged into one wild wail, in chorus.   It was a squalid resting-place!   His mind returned to the far away groves of Leigh Hurst, as he awaited the return of his guide!   "*There may be a chance to send a letter on at once, by the train,*" thought the young Squire, and then he sought in his dispatch bag, for envelope and paper.   He traced a few loving lines in pencil and inclosed the scrawl in an envelope, which, with loving prevision, he had already prepared, with the postage stamps affixed. "*It will at least serve to tell Beth of my wanderings,*" he mused, "*and to explain the telegrams I shall send, the very moment I reach an office.*" The search in his bag for a bit of wax to seal the few lines from prying eyes caused him to pick up a little packet, in the smaller compartment of his dispatch satchel. "*Ah! I have broken one promise!*" he muttered. "Mr. Robert Ross I am, *no more! I promised Beth to always wear her ring! And—a Leigh must keep his plighted word.*" He slipped the little token upon his finger and gazed lovingly upon its two joined diamond hearts. He dropped the heavy seal ring he had drawn off upon the table, and his head fell prone between his tired arms.

The lonely hovel was silent, while Cyril Leigh slept there alone and unguarded, the beloved face of the Lady of Leigh returning to shine upon him in his uneasy dreams. The wing of the Dark Angel swept his brow, for murder and robbery now crept on the unguarded sleeping boy!

Out in the corral, Arizona Jack stood beside the two horses, which he had led within the inclosure. They were still saddled, but the girths were quickly loosened, and the bridles removed. A man sprang up from a dark angle and cautiously advanced, when Jack whistled softly, "*Pablo?*"

"*Sí, Señor,*" softly replied a Mexican, stealing up to the new-comer.

"*Where is Pepita?*" Jack anxiously demanded.

"Right behind the corral here, out there in the arroyo, *waiting for you* with both our horses all saddled," answered Pablo.

"*All is ready, then,* as I told you yesterday. *I may want to get away any minute.*"

"*Señorita Pepita understands all,*" responded the peon.

"*Listen now,*" said Arizona Jack, sternly. "I will go down to the arroyo, and see her. You are to take both these horses over there. Let them rest a few minutes. Put the bridle on my horse, and have him ready. Bring both the horses along. You are to be ready with them there. You will lead this other horse. *I will ride mine.*   And, Señorita Pepita will be on the lookout around the station. When I come, we will make for McLaughlin's Peak, *as fast as we can!* We will hide there in the old place—the Contrabandista's place—*the Grizzly's cave.*"

" *Si, Señor,*" mechanically answered the peon, moving away with the horses.

Jack stalked on ahead and measured the star dial of the night with a practiced eye. " *Midnight!   The sooner it's over the better*, for some one might come along. There's always chances to take in life and *only one chance is now left me*, a desperate one, to win back this half a million. *I hope to God that he'll be asleep!* If he is *not*, then there's only one thing left, *a knife stab in the back*, and then *a run for it.   These fools have all played into my hand* and *to-morrow night*, we'll be well over the Mexican line. *I can make my own terms* after that, and *then I can take Pepita away* out of here, *to Europe.* If the Blums *won't buy*, then Bent and Stone *will*, and this thing will be laid to road agents, for no one in the camp saw me take him away. *It was a neat trick to have Pablo secretly bring the horse.* One word to her, Pepita must know nothing of my work, poor child, of the whole affair. She will think I have been rubbing Aladdin's lamp *when* our luck turns!"

Little time had Arizona Jack for endearment when Pepita Morales threw herself into his arms with a smothered cry of joy. She was leaning against a tree and holding the bridle of her horse in her slender hand. All Arizona Jack saw as he kissed her trembling lips was the sparkling of the tears lingering on her silken lashes.

The gleaming white moon had swept over the Huachuca range, and the far desert shone out now white and ghastly with the black clumps of cactus and mesquit, taking on in the night, strange unearthly forms. To the west McLaughlin's Peak towered up bold and massive, with its splintered crags lit up here and there with a glowing ray.

" *Must we linger here, Juan?*" cried the affrighted woman, clinging to him in a passionate embrace. "*I*

will do as you bid, but, *Dios mio !* Juan, remember *you
are my whole life !* "

" It is for *you, mi querida,*" he fondly cried. " They
have robbed me of your fortune, and I swear that
nothing shall happen the young fool. I can get the
papers without a fight. *It is my last chance,* for he
drifts into their hands soon—*the very men who robbed me!*
But, *the papers I will have,* and *have them to-night.* He
sleeps even now. Now remember. You are to ride
gently around the station. If any one comes on either
road ride up to the door and call "Juan!" If there's any
shooting or noise inside, you must ride over to the
arroyo and be ready with Pablo. I'll surely get to you.
He has my orders to be ready on the instant. I will
only get at these papers, and perhaps fire a shot or two,
just to frighten old Miller."

" And how long shall I wait for you ? " fearfully said
Pepita.

"*I will come out to the forks of the road the moment I'm
done,* and *I'll blow out the light in the station.* Watch
that *light.* The moment I blow it out ride up and
wait for me at the cross-road. I'll come out to you
there. If there's any shooting, remember, ride straight
to Pablo, and *I'll be there in a minute !* I am only going
to play robber, that's all."

"*Ah ! Madre de Dios ! Juan !*" sobbed the girl with
a parting kiss, as he motioned to her to mount. And
in a moment, the faithful Mexican girl touched her
horse and disappeared around a fringing bank of willows.

" She may be deceived by my foolery," grimly said
the outlaw.

" *Now, for the wolf's work !* " growled Arizona Jack,
as he loosened his pistols and knife, and then strode
swiftly back to the station. " The old man is pretty
well dosed. *Pablo has done his work well.* The woman's
only a poor thing ; she does not even know me. The
boy's asleep, *poor devil,* by this time. He left his loose
traps at the Condor. The papers must be in that dis-
patch-satchel. There's nothing hidden under his loose
tunic. And I notice this satchel is the one thing that
has never left his body. *Fool, to hesitate* at trifles now!

I ought to search him well.　But, to do that, *I'd have to finish him!*　A knife, sent home between the shoulders, would do the trick *without any noise.*　Old Miller can't wake up.　Pablo has dosed him too well.　As for the woman, *a gag will do the business!*"　Loosening a broad silk handkerchief, loosely knotted around his neck, Jack thrust it ready in the bosom of his hunting-shirt.

"*It's a cowardly dog's work,*" he groaned, "*but it's the only way to get back my own.*"　Wolf-like, he prowled around the little adobe until he satisfied himself that all were asleep.　He was keeping the ceaseless vigil of a murderous hate, and he closely gripped his heavy bowie knife, ready to silently strike down any one who stood between him and the last original papers of the swindling contract of sale.　In the west wall of the adobe, two panes of glass roughly set in to the mud wall, gave him a fair view of the tired young wanderer sleeping there with his head bowed upon his hands.　The feeble glimmer of the dying kerosene lamp lit up the little back room.

The human wolf paused in his stealthy round. "*Asleep!*　If he only was a friend of the bottle, I might easily slip in, cut the strap of his dispatch case, *put the light out*, and then make a dash, *knocking him in the head!*　Pablo has let the horses out of the corral and they could not pursue till morning.*"*

Between himself and the moon, he saw Pepita's shadow flitting about the cross road on guard.　He hesitated a moment, then growled:

"*Pepita!　It's for her—I've killed men before!*" and he silently glided into the adobe past the sleeping woman who lay unconscious in her hammock.　Old Miller was still lying in a stupor, his head resting upon his squalid counter.

"*Now, it's got to be done, now!*" was Arizona Jack's last desperate resolve.　"*I'll just give him the knife between the shoulders as he sits there.*"　And yet at the threshold of his crime, some awful shade seemed to bear him back.　"*To kill an unarmed man sleeping, in cold blood.　And he never gave me even a hint of his home, his people.　They may wait for him, perhaps, even now in far away England!*"

In the doorway, the human wolf paused irresolute, for the red rusty gold of the Condor seemed even now to be stained with innocent blood. *"I'll take my even chances to get away with the papers fairly,"* was Arizona Jack's last maddening resolve. *" They're mine, I was swindled out of the price of a life, and I'll have them. But, he shall have fair play if he wakes !* I'm only taking my own, *with the strong hand."*

The veins were knotted on his brow as he glided forward to the table. He looked down at the stalwart lad.

The sleeper murmured, *" Lisbeth must know all !"* For the brave boy's dreaming heart was far away with the Lady of Leigh Hurst.

Jack had sprung back into the shadow as the unguarded man relapsed into the deep sleep of exhaustion.

" A letter! My God, no one must ever have a clue if it comes to the worst !" the watching wolf of the night swore, as he stole forward, with his knife poised, ready to sink beneath the shoulders of the dreamer.

With one glance, he read the superscription, the mark of a loving brother's care:

For MISS LISBETH LEIGH,

LEIGH HURST,

Pately Bridge, Yorkshire, England.

Europe.

The heavy seal ring of the Leighs lay upon the table, where it had fallen from Cyril's tired fingers, and then, with a gasp of anguish, Arizona Jack picked it up and leaned over the sleeping man, holding it to the light.

There in the glimmering ray he saw the crest and motto of the Leighs of Leigh: *" Loyal à la mort."* His bosom heaved in one choking sob as he noted the gleaming double heart of diamonds on the finger of the sleeping boy. A sigh of anguish rent his soul,

"*Can it be?   My God!*" he faltered, with trembling lips, as he grasped the letter and hid it in his breast. He dropped the murderer's knife into its sheath and grasped the sleeping man by both wrists.   "*Tell me, Where in God's name did you get that ring?*" he almost shrieked, as Cyril Leigh sprang struggling to his feet in a sudden alarm.

But, the mask was off and the agonized tenderness of the outlaw's face brought the answer to the young Squire's lips:

"My sister, Lisbeth Leigh, gave it to me, and *who are you?*   Who in Heaven's name are you?   *An Englishman?*"

"Are you Cyril Leigh, the boy whom I never saw?" the outlaw gasped.

"*I am Cyril Leigh, of Leigh Hurst!*" the young Squire said, his blood returning to its channels; "*and you, are?——*"   His voice sank into a sorrowful whisper.

"*God help me!   I am Jack Powning*, and *I gave your sister, Beth, that very ring!*" cried Arizona Jack, his voice dying in a hollow groan, as he threw himself into the rough seat Leigh had sprang from.

They sprang to their feet, in a sudden alarm, as a slight form glided in at the rear door.

"*Juan, Juan!   Mi querido!   Indios, ladrones!*" whispered Pepita, as she dragged Arizona Jack toward the rear door.   She dragged him along with a frantic haste.

"*My God!   Big Jim's gang, Cyril.   For your life, now!   Fly with Pepita!   Trust to her!   I will atone! Yes, yes!   I will atone!*"   He pushed the lad out of the door and whispered a sentence to Pepita.   "*Go, for her sake!*" cried Jack Powning.   "*For Lisbeth Leigh's love*, go!   I'll stand them off here, a bit, and get over to you at the corral!   *Ride off with her.   Away!*"

"*No!   I'll stay here and fight them with you!*" cried Cyril Leigh, his courage rising.

"*Away!   For Lisbeth's sake!*   I'll hold them here and *fool them!*   I'll join you at once in the arroyo.   Leave my horse there with my man.   *Let Pepita lead you on!* Never mind the firing!   *They can't hurt any one!*"

The Mexican woman signed to Cyril to spring up behind her, and with a bound, the two were lost in the darkness.

Jack Powning caught up Miller's Winchester rifle from a corner, and threw both the doors of the adobe to their places, shutting the front with an oaken bar.

"*This will keep them delayed for a moment,*" he decided. "*They'll try the rear way! Now, for the chapparal!*"

And, darting out of the rear door, he ran lightly out, gaining the bushes, having blown the one light out with a sweep of his handkerchief. Springing lightly from bush to bush, Arizona Jack kept out of the glaring moonlight, as he dodged along toward the corral.

"*If I can only reach the arroyo,* then they'll not find our trail until after daylight!" the bold adventurer quickly decided.

As he dropped into the gully, a mounted man galloped up to within twenty yards, and the rapid ring of a revolver told of the discovery of Jack's escape. But the gleaning barrel of the Winchester was raised, and a sharp rifle crack resounded as the rider, a fair mark in the silver moonlight, pitched heavily forward over his horse's neck. Then rose the wild yell of "White Heron," the Apache, as he sprang out to aid the man whom he had piloted to the point of vantage to cut off the escape of Jack and the Englishman. A second echo from the Winchester, and the Indian fell over the dead man, helpless, with a smashed shoulder, as the dead man's horse went madly clattering back toward the station-house.

Arizona Jack's mood was a mad one. He had tasted blood again. "I'd like to stay here and butcher that damned fool Willetts," he snarled, as he sprang away.

Running like a deer with the hounds in view, Arizona Jack soon traversed the bed of the arroyo, passing behind the corral to where, with his Winchester poised, Pablo sat ready on his horse, with the bridle of Jack's steed grasped in his left hand.

"*Which way, Pablo?*" cried Jack, as he leaped into the saddle. Pablo pointed to where the purple peak loomed up to the west.

"*Now follow me!*" cried the victorious plainsman, as

he set the pace, gaining the cover of a long knoll which screened them from all immediate pursuers. And fast they flew away over the silvery sands, their horses leaping madly along in the cool night air!

It was half an hour before Jack reined up his horse beside Cyril Leigh and Pepita. There was a glad cry from Pepita Morales, but Jack only motioned her onward.

"*What does all this mean?*" cried Cyril Leigh, whose night ride had at last awakened him to the dangers of his quest.

"*Big Jim and his cutthroat gang have been set on by Blum to follow and murder you, for the papers in your possession!* And they will kill our whole party, if they bring us to bay, and find out our trail. They have meant to murder you *from the very first.* Here, *take this Winchester, Leigh.* It's old Miller's. I've got plenty of ammunition in my saddle pockets. There's but one chance for all our lives."

Arizona Jack turned to see if there were any pursuers in sight. But the desert mèsas gleamed out lone and bare.

"*And that is?—*" said the bewildered Englishman, as he quickly took the rifle. "*To hide till daylight, and then try to get over to the Mexican line.* There's but one danger! *Those damned Apaches.* I shot one of them, but the others will trail us. I know only one place, where we can stand them off, and *we're going there now.*"

"Tell me how you came here, *You, Captain Powning?*" said Squire Leigh.

"That's got to wait, my boy, till we're out of danger. Ride on with Pepita. *Pablo and I will hold the rear guard.* Let her set the pace. She knows where we are going. *Don't you stop to do any fighting. Pablo and I will attend to that!* You'll have a fair chance at it yet. There's no show to make the railroad now. These fellows and their friends would lynch us both, *you* to get your papers, and *me*, because I have just laid out a couple of their gang."

"*Are there no authorities?*" demanded the still amazed Englishman.

"You hold your only authority in your hands now—the rifle! Ride on, Squire Leigh, *ride on!*"

"*I will not!*" bluntly said Leigh, "till I know how the heir of Powning Hall comes to me in such savage guise. You are now the last of the line. *The Hall and the estates are waiting for you!*"

"*My God!*" cried Jack, ranging alongside. "There were two lives between it and myself when I left England!"

"*All dead now,*" said Leigh, "and you have been given up *for long years.*"

"*Go on, Cyril!*" yelled Powning. I'll tell you all if I save your life; if not, *the story had better die with me. Your sister?*"

"*Waiting for me at Leigh Hurst!* She is the same beautiful darling as when you knew her, a budding girl."

The horses' feet pattered merrily on the hard jaspery ground as they raced along.

"*Thank God!*" gasped Jack Powning, "He does not know the story of my shame, nor, of the blight upon that angel's life! Miss Lisbeth Leigh," he softly whispered. "She has not married. *He shall live—for Lisbeth's sake—I will save him!* My own Pepita shall pilot him out to Mexico, and Pablo and I will fight these devils, *till the last cartridge is gone! I'll fool the brave girl into saving him and herself!*"

In his exaltation of reawakened love and remorse, Arizona Jack never asked the story of Robert Ross, the masquerader. For his eyes were sternly scanning the ground to the rear, and, with Pablo at his side, he watched, ready to make a stand, while the seamed sides of McLaughlin's Peak loomed up, nearer and nearer, in the still morning air.

Their pace had slackened and the steep walls of a defile rose around them, two hours before the first glimmer of the dawn was slowly creeping from the East. The tired horses now dropped their heads in the gloomy shade of the mountain crags as Arizona Jack cried: "*Here we are safe at least for a time. Ease your horses! They must have rest. Our lives depend on them now.*"

"*What is your plan, Captain Powning?*" anxiously whispered Cyril Leigh, as Pablo and Pepita led the way into the defile.

"For God's sake Leigh ! *Never use that name* until I have earned the right to use it again. *I am only 'Arizona Jack,'* and, I will live and die unknown. My first mission is *to save you !* We will reach my hiding place in half an hour, a refuge safe against any men, *but these ! Fool ! I see it all now.* I should have struck out from the Condor for Mexico. *Now, we must live or die together !* I will consult with Pablo and Pepita— brave girl !" Jack Powning heaved a sob of bitter anguish. "*My God !*" he murmured, "*I dare not tell him all I plotted !* We are trapped together, and my thieving plan will seal these scoundrel's title to the Condor, *with our own blood !* Pepita could have easily taken him out—*over the line to Nogales.* He is young, the last of the Leighs. "*What juggling fiend brought him here ?*"

"I will atone—I will atone ! Lisbeth ! Oh ! Heavens ! *What a vengeance.* The one dear defenseless hand, and, if he dies here—*Leigh Hurst goes to another ! My God ! He shall live !*" Arizona Jack's soul was racked with the pangs of Hades.

"*Will they pursue us ?*" demanded Leigh. The boy's fighting blood was up—the cool English nerve that has told for generations; the nerve that took the stormers into Ciudad Rodrigo; the unshaken bulldog courage of Inkerman ; the pluck that held up the thin red line at the Alma; the bravery derived from the hardy Norsemen of yore!

"*They'll surely be on us by noon !*" grimly said Jack Powning. "*Let me think, Leigh ! I must try and do the best I can for you !*"

"*See here ! Powning !*" said the gallant boy, "I don't know what took you out of England. I was only a child away at school. But, Cornelia Powning is watching there at home with my sister Beth, to-night, and *we will go through this thing together ! You and I !* Cornelia is all the mother that Lisbeth has known, and Beth has been sister, mother, and guardian to me ! It's shoulder to shoulder, now, for old Yorkshire ! We'll stand them off a bit—by Heaven ! I'm in a dream, but *I know Beth has been always thinking of you !* Why, she's even kept your picture hung up in honor—*all these long years !*"

Their hands met in the shaded gloom of the gorge, and Cyril Leigh never knew that the castaway's eyes were filled with unhidden tears. The hell of a useless remorse was gnawing at the wanderer's heart!

"*Here we are!*" cried Arizona Jack, his voice sounding hollow, as they drew up before an overhanging cliff. "Here's the Grizzly's Cave, and, perhaps, *our battle-ground!*"

With a few rapid words in Spanish, Arizona Jack gave Pablo his first orders, as he leaped from his horse, and then lifted Pepita Morales lightly to the ground. "*Stay here, Leigh, and hold two of the horses.* Pablo will soon hide them. They can rest a bit. *I'll make a light within!*"

"*Is there no help? Can't we try to reach the railroad?*" groaned Leigh. "*Why stay here to be butchered?*"

"There's a terrific mountain range between us and Crittenden," sternly said Jack. "It is *as impassable as the Alps!* If we reached Elgin, these devils would surely lynch us there as pretended horse thieves or rustlers. It's fifty miles down the valley over the desert to the Mexican line. They would overtake and butcher us all!"

"*Where are the soldiers?*" demanded Leigh. "*Could we not hide up here in these mountains till help could be had?*"

"*Right! There is a squadron of cavalry at Fort Huachuca! Let me think! Let me think!*" said Arizona Jack, dashing ahead into the cave.

In fifteen minutes the whole party was within a huge cave whose narrowed entrance was only a rift in the solid basalt through which the horses could hardly squeeze, when unsaddled.

Cyril Leigh could see little of the interior by the flickering light of a candle. "*You know the place?*" he muttered.

"*Yes! I've often been here before, in my contrabandista days*, and Pablo and Pepita waited *for me here*. I was going out to Mexico after I had parted with you. I trusted to my disguise. For, there's an old blood feud between me and the last of the Stage Robbers and the Rustlers' gang here. *I did not want to go down to*

Tucson with you, Leigh. I would be shot on sight if I did. If I had only known! " he groaned.

"But *you piloted me into the Condor mine!*" cried the surprised young man.

"I was trapped, fooled, led on, perhaps, even to my death. *You'll know all if it comes to the worst.* If we escape, then I'll tell you myself *at the right time. Here, you and Pablo* must guard the entrance."

There were a half dozen packages lying around the stony floor. Leigh gazed wonderingly at them. "Pablo brought all this stuff up here to help me on my way out to Mexico. Thank God, *We've got five hundred rounds of Winchester ammunition here.*

"Lie down and get some rest," coolly said Jack as he threw a horse blanket over a saddle. "*We are surely safe from attack till daylight. I'll make my final plan of action now.*"

In the mouth of the gorge, Pablo, the Mexican, lay like a couchant tiger peering down the glen, while Cyril Leigh clutched the Winchester rifle stock and silently waited for the dawn. Leigh curiously watched the four horses huddled in the farther recesses of the cavern whose vaulted roof opened inwardly. Arizona Jack was busied with them, aided by the woman, whose face the squire had not yet seen. There was the murmur of earnest voices, then the sound of Jack's deep tones, the pleading notes of a woman's loving accents, and, as the minutes dragged away, a storm of tears and sobs. Cyril Leigh soon knew that the stern plainsman was urging the woman against the pleadings of her own fond heart.

Suddenly, he strode across the cave, and sharply interrogated Pablo.

The young Englishman waited in suspense as the emphatic notes of Arizona Jack accentuated Pablo's calm impassive answers. With all the fatalism of his race, Pablo Guerra was now prepared for his master's final orders, and stood ready either to make a dash for liberty or to die "with his boots on."

At last, Jack Powning called Leigh to his side. Pepita Morales was sitting crouched upon the ground with her head supported in her hands, and softly wailing in the soft accents of her race.

"*Madre de Dios! Juan!*" she cried, her long hair falling over her clasped hands, the blinking light gleaming on her slender form.

"*See here, Leigh,*" broke out Jack Powning, his breast heaving in choking sobs. "*I owe to this loving woman my very life.* She has given me ten long years of hers. There's but one desperate chance left! The gang who are after us have not ever seen *her.* They also know nothing of *Pablo.* It's but fifteen miles to Fort Huachuca. There is two hours yet to the dawn. *Pablo knows every inch of the ground.* I'm going to send her away, but only *to save her life.* I'm *also* going to send Pablo to guard her. *They will take the two best horses.* By making a long detour to the north, they are out of the line of our pursuers. If they get safely past the north spur of the Huachuca range, they've got a straight run into the camp. They can make it in four hours. By nightfall we can have the cavalry here. *It will at least save her, poor girl.* You and I can then stand them off, here in the cave. I'll go down the gorge with them on foot. *It's that or nothing!* I could have made Camp Huachuca from Miller's Station, if we had not been attacked, and before God I did not then know that these devils were on your trail. I thought that they would only try to trick you at Tucson.   If you had told me that you had quarreled with Blum at the Condor, I would have known when he left with his gang that you would never reach the railroad alive, and we would have raced into Fort Huachuca. But it's too late now. *It was a fatal mistake!* Are you content to stay with me ? *I'll give you your own choice.* You can try to go in with them. But, I really believe that they can make it. Even if they are observed, they may outride the pursuers. Pepita will ride my own horse. The best in Arizona. She rides feather-weight, too. She's to make the last running. Pablo, like a man, will stay and fight if they are stopped, and if she gets five miles start while they are getting him out of the way, we will be saved. He is the gamest Mexican I ever saw!" Cyril Leigh scorned to leave the de-voted man alone to his fate. He answered frankly:

"Powning! *Don't ask me to go.* Tell me what to do.

If *they* risk their lives to save us, I'll risk *mine* to stay here with *you*! As you say, they may be taken for simple frontier wanderers. But you and I have got to live or die together. Tell me now what to do?"

"Only begin to solidly block up the door of the cave when we go out. There's loads of loose stones lying around here. And now, write instantly a note to the Commanding Officer U. S. Forces at Camp Huachuca, and tell him that an English gentleman and his guide are beset by a band of Indians, thieves, and robbers at the Grizzly's Cave, in McLaughlin's Peak. Sign it with your full name and address, and tell him that the help must come on the run. We can hold out possibly till night. There's water in here, and pinole and jerked beef enough for a week. We've got two Winchesters and three pistols, and there's all the ammunition we can shoot away. Pablo will take his Winchester and one pistol."

By the flaring light of the single candle, Cyril Leigh traced the fatal message of despair. He choked down a sob as he signed his name firmly, for the last lines were: "In case of my death, notify Miss Lisbeth Leigh, Leigh Hurst, Pately Bridge, Yorkshire, England."

The hidden bonanza of the Condor Mine was forgotten as the young Squire saw Jack Powning's strong arm supporting the half fainting Mexican woman.

"*Here's the note! Tell them the same thing in Spanish, Powning,*" cried Leigh. "*I must now go to work!*" They started as a wolf's long howl rang out below them in the glen.

"*Won't you sign it, too?*" demanded Leigh, as he gave Arizona Jack the letter.

"*I have no name!*" bitterly said the outlaw. "*I died ten years ago!*"

Pablo had led the two horses selected by his master out through the cleft, and Arizona Jack tenderly forced the loving woman toward the entrance.

Suddenly she sprang toward Cyril Leigh, who stood there and held aloft the candle. With a trembling finger she traced the sign of the cross on the young man's forehead, "*Sea por Dios y la Santissima!*" she sobbed, as the young man clasped her hands in a mute adieu.

Pablo was already leading the horses down the defile, when Arizona Jack cried: "*I'm between you and them. Don't forget! I'll be back in ten minutes!*" We will not be attacked till after daylight."

The rattling of the horses' feet on the ground was all the sound that followed their exit, save the wail of the woman, whose voice sank away in despairing sobs. And Cyril Leigh sprang to his work, toiling to build a secure breastwork of stones in the open cleft of the cave.

There was a breast-high barricade when Arizona Jack clambered back up the glen. "*I waited till they were off,*" he gloomily said, with a hollow groan. "*And now, Leigh, I am ready to die*, for I have said good-bye to the woman who has given me more than life! And let us finish our work, for they'll only dig me out of here *when the very last cartridge is fired!*"

Cyril Leigh worked on with a desperate energy till the entrance was completely blocked. He turned toward the companion of his vigil, who had stooped to light a fresh candle. The face of Jack Powning was green and ghastly in the glimmering light.

"*Out there, under the stars, I have just parted with all I held dear!*" groaned the wanderer. "And when I unwound her arms from my neck, I swore to God to avenge her, *if they harm a hair of her head!* The day is beginning to break faintly. They are safe not to come on us for an hour yet! I've something to tell you, Cyril Leigh, but I must first make my peace with God for sending that child away to die, perhaps, for me!"

"*Surely no men would harm a woman?*" faltered Leigh.

"*My God! The only ones I fear are the Indians! Those damned Apaches!*" shrieked Arizona Jack, and he fell on his knees in unfamiliar prayer.

On guard, rifle in hand, at the entrance, Cyril watched the outlaw, racked with vain remorse, while five miles away Pepita Morales, leaning lightly forward, her hair falling over her shoulders, raced along, the big red roan horse, bounding lightly on, while Pablo, rifle at a poise, gazed out on the glimmering sand hummocks, with a defiant light in his eyes, as the rosy dawn slowly blossomed into the growing light of the day.

BOOK III.

"WHERE IS THE PROMISE OF MY YOUTH, ONCE WRITTEN ON MY BROW?"

CHAPTER XI.

"SAVE JUAN! RIDE! RIDE!" TOM GUILFOYLE'S TROOPERS.

CYRIL LEIGH watched the movements of the man who sprang to his feet, as a faint streak of morning light lightened the eastern skies, for Arizona Jack had silently finished his last preparations for defense. His face was veiled in the gloom of the cavern, but Leigh had listened to his agonized mutterings. "*Adios, mi querida! Adios, mi querida! Poor Pepita!* Here is water and some food. Drink this. *It will do you good!*" entreated Jack, as he poured some pinole meal into a gourd of water. "Here is also bread and meat. The very moment that it is light enough I'll show you all the arms and ammunition. Then, I'll first tell you what you must know, and, if we escape—you *alone shall be my judge!*"

They had been crouching behind the barricade ready to meet any onslaught. Jack Powning's urging had forced the young Squire to yield to the drowsiness of fatigue, while the borderer's mind had followed Pepita and Pablo out over the mist-veiled valley of the Canille Range. A thousand different suggestions had tor-

mented the entrapped outlaw. He had been face to
face with his past life while the tired boy slept at his
side, and many grisly phantoms haunted the now repentant man. His heart was racked with the memories of all the fresh hopes that had failed in the long
years before, and all the loathsome horrors of his
downward path returned in the night to torment him.
When the sleeping boy stirred and fondly murmured,
"Lisbeth, darling !" Jack Powning's hand sought his
pistol butt.

"*No! I'll save him. By God, I will !*" swore the
man, whose ecstasy of agony was verging on delirium.
"*Must he know? Dare I tell him all?*" the castaway mused. "*I have lived like a brute, but I will die
like a man !*" he sighed, as he watched the light beginning to gleam through the loosely chinked stones of
the barricade. With tin cup and bowie knife, he had
toiled alone in throwing up a bank of earth behind the
piled-up stones. Suddenly, a faint cry was heard ringing out far down the gorge.

"*I must awake him!* For they're coming at last !"
growled Jack. "Those damned Apaches have now
found our inward trail!" He smiled grimly as he remembered his last injunction to Pablo to ride along
the foothill for a mile or so before breaking out on the
mèsa northwardly. "*The inward trail is all right,*
as long as they don't find Pepita's outward trail!"
He turned away in the gloom and kissed a silken tress
of Pepita's raven hair. It was her last token of an unbroken faith. "*Poor child! God be with her !*" he
groaned. "If she gets safe through, then the five
thousand dollars that I have already made safe in
Magdalena, and the other five she has now with her,
will keep the wolf from the door. The price of my
honor, the price of a human soul, perhaps, the bitter
blood-money of our two lives. Fool that I did not see
that I was being hoodwinked! For this messenger of
the English ownership first out of the way, then my
own life would have been sacrificed. And *dead men
tell no tales !* They must have discovered my secret."
The parting under the stars from the child-wife who
had led him once out of death's jaws, was bitterer

than the coming death, and, rifle in hand, he stood grimly at bay behind the barrier, murmuring, "*It's time to pay off all the old scores and some new ones!*"

He roused Leigh and said, quietly: "They've found out the trail and are now coming up the canyon. Here are all the arms and ammunition ready at hand. Put this belt on and this pistol. *Keep it to the last.* I've taught you how to handle the Winchester. You are to do no shooting till I tell you. They can't either smoke us out or burn us out, and their only chance is to break down our barricade. They can't do that till it's dark! And I've left one or two lower loop holes that I can draw the plugs out of and astonish them a bit. Here are the best stations for each of us. Thank God! They can not get any plunging fire on us. *The other wall is vertical.* Now tell me how you came over here as Robert Ross. If I had known your real name I would have saved you and made your sister's fortune."

"My uncle, St. John Gladwyn, bought this half of the mine from Chandos Brandon, with the twenty thousand pounds he intended for Lisbeth's dowry," said Cyril. "It was the Hugh Dalton interest transferred by Ryley to Brandon. Now when this smug rascal 'Arthur Lemon' sought us out, to buy it for five thousand pounds, we became at once suspicious, and I came over to verify the facts under the name of Robert Ross. I naturally feared money trickery, but not this death trap," the boy said, bitterly. "It appears that their idea *now* is to destroy all the original title papers, and to defend the possession to the mines. Duped as I was, these two drunken miners at Bisbee told me of the buried riches of the Condor, so I fought shy at the mine and Blum finally raised the bid to twenty thousand pounds. I refused this unless I saw the mine and examined it when cleared of water. That's all. *He* went away, and here we are. *He made no threats, though, the* cowardly liar."

"My God! You should have put off your answer till you were safe at Tucson, there you could have had proper protection," groaned Jack.

"*And you?*" simply said Cyril Leigh.

"*I was sent to follow you on, and to simply try to deprive you of the papers.* If I had known *who* you were, my boy, I would have died first, but you were close mouthed, and I masqueraded, for there is an old blood feud between the Tucson hangers-on of this scoundrel Blum and myself. I dared not go on to Tucson with you. It would have only invited my butchery. *I see it all now!* They would have killed you on the roundabout way from Bowie to the mine, but they wanted first to try and get your legal title easily *by hoodwinking you.* That was Blum's game and this scoundrel Lemon wished to defeat Blum by getting the original papers spirited away from you. I was afraid to even hint at England to you, for the wretches whom Blum had sent to meet you would have at once *murdered me* had they known who I am. For, Cyril Leigh, I have masqueraded as 'Arizona Jack,' in Texas for a number of years, and this devil Lemon must have gone behind Blum to betray him. *He knew, the Judas, that you would later surely be murdered,* if you did not tamely submit to the swindle. Your chance meeting with the revengeful miners has lost them the whole game. And now they would wipe it out in blood. *We will see!*"

"Now I have left that untold which I can only tell you *at the last,* if you are saved. If we *both* are saved, you shall know all *at the right time.* If I die here in this cave, you must know that I was blameless when I left England. You were a child, away at school. Only Cornelia Powning knows that I loved your sister Lisbeth more than my life! I will now lay it down to defend you, and that I left England *for her sake!* I was in the jaws of Fate, and no shadow of shame ever came to darken her gentle soul through me."

"*Cornelia thinks that you are still alive.* She waits lovingly and watches for your return. *And, Lisbeth has always been faithful to her* silent heart's promptings," faltered Leigh. "*Now, I know,* at last, *why she never married.* I've been but a blind boy. But, what could I know?"

Arizona Jack grasped his arm. "*Hush! Hush! They come,*" he whispered, as he crouched like a tiger there behind the barricade. The clatter of climbing horses' feet was heard, and loud oaths rang out below them in the still dark defile. "*Back! Back!*" imperiously cried Jack. "*Let me begin my atonement. Not a shot till I tell you!*" He pushed Leigh behind the shoulder of a basalt boulder.

With measured deliberation, Jack Powning pressed the trigger, and a wild shriek of pain, rose, followed by a blood-curdling yell, which rang through the cañon. "*They've got more Indians,*" huskily cried Jack, as a volley of rifle bullets rattled against the upper stones of the barricade. "If our message does not get through, then they count to wear us out, or else make a rush at night, and batter down our barricade." There was no word spoken for an hour, as the two men guarded the different sides of the barricade. Fifty shots had glanced off the rough breastworks, and but thrice had Jack fired at an exposed limb. Cyril Leigh had twice sent a ball whizzing where a shock head or a flying form was momentarily exposed, and both the defenders had drawn blood. The assailants were driven to cover.

His bronzed face set and stern, Jack Powning guarded the post of honor.

"*They've lost one man killed, I know,*" he growled, "*and they have not tried a rush!*"

Neither of the men dared leave the shooting holes for a moment, and two hours wore away with only an occasional shot.

"*I see it all,*" gloomily said the plainsman. "*They are working at some safer plan.* Perhaps they've begun some scheme to surprise us at night. For they can rest at will, and when the night comes, their chances of a successful rush are better. If they have not cut off our messengers, then they must be near the camp now. I can see that they have plenty of men, and they'll surely make a rush at night."

Cyril Leigh, chilled and stiffened with his death-watch, only doggedly answered:

"*We will fight them to the bitter end. Let us die like Englishmen.*"

Arizona Jack suddenly raised his hand.

"*I hear voices,*" he whispered. "*Come over here and take my place. Drop down behind the bank!*"

Leigh crawled to Jack's side and then the scout threw himself prone on the ground.

"*They are digging*," he whispered as he rose up behind Cyril Leigh. "They have crawled up as near as they dare, and *are digging their way along so as to undermine our barricade.*"

"*Can we not build another within?*" demanded Leigh.

"*I see their whole game now*," growled Arizona Jack. "When night comes, and we cannot see to shoot, they will drop the stones of our barricade into their trench, then come in with a rush, and then—*the thing is over. And they'll make sure work of it, before morning.*"

"*My God!*" Jack sprang up as Cyril Leigh's rifle rang out, and an answering volley rattled on the higher levels of the bulkhead.

"*There, you devils, take that, and that,*" yelled Jack as he dropped two men who had rushed forward to pull back a writhing form which had rolled into plain view.

But, Cyril Leigh lay unconscious at Jack Powning's feet! Only one rifle was on guard now, and a chorus of ferocious yells outside greeted the murderous work of Arizona Jack's hand.

"*Burn the damned hounds out now! Smother them; get up there, all of you,*" was the cry of a leader, whom Powning recognized as Bill Murfee.

"*Is he dead?*" was Jack's horrible misgiving as he tenderly called: "*Cyril! Cyril! Speak to me, my poor boy,*" and then his heart leaped up as the young fellow moaned and began to move.

"*Don't rise. Just roll over backwards. Roll out of the way,*" said Jack, his one rifle ready to sweep every portion of the narrow glade before the blocked entrance.

Jack slipped the extra cartridges into the magazine of his Winchester, and stooped and picked up Leigh's rifle.

"*We've already laid out four in one way or another,*" he growled, and then turned his head to see Cyril Leigh seated out of direct range behind the curved stone walls.

"*Only creased the top of my head, Powning,*" murmured Leigh. "*It stunned me.* I'll be all right in a minute, but *I killed one of them.* I saw him fall flat. The shot only glanced in, which grazed me."

"*Thank God!*" cried Powning. "Wet your handkerchief and lay it loosely on your head, folded under your hat. There's a pool of cold leakage water back there, over there by the horses."

And suddenly Powning cried: "*Fool! I forgot the horses! We may have to fall back on them.*" He darkly glowered over a plan which was a forlorn hope —a last resort!

In half an hour, both men on the watch were astonished to see the upper light suddenly shut off from the rock barricade, and a choking smoke began to drift in from bundles of gramma grass, lowered down flaming from above the cleft. Arizona Jack laughed grimly, as he merely coughed, while several flaming meteors fell one by one outside.

"*They have burned off all their lariats now.* This cave runs back hundreds of yards in its windings, and *there's no other outlet!* As soon as the night-wind raises, *it sweeps down the gorge!* This smoking-out is a failure! *I only fear their digging!* It's slow work, but the floor of the canyon is covered with soft earth only, and I know that they will undermine our wall to-night, and drop it, *from the outside!*"

The two men were watching through their loopholes.

"*I'm only afraid of the long head of Bill Murfee!* He's an intelligent man and up to all of an old miner's tricks!" the outlaw whispered to the brave English boy. "You see that they have got plenty of men and horses, and they can soon get what they want! *The rush will surely come to-night!* And, if we don't have help before then, there's but one course left for us— *to die like wolves at bay—fighting to the last!*"

A terrible fear haunted Arizona Jack now. The terrors of the unknown appalled him. The assailants were busy digging and working. For whatever plan had been adopted, the assailants kept under cover, and the hours of horrible suspense crawled on till noon. It was only a half dozen times that a flitting shade or an exposed limb justified a shot, in return to the dropping fusillade which was kept up, solely to wear out the two entrapped men, by keeping them both on always the defensive.

"*Where in God's name is Pepita?*" groaned Jack, who began to count the minutes after noon, for the sun was leaving the gorge which opened to the South-east, and the shadows deepening in the cavern.

"*Cyril, my boy,*" gravely said Powning, "*something may happen at any time.* These fellows have brought up their wagons. I can hear them digging with the pick and shovel that goes with every frontier outfit. *They are surely getting ready for some systematic bold attempt.* I know Pepita's dauntless heart; I know the distance, too; I know my own horse's speed; *I know poor Pablo's nerve.* If help does not come to us by three o'clock, then we may know that our messages have *miscarried.* You've got your belt and pistol. You know where the *cartridges are*—the food, too. I may be killed by a chance shot, *if these fellows rush. Make your peace with God, my poor boy!* It is a strange fate that brought you here, *to die by my side!*

"I've nothing to tell you more, save that Pepita Morales has been my wife—my loyal wife. I married the child when she saved me from the vengeance of the brutes here in Arizona, eight years ago. I killed one of their gang in self-defense. For me, *there is no hope!* You they might have spared, but *for our work to-day!* And now they will hide all evidence of the crime. *The papers they will have!*"

"*By God, I'll burn them now, first! God will avenge us!*" cried the excited boy.

"*Hold your hand!*" said Jack. "*You have not yet signed over the title! While there is life there is hope! Find some soft place in the floor of the cave!* Bury them there. *Dig a hole with my bowie-knife!* And *don't forget the place!* For there is always a last chance! We'll take that. That girl wife of mine will reach Hua-chuca fort unless—*unless*"—he cried, with a choking sob—she now lies dead on these burning sands below, with the Arizona vultures swooping down on her. *Adios, Mi querida! Adios, Mi querida!*" muttered Jack, speaking as in a dream.

"*They might spare you*, even now," continued Jack, his hollow voice sounding ghastly, "to force a transfer of the mine from you. They may also fear the long arm of the English government. Even this brute Blum may see that you will be missed, that your friends will follow on your traces, that the English Legation will act at once. And so, they might be disturbed in holding on to this accursed mine. *Nothing but blood and tears has ever followed the Condor so far!* If you survive me, there's but one word for you to say. Never mention my life here, but say—and *say the truth*—that I left England to save your sister Lisbeth, my *first, my only love*, a sorrow which the canting tongues of society would have made a bitter public shame."

"Let me sleep in the grave, undisgraced in her eyes, *that is all I ask!*" And then, with a last effort, the bold defender of the barricade solemnly said: "*Lisbeth Leigh may know that I married this gentle, simple child, but only to repay her for saving my life* with the poor protection of a wanderer's name, and my strong arm has been a shield to her *until to-day!* To have kept her *here* would only have been to have doomed her to a later torture more brutal than the rack. If death overtakes her on the way, poor darling Pepita, pray God that it may be a ball that makes her exit from life *only one momentary pang!*"

"*Is there nothing more that we can do?*" groaned Leigh.

His heart clung to the beautiful dark-eyed sister praying at home for him. His young blood chilled in the gruesome waiting for that final rush and the sense of being penned up like a rat in a cage.

"*Our shots* won't reach them digging there below," groaned Jack. "It's certain death now to show our heads. If we lower the barricade, then, they can shoot *in*, as well as we can *fire out!* Our breast height bank here has stopped many a ball to-day. They have no timber for a battering ram. They don't dare to show themselves out in front before dark. *After that*, we cannot see to shoot, and they will have an easy job then, for they will not be in the light."

"*My God! It is horrible to die like a dog at the hands*

of these cowardly villains!" groaned Cyril Leigh, as he stood on the left side of the barricade, his rifle laying ready in the loop-hole.

"*We are in the hands of God, Cyril Leigh!"* hopelessly said Powning. "And I have said good-bye to life *many a year ago.* But for Lisbeth Leigh's sake, *to save you* now I would give my life up to these brutes! *Shall we parley with them?* They may spare you."

Jack stood ready to leap over the barricade.

"*Never!"* cried Leigh. "I know their faith *now!* They would lead me away, butcher you first, and then when I had been forced to sign the papers, slaughter me and bury me here out of the sight of men forever, in these wild desert sands! All that would be needed to finish the story would be supplied by Blum, 'Lemon' & Co., and the facile courts and suborned officials here. *I see the lure now!"* Too late! *Too late!* It's not for myself—*it's for Lisbeth I sorrow!"* groaned Cyril, "for the law turns her out *for the stranger heir.* Her dowry money is sunk here in those gray hills that we left. I wanted to cut down the timber, and so, give her a fund invested. But she so loves Leigh Hurst—the dear gallant girl—that she would not have it. And tell me, Powning, do *you* never mourn for your old home?"

The borderer gasped, "Spare me! For God's sake, *spare me, Cyril.* The temple of my life has been lying shattered for years, and even in my sorrow, I've not dared even once to turn back *in thought,* for I left all behind me then—home, friends, your sister, the golden morning light in her loving eyes. I could not do otherwise but *sink into the unknown.* A sacrifice *to a fiend* in *human* form!"

"*They all thought you to be dead,"* softly murmured Cyril Leigh. "Even the commander of your regiment, Granville Leger. I heard him tell my uncle Gladwyn that he feared you had been the victim of some mysterious crime. Poor Leger mourned unceasingly for *you* till his own death. And darling old Cornelia Powning waits and watches at home in love for your return. She wrote every month to Madam Leger for news of you. The officers of your mess never have taken your name off the roll, and Mrs. Powning has held back the seven years' adjudication of your legal death. The Horse Guards' decision was simply 'Missing.'"

"*What was Marie D'Orsay's opinion?*" tremulously said Arizona Jack, his hand on his rifle barrel. "*Mrs. Leger, I mean!*" concluded Powning.

"She always mourned for you, until her horrible death in the Ringstrasse Theater fire at Vienna. And Major Devereux Sidney, too! Poor Sidney! He was killed at El Teb! I was to go in the army, *you know*," said Leigh, with a last despairing groan.

But Arizona Jack's quick eye had now caught sight of a novel object, a huge, moving cylinder of nopales and tufted prarie grass bound with raw-hide ropes. It was being rolled up to the entrance of the cave.

"*Shoot quick! Shoot at the hands,* and then *at the body, if you can!*" sternly cried Powning, as the two rifles rang out in their quick magazine repetition. "*By God! They'll not try that game again,*" yelled Arizona Jack. "*Crouch down!*" A storm of lead rained down upon the entrance of the cave, as Arizona Jack gave out a wild yell of disdainful triumph.

"*There is one 'spread eagle' laid out there. The rolling-up game don't go.* They may have seen something. *Perhaps the soldiers!* Now, Leigh, I'll play our last card. They may get at the rockwork by dark. It's now three o'clock, and *no hope of help.* I'll show you a trick. *You keep the front covered till I come!*" In a few moments he returned, dragging one of the unwilling horses.

"*Stand back a moment,*" hoarsely whispered Arizona Jack, as he drove his heavy bowie-knife into the base of the horse's skull, instantly severing the spinal cord. The brute pitched over dead, blocking the entrance.

"*Now, bring on the other one,*" ordered Jack; and in five minutes, the two carcasses were an almost impassable barrier behind the rock wall of the entrance. Their last hope of escape was now gone! It was a "stand-off" till death! Lying covered with blood on the warm body of the steed, Jack Powning glanced out over the barrel of his rifle. "*No thoroughfare,*" he grimly said. "We don't get *out,* and they don't get *in.* There'll be a fight to the death *now,* Cyril, before three hours!

Why should they wait ? It will be pitch dark here at sundown."

"*If we only had good lights?*" vaguely said the brave English boy.

"*Useless, useless*, my poor lad ! " sternly said Jack. "*We will die in the dark!* It would only help them to fire in. *The end is soon coming!*" And, with a feverish haste, he gave the young man his last orders, "*Keep your pistol fully loaded to the very last.* We will fight as long as we can here, *at the entrance.* Fill your pockets with loose cartridges; we will get back further in the cave *if they force this way in.* Now, *leave me here* and grope your way back and find out the narrowest place to make a last stand in. I will go back myself and see it, *after your return.*" While the Briton crawled away, Arizona Jack's blazing eyes were fixed on the entrance. "*Dead! all dead!*" he murmured. "*Granville Leger, Sidney Devereux, too,* and *Marie D'Orsay*—the beautiful Mrs. Leger. In the awful holocaust of that Viennese fire. My God ! and then, if the boy is right—*no one ever knew!* There's one gentle heart saved a world of bitter shame—of vain regrets ! And now—to die—betrayed, penned up like a dog, in this loathsome hole. They shall feel my hand, *damn them*, heavy to the last. It will be all over, though, *to-night.*" And one wild burst of passionate appeal told of the baffled rage of the doomed man. "*Pepita ! Dead!*—dead—poor child, for, *if she had not failed*, the troopers would have been already here *now!*" And, when the boy returned, Jack Powning said, with a choking voice, "*I ask only one last favor, Cyril!* We will die like Englishmen ! *Game to the last*, but let me have my own way, and *keep between you and the door.* Only over my dead body will they reach you, and this I ask *for Lisbeth's sake!*" In the growing darkness, the Master of Leigh Hurst grasped the outlaw's hand in a pledge of loyal faith, to the grim death. "*I did not lead you into this trap*, I swear, it Cyril. I *am innocent of your blood*," said Powning, when he came back from his exploration, and then like two tigers they crouched ready for the death struggle. Though neither spoke, they knew that the final plans of the enemy were rapidly moving on. For many voices now rang out in harsh contention, below them in the defile. "It will not be very long, now! *Be ready!*" was the grim order of the "man in the gap." And Cyril Leigh refilled his rifle's magazine and waited there, his weapon ready for instant use.

Daybreak glimmering on the mountain tops found Pepita Morales watching the northern spur of the Huachuca range as the bronzed Pablo, riding at her side, urged her to remember Jack's last orders. "*Well to the north,* so you will not fall in with their party! One hour *due north,* then *northeast* till you are abreast of the Huachuca range! Keep the horses cool, and well in hand. A straight run in only when you strike the level, hard ground to the east of the Huachuca range," so the stern husband had enjoined them both. Pablo well knew his own forlorn-hope duty.

"If you are attacked, then Pablo stays to fight—to delay them to the last—and *you ride on! Pepita querida!*" he had whispered. "Remember, only at the last, give him his speed! He will then be fit to make ten miles on the dead run quicker than any other horse in Arizona!"

Neither messenger spoke as they plodded on in the silent night. Pablo ranging up only to check the speed of Pepita. For with streaming eyes and a heart beating in a transport of love and tenderness, the Mexican girl murmured, "*Juan! Juan! Mi marido querido!*"

As the gray sand hummocks became at last visible in the growing light, as the tall nopales lifted their forked stems in the air, and the mesquit groves shone out black against the yellow sands, Pablo led the advance craftily, hiding their progress by following every dell and arroyo bank.

The cactus clumps showed patches of gorgeous white and crimson and yellow flowers, and the gray desert hawk towered high over their heads in the heated morning air. The horses were still fresh as they clattered along; the lean coyotes gliding away timidly before them, and now and then a mountain wolf rushing noisily across their way. Pepita's eyes were riveted on the broken crags of the Huachuca range as they carefully skirted them by nine o'clock, and turned out of the occasional cover into the broad expanse of level pebble-strewn desert, where only the sagebrush and greasewood gave a grateful shade to the bloated rattlesnakes swollen with the venom of the July sun.

And then Pablo's face grew stern and set! For, now in the open, from the hills of Huachuca range, what glittering, thievish black eyes might not be riveted upon their onward movement? They had long crossed the road leading from the Condor mine to Elgin, and Miller's Station was left ten miles to the southwest. Pepita's heart beat in hope as Pablo pointed significantly to the rolling hills far to the east where Camp Huachuca lay, the great lonely mass of Broncho Hill rising black against the fierce glowing rays of the sun which now flamed down upon them like a fiery furnace. Pablo's horse began at last to drop his weary ears, but Jack's big red roan still sprang lightly over the hard gravelly soil, with the feather weight of the slender woman a mere bagatelle as a load for the superb charger. Pepita's tear-stained eyes were blurred in the blinding rays, and her face was ghastly pale in the reflected glare of the desert. They were loping along steadily now, the roan, ever and anon, stretching out his neck in one wild impulse to race away and roam the desert free as air. He seemed to know his mission of life and death!

They had smartly gained a full league toward Fort Huachuca, and Pepita, her slender hand straying to the folded letter in her breast, was gazing onward toward the hills but two leagues away where Port Huachuca lay, with the only help within a hundred miles, when Pablo, turning his head to the South, grimly pointed to four black objects between their course and the north spur of Huachuca Mountain!

The Mexican was heir by his blood to three hundred years of an undying feud with the Apaches. Well he knew the grim sign of the single file—the creeping on of those four baleful black specks, moving now directly athwart their course. But the devoted servitor never paused a moment to think of himself! A foe was coming on now who *never asked for quarter*, whose brutal nature *knew no mercy*.

His voice rang out clear and steady as the clang of a silver bell: "*Ay estan los Indios. Madre de Dios! Señora! Vamos al norte! Pronto! Pronto!*"

He pointed to the northern limit of the first Huachuca reserve, then jerked out his Winchester from its sheath, and steadily rode away, his tired horse turning quartering to the south, and cutting off the Indians' further advance.

Only a sweet voice like an angel's rang out:

"*Adios! Adios! Pablo! Vayase V con Dios! Dios ayudarnos!*"

Then, loosing the reins, the appalled woman gave the noble horse his lead, and, lightly as the swallow skims the lake, he bounded away, madly racing on for the last goal. Pepita's heart throbbed in a wild ecstasy of terror. She dared not even turn her head, and it was ten minutes before she stole a fearful glance at the southern plain. The maddened steed was now wildly dashing on, for she was lightly leaning forward on his shoulders, and the gallant roan sped away as if he thrilled to the anguished cry of the despairing wife whose heart was back in the gloomy cave where Powning and Leigh were answering the marauder's challenge with the ring of their ready rifles!

One wild scream broke from Pepita's lips as she saw, far away to the south, puffs of white smoke rising around a little hummock, and her heart told her that there, the lonely Pablo was fighting for his life alone, surrounded by the grim foe, selling his life at odds; the self-devoted vaquero knew at last the fatal plot of the Indian trailers. For, while one Apache had already fallen, and lay prone, with staring eyes, outstretched, lifeless on the sun-baked desert, and two others were fiercely waging an unequal duel to the death with Pablo, a black shade between him and the Eastern sun told the doomed vaquero that the remaining Apache had stolen away like a werewolf on the track of the now defenseless woman! The helpless Mexican crouched grimly in his little mesquit thicket, his frenzied eyes now watching every moving tuft of grass, as the snakelike foe wriggled up slowly toward him, but he knew in his heart that their lightest rider on the swiftest horse was stealing on toward the unarmed woman.

"*Séa por Dios y la Santissima !*" gasped Pablo, who now saw the death trap closing in on him. One of the murderous Apaches was crawling up on one side, and the other at the opposite points of the compass. Pablo was "*muy bravo.*" He had faced in years gone by the grim Yaquis, the ferocious Comanches, Kickapoos, and Lipans. He had fought the red Hualipais in their gloomy canyons, and too well he knew the awful horrors of the Apache's vengeance. "*The horse will save her, please God. It is a noble brute !*" he voiced his last hope as he prepared to sell his life dearly.

He was crouching down wolf-like, his Winchester at a ready, his heavy Colt's revolver hanging by the guard in his left hand. The clump of mesquit bush where he stood at bay was only a rod in diameter, and yet the grisly foemen feared to come to a close grapple with the desperate man whose horse lay dead at the foot of the little hummock.

Suddenly, there was a crackling sound as of the branches parting. Pablo's stern eye caught the gleam of copper hued shoulders and then his rifle rang out three times. Springing quickly to his feet he whirled around in a last fury, as a lithe form bounded toward him. The revolver was ringing out sharply as the brawny Apache dropped his gun after one discharge. The two men then closed in a silent death grapple and as the Indian's knife was driven to the hilt in Pablo's side, with a last supreme effort the Mexican pressed the trigger of the self-cocking pistol for the last time ! The report bellowed out and rang sharply over the lonely prairie. There was no shout of triumph, for the deadly triangular duel was now at an end ! "Standing Bear" lay locked in his foeman's death grasp, and two Indian ponies wandered idly about the hummocks nipping the gramma grass. There was none to heed the truants as they wandered slowly away to the shade. Only the gliding lizards of the mèsa, only the circling vultures of the lonely desert of death had marked down the grim harvest of death. The prowling coyotes gathered behind the sand hummocks and gliding from cactus clump to bunches of nopalitos, stealing through the greasewood and dusty parched sage brush, watched with dubious delight and a cowardly prudence, the angular forms of the dead lying upon the flinty plain. But, as the heat currents moved the air, these Ishmaelites of the desert, with joyous howls of delight, closed down for a wrangle over the ghastly spoils of the "land of gold and blood!"

There was a wild-eyed woman madly urging on an exhausted steed, as the limits of Fort Huachuca reservation were passed at last! Pepita, with a fearful fascination, had glanced at the flying pony coming in on the southern quarter, to cut her off from the reservation road. The great roan forged on feebly now, but his resolute shoulders were plunging bravely on, as he drew up his hind legs wearily in his frantic terror. For the blooded steed scented the coming Indian, and the bushy black head, crouching on the withers of the Apache's stolen horse, was a horrid menace of death and torture. The ferocious warrior had craftily cut his saddle away, and even thrown aside his gun. In his hand a revolver was clutched, as he raced madly on, the catskin quiver gleaming on his bare, red shoulder. There was the glare of a line of white tents looming up beyond the bushes. Pepita then drew from her bosom a poinard, and drove it into the flying horse's neck. The steed reared madly, and sprang onward in a fresh terror, as the Indian, crouching on his pony's back, now sent arrow after arrow, whizzing after the hotly pursued woman. As they swept out of the fringing bushes, in sight of the camp, the Apache wheeled his pony and darted back into the cover of the mosquito scrub. Flinging himself into the nearest arroyo, he skulked away through the deepening gully, to hide like a wild beast, in the nearest hole, until the shades of night would cover his retreat to the Eastern spurs of Huachuca range. The coward had feared to use his revolver, lest the guard should close in upon him!

Private Doyle of the Fifth Cavalry brought down his carbine, with a wild yell of "Halt! *Halt!* HALT!" as Pepita tore past him, racing on toward the guard tents, the great red roan staggering and throwing his weary head from side to side. *"Howly God! 'tis a woman!"* he cried, as he fired his gun in the air, screaming, *"Corporal of the Garrud! Number wan!"*

Her wild scream, *"Indios! Indios!"* turned out the whole startled guard, and a stout sergeant clasped her fainting form, as a dozen strong arms aided her descent. The bugle call, "Boots and Saddles," rang out in a wild wail, as Pepita tore aside the bosom of her dress. There was blood upon her trembling hand, as she held out the letter. *"Save Juan! Ride! Ride!"* she gasped. *"The Grizzly's Cave! To McLaughlin's Peak! Indios! Ladrones!"* Lieut. Tom Guilfoyle held her head, as she sank slowly to the ground. *"The Surgeon! Quick! Quick! She is dying,"* yelled the officer, as the line of men in blue and yellow began to form up. The brave red roan, with glazed eyes and heaving flank, dropped his head to the hand reached forth to caress the gallant animal. *"The horse is wounded in the shoulder, Lieutenant! Indians, sure!"* cried a trooper, and then Captain Armistead turned to the forming squadron, as he read the blood-stained lines, *"One platoon off to McLaughlin's Peak! Ride for life and death!*

"Here's your own horse, Guilfoyle! You go in command," said the bronzed captain. *"Spare nothing! I'll send an ambulance on* after you. *Take this letter."* The rattle of Guilfoyle's saber, as he sprang on his horse, awakened the dying woman.

"Ride!" she cried. *"Tell Juan I died for him—so happy! Ride! Ah! Madre de Dios!"* There was the sigh of a parting spirit as the Mexican girl's had fell back. Tom Guilfoyle was five hundred yards away, following his troops as Surgeon Dewitt turned his grave face to the commanding officer. *"An arrow buried in her right side, Captain, and nothing but the rattlesnake poison of the envenomed head did the work.* Look to your camp. This woman was wounded, so near our lines that they feared to use the rifle or revolver. This poison kills in half an hour!"

"Double the guard! Hold all the troops ready, Anson!" briefly ordered the Captain, as the officer of the day came clanking up.

"*Take her to the hospital, Dewitt,*" sighed the Commander. "*Can you do nothing? She has been very beautiful!* And spoke broken English! Some traveling party of the better class of Mexicans has been cut off!"

"*Ah! There's nothing left here for me to do,*" sighed the surgeon. "These fiends soak their arrow heads in the poison of the summer-bloated snakes. It always kills in twenty minutes, *when the arrow cuts a vein or artery.* See! Poor child! *Her hands are even now turning black!*"

And the platoon, led by Lieutenant Guilfoyle, was half way to McLaughlin's Peak before the alarmed pickets came back from scouring the lines of the reservation. There was an unwonted vigilance in every corner of the camp. But no sign of the thievish, devil-hearted foe was found. By the side of the dead girl, who lay now with her slender hands crossed on her breast clasping a crucifix, sat Armistead with his fair-faced wife.

"*It is a strange, strange case!* Followed probably for robbery and murder!" sighed Doctor Dewitt. "Here is the package of five thousand dollars, in large bills, which the Sergeant's wife found upon her! Rustlers, thieves, deserters, and renegade Apaches, I suppose! But, Tom Guilfoyle will make quick work of the gang *if he gets there in time!*"

And there, beside the body of the murdered wife, who had died almost in the moment of her gallantly earned victory, the three prayed that the last despairing cry of Pepita—a prayer, a benison, and a blessing —might avail to save the doomed men! The platoon was pricking briskly over the mèsa westward.

Lieutenant Tom Guilfoyle called up around him the dozen men of the platoon who were leading when the sun began to sink over McLaughlin's Peak. Twenty of the platoon were straggling along a mile behind.

"*Here, Sergeant!*" he cried. "Leave one good man here, *with the slowest horses.* Give *me* the six lightest men and the freshest horses. *Off with all the saddles!* Nothing goes but the carbines, belts, and canteens. The ambulance can bring the saddles on later. Let the man build a fire. You lead on the rest of the command as rapidly as you can. The ambulance will pick the man up."

His own saddle was the first on the ground, and Guilfoyle then tossed away his useless saber.

"*Now, men, not a horse's nose in front of mine! Come on!*" and the seven avengers dashed away, while the grizzled Sergeant O'Brien forced the remainder steadily along at the height of safety speed.

"*I hope to God the Lieutenant has enough men,*" he groaned. "'Twas the way poor Cushing died—the same headlong bravery. He's a dead game boy, though, and *he will have his way.*"

And Tom Guilfoyle's troopers dashed on like the wind after the brave leader, riding pistol in hand now.

In the noisome Grizzly's cave, Jack Powning, at bay, waited for the last rush which he now feared every moment.

"*Can you hear anything ?*" whispered Leigh, in a hopeless voice. "I know that our messengers have failed. It is six o'clock. *I rang my repeater just now!*"

"*Then, God have mercy on our souls,*" slowly said Powning. "*They have some scheme, but what it is I can't——*"

Arizona Jack was hurled back, as a violent explosion tore away half the front of the stone barricade.

"*Dynamite, my God!*" yelled Jack. "*Now, Cyril, now !*" he screamed, as a half dozen heads appeared swarming over the crest of the debris.

There was the sound of panther-like yells as the Winchesters rang out, and the crowding assailants were baffled by the bodies of the two horses blocking the norrow cleft.

"*Get in, get in—go ahead, you damned cowards !*" yelled Bill Murfee, his voice ending in a scream of dying agony, for Arizona Jack, throwing down his rifle, with a pistol in each hand, now poured in a lightning volley of shots at half range. And then, as Leigh had fired the last round in his rifle magazine, suddenly rose on the evening air the shrill ringing wail of the cavalry bugle, almost under their ghastly blocked archway!

"*The cavalry !*" screamed Arizona Jack, as he

slowly toppled over the dead horse, and, his grasp relaxing, rolled down upon the floor at Cyril Leigh's feet. There was no frantic wretch now thrusting an arm over the shattered defense, for down in the canyon below the carbines were cracking, and Cyril Leigh, lion-hearted, stood, pistol in hand, blocking the pathway to friend and foeman.

"*No thoroughfare! I tell you, again, no thoroughfare!*" moaned Arizona Jack, as he twisted over and feebly tried to rise. "*They've done for me, Cyril! Save yourself! Get out of this deadly country! Trust no one—not one!*"

The young squire listened in the darkness as the bugle now rang out joyously at the very entrance of the cave. A manly voice cried out, "*Here we are, friends! The cavalry!*

"*Come in, someone,*" shouted Leigh. "*They've killed him!*"

It was Tom Guilfoyle himself who clambered over the dead horses and first grasped Leigh's cold hand. "*I'm Lieutenant Guilfoyle, United States Army,*" hurriedly said the explorer. "*Who are you?*"

"*Cyril Leigh of England,*" faltered the exhausted boy, "*and they've killed my friend, Jack Powning.*"

Guilfoyle struck a match. "*He's only fainted. His shoulder is smashed, that's all.* We'll have an ambulance here soon." Then turning to the cave's mouth he shouted, "Build a good fire out there. Come in and clear the way so as to get out. *Who's got any whisky?*"

And then, private Patsy Casey, who had been the first in the fight in the canyon, mutely unslung his canteen.

"*Get all the whisky into him you can,* Casey," said the officer, after he forced Leigh to swallow a few mouthfuls.

"*The woman, that brave woman?*" said Cyril, as the men propped up Jack Powning's head.

"*Died at the guard tent, wounded by a poisoned arrow, almost in our very camp.*"

"And, *Pablo, the man who went with her?*"

"*They must have murdered him,*" said the officer.

"But, I know we killed four, and *there are seven dead bodies lying out here!"*

CHAPTER XII.

THE TALKING WIRE.

CYRIL LEIGH heard the words of the young officer, and his nerve gave way at last. He sobbed like a child. *"They died for us! Poor girl! This will drive him mad."*

"Rest here and watch over him." kindly said Guilfoyle. "You had better make ready to leave the cave. I must now give my orders, and find out the whole state of affairs. The surgeon will be here with the ambulance in a couple of hours. *Tell me what has happened!"*

Sergeant O'Brien was busied with a couple of handy men in examining the wounded man. A fire now lit up the interior of the cave, the troopers having dragged away the dead horses. The larger boulders had been rolled away, and five dejected captive ruffians were herded in the rear of the cave, by a couple of sentinels.

They were morosely silent as the Englishman answered : *"We were attacked by Indians and ruffians at Miller's Station.* I was on my way to the railroad at Elgin. My friend sent off the Mexican girl and a vaquero named Pablo to summon help, while we defended ourselves here. *That's all I know!"*

Tom Guilfoyle conferred in low tones with his sergeant.

"Now, if you have him bound up as well as you can, I'll lay out your work, Sergeant," said the smart, soldierly Lieutenant. *"There's no fight left in any one around here!* You take five of the weakest horses and the men who are most knocked up. *Set off at once for the fort!* Pass by Miller's Station. Get the whole story from the woman there. Old Miller is always drunk. Report to the officer of the day that I'll be back before sundown to-morrow. If a party search between the fort and the north spur of the Huachuca Range I think the buzzards will tell you where the poor vaquero lies! Take a man down to the mouth of the canyon to guide Doctor Dewitt up here. Tell him Captain Powning has a bad gunshot wound of the right shoulder. It's all smashed. He'll never hold a rifle up again."

Sergeant O'Brien gazed in wonder at his commanding officer.

"*Captain Powning, is it?* Shure, *this man's no other than 'Arizona Jack.'* I knew him for a deadly gun fighter, *when I was in the 'Third,'* at Fort Wingate, New Mexico, and *a hell of a man to run up against! There's the mark of his hand outside, Lieutenant,*" whispered the sergeant, lowering his voice. "*Seven fellows laid out stiff. This boy never did that work!*"

"Go ahead. I'll question the prisoners and set a guard here. Tell Doctor Dewitt to hurry. Say nothing about *who* this man is. Remember," sternly said Guilfoyle.

Cyril Leigh laid his hand on the officer's arm.

"*Lieutenant!*" said he. "I wish you to take us over to the fort. I can only explain to your post commander. I know too well that the so-called civil authorities will demand us that this gallant man would be butchered and I would be 'lynched,' if we ever fell into the hands of a posse. I alone know what has been behind this outrage. Think of that poor dead girl and the brave vaquero. The Indians were set on to do this work, but we were a little too much for them. I claim the protection of the British Legation and Her Majesty's Consul General at New York. As for my friend, *Arizona Jack or not,* he is Captain John Powning, of Powning Hall, Yorkshire, and late of the Twenty-seventh Hussars. He, too, is a British subject, and I will live and die *sharing his fate!*"

"I can understand all but Bill Murfee, *the Condor Superintendent,* being found dead here. The others are a damned bad lot, dead and alive," slowly replied Guilfoyle. "*You've 'done the State some service,'* as Shakespeare says. You had better get out of Arizona by Nogales. Get down to Guaymas and take the steamer on to New York, or from Panama, to London.

You would stand a 'slim show' in the hands of 'frontier justice,' Squire Leigh. *Depend on me. You are safe* now. Can I do anything for you?"

"*Yes*," cried Leigh. "Send an intelligent man on the gallop to Elgin. Send your own dispatch to the telegraph office at Tucson to repeat all my messages now lying there to Fort Huachuca. *Can I telegraph from there?*"

"*Yes*," said Guilfoyle, "over our own military line to Huachuca Station."

"Then, *all is well!*" thankfully sighed Leigh. "I can verify all my statements. In the meantime, I charge you, on a soldier's honor, to keep our names secret. I will write a cable dispatch. *I've plenty of money!*"

"Get the dispatch ready. The man will leave at once. *I'll keep this thing quiet*," said the officer. "There were a few Indians who scuttled away, hiding in the rocks. They won't talk. The other marauders, dead or alive, are all here."

"*Yes*, and the dirty coward who planned our murder is to be held scathless, I suppose, by 'frontier justice,'" bitterly said Cyril, as he hastily scooped his papers out of their hiding place.

"I dare not break the seal of the past—*not till he bids me!*" murmured Leigh, gazing at Jack Powning lying there at his feet moaning under the growing fever of his wound. He wrote the address of his guardian angel at Leigh Hurst, and then thought long over each word. "That will do!" he grimly said, as he read the lines. "It's plain enough, anyways."

Treachery here. Property very valuable. Title all safe. Been attacked. Safe now with Government troops. Will answer your messages from Fort Huachuca. Next address, Guaymas, Mexico, care British Consul. Am coming home. Will wait your advices, first.

The mounted trooper was waiting at the cave's entrance when Lieutenant Guilfoyle returned from a parley with the five prisoners. His face was very grave. "These men claim that Miller's station was attacked by horsethieves, and that Murfee, returning to the mine, followed on the trail, attacking your traveling party, imagining you to be the thieves. One friendly Indian, 'Lame Wolf,' and Lem White, the Condor Company's assistant foreman, were killed at the station. *What do you know of this?*"

"*Nothing!*" firmly said Leigh. "I was aided to escape from trouble by my friend, and was on my way to Elgin to go up to Tucson, when we were attacked here. Captain Powning thought the band to be some escaped reservation Indians on a raid across into Sonora."

Gulfoyle thoughtfully studied for a few moments in silence. "I'll have all my men examine the seven dead men. *There will be a fearful row kicked up about this!*" In a few minutes he returned. "*There's another respectable* citizen lying dead out there! Big Jim Willetts, the freighter, is a corpse. *It was a fearful misadventure.*"

"They knew their business. They blew away our barricade with dynamite," stoutly replied Cyril Leigh. "Whatever they claim to have thought, their real object was *murder!*" And then and there, he made a vow to make no reference to the Condor mine. "There's only that traitor spy, 'Arthur Lemon,' and Blum, and I who know the real secret. Even poor Jack knows little as yet. I will wait *for the enemy's story!*" He coldly stated, "*I shall telegraph to the British Minister, through your commanding officer* and *demand that an attaché be sent here to insure our safety.*"

"*Don't mistake me!* Squire Leigh," cordially cried the officer. "I'll answer for your safety with the last drop of blood in my command. *As for the future*, take my advice. *Keep your private affairs to yourself.* Get out by Nogales *as soon as possible.* You will find that Armistead will send you down with an escort. In a week your friend can be moved. He is a giant in physique, and a peerless specimen of a man."

"*Thanks!*" answered the Englishman. "I will certify to Powning's real rank and standing; how he came here is his own business."

"*Right you are,*" laughed Tom Guilfoyle. "I've had an Austrian count, a German baron, a French marquis, and a lord's younger son—all in our regiment as common troopers at the same time. *Picturesque devils too!* A trooper's jacket covers many strange secrets, out here in the trackless West. Hello! *There's Dewitt!*" cried the officer, as a cheery hail rang out down the glen.

In a couple of hours the relaxed nerves of the perplexed Briton gave way, and he slept like a log, lying on a trooper's blanket, while grave Doctor Dewitt and the untiring lieutenant made plans for the homeward march. The lonely owl screamed to its mate in the rocky pinnacles above them, the gray wolf's howl rose from the glen by the cave, and the chattering coyotes snarled in chorus on the moonlit desert sands below!

A trooper watched over the ghastly line of seven motionless figures, while the moonbeams glistened on the carbine barrel of the sentinel watching over the cave where the five "rustlers" were hobbled within like Indian ponies.

"I suppose, Dewitt, we had better leave a corporal and three or four men here, till the wagon comes out to bring in all the evidence of "Mr. Arizona Jack's" wicked shooting. It's a desperate thing to run up against a nervy man well posted!"

"I fear that these poor devils will never express their opinion," said Dewitt, thoughtfully knocking the ashes out of his pipe and gazing at the nameless dead. "*Let us turn in*, for *Powning* or *Jack*, or *whoever* he is, will be raving by morning. He is burning now with the coming fever."

And so, friend and foe slept under the eyes of the watchful sentinels till the bugle roused them for the homeward march. With rare delicacy, Guilfoyle asked no further questions, but led the advance, with Leigh mounted on a captured horse.

"All your property will be brought in in the ambulance of the Condor Company. We will trace out the whole story when all our scouts get back."

Doctor Dewitt followed the advance guard with his patient strapped down in the ambulance, for bold Jack Powning was again fighting his foes in his fevered ravings.

"I wonder if one man in five who takes to the plains

ever has a legal right to his local name?" mused the surgeon, whose face grew tender as Jack cried: "*Adios! Adios, mi querida!*"

"A strange life-history; this man's whole appearance shows good blood. Probably a moral castaway—'*a mauvais sujet.*'"

But the good doctor listened only with his "professional ear," and the sick man's revelations were merged in the countless strange memories of an army surgeon on the frontier.

And they wound homewards over the lonely mèsas.

It was night when the cavalcade drew slowly into the unpretentious military cantonment of Fort Huachuca. Captain Armistead stood at the door of the Post Hospital where Lieutenant Guilfoyle dismissed his men, and asked what disposition he should make of Cyril Leigh.

"*You will be Dr. Dewitt's guest,*" soberly said the commanding officer, "and on parole of honor, not to leave the Military Reservation. In fact, I have had a dispatch from Tucson that the sheriffs of Pima and Cochise counties will be here to demand both of you. So your safety lies within these lines. I will send all your telegrams over to you, and Lieutenant Guilfoyle will afford you all facilities to communicate with your friends. When I am ready to see you I will send him for you."

"It is strange," firmly said Leigh, "that such quick action was taken. Some one of the fleeing miscreants must have telegraphed the news to interested parties."

"It is rather strange, Squire Leigh," said Armistead, "but out on the frontier you soon cease to wonder at anything. I will send down to the Condor mine and have all your luggage delivered to you here, *at once.*"

Cyril Leigh stood beside the bodies of Pepita Morales and the undefeated Pablo. The girl-wife's face was marvelously beautiful, while the grim vaquero's countenance was still set in his last defiance of the grizzly foe.

"*He was a regular bravo,*" said Surgeon Dewitt. "They found three Indians dead within a hundred yards of him, and his hands had to be pried open, for he clutched the nearest foe in a death grasp. *They never lived to take his scalp.* You see, he died victorious!"

Cyril Leigh led the surgeon aside.

"*I will be responsible for all.* Let this man have decent Christian burial—the best that may be had. As you say I may not see Powning, *I will ask but one favor.* This brave girl's mother lives at Magdalena, Sonora, where her dead father was Jéfe Politico. She must be conveyed there for burial, and this man who saved my life must look again on the face of the wife who died for him—*the woman who saved both our lives.*"

"*I understand,*" said the surgeon. "*And, I will see the commander.*"

"There is one thing *more,*" cried Cyril. " I wish that horse that she rode to be treated *as a prince among horses,* for I will ride him in the Yorkshire valleys if I live to see old England *again.* *He shall not be forgotten !*"

Before the stars sank to the west, Cyril Leigh, in his room had read over the dozen warning telegrams forwarded from Tucson. They were accompanied by one addressed to the Commanding officer," signed British Consul General, New York City, begging him to afford all aid and protection to Cyril Leigh, of Leigh Hurst, traveling under the name of Robert Ross. A similar dispatch from the British Minister at Washington, and the British Consul at Guaymas, caused Lieutenant Guilfoyle to say, frankly: "*It seems very strange* that all these open telegrams contemplated some trouble in your case. Captain Armistead must confer with you to-morrow early, for the sheriff's posse is on its way *here.*"

" I think I can see the drift of the whole thing *now,*" grimly said Leigh. "I will let the light of day shine in upon the affair *very soon.*"

It was midnight before the young men separated. Cyril knew the whole story of the prairie record of Pablo's fight to the death, the capture of the four Apaches' horses, the brief relation of the sad-eyed drudge at Miller's station, and the reports of all the scouts. "By to-morrow night, the dead and the prisoners will all be here, and the Grizzly's cave will be ready to receive its future passing guests. But, I advise you to *write no letters*. Trust to the commander. Use his telegraph *only* and *keep silent*."

The little room in the whitewashed hospital ward seemed a palace to the rescued tourist, who drifted away into dreams wherein Lisbeth's loving face leaned over him in blessing, when Doctor Dewitt made his last report. "Your friend is getting on all right. You can move him in a week. *Better take him back to England!* He'll never lift a gun again. And—he would not live ten minutes if he were to fall into the hands of the gang that's now coming down."

When morning came, Cyril Leigh was awakened by the ringing bugles of reveillé. His frame was racked and stiffened, and, only one thought possessed him. "Lisbeth has no longer any fears. But—if I could only trap 'Lemon' at El Paso."

He pondered over the method while at his cheerful breakfast, but he did not know that "Mr. Arthur Lemon" had already sped away, northward, from El Paso. A telegram from the disheartened Morris Blum reached him with vague news of the disaster. Dalman had used his long days of weary waiting in corrupting the easily tempted José.

Faro and mescal were José's cardinal weaknesses, and leaving his heavier baggage to be sent on by the hotel, Moses Dalman leaped aboard the east-bound train while José disported himself gayly at a fandango across the muddy tortuous stream of the Rio Grande.

"*Damn them all!* I hold them in the hollow of my hand. They shall pay for my knowledge now," growled the lawyer, as he dashed off a telegram to Isidor Blum. "*There! I think the fat-witted fool will understand that!*" he said. The words were explicit:

"Resident partner has ruined all. Your other associates have betrayed you. Legal fight alone will save you. *Do nothing till I come.* Guard absolute silence. Address: *St. Charles Hotel, New Orleans.* On my way home."

"I am the only human being who knows that the power of attorney to Walter Ryley *was never recorded!* I shall milk them all of a big golden fee. I will demand ha.. of the interest which they have failed to save. And Mr. *Arizona Jack, damn him, lies buried under the walls of the cave.   That settles his title forever !*"

Moses Dalman breathed freer and freer as every mile of the track receded, and he welcomed the gloomy moss-hung cypresses of the Louisiana bayous, as he neared New Orleans.   "*Bah !*" he laughed, " I can telegraph from here to my office my return from a trip to Denver.   I register under my own name, and once in New York City, I can defy the devil himself.   No one knows where I have been."   The acute scoundrel, laughing at the helplessness of his intended dupes, would have been disturbed, as he luxuriously dined at the St. Charles, if he had seen the official dispatch of the Chief of Police, in Chicago, to the commanding officer of the United States troops at Fort Huachuca.   " No such person as 'Arthur Lemon' known here in reputable circles.   No such member of Stock or Mining Exchange."

The garrison annals of Fort Huachuca never chronicled such a state of fiery excitement as when a mob of fifty "prominent citizens" were herded at the guard tents by a doubled guard, under the watchful Lieutenant Anson, while the commanding officer spent a long day in interrogating Leigh, Dewitt, Guilfoyle, and Sergeant O'Brien.   Even the five prisoners were, one by one, passed before the stern review of the old veteran captain's eyes!   When the main inquest was over, a last half hour's conference with Cyril Leigh, prepared Captain Armistead for a perfunctory interview with the disgruntled Sheriffs of Pima and Cochise counties. Armistead had busied his Post-adjutant, Guilfoyle, with telegrams that wearied even the " talking-wire," and the department commander had "deigned to reply."

Cyril Leigh happily watched the protecting flag lazily floating on the parade, and then his eye wandered away to the grim bastions of the uplifted Huachuca mountains, where his sister's buried fortune lay hidden.   It was hers now, by the added title of the innocent bloodshed to regain its possession and to defend Lisbeth Leigh's lost dowry.

"*You'll not turn us over to that brutal mob, Captain ?*"

said the Englishman. "Let me face any United States authorities, but a frontier mob, *never!* There is much that I could tell you, but my legal rights will now be handled through Her Majesty's Legation."

"*My dear boy!*" said the gray-haired commander, "*Officially, I can say nothing. Personally*, I don't think you will have any cause to complain. *I am just going to put you out of the United States of America in good style*, as soon as your friend can travel, and I'll send Guilfoyle and ten men down to ˙Magdalena *with you.* I will telegraph to the Mexican commander at Hermosillo to send an escort up there, and you and that king-of-snap-shots, your friend 'Arizona Jack,' will be duly receipted for, in good order, at Guaymas, by the British Consul."

"*May God reward you!*" cried Leigh, impulsively, seizing the veteran's hand.

"I have heard officially from the Secretary of War, and the British Legation, as well as General Rankanfile, our Department Commander. Your statements have been verified, and I wish you would be my guest at dinner *daily*, while here. I hope to show you that all Americans are not thieves and robbers. I can discern the drift of all these past 'accidental happenings.' I know the gang here, but I have to keep silent," he sighed.

The two hours' animated séance of the commander and the sheriff ended in the application of the "*fortiter in re!*"

Armistead himself, at sundown, watched the angry mob file away toward the Condor Mine, bearing off the bodies of the slain assailants as the only fruits of their official raid.

The stalwart appearance of the four paraded platoons of Armistead's famous squadron of the "Fifth," impressed the furious posse with the necessity of bridling their wrath, and, their feet were soon beautiful on the mountains. The guarded assurances of Armistead that the whole affair would be carefully reported "*through the usual channels*," was duly conveyed to that maddened capitalist, Morris Blum, who was now engaged in choosing a new foreman for the mine.   The fact that his destined prey had escaped him, was emphasized by the flood of incoming telegrams from the wily old Bent at New York—and even Senator Stone at San Francisco.   For the affair at the Condor mine had been noised abroad, and, hideously distorted, reached, finally that fifty millions of Americans who live upon the lurid telegrams of the "journals of civilization."   A family blessing in the shape of a dispatch from Isidor Blum added oil to Morris's blazing wrath.   It was what is profanely called "*a hummer!*"

"*You have been a fool!   Do nothing.   Coming on myself*," and the bottled wrath of the "man who ran the whole of Tucson," blazed out when his future telegrams to Moses Dalman were treated with a contemptuous silence.   *It was his Waterloo campaign!*

In the little hospital at Huachuca, Cyril Leigh now waited on watch at his wounded friend's bedside.   The days gliding by found him there untiring in his devotion.   Surgeon Dewitt was now all ready for the sad home-coming of Pepita Morales, and Lieutenant Guilfoyle had selected his troops and transportation.   In their brief rides around the reservation, the two young men had grown to be brotherly, for the big red roan was now rebaptized as "Pablo," and daily grew to know Cyril Leigh's guiding hand.   Cyril Leigh's own heart was calm and tranquil.   He had leaped into a stern manhood with a bound.   He had warned his delighted sister to await his arrival at Guaymas, and the arrival of Andy Faxon, the teamster from Bisbee, placed in his possession the five cans of tell-tale golden borings of the diamond drill, as well as his own surrendered luggage.   A long day spent in conference with the honest freighter gave Cyril Leigh the knowledge that a liable friend would watch the buried treasures of the Condor.

"I'll leave you money—*all that you need*.   It's worth a hundred dollars a month to you, Andy," said Leigh, "to ride up there every two weeks and just see that the mines are *still full of water*.   All that you have to do is to telegraph to the British Consul at Guaymas if they begin to work at the mine.   *Now, my side of the fun begins!*   I will make them wish that they had never waylaid me."

The safe arrival in New Orleans of the two witnesses was verified through Andy, and the watcher knew, at last, that the two miners' depositions were in the hands of the British Consul at New Orleans. There was only the wounded man to wait for now.

Leaning over Jack's bed, Cyril Leigh listened, in reverence, to his sister's name falling from the sufferer's lips. For Jack Powning's mind had wandered away back to the fragrant hay-strewn meadows of Nidderdale, and the Master of Leigh grew pale and tenderly sad at heart as he listened. "The burden of an old sorrow. The sad memories of a broken life. I must 'respect the burden' on this man's darkened soul." In vain, Cyril repeated the old refrain, "Tout passe, tout lasse, tout casse!" The wounded man's heart had called her back again—the loving girl who had wandered with him under the oaks of Leigh. "Their sorrow is sacred. None but Lisbeth shall break the seal of the past," mused Leigh, and yet, he yearned to know of what past misery the dark shadow still lay floating on the troubled life stream of Jack Powning's gallant heart. Gazing down at the wasted frame, ravaged by fever, watching the silver threads woven on his comrade's temples, Cyril Leigh bowed his head. "He has paid the price. I will leave him alone with his sorrow—*for Lisbeth's sake!*"

He had wandered away one evening to watch the sunset glow fade away upon the rugged outlines of McLaughlin's Peak, the sun-god sinking in flaming gold and crimson toward the far blue Pacific, when the soldier nurse called him back in the tranquil evening hour. "*He is asking for you, and, the fever has left him!*"

Leigh strode swiftly to the bedside of the man who had stood between him and a horrible death.

"*We stood 'em off for all we were worth!*" feebly whispered Jack. "*How did I get here? Where's Pepita? Bring her to me! Call her! For she rode straight! God bless her! Yes! That's the bugle! They're coming now! 'Tis the cavalry!*" And then, his tired eyelids closed, and he slept like a little child, clinging to the hand of the man who feared the burden of the tale that must be told.   For, *Pepita's* light step would wake his slumbers no more!

In the surgeon's quarters that evening, the squadron commander sat late in a council with Surgeon Dewitt and Squire Leigh.

"You say that he will awake much stronger and refreshed to-morrow, Dewitt?" seriously demanded Captain Armistead, stroking his grizzled beard.   "I wish to move him over the frontier now *as soon as possible.* I am afraid of a 'habeas corpus.'   These fellows went away very ugly!   You are all right, Squire Leigh, but far safer over the border.   Your fighting friend is another matter, *he has some old matters to answer for*, that is, *if he's really the man they claim he is.*"

Surgeon Dewitt mused a few moments.   "Of course I can get him away in a day or so now, I only fear the reaction of learning how his wife died.   *Some one must tell him !*   I could give him opiates and get him over the line to Magdalena.   He could be told there."

"*That's the very scheme!*   I'll have the escort and transportation ready and you can go on to Magdalena in charge, Dewitt, so Guilfoyle, that young mad cap, will have company."   The surgeon's steady eyes rested on his commander's face.   "Armistead, we are both family men.   Don't you think Arizona Jack should have a chance to look once more on the face of the woman who died for him ?   *You are a husband and a father. Some one must tell him !*"   Armistead glanced at Cyril Leigh.

"*I can not,*" simply answered the young Briton with a choking sensation, as he turned his head away.

"*Then you must,* Dewitt, *I haven't the heart,*" shortly said Armistead.   "I want the whole party away as soon as possible.   *I can protect you now.*   I know from the statement of Miller's wife that the station was raided, and that your party were peaceful.   *I well know that the five thousand dollars in currency* which the poor girl hid in her breast, was the bait for the robbers.   Some one had evidently followed your party, and you, Leigh, were supposed to have funds to purchase a mine.   *Now is the time to get you all away.*   Doctor! *I will have all ready at noon to-morrow.*   You can make Miller's station to-morrow, stop at Washington the next day, and the third night strike Nogales. You shall go in command."

"*So, Squire Leigh,*" said Armistead, rising, "all I wish is to say 'Good-bye' and 'God Speed!' *I'll come over at noon!* Not a word of your destination to a soul! My officers shall be silent about Powning's identity. The escort will imagine that you go to Elgin, to go north. There's no telegraph at the little frontier town Washington. It's a pretty decent Arizona settlement. You'll be soon over the border, and, all your dispatches will be sent on to Magdalena and Guaymas. You can use the wire direct to me here. Your first letter to Europe probably escaped their notice. Any others you can write to-night. I will send them on to Tombstone before midnight by an express rider. I will send them and direct to the army headquarters building, New York City; they will instantly be mailed. They go under my own military seal."

"*Pardon me,*" queried Leigh. "Why can we not get aboard the railroad at Bisbee or Tombstone? They are only a half day's and one day's march away."

The squadron commander laughed grimly, "Because the mob, the posse, and the civil authorities would all be up in arms, and as your friend 'Arizona Jack' cannot shoot for himself, Tommy Guilfoyle would have to fight his way through these towns with his blue-coat troopers. You would have to run north to Fairbank, and then down to Nogales. County officials, deputy United States marshals, and others would lay hold of you both, for on your appearance at Tombstone or Bisbee, the roughs and villains would telegraph on to Benson and Tucson. 'Fighting Guilfoyle' would soon have a few indictments hanging over his head for murder! No, my dear boy, you have not yet developed all your mysterious enemies. That gallant girl nobly laid down her life for you! Pablo's desperate stand made this sacrifice of love an availing one, and my advice and directions to you are to get out, *by Nogales!* For I have given orders to Guilfoyle, if you are annoyed to get over the border *at once,* by San Juan, and then strike down through the Sierras of Sonora by the Antunez mountains to Magdalena. No one knows *where* you will cross the border, our troopers will protect you up *to the line* and *once over*, the Hermosillo commander will guard you, as an international courtesy."

"I will bring you my one letter in half an hour," answered Cyril Leigh. "I see that our lives are safe only while in your hands."

The two seniors watched Leigh's exit. Surgeon De-witt's eyes were moist as he shook his commander's hand. "You are risking your commission, Armistead, to do this. God bless you. They had 'put up a cold deck' on this brave, high-spirited boy, and, for once, 'a bad man from Bitter Creek' did some of God's own work *with the shooting irons!* Leigh is so constitution-ally cool and brave that he has not flurried under his trials. Now *I'll do as you wish.* I must give Arizona Jack a chance to see his wife's face. I've learned that she was the daughter of a fine old family down there. There will be no chance after we leave here, for I've done the best I could. *I will keep him up.* To-morrow a little opium will ease him along to the border. *Some-times a blessing, sometimes a curse,* is the king of pain, the poppy's gift. You fighting men lay heavy burdens on us doctors! This poor human waif will take it pretty hard. He is probably alone in the world. Playing a strong 'lone hand' against 'tough luck.' I've re-gretted I did not go into the line of battle instead of the medical staff. It's always the doctor who has to face these things that you real warriors dread! Last year you made me tell poor Thurston to say 'Good-bye' forever to his lily-faced wife when she went East, under the dread secret sentence of heart disease. And Jack Campbell's mother, when she arrived here, *an hour too late,* from Philadelphia! It was *I* who must lead her to the bedside when the only son's last word '*Mother!*' was *still ringing in my ears!*"

"Look here, Dewitt! *You're doubly a hero!*" warmly said Armistead. "Didn't I see you carrying water to the wounded down at Cibicu Canyon, when you were a mark for fifty Apache rifles?"

"Well! That was not 'professional,' *I admit!*" mod-estly replied the surgeon, as he rose to visit his patient.

"*We'll be on hand*, and you do well to send us off, Armistead. These two men would be 'lynched' if these 'prominent citizens' ever get them '*under their control*,' as the journals meekly say."

The train and escort were ready on the parade ground of Camp Huachuca, when Surgeon Dewitt, aided by his hospital steward, supported Jack Powning, as he hobbled into the darkened room where Mrs. Armistead sat by the dead girl's coffin. A motherly-looking woman was Mrs. Sergeant O'Brien, who met the "Commander's lady," here in the all-leveling presence of Death ! Arizona Jack never knew that every struggling, cherished flower of Officer's Row—and the "married men's quarters" had been culled by these diverse representatives of that suffering sex—ever "first at the altar, and last at the tomb." Mary O'Brien's fingers were busy with her rosary—but she could not see the blessed beads for her tears, as she listened to the sobs of the Commander's wife. For Jack Powning, strong in adversity, defiant in the eyes of death—was helpless as a child when he sank into a chair. The mute appeal of his eyes touched Mrs. Armistead's heart, for her gentle hands severed a tress of the silken hair, and she folded the white veil over the silent face whose waxen loveliness thrilled these chastened hearts. And, Jack Powning had kissed the pale lips, and his tears fell upon those slender hands folded in death, as he cried in the anguish of a strong man's soul. "*Adios ! Pepita ! Adios, mi querida !*"

Dewitt silently touched his arm, and they led the man, blinded by his sorrow, back to his lonely room. When the train drew out, past the sentry's beat, across which the dark-eyed girl had dashed in her whirlwind ride for life and succor, the flag hung at halfmast, and the whole garrison in escort turned back sadly, as the two ambulances and four wagons moved away over the sandy desert where Pablo's hero blood still cried for vengeance. Cyril Leigh lingered, an orderly holding the big red roan, who tossed his proud head as he saw the glancing ranks of the cavalry platoon receding.

Lieutenant Anson and the Post Commander heard Cyril Leigh's last words : "*The ocean may divide us, but we are brothers of the blood—after all !*"

It was then Leigh made the silent vow, as he rode smartly away, in the sweltering glare of the late July sun, which caused the "officer's mess," as well as the men's quarters, to think, at Christmas, that they had entertained an angel unawares! And, Sergeant and Mrs. O'Brien proudly treasured the token which was as loyally sent from Leigh Hurst, as well as the reminders for Anson—the Commander—glorious old Dewitt, and that pink of light cavalry Lieutenants, "Tom Guilfoyle!"

In the three days before the little command astounded the town of Nogales by marching through it over the Mexican border to Encima, without a single moment's halt, Leigh and Surgeon Dewitt had many quiet half-hours' chat as they watched over the slumbering man to whom the Surgeon had given the blessed "nepenthe." Long before the Mexican railway train sped into Magdalena, Post Commander Armistead knew from Guilfoyle's telegram that the two men in jeopardy were at last safely *over the border*. A telegram to the *Jefe Politico*, of Magdalena, had prepared all, and the two military escorts, with the whole "*gente de razon*" of Magdalena, accompanied the catafalque to the crumbling old yellow church where Pepita Morales had been baptized. Its jangling bronze bells, its quaint tower, its alcoved interior, spoke of the vanished Conquistadores and the zealot Padres who pushed north bearing the cross in defiance of the Yaqui's spears and the grim Apache's arrows. The wind-blown dust of the mailed cavaliers and the cowled priests of old had mingled for hundreds of years with the meaner clay of the wondering Aztecs and the stunted hill Indians who had hewn the rock and borne the burden when Nuestra Señora de Magdalena first was blessed with "bell, book, and candle." And hordes of black-shawled women knelt in silent watch through the last night, while the acolytes chanted the prayers for the dead. Pepita was "home at last, and home forever!"

Cyril Leigh and Surgeon Dewitt were joined by the British Vice-Consul at Guaymas as guests of the Jefe Politico, while Arizona Jack was guarded in the old

home of the Morales. The wrinkled dame with silvered hair, who wailed with "Señor Juan," wondered
at the flood of sudden wealth which had poured upon
her. Jack Powning, under the watchful eyes of the
hospital attendant, had told the brief story of the
tragedy which left them alone in the world. His gift
of the second five thousand dollars which was to be
the price of a crime, made the sorrowing mother the
financial princess of the little town. The simple words
"*Ladrones, Indios!*" explained the death of the beautiful woman still in her flower. For, in three hundred
years of rapine and blood feud, the Apaches and
Yaquis have taken a fearful revenge for the sins of the
guilty upon the innocent. The paths of Arizona and
Sonora have been watered with the blood of the traveler for a century, and the baleful watchfires of the
savage gleaming on the hills, carried horror to the
bosoms of the unprotected.

The Vice-Consul had instantly forwarded Cyril
Leigh's cable dispatch to his sister announcing his safe
escape from the bloody sands of Cochise County.

"*My orders are to personally escort you to Guaymas,*"
said the official. "*And with the twenty Mexican soldiers
given me, you may now dismiss your American escort!*
I presume that you wish to explain matters only to the
Consul in person?"

Then, for the first time, Cyril Leigh took thought of
the future of the Condor Mine, of Arizona Jack, and of
his stern necessity for prompt action. His blood
boiled at the memory of the crafty cowardice of the
schemers who had entrapped him.

"*If I act, it must be through others,*" he decided.
"My first duty is to get Jack Powning to a place of
safety. And *then—will he speak? What has he to tell
me?*"

But, Jack Powning was silently watching alone by
the dead girl's bier.

When the morning came, Cyril Leigh sadly watched
the last rites of the grand old church, whose history is
that of Christendom. With a swelling heart, he marked
Jack Powning feebly tottering to the seat, where the
shrouded figure of the silent mother sustained him and

grave Surgeon Dewitt guarded the convalescent's every movement.   The sad shrill chants of the acolytes, the unfamiliar incense, the candles gleaming before the silver-crowned virgin there, with outstretched arms of love, the deep tones of the Padre's voice, all bore Cyril Leigh's chastened thoughts far away from the present.   The ordeal of the last adieu was over at last! The long procession wound its way to the Campo Santo, while the four friends tenderly bore the wounded plainsman back to the residence of the Jefe Politico.

Already the special train for Guaymas was in waiting, and Tom Guilfoyle's troopers were mustered for the homeward run.   Surgeon Dewitt and the Mexican military doctor from Guaymas had inspected the last arrangements.   Jack Powning slept the sleep of a hopeless exhaustion.

"*There is only one thing for you to do,*" gravely urged the two American officers.   "*This man's whereabouts are known!   The Arizona scoundrels are not above assassinating him even here, in his helpless condition!   Only in the British consulate at Guaymas will he be safe!*   As for you, lose no time to get upon the Englishman's safest place—*the sea, under the Union Jack!*"

Cyril Leigh's cheek flushed when the Americans intimated that he should for safety go home by Panama.

"They might have you stopped and arrested if you went over to New York by the Central Pacific Railroad."

"I am now under the protection of the British Ministers at Washington and the City of Mexico," proudly said Leigh.   "*And, the hour of vengeance will come!* As for the man who has been crippled for life in my defense, his future *is a trust of honor to me.*"   The young squire's face was ashen pale as he said adieu to the mother of the woman who had died for him, but her grateful tears were mingled with his last good-byes as the Jefe Politico explained that the "English Lord" had left him a considerable sum of money to erect a monument over the grave of the dead Sonora beauty.

Padre Fernandez knew of the Briton's gratitude for the largess which made the old church ring for many a month with masses for the repose of the parted soul.

The whole official circle accompanied the wounded man to the train. Señora Morales knew that the man whose bounty had enriched her, would return to see the flowers blossom on the gallant girl's grave. It was the Jefe Politico who reminded her that she was now the richest woman in Magdalena. *"And I will take you down myself to Guaymas to see Señor Juan. For, he must rest in quiet. Està muy enfermo!"*

Jack Powning's feeble hand pressed the doctor's as he faltered a last "good-bye." And Tom Guilfoyle stood beside him as the train began to move. *"Doctor, you saved my life, which I owed already to Guilfoyle and his brave troopers! I'm alone in the world now, but life is not long enough for me to forget either of you."*

"You'll be pretty spry on your pins, old man," cheerily said Cyril Leigh, "if you get away from me. And *my house is yours as long as I've got a guinea!"*

It was Cyril who gave Surgeon Dewitt a little package as the train moved out with three cheers from the troopers, who had learned Leigh's liberal heart by their own entertainment. Neither Dewitt nor handsome Tom Guilfoyle ever knew, when they decided by lot, Arizona Jack's last memorial of a superb diamond ring and a glittering bosom-stud of great value, that the peerless "gun fighter" had won them as substantial tokens of a thirty-six-hour séance at the amusing but expensive game of poker. A young lady, who afterward joined the "Fifth Cavalry" as Mrs. Tom Guilfoyle, wore the reset ring, with great pride, as an evidence of her fighting husband's prowess, but the sober-faced Surgeon Dewitt only decorated himself with the diamond bosom-stud on Fourth of Julys and other most festive occasions!

It was a long two weeks before Arizona Jack was able to sit at his window in the British Consulate in Guaymas and watch the sapphire blue waters of the Gulf of California, his eye resting sadly on the Union Jack flying from the mizzen gaff of a huge steel four-master, loading wheat and hides for Liverpool.

"I can't make out, for the life of me, what's come over that man!" cried the hospitable consul, Mark Broadwood, to Cyril Leigh. *"His heart seems to have withered in his bosom!"*

"*It is so!*" gloomily, said Squire Leigh, who had daily reported by telegraph to Surgeon Dewitt at Fort Huachuca. He was now in possession of certain telegrams which contained the absolute mandate for his instant return, from the loving Lisbeth Leigh. There was a positive command to return *at once*, backed by Cornelia Powning's own signature. For Leigh Hurst, fair and splendid domain, now awaited its master in the peaceful Nidderdale, far from the bloody sway of frontier desperado and lying schemer.

"*How can I lie to them at home?*" mused Leigh. *For, both his sister Lisbeth and* the grateful Cornelia Powning demanded that he bring home with him that gallant saviour of his imperiled life, "*Arizona Jack.*" And Leigh's gloomy heart fell, for, to his entreaties, Jack Powning only answered by turning his wasted face to the wall.

"*Can it be that the bullet was also poisoned?*" mused the Squire, for Dewitt had told him of the hideous liquid made by the Apaches, in boiling the heads of the summer-bloated rattlesnakes. "They poison arrow-heads with this liquid fermented in the sun, *why not also, their bullets?*" But the sadness of the present weighed no more on Arizona Jack's heart than the shadows of that past which barred to him the gates of Leigh Hurst and the rich domain of Powning Hall.

"*I, the heir at law, am the only man in the world, who is there a social Pariah!*" groaned Arizona Jack. And the shadow of his once contemplated crime now rose up to curse him—the unfinished crime by which the ten thousand dollars was earned for the aftermath of which Pepita Morales *gave up her innocent life.*

Cyril Leigh had fathomed the last wiles of the " enterprising firm of Blum Brothers." He had received teamster Andy Faxon's reports and the tell-tale proofs of the golden ores. The astute Hugh Broadwood now knew the whole story, and Leigh was fully aware that the mine still lay full of water, and apparently deserted.

"Just have this man, Andy Faxon, run down and see me as your agent, my boy," said the veteran Consul. "*Get home to your own country!* Have a good

mining engineer of London—*a well-known British one—
mind you ;* notify the firm that he is coming out to make
an examination, and report. And *charge them, now,
boldly with fraud! They will buy you out for a fortune;*
but never trust yourself over the Atlantic, *again,* till
the thing is openly settled. They are powerless, and
detected now! Take home your *borings, to show what
you have got!*"

While the two friends watched for Jack Powning to
indicate his wishes, the physical healing process was
rapidly advancing. It was evident that any future
practice with gun or rifle however would be left handed,
for the good right arm was crippled. "*You can't stay
here forever, Leigh,*" bluntly said the Consul, "*the
sickly season is coming on and—by Heaven—both of you
should go !* You see your sister will start for Panama—
if you do not telegraph her of your intended departure. *There's her last unanswered dispatch! Now
I will have a shy at Arizona Jack.* If he's got any
heart left, *I'll touch it!*"

But, Jack Powning nursed his bitter past in a self-
accusing silence.

The long delay at Guaymas was now a source of
maddening annoyance to the bejeweled capitalist,
Isidor Blum. He had fallen into Counselor Moses
Dalman's adroitly laid trap. The lawyer now "orna-
menting the New York bar," had skillfully hedged.
Isidor Blum knew all of Morris Blum's blundering
failures, "along the whole line." Dalman secretly
chuckled over the twenty-five thousand dollar check
extorted from Isidor as a first "*hush money.*" "Get
over to San Francisco—see your partner, Morris,
see Bent, and Senator Stone. Tell them I alone can
save your mine. They are sharks, *it is true,* but not
fools, like the great brother *Morris.* Get them to
agree and for a quarter of the profit, I will beat the
English title. *I alone can,* and *so, away!* for you'll hear
from this Englishman. *He's no fool,* and he's got his
fighting cap on *now,*" and, there was a cool-headed
Junta of three men pondering in San Francisco, when
Morris Blum was called up there to recount the failure
of the trap which was sprung at Miller's Station,

Wary old William Bent and his smooth associate, Senator Stone, were left groping in the dark by Bill Murfee's violent taking off. His private reports had failed at the critical moment, and so perforce, the Condor Mining Company's junta "authorized Isidor Blum, Esq., *to take the necessary steps to protect the Company's interests.*"

The two sly conspirators feared to arouse the ire of Isidor Blum, who was duly fortified with the hinted disclosure that Moses Dalman (now "retained for the defense"), had a positively impregnable legal citadel, from which he could defy the attempt to prove up the English title to the half of the golden hoard, which they now dared not touch.

"*We must trust to Moses Dalman,*" groaned Isidor Blum. "*He is expensive,* but we cannot fight these people *without him.*"

"No, nor have all our own operations exposed," smoothly added the judicious Senator Stone. "We risk a good deal when we face the press—*the only thing, I fear as a public man,*" he whimpered.

Cyril Leigh explored the unfamiliar scenery of the dreamy old Mexican seaport, while stout-hearted Hugh Broadwood labored in friendly conference with Arizona Jack. The Squire saw a dark omen for the future of the line of the Pownings in Arizona Jack's solemn injunctions to conceal his history even from Broadwood. The skillful Consul wondered at Arizona Jack's strange conduct, and he, as well as Leigh, knew not of the seal of honor placed on the lips of the American officers by Jack Powning as to his real name.

"Let my dead past lie under the stone of Oblivion. I, *alone, must live to suffer and atone*" was Jack's last reply to Cyril's pleadings.

But the Consul was astounded, after he had frankly divulged all of Cyril Leigh's business plans to the convalescent "gun-fighter."

"*You are going to lose the mine for him by your stubborn conduct!* You *must* go to England *with him!*" said the angry official. And then, Jack Powning straightway sought out Cyril Leigh.

"*I am going to shoot myself,*" he said, "*if you do not*

promise me to go home to Lisbeth Leigh, and still count me among the dead! There is but one face I must never see—*your sister's.*" But, *I will save your mine!* Senator Stone and millionaire Bent at San Francisco will protect me. *Let me go there in your interest.* I can end the whole struggle, *for, I am 'Hugh Dalton,'* and *the mine was once my own!*"

CHAPTER XIII.

ARIZONA JACK TRUMPS MOSES DALMAN'S LAST TRICK.

THE two men wandered away toward the shore together, and Hugh Broadwood laughed in his heart to see the feeble plainsman leaning on the young Squire's arm.

"Things are surely moving now *in the right way,*" briskly cried the Consul as he sat down to write an unromantic report to Her Britannic Majesty's Home Government on the "Export trade of Sonora."

It was out on the rocks, that Jack Powning told the story of his life as he had summed it up for the recital in all these weary days of illness. The waves softly lapped the silver sands of the beach below, and they gazed out on the blue waters where the Acapulco galleons of His Most Christian Majesty of Spain had fled once to avoid the fierce sea cormorants of Francis Drake, the boldest of Good Queen Bess's sea-robbers.

"You say that you owe me something, Leigh," began Arizona Jack. "Then, *I'll tax you lightly. Give me that ring, the doubled hearts of diamonds.* For I gave it to Lisbeth Leigh, *your sister*, the one woman in the world who must never know the story of my downfall. *I'll touch lightly upon it.* The story of the old days. And, if you do owe your life to me, if I restore her fortune to her, *let this alone be my pay!* That I go down to the grave as Hugh Dalton is my prayer. Promise me on the faith of the Leighs, '*Loyal à la mort,*' that you will never tell my story to Lisbeth."

"*I promise,*" said Cyril, his dreamy eyes watching a

pelican gliding with graceful sweep along the sapphire waters.   " I will never tell my sister.   But before you bid me speak, let me ask you if you think your wasted life has been the only sacrifice ?   Think of Cornelia Powning's breaking heart before you seal your lips forever. *Think of Beth !* "   He stopped in a sudden terror when he saw Arizona Jack's agonized face.

" And you will go home *on the next steamer,*" continued Dalton.   " Take my horse Pablo with you as my parting gift.   Let me face these scoundrels, the Condors, at San Francisco, for I dare not tell you all *now*, but I will say that, if *I live to see Stone and Bent,* your position is the dominant one.   Now *I can strike back, strike for you,* and *for the always beloved woman whose life I have darkened.   It's my turn now,*" growled Jack.

" You *shall be Lisbeth's agent,*" warmly cried Leigh.

" Her *unknown* agent, Hugh Dalton only ? " queried Jack.

" *Yes !* Until you break the seal of the past," solemnly said Cyril, " I will go and leave this all in your hands with Broadwood to advise.   We will simply tell him that we are agreed on my future course."

" It's a strange path that led me to McLaughlin's Peak," said Arizona Jack, " when I came back from India ten years ago.   I was in the thralls of a sin of which *two* shared the blame before God.   It was, of course, hidden *from man's eyes.*   Out there in India, after my boyish courage had made me a man of note among my fellows, I fell under the spell of a woman who leaned down from her social throne, to notice the youngest staff officer of the Commanding General.

" For, in that flaming lotus land, prudence, pride, and womanly restraint often wither in the fierce fires of passion born of regal luxury and Capuan idleness.   We were at last ordered back to England.   Chance had brought me nearer to the family succession than I had ever before dreamed, and my medals and distinction made me the idol of one whom you know, dear old Cornelia, the Queen Regent of the Pownings.   God bless her ! "

" Amen," cried Cyril.

"And while you were away, a child at school, I first saw your sister Lisbeth in her girlish flower of exquisite promise. It's vain for me *now* to tell you that the chains which had once been of roses, bound with golden links, then weighed heavily on me. For your sister's love was a consecration of my wild life! The 'red star which burned over the midnight hours' of the shameless love I had long cherished was eclipsed forever. *I have never learned to lie!* I made one mighty struggle to free myself. And, God help me, I never knew *before*, the furies of 'a woman scorned.' The bolt that shivered my bark of life came down from clearest skies. There was, of course, *a last meeting*. I could not avoid a farewell with the one who had queened it over me for three long years. And I took desperate risks when I stole like a thief in the night to the meeting which was to be *one of final parting!* Some one had whispered to her of my visits to Leigh Hurst, the attraction which drew me to Nidderdale was not unknown—and Cornelia's doting fondness, your father's frank welcome, all pointed to a possible union of the houses of Leigh and Powning."

Arizona Jack's face grew set as stone when he quietly resumed, after a search for fitting words, "That I was coldly trapped; that I was met after the false alarms of a Delilah, by the man, *who later became 'first favorite'*; that my alternative was exposure to my commanding officer, or 'my social disappearance'—all these were steps of the throne upon which the man who ruined me mounted by the side of a woman who chose her own cruel vengeance."

Arizona Jack groaned as he muttered: "I was young. There was chivalry in me yet! I dared not face the 'commanding officer,' for, to fight him in that cause were sheer brutality. It was his home I had ruined! The 'honor of the corps' demanded a victim! Even in the shameful trap, for I was either burglar or lover, I caught eagerly at the one chance of saving Lisbeth Leigh from believing me to be *utterly vile*.

"That they are all dead, you may presume or not, *as you will!* I 'saved the honor of the corps!' I saved the name of a woman who had given me three years of

a life in which I was a willing Tannhäuser! Stealing
over to Hull, on a midnight train, I took passage on a
steam collier for Norway, and thence gained New York.
My knowledge of the foul snare came only after I had
been driven out of Arizona by these brutes, who have
sworn to reap the riches of the Condor at all costs.   It
may have been boyish folly, but no stain has rested
on Lisbeth's name through me, no shame upon her
heart!   How could I have faced the Horse Guards, the
corps, and society?   I could not in any way protect the
woman whom I fancied I had injured!   I saw no way to
make the shameful confession to Lisbeth of my hidden
intrigue, and I *could* not prove to her that I had not *lied*,
when I told her, under the oaks of Leigh Hurst, that
she was all the world to me!   *I had put the old life*
behind me, for her dear eyes had drawn me up out of
the mire of the past!   And her pure love had long con-
secrated my life to a better future.

"So, I silently accepted a social annihilation, trusting that Lisbeth Leigh would in time marry in her own
rank, and wed a better man, even if it were one who
never could know the burning love that thrilled to the
core of my heart.   *I went away for her dear sake!* There
was no stain on my name, no alleged crime at my door.
My course would have been always the same. A man is a
cur who leaves a woman to bear the *certainty* of shame,
however merited, when due to her *self-surrender* at his
bidding! *I paid the whole price*, and even if my money-
thirsty Delilah was *not unmasked*, I was *not innocent!*
The passing years have told me that the revenues of
Powning Hall were perhaps counted on by her to aid
her in shining in the fierce lights of London town.   My
detector—the man who acted as the blind puppet of
my tyrant—was sure to keep the faith after he had
won the *price of his infamy.* Oh, it was well done! He
was rich enough to serve the turn—an officer next in
command of the corps, *married* and *judicious.*   Once
that I had turned my back on England *they were safe*,
for they knew I would not drag Lisbeth Leigh down to
the level of my past life.   *I could not lie to her*, and so
it was worse than death to me when I became Hugh
Dalton, *the wanderer.*   God has set the seal of the

tomb upon lips that might have lied even now. Lisbeth lives in untroubled honor. And, *now, I am only poor Arizona Jack!*"

Cyril Leigh drew off the token of Lisbeth's parting instructions. "*It is yours, Captain Powning.* Wear it till we meet again. I will have the Consul draw up the agency papers and give you a letter to the British Consul at San Francisco. I leave all the details of the attack on the scoundrels in your hands. Is there anything else I can do?"

"Yes," said Arizona Jack. "I will telegraph to El Paso for José to come on here *at once.* He can be left here with the Consul, and, making his headquarters at Magdalena with Señora Morales, he can communicate with Andy Faxon. So we have a safe messenger—as José knows every inch of the Territory. You and I cannot safely return to Cochise County until my visit to San Francisco has muzzled those tigers, by unloosing upon them, the wily Senator. Now, let me sketch the mine's history. I was known as Hugh Dalton (the name was assumed by mere chance), for we buried at sea a dead passenger of that name. I then appropriated his useless cognomen. In the wild life of the 'eighties' at Tombstone, I never knew till later, that the man whom I killed, was set on by Bill Murfee to slay me, so that I could be robbed of my half interest in the mine. As frontier duels go, *it was a fair fight.* Pepita saved me, and we reached El Paso. A fugitive and proscribed, I took the name of '*Arizona Jack,*' as I was driven to the society of the smugglers and gamblers of the border. I spread the news of my death at El Paso to stifle a legal pursuit. I married the poor child who saved my life, and *a provision for her future was my only dream!* I always looked forward to being killed at any chance time. The better class of Mexicans on the Chihuahua side aided me for the sake of the sweet-faced child who died for us. One star alone shone down on my darkened way. Her fidelity touched me. I had intended to send her back to Magdalena with the money honestly gained from the sale of the Live Oak and Magnolia! Ryley, an easy prey to drink and

women, either swindled me, or else was plucked bare
in London.

"This scoundrel, Arthur Lemon, in some way has
pierced the secret design of the wretches now quarrel-
ing with each other.   He first sought you out, then he
traced me at El Paso, and he hired *me* to steal the title
papers back from you.   *I knew not who you were*, Cyril.
I had only received three thousand dollars for my half
of this hidden treasure, and so, I obtained, in revenge,
the ten thousand dollars which poor old Dolores
Morales now rejoices over, by a promise to aid Lemon
in swindling his own hidden employers.   The destruction of the English title papers was to leave the title *in
my hands*, and *we were to divide equally*.   But, an
Ishmaelite of the desert, I soon saw that other schemes
were woven around you.   Bill Murfee, who followed
us from Bowie, was working in Bent and Stone's interest, while Morris Blum sought to butcher you
simply because you would not sell.   Your leaving your
sister's letter on the table at Miller's Station, the tell-
tale reminder of Lisbeth's love shining on your finger,
told me *who you were*.   *I intended to deftly rob you of
these papers* and to *make for Mexico*, leaving you to find
your way out alone to Elgin.   Your accidental meeting
with the two miners at Bisbee has turned the scale.
But for that, Blum would have fawned upon you, welcomed you to Tucson, and you would have been probably drugged and plundered, if not *murdered!*   Of
course, 'road agents' or Indians would have been
blamed.   Now, you have the indubitable proof of the
value of the property.   Leave one can of the borings
here.   Take *the rest* on to London with you.   Let us
go in.   I shall only give my real name to the Consul
now as *Hugh Dalton*.   Let that be used in the agency
papers, the letter of credit, the letter to the British
Consul at San Francisco.   It will serve as a checkmate
to Mr. Arthur Lemon's rascally schemes."

Squire Leigh grasped Powning's hand, "You will
remember that your proper share of the mine shall
come *back to you*."

"Let us first win it back *for Lisbeth's sake*, Cyril,"
sadly said Arizona Jack.   You have much yet to do.

The Acapulco steamer sails *to-morrow*. I go up to San Francisco on the coaster calling *here in three days*."

"Will they not pursue you there about the old fracas at Tombstone?" fearfully demanded the young man.

"I've found a way to muzzle them, even if I'm now crippled for life," said Arizona Jack. "I will show no mercy. The sharks shall eat each other up. Never fear for me. I am safe now!"

"And your fair inheritance—Powning Hall—dear old Cornelia's open arms. She has 'burned the lamp of Love' for years in the window of her heart." Cyril Leigh was beseeching in his pleading.

"*My future is in God's hands!*" solemnly said the wanderer. "If there is a way out of the depths, He will show it!"

"I ask but one thing, in return for my silence," pleaded Cyril. "When this matter is arranged, you must go to a safe refuge somewhere. Will you not come to Europe? You can remain hidden in Paris, or Brussels. I can come over to you there, and, if Cornelia should be summoned suddenly, you could reach her bedside, even if you do not care to make yourself publicly known. Lisbeth loves her as a mother. Even if you still linger veiled from others, you dare not let Cornelia go, hungry-hearted and sorrowing, to the grave. You have saved *my life*. Let me help to save *your soul!* I am going now to Broadwood to arrange all. I'll send Manuel down here for you. Let *this* plead for me—and look into *that face*—and then tell me, if *you dare*, to let Cornelia Powning go, haunted by sorrow, to the other shore? She has tenderly guarded the woman you once loved, while you have wandered—the woman whose noble heart has been locked by an unbroken faith in your manhood!" There were tears in the boy's brave blue eyes, now.

Cyril Leigh strode away, leaving Arizona Jack seated there with his head bowed down. For through the mists of his own blinding tears, he could not see the pictured face of Lisbeth Leigh.

"*Lisbeth, darling! After these many years!*" gasped the crippled wanderer. And the sunshine on the murmuring waters took on a newer richness in its golden glow as he sat there face to face with his lost love—the woman who had not yet learned to forget. Still in the golden prime of early womanhood, there was the story of a sorrow-haunted past lingering in the splendid eyes and in the steadfastness of that sweet and shadowed face. Poor, crippled Arizona Jack was reconsecrated to manhood by the mute appeal of those eyes calling him back across the wild waters!

Consul Mark Broadwood essayed a Mark Tapley jollity when the three friends sat at Her Majesty's mahogany that night. The message recalling José had been repeated back as duly delivered, and even the astute official could now add nothing to the completeness of Hugh Dalton's credentials. With a delicacy which was born of a sudden intuition that the two men were now in thorough accord, Broadwood bustled away to make official passage arrangements for his proteges. The message—

"Leave for home to-morrow *via* Acapulco, Panama, and Colon, West India Company's steamer to Southampton. Left business agent here to follow on. All well. Property safe"

was delivered at Leigh Hurst before the *General Diaz* puffed away toward Acapulco. Its positive terms alone prevented the impending departure for Guaymas of Lisbeth Leigh. And, in the twenty-four days before Cyril Leigh and his great roan steed, "Pablo," reached Southampton, there had been five hundred joint readings at Leigh Hurst of these blessed tidings.

There was nothing left hidden between the comrades who had defended the gorge at the Grizzly's cave, when the *General Diaz* sailed away. Some subtle philter of life seemed to have animated Arizona Jack's drooping frame. It was the magic of Lisbeth's pictured face, the message of her softly shining eyes! The two Yorkshire men had communed the livelong night, for the picture of Lisbeth, now hidden in Jack's bosom, was a talisman, and on his wasted finger shone the ring which had saved Cyril's life.

"*Never forget!*" murmured Jack. "You owe your life not to *me*, but, to *her!*"

And his pride breaking down, he drank in the story of the beautiful life of the Lady of Leigh in the ten years which had changed her from the girl he knew to the Pride of Yorkshire. And so in loving review once more passed cherished forms that had trooped out of sight hidden in the misty years of a soul's eclipse.

"It is '*Cor unum, viae diversae,*'" said Powning, as they stood in the parting moment at the gangway. "*One heart* joins us forever, on our '*diverse paths.*' I *will* do as you wish, Cyril! I will come to Paris, but only, after I have made this imperiled treasure sure. I will come back here, to go to Magdalena, and see the grave of the gentle one who sleeps there. *Write always here to Broadwood's care.* It will be the safest. And I'll have José and Andy Faxon to help me. Then I'll come on by Panama, and remain in mufti, as Hugh Dalton, at Paris.

"And as I have promised a solemn faith to you, so do you promise me. *Keep silence,* and I will be near you soon. And Cornelia shall know, if it please God, how I have always loved her. And now we make our last pledge——"

"*For Lisbeth's sake !*"

The two voices rang out, and as far as Leigh could see, as the Mexican steamer sped away, the stern and soldierly form of the lonely man was there, mutely appealing to the messenger of a long buried love.

"*And, now for José,*" cheerfully cried Arizona Jack. "I will have a full day with him, for he comes to-morrow. Then, off for San Francisco and the Palace Hotel! The Senate is out of session. The glib Senator is hidden away, as usual, in the private poker-room there, his one sport when not weaving his Senatorial spider-webs. And I think that I can now furnish him gratis with what Rabelais termed '*a mauvais quart d'heure.*' They shall cross each other's lines, and emulate the Kilkenny cats. But, *he is the one 'kingpin' of the new 'star combination.'*"

That night, Arizona Jack sat alone in his room, mutely worshiping the picture of Lisbeth Leigh's ripened womanhood.

"*How can I avoid her ?*" he mused. The gallant

boy's docile promises never deceived him for a moment.

Cyril Leigh, on the deck of the *General Diaz*, was wrathfully objurgating the pride of the "mad Pownings."

"There will be a way out of this," he smiled over his Tepic cigar. "I promised him that I would not tell my sister, but, I did *not* promise *not to tell Cornelia!* This is not a case of 'no thoroughfare,' like Grizzly's cave. I can tell them all the story of his gallantry, and if Cornelia is the least bit of a woman, then, dear Beth can guess the rest."

Arizona Jack's heart throbbed in a nameless bliss as he adored the picture of the woman who still was true.

"She worships only herself, God bless her, in keeping true to the ideal man to whom she gave her heart. And, *I will never undeceive her.*"

He had steadily refused all offers of Cyril Leigh to provide for his future from the mine.

"*Remember!*" said Leigh. "Our family honor is as bright as yours. '*Loyal aux morts,*' as well as '*Loyal à la mort.*' If Cornelia should leave Lisbeth, her treasured funds, *they* shall come back later to *you.* The dead heart shall not be robbed, and *as a Yorkshire man*, I'll not see a stranger rule over Powning Hall. You may live as an 'absentee' if you wish, but '*the King shall have his own again!*'"

"That is a long, long way ahead, Cyril," kindly said Arizona Jack. "Let me be Hugh Dalton till I've made Lisbeth a rich woman. I have your promise. Remember that!"

Hugh Broadwood marveled at the change in Arizona Jack's appearance when the preparations for the San Francisco voyage were all completed. In his planter garb, with his flowing locks trimmed and a crisp, soldierly mustache alone shading his lip, the stately plainsman now looked like a Castilian Spaniard of "blue blood." The rapid healing of the shoulder wound left him only crippled in raising the good right arm. The sad-eyed José, mutely listening to his master's directions, wondered over the strange fate of his compadre Pablo and the idol of his heart, the child.

faced, Murillo-eyed Pepita. A fierce desire for personal vengeance burned steadily in José's heart and he joyfully contemplated carrying out a personal vendetta on his own account. For, the five prisoners liberated at Fort Huachuca were vicariously known to José, and he hunted for them after he had diligently gone about his master's business. It is true that with the aid of several other unfortunate Mexicans he finally put out of sight, three of the baffled marauders.

There was nothing left now, to prevent Arizona Jack's departure, and when Consul Broadwood saw the San Francisco bound steamer fade away, hull down, on the southern horizon, he was free to speculate on the real rank of his mysterious visitor. For José had aided with one or two mysterious hints the idea that Arizona Jack was of the *gente de razon* in merry old England. The Consul was not above keeping a secret of his own, and the departed secret agent had not reached San Francisco before Broadwood was privately possessed of a pretty fair history of the doings of "English Hugh" in the old days.

"*Fiction,*" laughed the Consul over his pale ale. "*Fiction is tame, a mere child's story*, compared with the *wild scenes of real life.* We are all of us only phases— *flitting phases*—mere shadows on the *glass of Life.*"

But the stout Englishman sealed up his social discoveries and duly reported to the Minister's at Washington and the City of Mexico the safe departure of Cyril Leigh, *alias* "Robert Ross," and his companion, "Hugh Dalton."

The Occidental Hotel at San Francisco, California, never harbored a more striking-looking personage than that reputed Mexican grandee, Señor Hugh Walton, of Guaymas. Upon his arrival, that soldierly-looking guest was at once received into the manager's confidence, and the visits of the British Consul placed "Señor Walton" upon a lofty social pinnacle. With some grim coquetry of his own, Arizona Jack had furbished up his outer-man with the latest fashions. His slight accent, his picturesque Mexican servant, the evidences of his recent wound, ascribed to Mexican revolutionary episodes, all confirmed the popular rumor that he was an Englishman born, but now an officer of high rank in the Mexican national army. The corded muscles and sinews of the handsome athlete gave a distinction to his bearing, and there was now a manly sparkle in his eyes, and his step was elastic.

The receipt of a dispatch from Colon, announcing the sailing of Cyril Leigh on the *Orinoco*, for Southampton, and the well-being of "Pablo,"—that traveled charger—was a bugle call to action, when Señor Walton had duly answered his comrade's dispatch. Certain afternoons spent with the British Consul and his lawyers, as well as the manager of a great international bank, had prepared Señor Walton to encounter that most wily of Pacific statesmen, Senator Stone.

It had been no mere slip of the pen which caused Arizona Jack to register at the Occidental Hotel as *Hugh Walton!* It had been the prudent outcome of his desire to gently surprise Messrs. Bent and Stone with his veiled personality. The early-gained knowledge that Isidor Blum, Esq., of New York City—the millionaire merchant—was a guest at the Palace Hotel, had given an added value to the temporary subterfuge. "Arizona Jack" was "*laying low*," *like* "*Brer Rabbit!*"

There was much adverse criticism as to the wealthy Mexican traveler's social isolation, on the part of various "professional beauties" of the splendid old caravansera, where the señor lingered while planting his torpedoes for the delectation of Senator Stone. Arizona Jack had decided to begin operations upon this oily statesman who timidly feared the light of day in many of his most profitable transactions.

"Old Bent and Blum are rich, crafty, and unscrupulous! *They fear nothing!* They have neither character or reputation to lose, and the only thing that they cling to is their money; but, the Senator is wrapped up in an unsmirched toga; he 'moves in a mysterious way,' his wonders to perform! and, I think that he is the weakest point of the trinity," so decided the undaunted secret agent. And, it was his own preoccupation in preparing the toils, which caused "Arizona Jack" to ignore the smiles and blushes which invited "the distinguished stranger" to meet sundry "kindred souls" on that judicious battlefield of flirtation, the vast hotel parlor, with its adjacent corridors, haunted by some of the loveliest, and, *not the most prudent*, of their charming sex. The prairie bronze alone dyed the señor's cheeks, and, in his "richly illustrated" form, he was, at thirty-eight, a far more commanding figure than "Jack Powning of Ours!" But Arizona Jack smiled softly, and failed to "catch on," to the gentle impeachment of his indurated heart.

It was through the personal arrangement by letter of Her Britannic Majesty's Consul, that Señor Hugh Walton was ushered into the awesome presence of Senator Stone, at ten o'clock, on a breezy August morning. The Senator's face was wreathed in happy smiles, for the morning mail had brought him the welcome and "*not unexpected*" intelligence that a "lady in whom he was deeply interested" would honor his theater box, on *that very evening*. The corner suite in the huge hostelry was the abode of an "easy and refined" luxury and the good humored Senator extended his box of Henry Clays with his usual *bonhomie*. The cool visitor was slightly off his guard, for, as he turned the angle of the Senator's private corridor, he had stumbled upon the bustling "Mr. Arthur Lemon," evidently proceeding from the Senatorial lair.

But, the splendid "make-up" of the visitor had deceived Moses Dalman, who could not recognize in the elegant figure of the neatly shaven swell, the breezy outlines of his accomplice, Arizona Jack.

"I must come down to business *at once*," hastily decided Jack. "*What the devil is Lemon doing here?* And I must frighten this fat fellow."

"I have called to see you in regard to the Condor Mine, in the Huachuca Mountains," politely remarked the visitor. A crafty look at once stole over the Senator's face.

"*Hold on!*" he cried, earnestly. "*Our lawyer was just here. I'll call him back,*" and the portly Senator raced down the hall. "*Too late!*" he remarked, as he came back puffing. "Go *ahead! What can I do for you?*"

"Who is your lawyer?" quietly inquired the stranger.

"*Mr. Moses Dalman of the New York Bar,*" said the Senator. "He just *went out,* as you *came in.* Now, Sir," said the statesman, dropping his man-and-brother-free-and-easy style, "What is there about the Condor Mine? I received you, because the Consul wrote me that you wished to see me on a very important matter!" The round gray eyes were flinty hard in their sheen, but the Senator gasped and dropped his cigar, when the stranger curtly said:

"It's very important to you! *I am Hugh Dalton,* the very man who located that mine!"

"*The hell you are!*" roared the statesman. "*Then, you're the man who killed Bill Wakeman!*"

"*The very man,*" quietly answered Arizona Jack, "and I have come up here to make you and your associates, *disgorge!*"

"*Ah!*" sneered the Senator, rising. "*That's enough!* A coarse bluff, a windstorm. If you're in this town, *to-morrow night,* you'll be taken back to Tucson on a requisition *for murder.* There's an indictment hanging over you still, and they'll lynch you down there. Bill Wakeman was a *very popular man.*"

Senator Stone was astounded when Hugh Dalton quietly lit the cigar which he had accepted, and proceeded to smoke, as if a pipe of peace had been offered.

"Don't threaten, Senator. *It's very bad form.* Now, *to begin with,* I'll play with all my cards on the table. I'm a British subject, and I have an irresistible backing. I am also well armed, and *I'm a pretty good left-handed shot! I propose to open your eyes!* I know that both Bent and Isidor Blum are here in town. Perhaps, also, that sneaking assassin at second-hand, *Mr. Morris Blum!* I will give the whole affair *to the press,* to-morrow, *if you dare to rise and touch that bell!* First, let me say that I'm the man who 'laid out' a few of your paid assassins at the Grizzly's cave, *not a month ago!* If you want to know how neatly the two Blums have swindled and betrayed you, let me give you a few 'pertinent facts,' and to your villainous lawyer.' I wish to see the whole lot of you, face to

face, together, as soon as I can, *lawyer and all.*
Don't forget that conspiracy to murder is a serious
crime. My bankers and the British Consul have
already consulted the Chief of Detective Police. *I am
under the care of the British Legation,* and *I defy you!*
Now, before you call your brother Condors together,
let me open your eyes to the operations of the Blum
scoundrels. If you and Bent are to be robbed of what
you really own, *with your eyes open, all right;* but I will
remain here till I have that indictment dismissed, and
*then I will proceed against the whole lot of you! The
tables are turned, Mr. Senator!*"

"*Who will have it dismissed?*" sneered the Senator.
"*A likely tale!*"

"*You will!*" politely remarked Hugh Dalton.

"*You are lying to me!*" roared the wrathful statesman. "*Dalton was killed at El Paso—killed years
ago!*"

"I circulated that story myself to get out of the
clutches of the killers who run with the Blum gang,"
laughed Jack. "Now, let me tell you! I am the ac-
credited agent of Miss Lisbeth Leigh, of Leigh Hurst,
Yorkshire, England, the lawful owner of half the Condor mine, and it was her brother, *Cyril Leigh,* otherwise
Robert Ross, whose murder, your gang plotted. The
papers are now in the vault of the British Consulate.
He is safe on the ocean, half way home to England,
and *I am here!* Now, sir, *by Jove,* I'll turn the
whole American press loose on you! I owe you
something for this stiff shoulder, but your gang is
seven men short. The commanding officer at Fort
Huachuca has got the whole facts, and even *you,* cannot muzzle an army officer. *Do you want to hear now*
how the two Blums have swindled *you* and *Bent?*
Don't forget that I know all your joint operations for
ten years down there."

"*I must first see the Consul. You talk like a madman!*
I must see our lawyer, *Moses Dalman!*" faltered the
frightened Senator.

"*See here,*" laughed Dalton, "you can hear the
rest after you have telegraphed down and had that indictment dismissed. A formal *nolle prosequi* can be

sent later to the British Consul.   *If you are sane* you'll have a private talk with *Bent* after *you see the Consul!* But *first, please,* ask Counselor Moses Dalman if he knows a man named '*Arizona Jack.*'   I've got him here as a witness.   *Just note the effect,* please do!   It will be highly amusing.   *You'll find it so!*

"Now, Sir, I'll give you just *one* day to get over your scare," said Dalton, rising.   "In *two* days, if you don't come to time, I shall take the train to Washington, and lay the whole thing before Her Majesty's Minister.   *I* have as much money and power behind me as *you* can muster.   *As to the press,* I will turn it loose on you, *when I go! On second thoughts,* you can suit yourself about the '*nolle prosequi.*'   You will find me at the Occidental Hotel.   You can spare the time to come over, I think—just see the Consul—and then ask that *little question* of your *estimable* lawyer.   I'll be glad to introduce him to Arizona Jack!"

"Won't you come here, Dalton, and dine with me *to-night?* I'll have Bent over here to meet you," said the smooth Senator.

"*Ah! The old dodge,*" smiled Hugh Dalton.   "*No! Thank you!* Now just go ahead with that extradition, I'll be glad to have you begin.   I will see you *alone,* and—you had better go and see the Consul."   As Arizona Jack sauntered away, he heard a pleading voice at the door: "*Be reasonable, my dear fellow,* and *let's talk this thing over a bit—quietly—you and I.*"

But the "star guest" of the Occidental sat chatting with the British Consul that night, in his own house, while Senator Stone and William Bent, Esq., conferred until the wee sma' hours.   There was a lonely lady in a theater box that evening, who shrugged her pretty shoulders, at the apologetic bouquet, and the curt note: "Public affairs prevent!"   "*He is the very smoothest liar in the world!*" said the resentful beauty.

The two sly old foxes who had been vastly alarmed by Arizona Jack's cool denunciation of their partners, were now of the mind that they had better, *at once,* seek for an alliance with the English interest.   The Condors at San Francisco were thus divided into two camps: Messrs Isidor and Morris Blum still blindly relying upon the reserved artillery of Counselor Moses Dalman.

"*Don'd get frighdened, Boritz,*" said Isidor. "We have only blayed doo glose a game. Ve vent in to shear dese English beeple *too glose*. If Dalman had given dem dwendy dousand pound out *dere* in London we had den de whole didle, *all right. It's doo late, now.*"

The three American Hebrews earnestly discussed all the points of the deadlock.

"*There's no harm done after all,*" said Dalman to Isidor. "*Don't abuse poor Morris for his stupidity.* He did the best that he could. It's true that he *failed,* and the Englishman *got away!* But, Bent and Stone *are baffled, too.* If they played false with Lem White and Bill Murfee, both these fellows are *dead.* And Bent and Stone have no 'private reports' *now,* and no way of proving these past ugly stories of Bill Murfee. They won't dare to admit that they were undermining you. So, *we all start even* as to the outlying half of the mine. *Keep quiet!* Watch Bent and Stone, and if this Englishman turns up here, why, just throw the whole thing into the United States Circuit Court down there, get a bond accepted, made up of fellows who are *penniless,* that's an easy trick, then go ahead and gut the mine and *let these people whistle!* I'll bring you out *all right yet.*"

"Ah! But we don't dare to incorporate the mine," sighed Morris. "*These people own an undivided half.* We are liable as partners to them. We can't incorporate, gut it, and get rid of our stock."

"Just show the 'stiff upper lip' with Bent and Stone! They are *now* evidently concocting some dirty trick! My 'kingpin' secret, though, holds the mine *safe,* and I will not show our hand till we are forced to!"

So for three days, a veiled hostility slumbered under the white flag of truce, for Senator Stone had returned astounded, from a visit to the British Consul. That functionary coldly said: "I do not hold a man of your public character responsible for the atrocious villainy of this Blum gang, and their dishonest agent. But I know all the whole situation now, and officially, too, for the consul at Guaymas has verified these facts, and I am acting under the strict orders of the British Minister. The Anglo-Californian Bank will back Cyril Leigh's agent *to any extent.* He has selected the very best lawyer on the Coast, Paul McMasters. I would, therefore, advise you and Mr. William Bent to make terms with the English interest, and to clean out these three buzzards who have played Condor down there."

The Consul's brow grew black as Senator Stone affected the lofty "moral tone," which he used on "public occasions."

"*See here, Senator!*" curtly said the Consul, "Western mining morals are *at a low ebb*, but I'll tell you for your own protection, *you* have something to lose. Hugh Dalton has the pocketbook taken off Bill Murfee's body, and some old letters are there *from you.* They throw a little light on the homicide of Bill Wakeman! It appears all would have gone well if Wakemen had only killed Hugh, *in that old fracas!* You have something to lose. Instead of this Dalton being a pretender, he has Leigh (a millionaire Yorkshire squire) at his back, and '*Arizona Jack*' under his hand! *You are the only one who has anything to lose* in the way of character. Bent and you stand as one in interest. If the press gets hold of this story *your public life is at an end!* And *you don't know Yorkshire grit* if you think that Cyril Leigh will not have all his sister's rights. I am determined to protect every British interest here, so *let us not meet as foes.* I now advise *you* and *Bent* to be both *liberal* and *prompt.* Your own safety *demands* it!" And then, he coldly bowed the great statesmen out.

The mantle of a sour silence settled down over the faces of Senator Stone and the uncommunicative William Bent, when the Senator returned from a persuasive séance of four hours with Hugh Dalton, at the Occidental Hotel.

"I am indulging in the luxury of a private detective here, *as a guard*, and I have invited the official presence of the Chancellor of the British Consulate! These gentlemen will both remain in my sleeping apartment—and, thus, I'll have no more Grizzly Cave traps!"

The Senator's rosy face was a study in fats and oils, as he blandly said: "*See here!* I've telegraphed to the District-Attorney, down there at Prescott, to have a *nolle prosequi* entered in the case of 'People of the Territory of Arizona vs. Hugh Dalton, alias English Hugh.' The official document, countersigned by the Secretary of the Territory and the Governor, with the seal of the Court, will be delivered to the Consul here. So, *that clears up the old matter forever!*

"Now, Isidor and Morris Blum as well as Moses Dalman (our lawyer) are here. We have all got to separate soon, for our own affairs, and I have called a meeting of the owners of the Condor Mining Company to-morrow at noon, at my rooms at the Palace. Will you attend with all the papers and credentials that you have? There ought to be some way found of fixing up this affair *in an agreeable manner.*"

"*There is an easy way,*" dryly said Arizona Jack. "I will have the Chancellor bring my full powers there and exhibit them. The papers are in his legal custody. Then, I will be ready with my propositions and also some information of value. I warn you all of the one mistake in this game of hide and seek. Poor tools, poor dupes only have been sacrificed so far, but if there is any tragedy to come, *I'll murder the first man who lifts a finger,* regardless of rank or financial standing. And so I shall have my own '*personal credentials*' in my pocket. *I'd just like to have one crack at Morris Blum!*" Arizona Jack smiled grimly as he showed how easily his left hand could manipulate a Colt's police pistol.

"*It's not loaded, Senator,*" laughed Dalton, "*but, it will be to-morrow.*"

There was one delicate point on which after three hours of an earnest conference the two men differed. Arizona Jack had plied his august guest with wine and cigars, but he gently smiled and shook his head when the Senator begged him for Bill Murfee's pocket-book.

"*It will remain sealed* in the achives of the Consulate, until the Anglo-Californian bank forwards it to London *with our first remittances.* You see I would like to oblige you, but I am only Cyril Leigh's agent, and Miss Lisbeth Leigh will naturally *wish to keep that book. It was a fair prize of war!*"

"But *after I have delivered you the dismissal of the indictment?*" pleaded the weary-eyed Senator.

"*I couldn't think of it,*" gravely said Arizona Jack. "*I may need it later to obtain some indictments for conspiracy to murder.* No! Senator Stone! You and Bent had better come to the scratch. Be prompt *and liberal.* Remember this is a case of '*dog eat dog,*' and the mining reporters are already on the track of the murderous affray at the McLaughlin Peak. In other words, Sir, *you have no time left for trifling.* As for 'bluff' or threats, *that don't go.* '*It is played out.*' Your local bully, Morris Blum, needs a stiff hand, and I'll give him a good twist. *I owe it to him!*"

The various hangers-on of Senator Stone vainly impinged upon his door panels that evening, for Bent and the statesman were now busied toiling over the midnight lamp to privately arrange "the dish of crow," so that the other Condors would digest the major portion.

So oily was Senator Stone's "*suaviter in modo,*" that when all the "high contracting" parties were assembled at the long green table in the Senator's corner room, it was from the statesman's own private rooms that "Arizona Jack" entered, followed by the Chancellor of the British Consulate. The two Blums gazed furtively at the elegant figure of the plainsman, who took a seat directly facing Mr. Morris Blum.

Moses Dalman sat as if stunned, his face pallid, and with trembling lips, when Arizona Jack, in silence, handed a packet of papers to the Senator. They went the rounds, while Hugh Dalton's professional "poker eye" calmly sized up the shivering ornament of the New York Bar.

"*These documents are in perfectly correct form,*" curtly said Dalman, as the Senator gazed moodily at Bent.

"*I guarantee all the official indorsements and seals,*" said the young English official, who then disappeared with a polite nod, directed generally to the unhappy group of "Condors."

"Before I enter into any discussion for my principals," said Jack calmly, "I would premise that the evidence of Tom Faison and Barney Farley—the two miners who explored the bonanza, now lying under water in the Condor—has been taken before the British Consul at New Orleans. The map of the ore body and the documents are on their way to England, but certified copies of both are in the hands of the Anglo-California Bank here, as they are our financial agents."

Morris and Isidor Blum gazed at each other with a sickening smile of doubt, when Jack quietly added:

"I have *one* case of the boring samples here, and *four* other cases are now on their way to London for assay. So, gentlemen, we know just what's in the mine, and also, why Mr. Morris Blum has filled it with water!"

The burly bully was half way out of his chair when Arizona Jack remarked:

"*If you leave that chair, or lift a hand, I'll see that you regret it.*"

He calmly laid his revolver on the table before him.

"*I'm in a den of thieves, and I know it!*"

Morris Blum's face dropped on his hands. He remembered the sudden "taking off" of Bill Wakeman.

"I will make now my first and only proposition," began Arizona Jack, when Moses Dalman astonished all by saying, "*Will you step into the next room with me for a moment?*"

"*Certainly,*" remarked the elegant apparition, in whose splendid guise, Dalman had at last recognized "Arizona Jack."

They were alone together when Dalman whispered, hoarsely:

"One hundred thousand dollars, if you will swear that you never made a power of attorney to Walter Ryley. *Don't be a fool!* I'll take care of the rest. *Put off this conference a day*, and I'll deliver you the money, in gold coin, to-night, when you sign the paper."

"*Not for a million*," contemptuously said Arizona Jack, as he returned to the room. And Moses Dalman took his seat later, blandly remarking: "I only wished to ask one question about the form of the agency papers."

There was a cunning gleam in his foxy eyes now—a gleam of triumph. The reserved artillery was in a position for action now, and Moses Dalman's green eyes shone out like an adder's.

"We will take two hundred and fifty thousand dollars in United States gold coin, to be deposited at once to the credit of Miss Lisbeth Leigh, of Leigh Hunt, Yorkshire, England, with our agents, the Anglo-California Bank, and fifty per cent. of the net value of the ore body, for our clear title to one-half the Condor Mine. You to appoint *one* expert, we to name *another* from London, and the British Consul here to name *a third*. We are to pay no share of pumping the mine. Average assays from every gallery and cross-cut to determine the value of the whole ore body, and twenty-five dollars a ton to be allowed for working.

"We are to appoint an inspector of the mine, and the experts are to be paid jointly out of the first proceeds of the mine. *That is our whole proposition !* The details to be carried out by the Anglo-California Bank !" And Arizona Jack calmly lit one of the Senator's Henry Clays.

"The cash payment is to be shared ?" said Bent, raising his eyebrows.

" *You pay that,*" sternly said Dalton, " for what you have *already* taken out of the mine! *Do you want any further details ? I can give them !*"

Jack was softly smiling now, with his hand lingering near his revolver.

" *Before you agree to such an insulting proposal,*" said Dalman, his voice ringing out suddenly and as sharply as the cut of a steel blade, "allow *me* to say, that I shall, on behalf of the Messrs. Blum, oppose any such agreement. There is a fatal defect in this trumped-up title of the Leighs' *There was no power of attorney ever recorded in England !* Ryley and Gladwyn are both dead. There is no power of attorney from Hugh Dalton to Walter Ryley *in existence,* and no *record of such a document can be found anywhere !*"

And then, Isidor and Morris Blum gazed in an exulting triumph at Bent and Stone, while Dalman sneeringly rejoiced in his possession of the paper stolen from poor Ryley's dead body!

"*That fixes him, the fool!*" thought Dalman, as he gloated over the destruction of Andrew Harrison's records at Tucson.

There was a murmur around the board, but with flashing eyes, Arizona Jack sprang up and faced them all, "Allow *me* to remark that I am '*Arizona Jack*,' otherwise '*English Hugh*,' otherwise '*Hugh Dalton*.' And, I very carefully recorded a certified copy of that Power of Attorney to Walter Ryley in the office of the U. S. District Court, at *Prescott*, Arizona, before Ryley left for Europe. I did not want Mr. Bill Murfee to know that I was trying to sell the *other half* of the mine! A certified copy of that record is now on its way to England, and the records are still intact, for the British Consul has *another certified copy, now in his safe.* And—gentlemen of the Condor—if you doubt Miss Lisbeth Leigh's title—I may say that I have redeeded the identical property direct to her, since my arrival here! I will give you *now* one day to consider my proposal, before bringing an action against you *jointly*, for theft, and conspiracy to defraud, as well as seeking for indictments for conspiracy to murder! '*Mr. Arthur Lemon*' there, alias '*Moses Dalman*,' can now explain to his employers how he tried to hire *me* to murder the very man whom I was secretly protecting, Cyril Leigh, my neighbor in England, and, *a distant relative.* I shall go down from here to Tucson, Arizona, under the escort of Deputy U. S. Marshals—if I go. *Let '* Arthur Lemon, of the Chicago Stock Exchange *'* explain his swindling voyage to Pately Bridge, his secret journey to Bowie, where he paid a stranger ten thousand dollars to butcher this Robert Ross! *False—even to the thugs who hired him! Blum Brothers of New York and Tucson!*" Arizona Jack lit a cigar and sauntered away. Before another day was over, the talking wire had told Lisbeth Leigh that she was rich beyond her wildest dreams. The "*quiet settlement*" was effected, and the caution money was deposited in the Anglo-California Bank.

CHAPTER XIV

"WHY WILL HE NOT COME?"

THERE never had been such a Christmas Eve of jollity at Leigh Hurst since the old days when the last squire and his beautiful second wife had watched Lisbeth in her girlish flower, dancing "Sir Roger de Coverly" with the young heir of Leigh Hurst. For the return of Cyril had brought a whirlwind of startling rumors to agitate the sleepy circles of the old country families. It was generally conceded that Squire Leigh, a gallant young knight errant, had been the hero of a strange latter-day romance as wild as the moving scapes when Amyas Leigh threw his sword away. This "Westward Ho" story seemed also to place upon the brow of beautiful Lisbeth Leigh the glittering coronet of Plutus's magic investiture. The brother and sister sat behind the great oriel window of the library at the midnight hour tenderly gazing in each others eyes and listening for the touching song of the Christmas waits. Their thankful hearts beat in a loving unison. They could see the far-off tower of the old church, where "deep on the convent roofs, the snows were sparkling to the moon!" A cherry-red gleam twinkled beyond the leafless, hoary oaks where the rectory opened its hospitable doors to all. And the silver notes of the Christmas chimes had floated out over the dales through the crystalline air with their message of peace and good-will!

There was a great house party at Leigh Hurst, for the keen-witted world wags on ever in the same old fashion. The news of beautiful Beth Leigh's fairy gift of fortune had drawn together all that willing suite of suitors whose motto is "Beauty and Booty." There was Major Vyner, of that classic band of intellectual aristocrats, the Royal Engineers; the polished Harry

Poynter, of the F. O.—a coldly gleaming swell of swells; young Sir Hope Maxwell, a canny Scot from the marshes of the Tweed; Phil Fitzgerald, of the laughing eye—that roguish and romantic Irish literary genius of the "London Symposium," and others, "*too numerous to mention*,"—as the society journals have it. All these had attended the "Christmas Eve" reunion.

For steady drawing power, give us always the good, red gold, the coveted "shekels" of the Philistines. And, so it had fallen out, that Cyril Leigh had reached county fame, by a single bound, and the magnetic influence of the splendid heiress of the Condor Mine had also spread in gentle ripples, even as far as busy London. She was now a "personage!"

Certain Yorkshire bankers, and even those conservative solicitors, "Messrs. Carstairs, Lyon & Carstairs, of Sheffield," had proudly let fall a hint here and there, very stimulating to these Lochinvars, young and old. And, so, with "sweet wonder in her eyes," Lisbeth Leigh found that she had developed, under the glowing colors of romance, into a "social star of the first magnitude." "'Twas ever thus from childhood's hour," etc., etc.

Adulation is contagious, and, nothing succeeds like that success which has already succeeded! The beautiful Yorkshire dales were besieged by willing cavaliers of note. The splendid dark eyes of Lisbeth Leigh, however, only shone with an equal splendor upon her gallant wooers, but, there seemed to be no indication of "wedding favors" in the near future. The brother and sister had been "drawn closely heart to heart" by the vanished sorrows of the exciting summer. None but Lisbeth knew the whole story of Cyril's wanderings from El Paso to Guaymas, and the whole country side marveled still to see the Squire dashing along the road in all the bravery of a superb Mexican outfit, which had been conveyed to him by the sad-eyed José, whose endless consumption of cigaritos now astonished the piquant soubrettes of Paris. That superb red roan charger of Jack's, whom no one dare to mount save Squire Cyril, was more than a seven-days' wonder in Yorkshire. The endless illustrations of "buck jumping" and "equine cussedness" gave to Pablo, the famous horse, a lurid renown all his own!

"*See, Cyril,*" said Lisbeth, suddenly. "*Powning Hall is all lit up! What a good omen!*"

They gazed out over the meadows of Nidderdale to where the old stronghold of the mad Pownings now shone out in all its massive splendor. There was much sage wagging of beards when Cornelia Powning had sent forth her invitations for a grand Christmas dinner, the precursor of her open-handed largess to the tenantry. As the chorus of the waits rang out, Lisbeth turned to Cyril.

"*She never will give up hope!*" the Lady of Leigh dreamily said. "*What an untiring love—what a faithful heart!*"

It was in deference to Cornelia's loving kindness of the past years, that the whole house party of Leigh Hurst were to gather around the table at the great Hall, and see the boar's head brought in.

There was but one shadow resting on this happiest of all the later Christmas days, and it found its voice in Lisbeth's pleading cry, as the brother and sister stood a moment before the hearth where the Yule log was still blazing, fringed with its whitened ashes. The soft wax lights gleamed down on the dented armor of the dead Leighs, and the great stained glass window shone out in all its aureole of splendid color—bearing that proud, unbroken legend of their race, "*Loyal à la mort.*"

"Why will *he* not come to us?" softly said Lisbeth. "*Shall I never see his face?* The man whose brave breast was a living bulwark to you in those awful hours." Cyril Leigh turned and gazed at the gleaming lines of light, where the gray turrets of Powning Hall shone out over the peaceful valley.

"*I will ride down to Pately Bridge, Beth,*" answered Cyril, "*the first thing in the morning;* I hope even *yet* to hear from Paris. Hugh is a very *strange fellow* and I hope yet to break in upon his gloomy reserve. You know that he has been all this time in the surgeon's hands. The splinters of bone are still loosening from his shattered arm.   We must trust to time."

"And Cyril, if I can not meet him face to face and thank him for bringing you back to me—for saving my fortune of fairy gold—*why should I not look upon his face?   Is he so proud* that I may not have his picture—the man to whom you gave my ring?"

"*Lady Bird,*" fondly said Cyril, as he caught her to his breast.   "Trust to me—trust to time, and *all will be well!*   Now, *off to your beauty sleep*, for to-morrow you must look your very best.   The whole country side will be there, and none may outshine the Lady of Leigh.   Besides, I want to talk with you to-morrow afternoon—about myself, about the army, and *all that.* And, *I've much to say to you!*"

The Squire's eyes were dancing with all the joy of a half-hidden secret.

"Does your morning ride take you as far as Lord Trevor's castle?" laughed Lisbeth.   "Bonnie Mary Annesley must have her Christmas greeting—and her Christmas gift."

"*Stranger things have happened,*" admitted the master of Leigh.   "*You are a witch of witches,* and *the sweetest and dearest sister a man ever had!*"

He fled away, fearing further questions.

Lisbeth Leigh had stolen in to see her fairy god-mother, Cornelia Powning, before she sat dreaming by the dying fire in the boudoir.   A sudden thought had crystallized into a determination.

"Cornelia has soon to go down to London *on important legal business*, dear heart," she mused.   "She shall take me, and *we will go over to Paris.*   Then, without a word to any one, we will storm the castle of this wounded knight errant.   But Cyril, shall not know.   He would never consent!"

Against all the laws of "beauty sleep," the Lady of Leigh sat there a long time with her heart fondly beating in the fullness of her happiness, and gazing into the fire.   On her lap, her hands lay idle, and her eyes were very dreamy.

"*He would take nothing but my ring!*   And yet, he will not even come once beneath our roof.   *What strange manner of man may this be?*"

And then she dreamed olden and happy dreams that night, for the angels were whispering to her of new hopes! Her womanly heart throbbed on in an exquisite mystery of bliss.

Squire Leigh took counsel of himself in his den as he stuffed the priceless pipe which had cheered him on the desert of death.

"*By Jove!*" he briskly murmured. "*This sort of thing can't go on forever !* For with everyone now playing at cross purposes, both Cornelia and Lisbeth may be betrayed by this finical adherence of mine to a pledge of honor. *There's the succession.* I'm not going to see Jack left a castaway—a pauper, with this wealth all his own *by right*, and if Lisbeth should marry some one of these fellows! *They're all in the running* now. No! By Jove! *I'll talk to old Carstairs !* He can perhaps be led on to make a discovery which he can use *later*, at his discretion. And *so*, I will be free of the load of care which I am carrying. For, *there's Mary*, and Lord Trevor *will* have me answer him by the New Year! It's either the *Army without Mary* or Parliament, perhaps, *with her*, for I'll be a year over age before the new election. And a single motion of Trevor's finger carries the borough. By Jove, if I was *only engaged to Mary*, I could confer closely with Lord Trevor. *He's the man—yes, the very man to help me !* I'll speak to Mary before to-morrow night and then it's all plain sailing. For Trevor is a kinsman of both our families."

With this pleasing prospect of "speaking to the Honorable Mary Annesley," the light-hearted Squire drifted out on the land of dreams.

Crisp, cool, sparkling, Christmas morning brought to Lisbeth Leigh the hasty embraces of her wonderfully excited brother. There was a dancing glee in his frank eyes which told a sweet story to the Lady of Leigh as she departed for the last look at the church decorations and the marshaling of the happy volunteer choristers. Madam Cornelia Powning was charged with the later bringing on of the guests to the morning service, for, laughing faces in the church were lingering over the last touch to the decorations, and sweet, uncertain, girlish voices were busied with the last trials of carol and chant. Queen of them there, serene and lovely, Lisbeth Leigh moved around, governing all, clad with gentle authority, the dreamy look lingering in the deep splendor of her wistful eyes.

Brave "Pablo" tossed his crested head and sped away over the roads fringed with snow-sparkling hedges |and fleeced in the unfamiliar snow. Merrily the steel shod hoofs rang out on the frosted ways as Cyril Leigh, with tasteful selection of words, arranged the flowery phrases with which he proposed to greet bonnie Mary Annesley. Her blue eyes and golden hair had haunted him since he carried away her image in his heart on the dreamy trip to meet the astute "Arthur Lemon" in London! And how much had gone on since then! The lightning shuttle of time was restlessly weaving strange pictures in the web of his life. Leigh was brave enough as far as Pately Bridge, and there, his thoughts were with his sister. For, a large hamper of cut flowers marked "San Remo," there awaited the Squire's orders, addressed to Miss Lisbeth Leigh, Leigh Hurst, Pately Bridge, Yorkshire, England.

"*By Jove! that's Jack's token!*" cried the happy Cyril.

The telegraph operator thanked the generous Squire for a golden tip, as the young man tore open Hugh Dalton's dispatch from Paris.

"Detained here by Doctor's absolute orders. Must see you soon *on very important business.* Write to me at once when you can come. A Merry Christmas to all at Leigh Hurst. My absence imperative. Let the flowers plead for Arizona Jack."

"Shall I answer him?" mused Leigh. "I think that I will wait till I have spoken to Mary. I can send a dispatch over after I've talked with Cornelia and Lisbeth."

It seemed to the enraptured youth that all the planetary system in some occult way now revolved about the "Honorable Mary Annesley," and, with a beating heart and memories of her whispers of the night before, when they stood in the shade of the great window after the last waltz, he galloped on, and "beat the local record" to the lodge gates of Carlyon.

The pretty speech which had been so neatly arranged to flow "trippingly from the tongue," suddenly faded away, as he threw his horse's reins to a groom in front of the overhanging archway of Carlyon.

"Just walk him up and down a bit," said Leigh, as he nervously sought for a certain pacquet which had been greatly on his mind of late. By the all-powerful witchery of young womanhood, bonnie Mary Annesley had seen that brave young rider drive up, and, she was strangely early astir for the aristrocratic hold of Carlyon. Her pretty head, "running over with curls," seemed to make the room a temple of beauty—"like a lily in bloom"—and Cyril Leigh, on the threshold of his maiden speech, forgot all the cunning of the orator, before the mute invitation of those loving eyes. The packet was *duly delivered*—and, in an awful moment of irresolution, the young squire, a beggar as to words, "crossed the Rubicon," and was soon aware that the scepter of his own life had passed away from him!

So, when the spell of loving lips encouraged him, he murmured: "*I shall speak to your father, at once.*"

The stately festivities of Carlyon claimed the golden haired angel of his heart, but, Cyril knew how artfully his all compelling sister had so engineered the social arrangements that the Honorable Mary Annesley should be allowed to grace Cornelia Powning's after-dinner ball, even if the little queen were only allowed

> "To tread but one measure—
> Drink one cup of wine."

And in the mutual apprehension, in which "they had snatched a fearful joy," the lady and her lover were vastly relieved at heart, even if "held tenderly apart," as the sweeping strides of Pablo bore the Master of Leigh homeward. Master of himself no more, he hastened away to his room and dispatched before wending his way to the church a formal letter begging Gerald Annesley, Lord Trevor, "to accord him an early interview upon a matter of the utmost importance." This grave dispatch once safely on its way, Cyril Leigh led his guests to the old church, the merry notes of whose inviting bells seeming to pour from golden throats. Leigh was not far wrong in his conjectures that the wily old retired diplomat, Lord Trevor, would at once summon his youngest daughter to the fatherly presence, and, with a delightful indirection, probe the agitated heart of the "Honorable Mary," with regard to "*a matter of the utmost importance.*" This gentle secret was a matter of general conjecture now!

The very merriest possible Christmas breakfast at Leigh Hurst followed the service, wherein Cyril Leigh studied the faces of his sister and the woman who waited for Jack Powning to return to the halls of his fathers. Cyril Leigh had kept the promise of honor to Arizona Jack, but he had not failed to bid Cornelia hope for the return of the vanished soldier! An apocryphal "Bank" in San Francisco had discovered certain traces that Captain Jack Powning, of Yorkshire, had been seen alive in western America since the limit of time which would enable the heirs at law to claim their own! This was the last straw wildly caught at by Cornelia's loving heart, now thrilled with new *hopes*. And, "*upon this hint,*" those wily old solicitors, Carstairs, Lyon & Carstairs, had interposed the most urgent legal objections to further proceedings, "*in view of recent information*" and "*probable future revelations.*" Thoroughly in concert with Carstairs, Cyril Leigh was about to gently lure Cornelia Powning down to London.

"Once there, I will get her over to Paris on the promise of a definite clew, and then, Jack can arrange hereafter to keep his own secrets, but one person in the world must never know this from me, and that one *is Lisbeth!* For Powning's such a Don Quixote of honor, he would 'shoot wildly from his sphere,' and perhaps, bury himself in the Big Horn Mountains. *God knows that he's capable of anything!*"

In the afternoon, the disingenuous Cyril sought out his sister in her own rooms. He had much to say to her, and yet he was deeply astonished to find her in tears. Her boudoir was a dreamy bower of floral beauty, the rich spoil of San Remo making it a summer glory in the winter snows, but, upon her hand, it seemed there sparkled again the little ring of doubly twined hearts with its diamonds gleaming as a familiar token!

"*He has sent your ring back? He is going away?*" cried Cyril, with a sinking heart.

"*It is a new one, Cyril!*" said the girl, and then, the loving brother struggled hard between honor and the dictates of his affection, for Cyril could see that the past had returned with all its sorrows to cloud her, and that with all a woman's quick divination, she was troubled at heart by the veiling mystery of the man whose pride held him afar beyond the green tossing channel. It seemed a useless torture of two heaven-plighted hearts!

"*Beth,*" said Cyril, anxious to take refuge from her questioning eyes. "I have the most important matter of my future life to arrange *now*. I have spoken to Mary Annesley and I shall see Lord Trevor *to-morrow!* I must decide between the Army and life at home, perhaps a career in Parliament, *if all goes well!* Now, the Anglo-California Bank wants me to come down to London. I have to see Carstairs, and the three experts have at last finished their work of valuing the great ore body. This matter of the Condor can be closed out in a few months, as that swindling lawyer, 'Moses Dalman,' the counterfeit Lemon, has been now dropped from all connection with the Condor. All have deserted the faithless adviser. The new attorney of the company is one satisfactory to the Bank, the Consul, and our inspector. If I go into the army, I want your affairs all settled up before I leave home, in which case you will rule at Leigh Hurst. If I marry Mary, it will not be for a year, until I am duly elected to Parliament, and you will surely guard the old Hurst for me till then. It's your home for life, you know!"

"Cyril, I have promised Cornelia to live with her at Powning Hall, if you should marry," said Beth, with a crimsoning face.

"Now, I will see Lord Trevor to-morrow. Our guests go away, and I can go down to London, and then over to Paris, to see Dalton. I need his advice *on these bank matters*, and I am going to take Cornelia to London with me to see about delaying the action to settle the succession. *I may be away for two weeks.* I only wish you to promise me one thing, that is: that you will no engage yourself to be married *to any of these men* now addressing you till my fate is first settled, and till your mining business is over, and your fortune vested in your own name. I've a duty, as head of the family, you know!" Whereat, Lisbeth laughed, and fondly kissed him her approval.

"*Cyril,*" said Lisbeth suddenly, "take *me* down to London and over to Paris *with you. I wish to see your friend Hugh Dalton.* I wish to ask him some questions about—*about——*" And then her voice died away, for, as the crimson glow stole over her face, she reflected that the secret of her lost love was known but to Cornelia Powning and herself.

The young Squire's nerves were shaken. The fond woman's loving arms were round his neck, and Cyril struggled bravely with his good angel!

"*I dare not now—I cannot Beth,*" he answered. "But I give you my word of honor that you *shall* see Dalton. As soon as I know of my future status, the moment this business is fixed so that Cornelia is protected, I will then take you over there—*alone* you shall go with me to London and Paris. You will have to go down to town soon to see your bankers if we accept the last proposition. I think that you should drop all connection with these banded 'Condors' of the Huachuca Mountains. The funds once capitalized, you will be as rich as any woman needs to be."

"There is one thing, however, that I *absolutely insist on,*" said Lisbeth, in a smothered voice. "You tell me that this crippled man, Hugh Dalton, is not rich! He is now unable to face the world! His wound must be a serious menace to his future prosperity? I warn you that I will never sign the papers; that I will *not* accept this fortune, unless he accepts a share in return for what he has done for me and *for you!*"

"Lisbeth! *For God's sake!*" cried Cyril. "Be not rash! You do not know the man! *Leave all to me!*"

"*I will not!* Cyril," said the splendid woman. "If he will not accept my gratitude, he shall, *at least,* accord me simple justice. And the first use that I make of these moneys will be to trace him out, and to force him to divide my prosperity. He shall share the riches which his blood has gained for us!"

"*I have no right to force the battlements of his heart*, Beth," sadly said Cyril, and, he left his stately sister vainly sorrowing there.

While the Master of Leigh ruled the golden hour, Miss Lisbeth's carriage swiftly rolled away to Carlyon, and, sweeping then back homewards in a circle by Powning Hall, she imparted to Cornelia, waiting for her there, the gentle assurance of Lady Frances Trevor —that Cyril Leigh had made his "calling and election sure."

"With Lady Frances and '*the Honorable Mary*' as advocates, surely Lord Trevor's only objection—*Cyril's youth*—will vanish. The houses of Leigh and Powning should have at least, one man at home, to rule over this God's paradise."

And then, Lisbeth Leigh was surprised to find, for the first time in her life, that Cornelia Powning would not grant a favor.

"I go to London only to see the solicitors. It is the old sad business, Lisbeth darling. Do not ask me to take you, this time, for I shall be under Carstairs's charge, and I have my coming disposition of all my affairs to arrange. In a month, dearest, we will go to London together, as you will. But, *not on this visit!*"

All through the splendors of the baronial dinner at Powning Hall, and while she watched Cyril proudly leading the Honorable Mary Annesley, a deliciously happy looking Hebe, through the shifting scenes of the dance, stately Lisbeth Leigh eyed the ring gleaming on her slender finger.

"*He would avoid* me, and *yet*, he keeps my old ring! *We shall see!* For there is a pride which will not be denied. I will meet him yet *face to face*, and he shall tell me why the sister of his comrade may not meet him with a grateful heart."

With her eyes fixed upon distant Paris, she could not see the kindly dissembling of her brother and the lady of Powning Hall. For Love was and is, and, thank God, ever shall be, fond and blind! Earth's one unfading charm!

When Cyril Leigh, upon the next afternoon had listened to all Lord Trevor's oracular arrangements for the future of the youngest branch of his family tree, the happy lover escaped only to share his joy with gentle Lady Frances and the rosebud girl who waited calmly confident of her noble father's consent, for the Honorable Mary was the darling of the old nobleman's heart. The "*Army*" went down in a trice, easily bowled out by county interest, and the future "*assisted*" Parliamentary career. Cyril had returned to listen to the wisely formulated plans of the peer for a marriage after the election, and the consequent amelioration of the Carlyon and Leigh Hurst estates.

"It's a shame to see the old families go down before these 'cotton spinners' and 'rolling-mill men!'" wrathfully said Lord Trevor. "Now, there's the Powning property—a grand old name, a superb estate, and the race has spent itself in foreign service. That old mystery—the Jack Powning affair—was a crusher. I had always nourished great hopes of him."

"*Did you know Captain Powning?*" timidly said Cyril, seeing his opportunity.

"His father was my best friend and my fag at Eton, and, besides, I led the way for young Jack the first time he rode to hounds. I've always thought that he was murdered! He was a gallant lad, too. *A brave soldier.*"

"You are wrong, my Lord," quietly said Cyril. "I'm going to meet him in Paris *next week!*"

"*Good God!*" cried the peer, springing from his chair. "*This is news indeed!*"

And, on the old noble's promise to guard the secret, Cyril then unbosomed all the story of "Arizona Jack." There were left some gaps in the relation which saved the picture from the darker shadows of a life record whose lurid pages had been tinged with blood, and these leaves were left unturned!

> "Leaves pallid and somber and ruddy,
> Dead fruits of the fugitive years ;
> Some stained as with wine and made bloody,
> And some, as with tears!"

"Do you know, Cyril, my boy," said Lord Trevor, "this thing is about as bad as compounding a felony. Here's that royal girl, your sister, who has long loved this promising man with a singular devotion.

"And he's just the same Jack Powning I knew—gallant, fantastic, hot-headed, and *reckless*.   Now, as you are about to be a member of my family,"—Cyril's face was rosy in a sudden alpenglow—"and we must look out for Lisbeth's future—do you suppose that I'll be content to see her anything less than the queen of Nidderdale?   *My dear sir!* she's an empress at heart! Now I know that the heirs-at-law are determined soon to oust dear old Cornelia.   Shall chancery lawyers eat up the splendid acres of Powning?   *I'll stop it* if I have to call it up myself in the House of Lords!   I'm a distant relative of this young Don Quixote.   Why he's a mere boy yet—only thirty-seven!"

Cyril Leigh had guarded the easily inferred details of Jack Powning's self-sacrifice in never betraying the woman who had trapped him to shame.   "As long as there were lives between him and the succession," growled Lord Trevor, "he might play the Disinherited Knight.   *I'll tell you now what I'll do.   I'll write him a letter* and tell him that I have learned the truth through our Ambassador at Paris and that he has been recognized.   Now whether he lives at home in England or not, all that is strictly his own affair, but the succession shall not go wrong. *Don't you see that Lisbeth still tenderly loves him?* There are some things that a woman cannot say, my boy, and some things that she cannot do!   But you must just whisk Cornelia carefully over to Paris with you.   Let her walk in on him with you and then hand him my letter.   *That's all!*   As I am his ranking kinsman, I have a right to call him back out of the dumps.   If you simply do this, all will be well; then give him his head!   But if he fights shy—why, you can send me a wire!   I'll telegraph to Dufferin.   We were boys together and he will soon magnetize this young Timon of Athens.   For, Dufferin is a magician and the king of golden hearts!

"In the meantime, only *you*, and *I*, and *Cornelia*, are to know of this.   Dear old Cornelia!   She must not be cheated out of the return of her natural love. When you have stormed the madcap fellow's battlements, just leave him *alone* with Cornelia.   Don't you even ever mention your sister's name. Let Time and Fate bring that all around. If you do, neither the *one* nor the *other* will ever forgive you. *I know women, that I do,*" proudly remarked Trevor, who had been a notable squire of dames in his day.

"*And, dear old Cornelia,*" said the happy Squire, anxious to escape the society of the imperious young Hebe of Carlyon.

"*Not a single word to her, as yet,*" hastily said Lord Trevor. "She would just fall on Lisbeth's bosom, and then set all the bells a ringing, and slaughter fatted calves by the score, as well as wear out the telegraph! Your phantom comrade would be off to Bulgaria, or God knows where, in a jiffy.

"*No!* I will write to-night to Dufferin, and send him a telegram, which can be sent to you at Morley's. Once that Cornelia is there with you, show *her* the dispatch, send your own usual advices on to Señor Hugh Dalton at the Hotel Choiseul, and then both of you *quietly walk in on him.* Then *trust to Nature for the rest!* He will never escape from Cornelia," grimly said Lord Trevor. "She's a woman of uncommon resolution. And, *as to Lisbeth! Ah! Celà va sans dire!*" laughed the peer. "Get away, now, to luncheon, with Lady Frances and my little girl. You will please ask Mary to come in and see me here, for a moment."

The wily old noble bent his head over the confidential note to Earl Dufferin, and he suspended his labors just long enough to receive a stormy shower of caresses from the "Honorable Mary Annesley," who was secretly delighted at the long drawn-out love-making in store.

"*Remember, Mary,* you must marry a member of Parliament, so you had better go in for my *Blue Books now,*" said the happy father. "*Not a bad idea,* this knitting up of the three families. *Ça ira!*" mused Lord Trevor, as he thrust his hands in his pockets, and, strolling to the window, contemplated the sweeping valley long ruled, further than man's eye could reach, by the Leighs, the Pownings, and the Annesleys. He could hear the "delight of happy laughter—the delight of low replies," as the Honorable Mary led her captive knight into the sunbeam presence of Lady Frances.

"*There's right good stuff in that boy*," murmured Lord Trevor. "But—Jack Powning—I'd give a pretty stiff sum for a faithful transcript of his adventures. For, he has certainly taken *a long dive into obscurity*." With a maliciously delightful hospitality, Lord Trevor sent Lady Frances over to beam in upon the agitated Lisbeth Leigh, and bear her away to Carlyon for a week's visit during the absence of Cyril and Madam Cornelia. "Next to being in love *yourself*," mused Trevor, "is the delight of being around people who are immersed in the honey dew of Paradise. Mary will keep Miss Beth busy—*in chasing rainbows!* It's the time of roses with my dear little lass."

The clouds seemed to be rolling away from Nidderdale now.

In a cozy apartment of the Hotel Choiseul, in Paris —a week later, Señor Hugh Dalton was stretched out upon a divan, ~moking the very last of his excellent Tepic cigars, and gazing idly out at the crowds pouring along the slippery street below.

The sad-eyed José moved around the rooms noiselessly in fond anticipation of his master's every wish, while "Arizona Jack" restlessly examined his watch from time to time.

"*Leigh is late!* He said that he would be here, *at eleven*," mused the wanderer, settling down his still painful shoulder into the softest cushion. His mind had wandered far away to the little grave which he had left, under the shadows of the gray walls of the Campo Santo, of Magdalena. The month in which he had taken leave of Señora Morales and the jubilant Consul Broadwood came back to him. He gazed out into the blue wreaths of smoke surrounding him, and muttered, "Shall I wander over the world further? Why not go back again to the cloudless glow of Mexico's skies? The world has nothing left to give me, now." He suddenly heard his name cheerily called by Cyril and as he struggled to his feet, a slender figure shrouded in black, wreathed itself upon his breast

"My dearest boy! God has brought you back to me!" cried a gentle voice and then the blessed swoon of perfect joy, saved Cornelia from her fond heart's violence—as her head fell upon his breast.

The castaway's tears fell upon the silvered hair, as Cyril Leigh gently said: "*Jack! It was the will of God! Love* is stronger than your pride! Lord Trevor has discovered your whereabouts, by chance! *Here is his letter!*"

"*And, Lisbeth?*" gasped Arizona Jack.

"*Knows nothing as yet! I have kept my promise to you not to tell her!*"

Cyril Leigh left the two alone, and descended to the pretty courtyard of the Choiseul. "If the prodigal won't come to his fatted calf, we shall finally have to serve it up here, *à la Français,*" thought the happy Squire. "I must now keep dear old Cornelia keyed up to concert pitch, and, his pride must be pretty strong, if it proves stronger than her quenchless love."

José was dimly aware in his placid mind that Arizona Jack was "*muy caballero,*" and so, he attached himself to young Leigh, as an English Hidalgo of great renown. The simple story of the wanderer's home-coming to Cornelia's heart was told in the gentle determination of her loving clutches.

"He'll not fly forth again—over the troubled waters of life—not *while Cornelia lives!*" mused Cyril, as he ordered the very best breakfast for three to be served in a private dining-room. When the obsequious *maître d'hôtel* had bowed himself off, Cyril sat down to a meditative cigar.

"I will go out and telegraph Lord Trevor to come over. That's the trick, and, I will let him take Cornelia back. For, Lisbeth will stand a good bit of watching now. *Does she suspect?*" Cyril stood in great awe of that unspoken love which had kept Lisbeth proudly silent in these years of Jack's social eclipse. "*Haste, now, would ruin all! We* must trust to *Time* —old Father Time—*the universal cure-all!*"

The sad-eyed José aired his broken English in giving the young Squire the latest news from Magdalena and Guaymas, until, with a cautious diplomacy, Cyril sent him up, as a forerunner. And so, Madam Cornelia Powning and Captain John were prepared for Cyril's bustling return, announcing the breakfast. He was poorer by twenty pounds, for José had confessed to the slaying of the three ladrones, the remnants of the band who besieged the Grizzly's Cave.

Arizona Jack led the young man aside. "*I have read Lord Trevor's letter.* He has a right to know that I respect Cornelia's superb battle for my shadowy rights. *Dear, noble, womanly heart!* She tells me that the Powning estate can only be saved now by the acknowledgment of my existence. Trevor is my leading kinsman. I know the fire of his frosty heart. *He will stop at nothing!* Telegraph to him, in your name and Cornelia's, to come over here at once. He can take her to Earl Dufferin, and *between them*, they can manage to stop off the cormorants. I'll fix up a golden bait, *for the next of kin!*"

"*The very thing that I would propose!*" cried the delighted Cyril, "for, I am to marry Mary Annesley as soon as I am 'slated' for Parliament."

"I know the young fairy! She has ridden her pony to see the hounds throw off with me in the old days," joyously replied Arizona Jack.

"*Will you go back with me to England?*" whispered Cyril.

Jack Powning turned and gazed at Cornelia, softly weeping the happiest of tears.

"There's a lonely grave at Magdalena that speaks to me of a past which is buried there. I have time yet to give to the beloved dead before I dare to take up the thread of a new life. Face to face with the past, it is only for Cornelia's sake that my soul whispers, 'Resurgam!' Don't you know, Leigh, that there are times when an absolute rest of heart and soul are the only medicine of a 'mind diseased?' I have made a bargain with this dear noble woman who has given up her whole life to holding up the honor of the Pownings. *For my sake* alone, she has not wedded. I was always her favorite. I will meet her half way, and she shall know that I am grateful for the watch and ward which she has kept in the old tower. I have already given to her my word of honor that I will not go away again, that I will await her summons at need, and, in the meantime, keep silent, for *Lisbeth's sake!*"

The wanderer's lip trembled, and he turned proudly away.

"*Ah! No! There is yet a gulf between me and my birthright!* I look along life's columned years, and see its ruined fane *just where it fell!*"

While the gentlewoman slowly descended to the *petit salon*, clinging kindly to the captured prodigal, Cyril achieved the dispatch of his telegram. "*There shall be no break in the programme!*" he vowed, for a sudden terror possessed him! "If Lord Trevor should be enraged, then, good-bye to all—to my parliamentary hopes—and to the Honorable Mary Annesley's hand!" For, the stern Trevor had both borough and heiress, to give away! Cyril was more timid before that rosy Hebe than he had been while fighting at the barricade.

Late that night, the two comrades in the siege of the Grizzly's Cave, communed long after Cornelia Powning slept happily, for Lord Trevor's answer had brought to her aid a tower of additional strength. "*Leave at midnight!* Be with you in thirty-six hours. Wait for me. Lisbeth will remain at Carylon," so ran the peer's incisive words.

With all the proud shyness of an Englishman, Cyril Leigh refrained from mentioning his sister's name, when the bell of Nôtre Dame struck midnight, and the Squire had explained all the final dispositions of the fortunate sale of the Condor interest, through the wise counsels of the Anglo-California Bank. But he could not check the tide of feeling which surged in his wildly throbbing heart, as he gazed at Jack Powning, seated there with his head upon his hands.

"There is but one secret, now, for me to keep, Powning," said Cyril. "*Of course*, before Trevor comes, I must tell you that he knows nothing—absolutely *nothing*—of what you told me in the cave out there. And I will *tell you now*, I will never give a promise of honor again in my life! There is a higher justice than mere self-interest or pride can ever fathom. And there are some things that a man has no right to promise to do!"

Arizona Jack sprang up and faced his friend. "*Cyril!*" he said, in despairing tone, "*Wait!*—wait—till I can feel my heart throb again, after the frozen death in life of these years. I will not show my soul, naked and ashamed, to the one whom I would not let foul scandal smirch. *I have paid a fearful price!* There is but one innocent one—*Lisbeth!* God bless and keep her—and I would sooner face Bill Murfee's banded murderers alone again, *to-morrow*, than to dare, as yet, to look into that darling woman's steadfast eyes! *Let me have yet a few months more!* Cornelia knows all now, and she may guide me aright! My dead self, my wasted promise, my ruined youth, shames me now. I shall put myself in Lord Trevor's hands and Cornelia's as regards the estate. His letter is unanswerable. You and them I can rely on; but if Lisbeth Leigh's peace is broken by any one before the time, *I shall disappear beyond the power of man* to ever find a vestige of my body! I have my expiation yet to undergo."

"*Trust to me!*" sadly said Cyril. "Remember, *Resurgam!*" and then, the Squire walked home through the gay streets where folly and vice chase the flying hours with feet unwearied in wicked straying.

"He shall not be left to wander a wreck on error's shore, a houseless specter, evermore!" mused Cyril as he watched the bright promise of the stars above him. "It must be something beyond them both, which will bring them both together—some blessed seal which sanctifies and consecrates."

With a growing confidence in the efficacy of that strong coming reinforcement, Lord Trevor, Cyril Leigh waited for the arrival of his kinsman. With no feigned reluctance, he prepared to hie back to the Yorkshire glades, where Lisbeth Leigh was enjoying the society of the Honorable Lady Mary Annesley. "*My place is there now, as soon as I can get there*," he gleefully decided, in view of his parliamentary and matrimonial aspirations, and his heart was haunted with grave fears lest Mary Annesley should be torn away from him by the gnomes and genii of the Black Countree!

Gerald Annesley, Lord Trevor of Carlyon, brought a distinctly breezy element into the councils at the Hotel Choiseul. Squire Leigh dutifully met the coming reinforcement at the Gare St. Lazare. While they were on the way to the Hotel Chatham, where the Lady of Powning Hall was domiciled, a few pithy questions gave the old peer all his points.

"Do you get up to the Choiseul, say good-bye to Powning, pack your traps, and then be off to Nidderdale! *Think of it, sir!* If the Danes or wild Scots should invade the North Countree, *you* are the only notable man left in the gap! You are to be my Warden of the Marches, and so, defend Carlyon, Leigh Hurst, and the Hall against all 'men of evil mind'! Tell Powning that I've gone over to see Earl Dufferin, and that I'll look him up *at once.* I saw my solicitors in London, and *I have my legal cue.* By the way, here's a letter from Mary!"—the delivery whereof plunged Cyril Leigh into rosy dreams. *The "paragon" was still safe!*

"Remember! You are to say that I will keep Cornelia two weeks in London, *or near there,* on a frolic, while the solicitors are arranging some business affecting us both. And so go home, and keep all the Yorkshire hearts merry. I will answer for all things here. Address us *at the Savoy, London,* and look out for my telegram. Let no one of our circle down to London, *on any pretext!* I have fixed things at the Savoy. But we must not be found out in this loving deceit."

Cyril Leigh was half way across the channel before Lord Trevor had finished his long vigil with Arizona Jack. The wanderer saw in the peer's honest face that the mere fact of his existence was all the knowledge possessed by the old nobleman. Cornelia Powning's own artless story had proved to Jack how closely Cyril had guarded the secret.

There was but one figure painted in the stories of sweltering sands, towering mountain passes, the dark midnight tableau at Miller's Station, the league in the cave of death, the contest of wits with Arthur Lemon, Senator Stone, and the brutal Morris Blum—it was the figure of Hugh Dalton—*an all-conquering hero!*

And Jack Powning was forced to bow to a stronger will than his own, when Lord Trevor cut short the attempted evasion of his present duties.

"*I've made it all easy for you, my boy*," said Trevor. "Earl Dufferin will at once issue you a passport, and they will inscribe the details on the Legation archives. You need not come to England till you so desire, but, *noblesse oblige*, you must recognize Cornelia's life-work. I will charge myself with the necessary legal details and insure the silence of all. I am, as your kinsman, the titular head of your clan."

With rare delicacy, Lord Trevor never obtruded the name of Lisbeth Leigh, but, the succession of Powning Hall was now made sure beyond all cavil.

It was late the next day, after a brief confidential interview at the English Embassy, that Lord Trevor announced his final plan.

"I will leave Cornelia with you and run over to London. A week or ten days will suffice me. Cling to your name of Hugh Dalton. So, your retirement will be guarded. I am going to send my yacht, the *Pathfinder*, over to Cherbourg to you about February first. You can coast around to Villefranche. And you'll find dear old Cornelia there, in my cottage at San Remo. A quiet month together will make another man of you, and then I'll run over and bring her home with me. So finish up your Parisian experiences, and after Cornelia leaves you at San Remo, you shall do as you will, only promise me that you'll stay near us on the Continent. Let me watch over both your interests, and my only reward is to know that the Powning blood still holds the old acres. And, '*Powning must be Powning*' always!"

With some magic of her own, the faded old gentlewoman found after Lord Trevor's departure that Jack Powning had been tamed. Silent as to the past, and non-committal as to his future, the wanderer was as wax in her hands. And yet, when she returned to Nidderdale, after the triumphant Lord Trevor had come back for her, there was no spoken promise of "Arizona Jack" that he would return to England.

"*Let us talk of that, at San Remo*," he said, as he

lifted her hand with knightly grace to his lips, when the visitors left for London.

The sad-eyed José, a month later, gazed in wonder on the glories of the Corniche, as he followed Arizona Jack, and his silver-haired kinswoman around the orange groves of Cap St. Martin. The adroit hand of Lord Trevor had guided Lisbeth Leigh into beginning the picking-up of all the threads of county influence for her brother. Cyril's coming of age, the growing pre-occupation of the two young lovers, and the investment of her now idle funds busied the woman who was now the center of a loving intrigue, and Miss Lisbeth Leigh was the loveliest country politician now, and deep in the Blue Books.

Hugh Dalton, "in the south of France, for his health," remained an enigma, and the period of his year of penance was drawing to a close. Many a light-hearted woman of fashion watched that stern, soldierly figure, as Jack Powning wandered slowly through the silvery orange grove with the old gentlewoman, and wondered why their bright eyes had no spell for him.

Sitting for hours alone, out on the crags, and watching the blue waves break on the enchanted coast, Arizona Jack faced the ever-recurrent specter of his past life. He would give but one promise, when Lord Trevor came back with the spring swallows to bring the tranquil-hearted Cornelia home. There was the fond pleading of a life's affection in the old gentlewoman's eyes, when she said, "*If I need you—at my summons, will you come?*" And the wanderer knew that his kinswoman saw the gathering shadows of their last parting. He bowed his head, and kissed her hands. "*At your call, I will come home.*"

CHAPTER XV

"YOU MUST SPEAK THE WORD."

THE days wore away quietly along toward Easter, and all the humble cottage dwellers near the villa at

San Remo knew of the open hand of the "Milor Inglese."　For, Hugh Dalton was forced to recognize the fact that he was a rich man now, the solicitors of the Powning Hall estate having acted on the advice of that energetic nobleman, Lord Trevor, and transferred a block of the accumulated funds to the credit of the man who walked by the shores of the blue tideless sea. José followed his master as faithfully as a Welsh collie watches the feeding sheep.　The silent wanderer had found the royal way to the squalid homes of the poor of the Province Porto Maurizio.

There was a struggle still going on in the hot and restless heart of the man who saw the "Golden Now" gliding by him.　Alone, out on the rocks, he sometimes dreamed of some strange far away land where he might throw his life away in battle for England—and then with a bitter sense of his helplessness, the wounded arm would drop as he stretched it toward the distant Soudan or the region where England's sons were forcing the silent mysteries of the heart of Africa.　"*Only a cripple, a poor human derelict*," he groaned.　In his unavailing fight against Fate, in following that false code of Honor which betrays, Jack Powning was yet a rebellious and a drifting soul.　He knew not of the clear gleam of the star of Duty, which leads the erring man on to soar over the clouded past, "and, conquering more than cities, arise the master of himself, at length."

His moral atonement had reached no farther than the self-denial of his hungry heart.　He seemed to find his life hollow, for in no hidden way, could he advance the future interests of Lisbeth, whose image shone still "faint, cold, and far," above him.　Her dowry in the Condor was all secured at last, and the golden harvest reaped now, was permanently invested in the "sweet simplicity of the three per cents."

"Cyril has a golden career before him," mused Arizona Jack.　"That delicious bribe, the Honorable Mary Annesley, and the coaching of Lord Trevor will make him a man of note.　Aunt Cornelia—God bless her—trusts in the God who has walked before her, in all the ways of her blameless life, '*a cloud of smoke by day, a pillar of fire at night*.'"

He knew that he had made Señora Dolores Morales more than secure for life, and the grateful poor of Magdalena had received a startling large largess of British gold. "This, at least, is *honest money*," he gloomily said, as he sent his bills of exchange over to Mark Broadwood.

In the feverish generosity of these hours of indecision, he made naught of his own good deeds. "All this came to me without effort, these revenues of Powning Manor." And he resolutely tried to put away the memories of the woman whom he dared not approach. Her picture, gently filched from the grateful Cyril; the ring which had saved him from the wildly devised crime planned at Bowie and conceived at El Paso; these two talismans were kept, with the letter whose every line still thrilled him to the bosom's core; the letter in which Lisbeth Leigh claimed the right to thank the man who had saved her brother's life, and aided to baffle the "Condors" of Huachuca!

He wandered, haunted still by one loving and lovely face through the dim interiors of the Cathedral of San Remo, the Santuario della Guardia also, knew his restless steps, and, in the Santuario dell Assunta, his troubled heart melted under the witching music of the pleading voices of the singers.

In the long corridors of the palazzo of the Marquis Borrea d'Olmo he gazed on faces, pictured there, which brought back to him the wistful eyes of the sweet woman whom he now worshipped with a despairing love. He found one face, the prototype of her own, and there, before that shrine of his heart, he lingered, his lips moving in the words of an old song,

> " Dearest, and always beloved!
>   Leave but one trace,
> Only come back to me, darling,
>   Once more, your face."

In the fragrant groves of palm, where the golden oranges gleamed and the silvery green of the olive trees rose above the lemon orchards, he marked the calm-visaged priests of the seminary sadly pacing along with their hopeless eyes dropped in self-abasement.

He had guarded till now, the dark story of his intended treachery to Cyril! He had never dared to unfold to Cyril the awful gulf of plotted crime which lay between him and Lisbeth, whose pure life had flowed on like a crystal river.

"If I suffer on alone, if my life atones, why should she know?" he groaned.

For he feared to face her splendid eyes and then, tell her a part only of the truth. In leaving Cyril's heart unshadowed by the whole story of his mad recklessness he had but followed out his last pledge to himself in the cave, "*For Lisbeth's sake!*" But he now writhed, Prometheus-like, bound to the rock, and one evening, when the deepening shades hid from his eyes the floating figure of the Blessed Virgin beaming down from a marvelous picture over the Cathedral altar, he went from confessional to confessional, till he found a priest who spoke Spanish. And there on his knees, to the unseen minister of God's grace, hidden behind the screen, he poured out all the story which burned yet in his guilty heart! The silent interior deepened into gloomier shades as he unbosomed his sorrows, but a light shone in his lightening heart, for he had *at last*, cast away the burden of his gloomy secrets. Some mysterious spring in his heart had loosened, and it seemed as if the murmur of that grave voice behind the screen led him on to a dawning peace. It was over—*at last!*

The agitated stranger told the whole truth, and then the astonished priest heard the frank confession that the man who sought the ear of God's minister was "*without the pale*" of the Roman Church!

"*I speak to you* only as my brother. We are all brothers here *in sorrow!* Do not wait till your duty *comes to you! Go to it!* Remember '*Deo duce!*' Your life is a trust. You have no right to cast it off. And remember, my brother, you hold a leading place in your family line. *Take up again the* broken thread of Life. Go back and be brave. For you can serve those to whom birth has made you leader and lord. You may not put away the cup of Life. You will find your work waiting for you there *at your own doors!*

And if you cannot live out your life *for yourself*, then *live for others!* And leave the dark past with Him who pardons. Let your noble future be your living prayer for the past. Go, my brother, and *go with God!*"

The stricken man on his knees started. He seemed to hear again the sweet, low, thrilling voice of Pepita, "*Vayase V con Dios!*

"*May I come to you again?*" he murmured.

"*When you will!* Come to a brother's heart," said the grave, sweet voice of the unseen priest.

Out into the serene starlight, Arizona Jack went, muttering "*Deo Duce!*" as he encountered the old sacristan lighting the evening lamps. He had read the name "*Padre Anselmo*" on the confessional box, and he then drew the simple sacristan aside and crossed his palm with a broad gold piece. "*Tell me of Father Anselmo,*" he said.

"Ah, Signore Inglese—there is an angel. And yet ten years ago he was the gayest cavalier of the Guarda Nobile. But, the Contessa Valeri—his promised bride—was drowned, before his very eyes, at Capri, and he buried himself for five years in Salamanca. Here in the cholera plague, wherever there is sorrow, he has won an earthly crown of grateful love. '*Friend of the poor*' they call him."

The next day, wandering by the shore, yet irresolute as to his return to England, for all his fears had returned to vex him with the golden day, Arizona Jack lifted up his eyes to see José running with a paper in his hand.

There alone, by the sea shore, he opened the telegram. Its signature "*Trevor,*" was the call to instant action. But he sat dazed with trembling lips as he read:

"Cornelia seriously ill. Come instantly. Will meet you at Dacre Station. Answer."

"*Deo Duce,*" he murmured, as he strode along followed by the anxious José. There was a passing carriage; he hailed it, and then bade the man hasten to the Cathedral. In ten minutes he led José into the presence of Padre Anselmo. "My poor old servitor! Take care of him till I send for him. Let him come to you with his simple wants. *I leave him at Villa Trevor.*" And when the priest opened the envelope which Arizona Jack had marked "*Por los Pobres,*" he smiled. "*Deo Duce.*" The ex-guardsman murmured. "His *faith* may be lacking yet, but he abounds in *good works.* All promises well, for *he is going home.*"

The two men had parted as brothers of the heart, and as the wanderer sped along the Corniche to sweep onward by the Paris, Lyons, and Méditerranée, he heard the gentle voice ringing in his ears. "*There is but one way, Deo Duce.*"

Arizona Jack turned his head to see the little city bowered upon its rising slopes by the sapphire sea fade away behind him. The last gleams of the setting sun flashed off in a golden glory from the red tiled roof of the old cathedral. The "fields which promised oil and wine" stretched out along the sculptured hills, and one faint silver star twinkled in the East shining out far beyond the Ligurian Alps hanging over the sparkling Gulf of Genoa. There in the "dim religious light," under the benediction of the outstretched arms of the Mother of Sorrows, Padre Anselmo lovingly prayed for the returning prodigal.

There was no plan framed in Jack Powning's mind as he was whirled along through the beautiful Midi. All these patient years of waiting of Cornelia Powning seemed now to appeal to him. It was the one rose which had blossomed in the arid desert of his life!

The fresh air of the Channel brought back all the old life into the yearning traveler's heart, and he stood, a martial figure with spray-drenched hair, on the deck as the steamer glided in under the white Dover Cliffs.

There had been a mercy in the missing of the telegram which reached the Hotel Choiseul an hour too late, to rob the voyager of his one last lingering hope —that he might see in the old gentlewoman's eyes the recognition of his loyal faith. For he had come at her call, a call which he dared not disobey.

When the train sped on, after he had dashed hastily through London, he realized that a "generation had arisen which knew not Joseph." For in all the vast hive of Lud's town, in the swarming life of St. Pancras

Station, there was no one to note the lonely man, whose soldierly, bronzed face and wounded arm spoke of "moving scapes by flood and field." He was a stranger in his own land!

"*There is no need for me to avoid my fellows,*" he bitterly murmured, "for, *Time has done its work!* My name lies buried under the drifted years. *There is the strange mercy of oblivion.* I am truly a stranger in a strange land."

It was in the early gray of the morning that he stood once more under the shadows of the grand old York Minster, and then he found that he had a heart left. For the familiar scenes of his boyhood had silently touched the sealed fountains of feeling, and he sat, wrapped in olden reveries as Marston, Wetherby, Spofforth, Ripley, and Darley flashed by, and then he awoke with a start to meet his kinsman at Dacre.

There was no notice taken of the tall stranger whom Lord Trevor hurried into a closed carriage. In silence the old peer pressed "Arizona Jack's" hands and as their eyes met, the wanderer knew that he had arrived too late for the last blessing of the dear old kindly eyes.

"*I have thought it best to bring you home to Carlyon,*" said Lord Trevor, "*for no one knows of your coming! The last sigh she breathed was your name.* It is two days now since she left us, and *to-morrow you will go to the church with me.* I have charge of all, and Easter morning follows her obsequies. I know you will approve all my actions, for your boyish rooms in the old tower are ready for you now at Powning. *No one shall know!* I will go over with you to-night from Carlyon. I have a letter for you—*the last which she ever wrote*—and I only know that she begs you to take up the care of your people here into your own hands."

Jack Powning bowed his head, and a flood of old-time memories swept over his softened heart. Down the beautiful valley of the Nidd, past the well-remembered Brimham Crags they moved on, until the wanderer's eyes rested on the splendid sky lines of Powning Hall rising over the oaks which hid Leigh Hurst from their sight.

"*Cyril?*" whispered the world wayfarer.

"*He knows nothing as yet,*" gravely murmured Lord Trevor, "*I left all to you!*" And the beating of his own heart was all the sound Jack Powning heard, as sweeping round the noble vale he saw again the gray turrets of Leigh Hurst shining in the spring sun. There his heart of hearts waited for him in all her gentle faith!

Leaning back in the carriage, the man who had come into his own again lingered in an unconscious joy, which thrilled through him like the most exquisite pain, for the breeze of his native vale had brought back to him all the wild, wayward charm of his younger days.

When they neared Carlyon, Lord Trevor gazed frankly into Jack Powning's eyes. "*There are moments in a man's life when his soul is on its knees,*" said the old diplomat. "*If you needed aught to call you back again—*there is no appeal left after you have looked upon Cornelia's face for the last time. I have done all that I could. And now, in the name of all these who have gone before—and we've been a rare old line—I ask you *do you go or stay ?* "

"With your aid, Gerald Annesley, and *for her sake, I will stay,*" slowly said the wanderer, who was at rest at last. "*I leave all in your hands.*"

"Then, this Eastertide will be a triumph of love!" murmured the old nobleman, who turned his head away, for in his own heart he had long since divided the burden of the sealed pages of the life of the man who was no longer Arizona Jack.

No one knew of the stranger guest's arrival at Carlyon, and in a set of guest chambers long set apart for this very purpose, Lord Trevor left his long-fought-for prize. "My own man will wait on you here *till after all is over.* He will secretly provide everything for you, and to-night I will take you over to the Hall. As executor of your aunt, *I have to take temporary charge,* but her will, which is known to me, places me in a position of the greatest responsibility. Your family solicitors will send their head down to you here at once, but, Cornelia's handsome personal fortune is left to be administered by me.

Captain John Powning saw the "begging of the question" in the old peer's eyes.. "*Tell me all !*" he said, simply.

"Your secret cannot be longer kept! The will, in due course, will be opened Easter Monday, and one-half of her life savings is left *to you*, and the other *to* ——" The old man hesitated and turned his head away. "*To Lisbeth Leigh*," he said as he went out, leaving the startled visitor face to face with the sweet apparition now called up by his throbbing heart. And in the rooms where Rupert's cavaliers had planned the desperate charges which well nigh wrested victory from Fairfax and Cromwell and Leslie at Marston Moor, the Master of Powning Hall read the trembling lines traced by a loving hand which called him back to life again! There was a touching faith is his buried manhood which bade him lift up his head in hope; and all the selfish pride of his stormy heart vanished before the simple words of Cornelia's loving letter!

The rising tide bore him out and beyond himself, and in the fading glories of the sunset skies, he knew a peace which he long had vainly sought.

"*There lies my duty before me*," he murmured, gazing out in the splendid richness of the patrimony, which was his to rule. "*It shall be as she wishes it.*"

And he bared his head in the soft rich evening air, and vowed himself to live for his people—among his people.

The evening stars were trembling in the quiet skies, when Lord Trevor led Jack Powning out of the entrance, whence Rupert's cavaliers had defiled to die at Marston.

"*Trust yourself to me*," he said. "*All is ready!*"

And in the solemn of the night, unheralded, the wanderer returned, led by his kinsman, to keep a last vigil of love.

There was a beautiful woman leaning from her casement that night, who watched the light gleaming strangely out in the old round tower at Powning Hall. Lisbeth Leigh was alone, and the letter bearing her name which had been Cornelia Powning's last trust to Lord Trevor lay opened before her. Across the fragrant meadows of Leigh Hurst, beyond the old oaks so dear to her girlish days, she could see these unfamiliar lights gleaming out in the tower there, while shadows wrapped the rest of the noble mansion.

"*Cyril knows nothing!*" she timidly murmured, and she knew by the glances of Lord Trevor's eye that Cornelia had kept the faith to the last. She gazed out in silence upon the peaceful scene, and then she read with a thrill of exquisite bliss, the lines which were, to her, love's last legacy. For gentle dead hands were outstretched now to bring the parted lovers face to face, at last!

"You will meet Hugh Dalton—for he has given me his word to come, when I call him. And when you are face to face—Lisbeth, you will know what I leave to the One who leads us right."

With a glance at the ring which sparkled upon her finger she murmured, "*If it should be—then ——.*" She had no words to finish but, blessed angels of Love and Hope ministered to her that night in her dreams. She dared not frame the hope whose very ecstasy thrilled her trembling frame with awakened transports of love.

The old gray church was crowded with those who held the memory of the gentle Lady of Powning dear, when Cyril Leigh led his stately sister, the next morning, to the great canopied pew of the Lords of the Manor. Beautiful Lisbeth Leigh never lifted her eyes while the service solemnly proceeded, her only wandering glances resting upon the exquisite flowers covering that dear dead heart. It was only when the gathered hundreds turned to leave, that she saw a stern soldierly figure in black at the side of Gerald Annesley—Lord Trevor—whose state pew filled the front of the opposite aisle.   And, as the tall stranger stooped to take one blossom from the wreath above her stainless breast, Lisbeth Leigh, with a quick gasp then knew that the dead woman's love had brought Hugh Dalton, *home at last.*" Slowly his head turned as he moved forward, on his kinsman's arm, and their eyes met! The bronzed, impassive face never changed, but, the pleading eyes turned to her own, spoke of all the infinite love surging through the chastened wanderer's soul. It was the cry of a new born human soul. "*Resurgam!*"

Lisbeth felt Cyril's arm convulsively tighten upon

her own, and he was ashen pale and speechless as he led his sister out to her carriage. There were left there behind them but those who opened the ancient vault of the Pownings to receive the ashes of the Lady Bountiful of Nidderdale. The sunlight streamed through the gorgeous windows of the old church, the pure flowers of Easter morning were already gleaming on the walls, and the lark soared high above, its gurgling song falling in floods of melody. There was no one in the lessening throng who knew the handsome young soldier of old in the stern, bronze-faced man there, whose sweeping mustache hid the lines of happy Jack Powning's once smiling lips. The Master of Powning stood there unknown, the bravest figure of all the countryside!

But, with her steadfast eyes turned upon Cyril as they moved away toward Leigh Hurst, Lisbeth whispered: "*That man*, Cyril, with Lord Trevor——."

"*Is Hugh Dalton, the man who saved my life*, the man who gave you back your fortune!" tenderly whispered the Squire.

It was on her brother's breast that the graceful woman's head lay as the whole innocent deceit of love was made plain to her. "Don't, don't speak to me now, Cyril," she faltered. "*Only, take me home!*"

She dared not own even to the brother the secret of her lifelong love, or the joyous new-born hopes that the bird soaring above them was singing in her awakened heart. That the gentle stratagem of the loved one now passed away had called him back after many years she knew, and she blessed the gracious memory of the true heart now at rest forever.

And as she sought the refuge of her own rooms, she gazed upon the little ring which Hugh Dalton had sent back to her as a token. "*He kept mine,*" she murmured, "*for the sake of the old days.*" And she now knew, with a wild bound of her joyous heart, why the champion of the Grizzly's Cave would *take no pay at her hands!* She knew instinctively that he had fought in that dark hour, "*for Lisbeth's sake!*"

And the startled Cyril found but one refuge in his sudden alarm lest "*things should now go wrong.*" "*I'll have 'Pablo' saddled* and *gallop over to Carlyon.*   Lord Trevor is the only man who can advise me *now.*   Even Lady Frances and *Mary* must soon know this.   I think I had better be out of the way *for a while*, for if Trevor don't know what's the correct thing to do, then *I'm without a friend in the world.*"

The beautiful Lisbeth Leigh saw her brother ride away and easily divined the innocent perplexity of his boyish heart.

When Pablo's springing form had swept on beyond the line of the fringing oaks to the west, the Lady of Leigh departed upon a pilgrimage to which an unseen hand seemed now to beckon her.   Her noble face was rose-tinged, as her carriage swept up to the grand entrance of Powning Hall, and it was no butler who received her, for, from the stern old round tower, the eyes of the plainsman had seen the approach of one who had mastered now her own beating heart.   She was only a woman, and her woman's pride would fain mask the love glowing in her heart!

There was not a word spoken as the Master of Powning led the woman, whose hand trembled in his own, to the grand drawing-room where all the fair women of his race looked down upon the sweet face of Lisbeth Leigh, lit up with its softly shining, tender eyes.   Their glances called back Jack Powning to the Heaven he had left, and which now glowed around him.

They were alone, and he stood before her, with his head bowed and holding her slender hands in his bronzed palms.

"You would not let them pay you *for me*," she said, in a low, sweet voice, "and so, I have come to say to you that I will not rest under this unpaid debt—the debt I owe for a brother's life—and for my fortune."

And then, she drew off the ring which she had received from Hugh Dalton.   "*Take it back*—and *give me back the ring which brought you home to me !*"

"*You must hear me first, Lisbeth*," said the man, who read the loving story of her eyes.   "*I am not worthy that you should come to me.*"

"*I will hear nothing*," resolutely said Lisbeth Leigh,

smiling through her tears. "Can't you see that I will have my ring? To-morrow the whole country side will know, and, in default of your pay, *I have brought you— myself!*" There was a sobbing angel on his heart whose gentle eyes told him how a woman's love had conquered a woman's pride.

It was an hour later when the carriage with Lord Trevor and Cyril Leigh drove up to the great arched door of Powning Hall. The old nobleman sprang out with the haste of a first well-wisher, for hand in hand, before him stood the lovers, who were destined now to rule together this dreamy paradise of Nidderdale.

"When shall I tell them all, of your return?" eagerly cried Trevor, as Cyril Leigh grasped his comrade's hands in a speechless joy.

"*You must speak the word, Lisbeth,*" tenderly said the new master, "*for, I have given my whole life now over to you.*"

"Let us go in. I must think this all over, if I am to decide!" said the beautiful Lisbeth Leigh, strangely timid and unready, for one who had so long been the queen of Leigh Hurst.

"*You must soon learn to decide many things, Lisbeth,*" said Captain John Annesley Powning, "for, henceforth *this is your own house,* and *our home!*" The four were seated in the great drawing-room, before the Lady of Leigh found words to express her decision.

"I think that we had better leave it all to Lord Trevor!" she said, and then she fled away, in a strange confusion, for her face was tinged with a crimson glow.

The three men were silent a moment, and then Lord Trevor's aplomb proved him at once the master of the situation. "We must work at this as a united family! I am luckily in legal charge here. I shall telegraph for Solicitor Carstairs to come down from Sheffield to-morrow, and I'll run over to York and bring back Jekyll himself. To-morrow is Easter Sunday. One of Jekyll's firm would, of course, come with the will. I'll bring the Chief with me. Now, we've a stolid and curious community of voters, and Cyril's prospects must not be hurt with any strange radical yarns I'll also bring back a 'special license' from York. Carstairs and Jekyll can easily make all their drafts and memorandums on Monday. I will give you Villa Trevor, and send the *Pathfinder* around to Porto Maurizio.

"It would be a relief to me to have you young people *out of the way*, for two or three months! Now, Captain," said the old peer, with a twinkle in his eye, " we will have the steward of the estate in. *You* shall only tell him to obey my orders during your absence. I've a deal to do, to arrange the affairs of Cyril and Mary. I propose that we should have you all over to dine at the Hurst together to-night, to-morrow you will surely be gathered together at the Easter services. I'll be back for church. Lady Frances will expect you all at Carlyon for Easter breakfast and dinner. Monday there is the legal business to arrange here, and on Tuesday, Cyril, I propose that there shall be a private marriage in the family chapel at Carlyon "—the would-be member of Parliament smiled as "coming events cast their shadows before "—"on Wednesday, after our family reunion at Carlyon, I advise you, Captain Powning, to take the London train and *go right on to San Remo!* To the county, I shall say *nothing*— absolutely *nothing. It is the only safe plan. Qui s'ex- cuse—s'accuse toujours.* You will be simply regarded as a modern Monte Cristo—that is all! Lady Frances will, on your return, gather ' *le monde ou l'on s'ennuie* ' to a celebration, in which Carlyon shall outdo even its old golden days. The whole official society of the Three Ridings shall be bidden.

" And *this*, the only sensible plan, is my wish and will *on behalf of Lisbeth*," said Lord Trevor. "Now, I will call in the steward of the estate. He's a new man. One whom you never knew, and *that's one comfort.* Then I'll be off for York and back to-morrow early. You, Cyril, can ride over to Carlyon on your wonderful horse, see Lady Frances, and then bring them all over to dinner at Leigh. I will leave Powning himself to drive Lisbeth back home to Leigh. There's some pretty fair horseflesh in the stable."

" *All this is very fine*," murmured the new master of

Powning, "*but* —— " the Captain glanced at the stately figure of the lovely woman who had found a refuge at a window, looking out on "My Lady's Garden," where the burnished peacocks strutted in pride.

"*You must take up the running yourself, now,*" kindly said Lord Trevor. "You may use *my name*, if you wish, but *I disclaim all future responsibility !*"

Jack Powning saw the delicate subterfuge of the graceful old nobleman who had thrown his social banner around him as an all-powerful ægis of protection. From the massive walls of Carlyon, Lord Trevor could defy the whole world of fashion in arms, for Lady Frances's gentle county leadership had never been questioned. Trevor's whole life had illustrated that one haughty line of action: "*Roy ne puis, prince ne daigne, Rohan je suis !*"

"Now, Cyril, let us go and hunt up the steward. I wish to give him my orders about the legal gentlemen's entertainment on Monday," briskly said Lord Trevor. "You can ride over here daily while these travelers are having a month on the Riviera and a peep at the Mediterranean. We must he joint suzerains, till Powning comes back and get into harness. I've no time to lose if I get my train to York. I can get the special license out to-night." They hastened to escape and leave the startled lovers alone.

"Arizona Jack" led Lisbeth Leigh out into the garden, and they wandered away into the bower where the dream hallowed figure of a graceful mother returned to bless the returned plainsman. There was a strange silence between them, for Lisbeth's heart told her of the struggle going on in her companion's bosom. "*I dare not tell you, Lisbeth,* of Lord Trevor's wishes, without promising to tell you first the whole story of my life—and—*tell it without sparing myself !* For I came back to you, *because of Cornelia's mandate.* She left me a sealed letter."

Lisbeth raised her shining eyes to his. "*And she left one to me !*" she murmured, in a voice soft as the falling dews of night. "*But I will not now, hear a word, not a single word,*" she said with a gentle insistence. "You shall tell me when *I wish*, and, only *what I care to ask.*   For, *I have my own secrets !"*   She paused, her hands filed with the flowers she had idly gathered.   Her eyes were downcast as she said: *"I knew long ago that this day would come."*   Powning sprang to her side.   *" When you would only take my ring from Cyril as your pay,* when you sent me back the new ring, which was its double, when I saw the light of happiness in dear Aunt Cornelia's eyes, then I knew that you had risen from the dead!   *I have been true to you,* in all these years, and *together, we will go on now, hand in hand.*   Tell me nothing sad now, *I can not bear it!*   There is but one thing I ask—*take me away from here for a time,* for I must be alone with you, *in our happiness."*

They were clasped heart to heart, when he whispered to her all the loving schemes of Lord Trevor to shield them from the hydra head of gossip.   *"I will do as you wish.   Let us go away.   It is best.*   And we shall find a new life out there, under the purple crags of Sorrento!"

"Let us forget the world," she said softly.   "There under the stars of the east, we will leave all sorrow behind us for a time."   The beaming face of Lord Trevor recalled them as they walked back hand in hand.   The lark was singing high in the scented meadows and the sun shone fair on the beautiful vale by the Nidd.   *"I can not go in,"* she shyly whispered, "without telling you the words of Cornelia's last message to you.   *Tell him that pride shall yield to love,* and *that my blessing will linger round you in the dear old halls.'"*   And, then, he knew why she had timidly come to him—to save him from himself, and to lift the dark shadows from his heart!

"I have been dead these many years, Lisbeth," earnestly said the Master of Powning, *"but to-morrow is Easter* and the grave of the old sorrow is sealed forever. Your love, you noble darling, has called me back.   It is your voice in my heart which has whispered *'Resurgam.'*   There is the golden prime of our lives before us.   And you *shall lead me on—lead me on yet, to be worthy of you."*

When the wondering steward had received his brief

orders, Lord Trevor took occasion to hint of a monster celebration at the home-coming of the travelers, which should revive the olden glories of both houses.

"Till then, Bradford, *absolute silence*, and enforce the same discretion here, *with all!*"

When Trevor was gone, Cyril Leigh sprang upon the fretful Pablo, who was now growing proud of the caresses of a slender hand, upon which shone the ring which Lisbeth Leigh had exchanged for Jack Powning's newer token.

"*Brave Pablo!*" she murmured. "He brought back wealth, life, and happiness to us all on that wild midnight journey."

"*Through night to light,*" said Powning, as he bent his head, and then whispered softly: "*Adios, mi querida!*"

He gazed into the steadfast eyes of the loving woman at his side, and a pang of sorrow racked his awakened heart.

"*Does she know?*" he sadly mused, and his thoughts flew far away to the little grave hollowed by the yellow stone-walls of the Campo Santo, in far away Magdalena—the grave where lay pulseless and cold in death, the gallant-hearted girl, who had died for them under the Apache's deadly arrow.

"*The innocent sufferer for the guilty! God be with you, Pepita!*" he prayed.

There was a famous dinner at Leigh Hurst on this memorable Easter eve, and only the presence of the Honorable Mary Annesley brought mirth and laughter to the board. For, Lady Frances was lost in following the wanderer's hidden path in the buried years. Captain Powning and Lisbeth were fain to escape the general observation, but the rosy Eros hovered daily near Cyril and Mary, and the flutter of his wings brought blushes to the young patrician's cheeks. The mother and daughter of the caste of "Vere de Vere" were perfect in the parts assigned them by that absent *deus ex machina*—Lord Trevor—and yet, before Captain Powning drove them home to Carlyon, Lisbeth Leigh's sweet secret had percolated through three gentle bosoms. Lady Frances said but little, as the break dashed on in the mellow starlight. Jack Powning was a "proper man-at-arms," and, he was "to the manner born," and yet, the gentle patrician still eyed him with a certain alarm, as if he were a stray inhabitant of Mars, and had taken an excursion train downward by the way of the moon.

The Honorable Mary Annesley, in the golden glow of her own mating time, had precipitated herself upon Lisbeth Leigh's bosom and opened the golden portals of her heart to "Uncle Jack!" It was her time of roses, and she bloomed for all, "a thing of beauty and a joy forever!" When the Easter anthems rang out in the manor church at Leigh Hurst, there were many glances of interest centered upon the stalwart visitor in Lord Trevor's pew, but, the busy gladsome season rejoiced all hearts, and only around the sumptuous breakfast table at Carlyon, was the identity of the "South American General" known.

Lord Trevor took Miss Lisbeth Leigh apart from all, into his library, and dropped the mask of his seeming lightness for a moment.

"*My dear child*," said the old noble, "you have nobly seconded me in my attempt to conquer that strange unruly nature which Jack has received from the mad Pownings. I know that which none but he, shall ever know! Some Italian said, 'there is in every man's nature the highest heaven and the lowest hell.' As the head of his house, and as a man who gave my dearest child to your brother, I can tell you now that Powning's fantastic honor *alone* made him a Western exile. As for the wild life out there, think of his lifelong reminder in that stiffened right arm which was raised in defense of your brother's life—and your fortune—when he made a living bulwark of his body, in the mouth of the Grizzly's cave! Jack has told me *what you need not know*, with all his shortcomings, and the follies of his wild days. *I call him a hero, after all!* These pearls, my dear child, were chosen by me for Hildegarde, and, since her bridal flowers withered forever, no one has even worn them. When I give them to you, I make you as she was—*the daughter of my heart!*"

And then, the courtly old peer kissed the trembling

hand of the dark-eyed beauty, who clung to his neck, sobbing in a transport of joy at the generous shield of his noble words.

The only calm, unruffled souls at Powning Hall on that Easter Monday, were Messrs. Jekyll and Carstairs, who conducted a professional duel of politeness in guarding the interests of their respective clients, when the will was opened which made Captain John Annesley Powning and Miss Lisbeth Leigh the equal devisees of the departed lady's very large personalty. With due punctilio, the presence of these secret lovers had been insisted upon, and finally, a knowing whisper from Lord Trevor caused the men of parchment to suddenly furl their hostile sails and hobnob together wonderfully over a state luncheon, while the family party assembled, as Cyril's guests, at Leigh Hurst, The scrivener which each had brought made acquaintance with his fellow, and so with "maimed rites," certain papers were drawn, the consideration of which caused the frosty old solicitors to laugh over their Madeira!

On the night before the wedding, while Captain Powning walked the terrace at Carlyon, where he could see fair Leigh Hurst lying stretched out below him, and the lights of Powning Hall far beyond gleaming over the sturdy old oaks which had shaded Rupert's cavaliers, Lord Trevor left his wife's side and then sought out the lonely man. Already the splendors of the Carlyon plate gleamed in the great banqueting hall in readiness for the wedding feast, and but one thing remained to be done.

Lord Trevor drew Powning away to the stone seat on the terrace, where stern Noll Cromwell had sat, and watched the prisoners defile by him after illfated Marston Moor.

"There's one thing I must say to you, my boy, and say it *to-night!*" the old noble began, eyeing his man keenly. "All these younger people have never learned a word of the cause of your going away. Frances herself never even dreamed it." "Arizona Jack" was now trembling with suppressed emotion! "Before you return I shall see that you are reappointed in some branch of Her Majesty's military service and that your record is thus made right at the Horse Guards. You can serve a year or so in some staff rank, and then resign *in honor!* I want these three families to hold up the ' good old fashion ' and so guard the noble heritage of their fathers. For, commerce may fill our coffers, manufactures raise up the middle classes, but England's true staying power and greatness depends on the conservative strength of her good blood! There is but one useless product of these Brummagem days, and that is *the imitation gentleman!* Eustace, my boy, will hold up our family name, and Leigh Hurst and Powning are now safe with you and Cyril. When I'm called away, Eustace shall leave diplomacy and reign after me here. *That's all I ask!* I've kept pretty well to the front. Now there are things which can't be written. One of them I tell you to-night. Sidney Devereux was Major of your Regiment!" Jack Powning started up in an agony. "*Hear me. I'm an old man!*" simply said Lord Trevor. "*Before he died*, he sent for me and told me of the shameful trap which was laid for you by a *fille de marbre. I know*, my boy, *that you remained gallantly silent*—that you, in a manly way, spared Lisbeth Leigh's pure and untroubled heart. Poor devil, Devereux was soon in the toils! He was played on by that female Iago, who only raged because Lisbeth Leigh would rob ' Her Ladyship of Vanity Fair ' of the revenues of Powning, for even then, it was drifting your way. Devereux was weak enough to bend to a devil's bidding! He was Marie d'Orsay's favored lover and, really ignorant of your dark bond of intrigue. She lied, even to him! After Leger died— after poor weak Devereux's eyes were opened—*he spared no pains* to find you. He lavished his own gold vainly to seek you out. Death had claimed them both and you had hurled your splendid heritage away. He believed that you were dead. Devereux bade me guard this secret, but, should your honor ever be questioned, to speak out, and so he died, the prey of a vain remorse. If ever erring man atoned *you* have, and now, leave your honor and your public standing *in my hands.* For, you have been ' *Loyal à la mort!* ' "

And then silently they clasped hands, after the fashion of Englishmen, and the old peer led his guest back into the circle where light and love awaited them both.

By the altar in the old chapel of Carlyon next day, Lisbeth Leigh was given away in marriage, Lord Trevor insisting upon his fatherly rights, while those gay young plighted lovers, Cyril and the Honorable Mary Annesley availed themselves of the opportunity of a rehearsal. The bride was not decked as the women of her race had gone to the altar, but her eyes met her husband's with all the light of an undying love. It seemed only like a sweet dream to her, a vague, passing vision, too beautiful to last, this new birth of a wrecked life, and her only visible evidence of a "changed state" was the signatures upon the registers, and the case of rare old jewels, which the master of Powning had brought to her, with the whispered words—"*My mother's.*"

Some good fairy had deluged the chapel, and wreathed the breakfast board with a wealth of magnificent flowers from San Remo. With the rare foresight of Lord Trevor, the servants and the luggage had been sent on to Dacre, and before the sunset hour, man and wife were on their way to Porto Maurizio.

"*Je m'en charge de tout,*" gayly cried Lord Trevor, as he parted with the married lovers at Dacre. "I've already telegraphed them to send the *Pathfinder* away to Gibraltar, and if you bring her back *within three months*, I'll send you both off to Iceland to finish your honeymoon trip. Johnson left this morning for Villa Trevor, and *he has all my orders.* You are simply to report the safety of the yacht *from time to time. That's all.*"

"There are some pretty nooks around Sicily, some little harbors about Amalfi, where you can find the heart of nature beating in as wild delight, as in the days before great Pan died." Even in the golden happiness of their chastened hearts they were touched with the rarely unselfish devotion of the brave old gentleman, simple, sincere, the flower of courtesy, and the type of his race.

As they swept down through the delightful Nidderdale, the memory of Cornelia Powning came back to
them with all the unravished fragrance of her gentle
and loving heart.   The bronzed wanderer knew now
from the happy whispers of the stately beauty at his
side, how tenderly unfaithful Cornelia had been to the
pledges extorted from her by the man whom she had
captured at Paris!   The peace in which her placid life
had ebbed away was born of the certain knowledge
that the two whom she had loved and cherished would
reign after her at Powning.

"*How can we reward her tireless love ?*" said the happy
wanderer.

"The highest title of the Pope is '*servant of servants*,'"
said Lisbeth to her lover.   "We have both learned the
shadow side of life!   Let us remember that around us,
there at home, *lies the nearer and the nobler duty!*   To
raise up those who look only to us in their time of
trouble."   And the future was as fair before them as the
cloudless glow of the sunset skies, for there were no
shadows resting on their happy hearts.   Fair and
clear over them rose in the east the evening star, a
trembling lamp of love.

The burst of local wonderment which expended in
increasing ripples after the adroitly concealed news of
Captain Jack Powning s return had been divulged, was
intensified by the severely legal and carefully drawn
notices of the marriage at Carlyon.   No man dared to
interrogate that most stately peer, Lord Trevor; and
the banded families of Leigh Hurst, Carlyon, and Powning Hall were all sweetly unconscious of public com-
ment.   "As some tall rock that lifts its awful form,"
so Lord Trevor fended off all injudicious inquiry; only
the family solicitors proudly wagged their wise heads
and "much implied by their retentive mystery."

The "Yorkshire *Post*" gathered up the echoes into
a romantic tale of the return of "General Juan Powning" from the South American wars, where he had accumulated glory, wounds, and untold wealth in the
romantic fashion of his impulsive family.   Sundry flat-
tering details of his "splendid matrimonial alliance"
with the "Flower of Yorkshire," finished off a tasty

piece of journalistic invention.   For, the Old World is
beginning to learn modern journalism from the New!

But, Cyril Leigh was too busy with his daily trips on
"Pablo," in the interest of his parliamentary ambition
to the gates of Carlyon, where that rosebud, the Honorable Mary, was now diligently studying Blue Books,
and Lord Trevor was too much occupied with plans,
present and future, to note this seven-days' wonder
which faded away, only to be reawakened by the
splendid preparations for the home-coming.

The swift *Pathfinder* had hardly reported at San
Remo before Captain Jack Powning's face flushed in a
glow of scarcely dissembled pride.   He handed to his
beautiful guardian her sheaf of home letters, and then,
hastily tore upen a brace of portentous looking official
letters.   The first, announcing his own appointment as
Major of the Yorkshire Yeomanry Cavalry Regiment,
of which Lord Trevor was the titular Colonel, was
followed by a second, directing him to communicate with
the Horse Guards in regard to a "staff appointment"
which the Field Marshal Commanding, H. R. H., the
Duke of Cambridge, had been graciously pleased to
request Her Majesty to grant to Captain John Powning,
late of the ———— Hussars."

The wanderer then knew the delicate artifice by
which his loyal old kinsman had reopened the doors of
all the "Clubs" to him, and he sighed:

"*Brave, dear old fellow !   Trevor is the very Lancelot
of friends.   Everything goes down before him.*"

"*Are you happy, beloved?*" said the man who had so
strangely been born to a higher life.

"*So happy—a double happiness,* because you *share it
with me,*" cried Lisbeth.   "*Because you have been brave
and true,* because you have *conquered yourself,* and *our
love has but one motto—' Loyal à la mort !* '*"

She kissed the ring upon her finger as she gently
said: " Let us go down and tell Padre Anselmo the
good news."

The priest was pacing alone the silent walks of the
Cathedral gardens, where the splendid Genoese beauties
had wandered with their lovers in the proud old days.

He broke off a blushing rose from the nearest stem,

and his dark, mournful eyes shone tenderly as he said:
"*The rose of Life—the flower of Love for you, Señora!*"

"And for *you, Padre mio?*" she said.

He turned his eyes to the blue and treacherous sea.

"*Peace, and one beloved memory,*" he sighed.

They wandered back when all their happy news was shared, leaving him standing alone, musing there, a black shadow among the summer roses.

Lisbeth's heart echoed to his watchword: "*Deo duce!*"

And as they silently walked along the beautiful slopes to the home where love had led their feet, she murmured softly to the beating of her happy heart:

> I smiled to think God's greatness
> Flowed around our incompleteness,
> Round our restlessness, His rest."

They sat alone, watching the daylight fade away on the sculptured hills, while the planet of Love softly swept over the darkening seas below. The sound of the vesper bell alone broke the wooing silence, and then, they knew that Padre Anselmo was praying at the altar for all Christian souls! "*What are you thinking of?*" whispered Lisbeth, as her hand stole into her husband's brown palm. A smile of tenderness wreathed his murmuring lips. She did not hear his words, for it was only a prayer he breathed as the bell's rich note called up a sleepless memory lingering on his loyal heart. He sighed as a wistful face came back to him— the face of the woman who had died for him, and then he bowed his head, and murmured, fondly, "*à Dios, Mi querida!*"

[THE END.]

LONDON:

PRINTED FROM AMERICAN PLATES BY WILLIAM CLOWES AND SONS, LIMITED,
DUKE STREET, STAMFORD STREET.